GODSPEAKER

Tessa Crowley

ISBN: 0692710809
ISBN-13: 978-0692710807

To my parents, Mark & Terri,
who are almost entirely to blame for this anyway.

GODSPEAKER

You and I, little one, we're not meant for a world like this. After all, it's in the nature of a shadow to hide from the light.

But you know that, don't you? You've been hiding from it, too, not so unlike me. And in a world full of light, you and I huddle together in the shadows, and even if you've never noticed it, I've noticed you. We're connected, you and I. I look forward to showing you.

You are so close to coming into your inheritance, and I to mine. I have waited all the years of your world for you, little one. Now that I have you, I know our destiny is nigh.

You and I, little one, we'll change everything.

BY MY ESTIMATION, I have about five days left to live, so I must write this quickly.

I never pictured myself ever writing an autobiography, though that may be due in large part to the fact that I never really considered I'd have a life worthy of one. But here at the end of all things, alone in my prison cell, while the very world crumbles around the city, I understand the urgency of giving this dreadful sundering a narrative and a context.

And I know - gods, I know - that I am the villain, the public enemy, and I know there's a good chance that these parchments will be burnt as heretical lies the moment they're discovered, but I must take that risk. I must pray that some value is found in this story. There are people yet living who I love very much, and who deserve the truth. Gods willing, this will find its way back to them - although in my experience, the gods want very little any of us should want.

My name is Silas of House Olen, and contrary to popular opinion, I was not spawned in the dark pits of Umbrion's Shadow with murder in my eyes and darkness in my heart. I was born in the usual way, two generations out from the First Andels, and my life was, for the most part, really quite ordinary.

"What is that useless contraption?"

(And of course, no fair account of my life could begin with anything but criticism from my grandmother.)

"It's a l-l-lens."

"Is that why you've locked yourself up here for the past two days? Glass?"

"Y-yes, Grandmother."

(Nor indeed would it be complete without my embarrassing inability to defend myself. I am striving for accuracy, after all.)

"Come downstairs," she said impatiently, and at last I tore my eyes away from my work and looked back at her, to where she was standing in my bedroom doorway. My grandmother was a beautiful woman, all long limbs and dark hair and cutting wit. I'd inherited everything but her articulacy, which was a shame. My life would have been much easier if I'd been uglier but without the stutter. "We need to discuss the festivities."

I could not imagine anything I wanted to talk about less, but as I've already demonstrated, I never had the necessary wherewithal to stand up to her.

"I'll be right d-d-d   "

But she was gone before the word came out. She never did have the patience for my impediment. I sighed and turned forward to my desk again.

I try to picture my desk in my mind and it seems like a distant dream, coming to me only in broad strokes and impressions, even though at the time I knew every detail of the chaos. As I recall, it was a mess of delicate instruments and large chunks of glass in various states of transition to a lens. I had just put the finishing touches on my new high-powered spyglass, and I snapped the final lens into place before I gathered it up and set off downstairs.

My home is something I remember with more clarity. Like most of the capitol, it was a building of sandstone, its rooms and halls carved from the living rock, lit with oil lamps. As House Olen was a family of some standing within the city, we were afforded certain luxuries. Incense that filled the house with the smell of jasmine, steam vents from the spring beneath the city to keep us warm, and of course there was the art: beautiful mosaics along the walls and floor, colorful tapestries, and potted ferns and flowers. It was a lovely home, and by rights it should have been an ideal place to grow up. Perhaps it would have been for a different child.

When I came up to the top of the stairs leading into the atrium, I straightened the front of my tunic with my free hand. It was a habit done by rote; I'd long since learned that my family would take any opportunity to criticize me, and that it was best to not give them a head start. Once my clothes were pulled right, I started down the steps.

"... three hundred seasons already. My goodness, how they fly." I recognized the voice as Father's. "I remember when you were squalling in my arms, and now my son is set to become a statesman and a sorcerer."

I knew they weren't talking about me – I was most assuredly nothing like a statesman or a sorcerer – and that left only one intensely unpalatable alternative: Perenor was home early from his training. I'd thought he'd be gone for at least another day, training with the other acolytes of Craft in the monastery on the hill outside the city.

"Careful, Father," I heard Perenor answer good-naturedly as I reached the bottom floor, "you sound almost maudlin."

"Silas, there you are."

At this time of night, the glass ceiling of the atrium let in only starlight and the soft ethereal glow of the sky-river. The bulk of the light came from the hearth against the wall, burning brightly and illuminating the faces of my mother, father, brother, and grandmother as they watched me arrive.

"G-good evening."

"What in Sol's Light is *that* ridiculous thing?" Perenor asked at once.

Self-consciously, I hugged the spyglass to my chest.

"It's f-f-for looking at stars."

"What is it with you and stars?" Perenor stanched it from my grasp and peered into the wrong end. I grabbed it back at once, before he could do any damage to it.

"Wh-wh-what are y-you even d-d-doing home? I th-th-thought you'd b-be g-gone for another d-d-day."

"Came back early to help plan our party, of course," he answered. "Are you excited, brother-mine?"

He smirked in a way I would charitably describe as shit-eating. I glared back at him.

"Behave," our mother said severely. "One would never guess that you two shared my womb."

Brothers were a rare enough thing and twins even rarer, and though I had some vague concept of a special bond shared only by siblings, I had never felt it with Perenor.

"We were discussing the arrangements for the party," my mother continued. She was lounging on the divan with a glass of what I guessed was mulled wine. If I was an echo of Grandmother, Perenor was an echo of Mother – she gave him his sandy hair, bronze skin, strong build. "Queen Nerisa has agreed to allow the party to be hosted in the palace."

A tremor of dread ran through me. "You w-w-w-won't make me g-go, will you?"

"Oh, honestly, Silas," my father sighed.

"You don't want to attend your own coming-of-age celebration?" my grandmother asked. She sounded cross, though not entirely surprised.

"I d-d-d— I d-d—"

"Don't like people?" Perenor interjected. "We've noticed."

I glared at him a second time for good measure. Not because he was wrong, but because I'd never forgiven him, or anyone in my family, for not seeing why and to what degree I didn't like people.

"You have to at least *show up*," Father said. "It's being hosted in the *palace*."

One of the benefits of having a mother and grandmother on the Queenscourt, no doubt. It was unclear to me, however, in what way this great honor was supposed to make me more likely to attend.

"I d-d-d-d—"

"You're coming," Grandmother said severely. "I won't have anyone noting your absence from your own party. Surely you can find less conspicuous ways to embarrass your family."

It was difficult for me to say which was the more unpleasant feeling – the fear or the shame. After three hundred seasons, I knew I was a perpetual thorn in the side of my house, gregarious politicians and policymakers all, but it never stopped hurting to hear them remind me. I shut my eyes a moment and took a few breaths to calm my nerves and stutter.

"I'm g-g-going to the b-bluff."

"I take it you don't have any opinion on the guest list or entertainment?" Perenor asked glibly, and I glared at him one last time for good measure, heaved my spyglass under my arm, and set out through the front door onto the street.

At night, Ellorian was a labyrinth of sandstone buildings and pools of orange lamplight, of cool night air and salty wind off the sea. Ours was a sleepy borough of the city, higher than the rest, commanding an excellent view of the capitol and the stretch of shoreline onto which it was built.

For me, the city was always best at night: quiet, dark, still, blessedly empty. In the day, it was too much – too bright, too loud – but at night, it felt almost sacred, alive with fireflies and gentle rumbling, as though snoring, from the veins of the hot spring just under the streets.

In any case, it was a preferable alternative to my family.

I stopped on my way out of the city beneath a familiar window, snatched a pebble from the ground, and threw it so it rattled the glass. I had to throw three more before I saw a silhouette move into frame and the window opened.

"You could just use the door," Soya said, leaning out the window, her long hair caught in the wind.

"Your s-s-servant hates me."

"You're not special. She hates everyone."

I grinned at her, holding up the spyglass. "I f-f-f-finished the new lens. Come down; let's g-go to the bluff."

"Maybe I have more important things to do tonight than get drunk and stargaze with the likes of you, Silas of House Olen."

"Name *one.*"

There was a moment of silence. Even shadowed by the light behind her, I could see the grin that split her face a moment later. She ducked back inside and shut the window.

I was only waiting a few minutes before I heard the door on the other side of the building close, followed by footsteps on stone. Soya came around the moment later, a bag over one shoulder.

"A little nightbird told me that someone's having their coming-of-age party in the palace," she said by way of greeting. I groaned.

"L-l-let's not talk about that."

"Oh, no, *let's,*" she insisted, and I started off down the road out of the city. "I'm sure you're absolutely *beside* yourself with anticipation. All the pomp and pageantry and people; that's all your favorite things in one event."

"They're m-m-making me go," I sighed.

"It's bound to be the biggest social event of the season," Soya continued as though she hadn't heard me. "And that's counting the upcoming Queensday Tournaments."

"Do you th-think you could come up with a clever l-l-lie to get me out early?"

Soya laughed. "Just tell them you want to get a good spot to watch the Godspeaker's arrival," she suggested, just as we pushed open one of the side gates leading out of the city. All at once, we were at the edge of the wilds stretching south out of the city, all softly waving palm fronds and whispering tallgrass. The path leading up to the bluff was dark, but one that we both knew well and had no trouble navigating.

"Is that on the s-s-same day?"

"I think so. I mean, only one of the Godspeakers has arrived so far. I heard that Greatmother Amira is due to come next."

Despite my best efforts, I couldn't really picture what it is a Godspeaker might look like, especially the Worldmother's. They were holy people, so far removed from the experience of a secondborn in the capitol that they were not so much actual people as ideas.

"I d-do want to see her arrival," I decided, making a sharp left at a palm to follow the steeply sloping path up the bluff. When Aemor's Godspeaker had arrived, it had been nothing short of a parade, so the arrival of the mouth and the hands and the will of the Worldmother was sure to be even bigger.

I walked in silence for the rest of the way, though Soya was chattering enough for the both of us. I never minded how much she talked; it made up for the fact that I, after ten years of training myself never to say more than was absolutely necessary, hardly spoke at all.

Ours was a path long memorized, and we made it to the bluff in good time, rewarded for our huffing and puffing with a breathtaking view. From so high, we could see miles and miles of shoreline – the endless, rolling, night-blackened waters glittering with pinpricks of starlight – and the whole of the capitol laid out at our feet, the veins of the city lit up with yellow-gold lamplight.

Most spectacular of all was the sky-river, stretching from horizon to horizon in an incredible arc of impossible colors.

I was never what you would call sentimental – in fact, I'd go so far as to say that mine was a mind more analytical than most – but ever since I was small, I had always been awed by the beauty and majesty of the nighttime sky. When I was a child, I would stay up late and stare out my window at all the little specks of light, dreaming of what they were.

The obsession had grown from there, despite (or perhaps because of) everyone around me telling me how ridiculous it was to be so fascinated with something as irrelevant as the stars.

I set up my spyglass, and Soya collapsed on the soft moss bed along the side of the creek that trickled over the edge of the bluff. During the monsoon, the creek was closer to a river and the moss was inaccessible, so Soya always made use of it during the dry season.

"You shouldn't go, you know," she told me as she got comfortable, rummaging through her leather satchel and eventually producing a skin of what was most likely mead.

It took me a moment to remember what she was referring to. "I d-d-don't have a choice."

"Sure you do. Just tell them to go fuck themselves and don't show up."

"That does sound like s-s-something I would do," I answered with a smirk, bending slightly to search the sky with the spyglass. The new lenses were perfect – crystal clear and much stronger than the last model.

Her voice was tender, suddenly; concerned: "You'll have to learn to stand up for yourself eventually, Si."

I spared her a half-glance and a quarter-frown. "You s-sound like my grandmother."

"Not that she isn't awful or anything," Soya said, "but she does make the occasional point."

I had more than a little to say to that, but quickly decided that I had neither the patience nor the inclination to get through them. Anything I couldn't say in twenty words or less wasn't worth saying. So instead I let her drink and searched the horizon for one of my favorite stars.

"Would it be easier if I went with you?" she asked suddenly.

I looked back at her again, smiling. "As my d-d-date?"

Soya snorted and took a long swig of her mead.

"K-keep showing up in p-p-public with me and people will t-talk," I said. "We're b-both of age n-n-now."

"No offense, Si," she answered, "but I'm way out of your league."

I laughed, but she wasn't wrong. As the firstborn of the noble house of Rhodan, Soya was out of a lot of peoples' leagues.

"No, just as a friend," she continued a moment later, settling down on her elbows. "I think I've gotten rather good at scaring people away from you."

"M-m-my favorite thing about you. Sure, you sh-should come."

"I would never turn down free food and alcohol."

I was about to set to the task of putting my favorite star back into focus when something caught my eye, skirting across the horizon.

"Wh-wh-wh-what's that?"

"What's what?"

"That."

Soya reluctantly lifted her head, and I pointed at it. It was just to the left of the sky-river, brilliant silver-white with a long tail, larger than any star.

I looked back at her in time to see her frown.

"It's n-n-n-not a star," I said, swiveling the spyglass around and hunting for it. Behind me, I heard Soya pushing herself to her feet. Through the spyglass, I could see the long tail with better detail – a streak of fading silver with hints of blue and violet, flickering as though they were on fire. "It's b-beautiful."

"May I?"

I moved out of the way to let her look. She ducked down and fell silent a moment.

"Wow," she said. "It's like it's flying. A flying star."

"It's n-n-not a star," I said again. "C-can't be." I moved toward the underbrush and kicked over a large shale rock, where underneath I left all my star charts, bound and wrapped with waxed leather to protect them from the elements. "S-s-stars don't just come and g-go like that, they have p-p-p-patterns..."

I knew as much because I'd written about them extensively, charting them in exhaustive detail for over two hundred seasons. This wasn't a star, I was sure of it – this was an anomaly.

I sat down beside my spyglass and flipped open the heavy book of star charts in my lap. The first pages went back to my childhood, with nothing but poorly-formed drawings of constellations, but the further on they went, the more precise they became, more expansive. By the time I got to the stick of charcoal serving as a bookmark, it was all careful notes and detailed equations. I scribbled a few sentences about—

"I d-d-don't know what to call it."

"A flying star," Soya insisted.

"It's n-not a star!"

"It *looks* like one."

I sighed. Until I knew for sure what it was, perhaps it was the best name. I kept writing, marking the location on the horizon and the hour.

"Maybe it's an omen," Soya said as I wrote, bending down and looking through the spyglass again. "From the Night Father."

"An omen about wh-what?" There were plenty of reasons the gods might give omens, but Umbrion was hardly one of the more communicative of the pantheon. He didn't even have a Godspeaker.

"If we knew that, it wouldn't need an omen, now, would it?"

She sat down next to me and offered her skin of mead as I wrote. I smiled and took a swig, and the honeyed flavor burned all the way down my throat.

In the brutally clear lens of hindsight, I know that was the moment where it all started. Soya had never been more correct – that flying star *was* an omen, and I stayed up on that bluff all night thinking about it, staring at it, charting it, until Soya bid me goodnight and went back to the city, until I was alone with the stars, until I fell asleep on that bed of moss with the wind on my face and vision of flying stars in my mind's eye.

And when I woke up the next morning, despite the fact that I'd fallen asleep nearly a league from home, I was tucked safely in my bed with a single nightlily in my hand.

I WOULD HAVE BEEN more surprised or alarmed but for the fact that this had been happening to me since I was very small.

I couldn't have been more than 100 seasons old when it first happened, so long ago that my memories of it are uncoordinated and hazy, in the way that only childhood memories can be. I had climbed out my bedroom window and onto the roof while the rest of my family slept, and I had fallen asleep admiring the stars.

And when I woke up the following morning, instead of being on the roof, I was tucked safely in my bed with a nightlily flower gripped loosely in my hand.

I was too young at the time to really understand how strange and impossible it was, and I went on with my day as though nothing was wrong. No one commented - no one seemed to know - so I never gave it much thought, even as it happened again and again. I would fall asleep under the stars, and wake up in my bed with a nightlily flower.

It seems strange, in retrospect, to say that I had just gotten used to something so anomalous, but that was precisely what happened. It was just another phenomenon of the world that I didn't quite understand, no more bizarre in my mind than the way the sun moved across the sky or rain fell from the clouds. It was unusual, but so was every other part of the world in its quiet, beautiful way, and in the innocence of my younger years, I never felt any compunction to fear it. I still didn't, all those years later.

So, as I did every time, I smiled, and I smelled the nightlily, and I rose to dress and get on with my day.

MY PARENTS, GRANDPARENTS, AND BROTHER all set to the task of planning the festivities, and I was forced into helping, which was unbearable.

Granted, their progress was often hindered by the nearing Queensday Tournaments, coming up at midseason. They were an auspicious event in their own right, and planning a party so close was a bit like lighting a match in broad daylight, so I took some comfort in the party's comparative insignificance.

Still, we were a well-respected house, and my brother, gregarious overachiever that he was, had plenty of friends that were all eager to help him celebrate his coming-of-age, especially at the palace. Every day I saw the guest list grow, and it only made me dread it more. By the time the awful day actually arrived, I was an absolute mess.

I am not exaggerating, by the way. Sometimes when I am too inside my own head, too wrapped up in my fears and anxieties, I can start to break down. I become a trembling, sobbing, fearful mess, lost in my own terror, and I want nothing more than to lock myself in my room and never come out. The episodes are awful; they leave me feeling vulnerable and delicate and hollow.

Such was the case on the day of the party. It was a good thing Soya found me when she did.

"It's about to start," she said, knocking on my bedroom door. "Are you in there?"

I couldn't answer, largely because I couldn't speak due to the wheezing and trembling.

"Si?"

I heard the door squeal as she nudged it open, and in the reflection of the mirror, I saw her peer through the crack. "Oh, Si..."

She left herself in. Some quiet corner of my mind noticed how nice she looked in her formal linens, dyed rich violet and embroidered with gold, but it was drowned out by the much louder parts of my mind that were screaming *no, no, no, can't, no, please, no, please, no, no, no.*

She came up from behind and hugged me tightly around the middle. My legs, already trembling from the terror thundering through my body, nearly gave out, and I had to brace both hands on the wall on either side of the mirror.

"It's okay," she said. "It's going to be okay. It's just for an hour."

It was hard to take comfort in her reassurances. All I could think about was the length of the guest list, of how many people would be there, and how many of them would be staring, judging, with their cold eyes and their cruel words, sharp as knives and twice as painful.

"Not even an hour," she continued, petting my hair. "We'll just go in for a little while. Just for a while, let you be seen, and then we can go find a good seat to watch the Godspeaker's arrival."

I did my best to believe her, to acknowledge that it would probably be fine. Awful as strangers could be – and I knew from experience just how awful they could be, especially to a strange, quiet boy with a stutter – I knew that most would prefer to ignore my presence entirely rather than harass me at a function hosted by my family.

And I wouldn't have to stay, I reminded myself. I could leave with Soya as soon as I was seen.

I could convince my mind, but my heart seemed to disagree.

"All right?" she asked a while later, once the worst of the shaking had stopped.

I forced myself to nod. Not because I was all right, but because I feared my grandmother's anger more than I feared the party, albeit by a narrow margin.

"Come on, Si. I'll make sure no one gives you a hard time."

I reluctantly followed her downstairs and kicked on my sandals before heading outside into the blindingly sunny streets of the capitol.

The clear skies of morning did nothing to cheer me; I still felt as though I was walking with a weight in the pit of my stomach, so heavy that it made every part of me drag. It certainly didn't help maters that the city was full and bustling with people at this time in the afternoon. I kept my head down and tried to ignore the way my heart was hammering in my throat.

"You look nice," Soya offered, in a valiant attempt to cheer me up.

It was just a simple, wrapping linen tunic in dark blue. It fit me well enough, but I'd never had much to work with. Each of my features on its own was nice enough, but they came together in such a way that wasn't so much attractive as it was peculiar. I wasn't handsome like Perenor; I was mismatched.

When I didn't answer, Soya sighed and linked her arm in mine.

"It'll be *fine*," she insisted, "you'll see. We'll go in, linger, chat, and then we'll be right out again."

"I'm all-all-all-all right," I said, because I hated worrying her.

She smiled reassuringly. "Yeah, you are."

No matter how many times you'd seen it, rounding that last corner onto the main artery of the city and seeing the palace at the end was a slap to the face. With its limestone spires and gleaming golden roofs, it was by several orders of magnitude the largest and most beautiful building in the city.

The wide stone road leading up to it was a mess of carts and camels and shouting merchants. I hated crowds, and they always set my heart beating faster. I must have gripped Soya's arm a bit too tightly, because I could hear her mutter something reassuring yet indistinct, inaudible over the dull roar of the street.

It wasn't a long walk from anywhere to the palace, because the palace was in the center of everything. When we came to the golden gates and the guards there posted, we were allowed through with little more than a glance in our direction. As the firstborn of a noble, Soya was allowed just about anywhere without question, and I clung to her metaphorical coattails all the way in, crossing the drawbridge over the moat and into the gleaming golden doors.

I wasn't terribly familiar with the layout of the palace. I'd only been inside on a handful of occasions, but it is the sort of building that always manages to exceed your expectations regardless. Gleaming marble floors and walls, broad windows open to the surrounding gardens, endless mosaics wrapping around the ceiling and down toward the floor, endless sculptures and pottery and tapestries.

Servants and functionaries were crossing in every direction, and just as I realized that I did not know where the party was being held, Soya gave my arm a tug and pulled me off to a flight of curving stairs leading to the upper level.

Down a hall and around a corner, and suddenly I could hear a low and ominous thrum of muted voices. Navigating the busy streets of Ellorian had been agonizing enough, but before we had even made it through the wide double doors, I knew it was going to be too much. Fear rose like bile in my throat, and I stumbled to a stop in my path. The doors were standing open, and I could see them – all of them, in my mind no different from a pit of vipers—

"I c-c-c— I c-c-c-can't—"

"Yes, you can," Soya insisted, tugging me along. "You can, Silas, it won't take long."

I could see them through the double doors, so many people, laughing and dancing and drinking wine, and even though none of them had looked at me, I could already feel the heat of their stares, the cold sting of their judgment, and it was *awful*, and I couldn't bear it, I just wanted to run away.

"I c-c-c-c—"

"Your grandmother will skin you if you don't at least show up."

And she was right, of course she was, but it took another firm tug at my arm to bring me inside anyway.

I've never really had any luck in trying to explain my strange fear of social interaction to other people, and there have been many who have asked. They always seem confused by the premise of it, never understanding the context of being an outsider in an insider's world. On more than one occasion, I've wanted to shake them by the shoulders and say, *look, look around, I am in a room full of wolves; would you not also be trembling?*

And that's what they were: wolves. My only relief at that moment was that none of them had spotted me when Soya dragged me in.

Although the party had only just begun, it was already settling in. It was hosted in a large ballroom with great, wide columns melting into a vaulted ceiling, with windows of colored glass and a gleaming marble floor. On the far end of the room was a band of musicians – drums, lute, harp, flute, chimes – whose song filtered through the crowd and echoed off the high ceiling in strange ways.

Soya pulled me straight to the refreshment table and urged a cup of wine into my hand. I wasn't an intemperate sort, but I eagerly took a swallow of it in the hopes it might calm my fraying nerves.

"See?" she said. "It's all fine. No one's noticed. No one's even going to—"

"Silas?"

I spun so abruptly that I nearly dropped my cup and coughed up my heart. A young man was crossing the ballroom toward me, dark-haired and distantly familiar, though I couldn't place his name. He was, for all intents and purposes, a stranger, and I desperately hoped that he wouldn't ask me any questions, because it was doubtful I could speak.

"It's good to see you," the stranger said to me. "Congratulations on your coming-of-age."

I made a small, strangled sound in the back of my throat and then masked it immediately with a swallow of wine.

"I'm Dorran," said Dorran (apparently), his smile fading fractionally when I didn't respond. "House Valnon?"

The name was familiar, but only vaguely. If memory served, he was one generation out from the First Andels, and his mother was also on the Queenscourt – or maybe she was a diplomat form Sessyr. I couldn't remember. Any critical thinking ability I have is compromised in the presence of strangers.

"Did they not warn you?"

"Probably not," Soya interjected, bless her. Dorran's eyes swiveled around. He frowned in confusion, and she continued with, "Sorry. Soya of House Rhodan. Friend of Silas's."

"Oh," Dorran said. Then, "*oh*. Lady Rhodan!"

"My father's the lord," Soya answered dismissively, "and he's in Avenos."

"It's a pleasure to meet you," Dorran said, offering a hand to Soya, who took it with a smile, "but I was rather hoping I could speak to Silas alone."

Soya shot me a brief, measuring look. I shook my head. I absolutely could not speak to him alone. Balance of probability was I couldn't speak at all.

"It's not private, is it?" Soya answered, taking pity on me. "Parties aren't good places to discuss private matters."

Dorran smiled nervously. "Well, no," he admitted. "It's not private, it's just – did they really not warn you, Silas?"

He looked at me as though he was expecting an answer. I could not fathom what he meant – I didn't know who they were or what they were meant to warn me about. And since there was no way I could possibly get a single word out, I just shook my head and tried to conceal the fact that my hands were shaking.

"Your grandmother and my mother have been commiserating," he explained. He looked a little more nervous, though not nearly as nervous as I looked, surely. "They were talking about - well, it's all sort of convoluted, tangled matters of diplomacy and everything - but my mother seemed quite keen on the idea of joining a Sessyrian house with an Imlandranian one. Interprovincial cooperation and all that."

It took me a moment to work out he meant. It took Soya a split second more.

"Wait," she said, "you're talking about - they're thinking of *betrothing* you?"

The only thing I handled worse than strangers was surprise, and this was surely the worst kind of surprise. I had come of age literally hours ago, and already my matriarch was planning a marriage for me - behind my back, no less?

In my shock, I found that I rather forgot to be afraid. At least until Dorran spoke again—

"Well, if all goes well." He smiled at me, and I'm sure it was meant to be reassuring, but it was not. "We were meant to get to know each other first. That's why I wanted to speak alone. Do you dance, Silas?"

I most assuredly did not dance, especially not with strangers, *especially* not while my hands were trembling so violently that I could scarcely hold a cup of wine. The fear came back as waves of pain, and I pushed past Soya, abandoning my wine on a nearby table and making for the hallway. Behind me, Soya muttered her apologies and scrambled after me.

Betrothal - the word was still spinning through my head. How could they set up my betrothal without my knowledge, to someone I didn't even know?

"Silas! *Silas!*"

Soya had always been faster than me, and by the time I was halfway down the steps, she caught up with me, wrenching me around by my shoulder.

"Silas, it's all right—"

"B-b-b-*betrothal?*"

"Look, it's awful for them to do this to you, but in case it's escaped your notice, your family in general is pretty awful."

I laughed bitterly and kept walking. Soya sighed loudly and kept following me.

"Th-th-this is a n-new low, even f-f-for them—"

"It's not like they can *force* you to marry him. If you just talk to them—"

"I d-d-don't want to-to talk to them." I didn't want to talk to anyone. I wanted to leave this godsforsaken place. "I w-w-want to watch the G-Godspeaker's arrival."

"Silas—"

"I kn-know I'll have to c-confront them," I said, "*obviously* I kn-kn-know, but Soya, c-can we just—"

I sighed, stopped again just inside the gilded doors leading out of the castle. Soya watched me in worried silence as I gathered up my words.

"L-let's just go," I said. "P-p-please?"

Soya sighed, but nodded. I smiled gratefully, albeit somewhat weakly, and together we pushed out of the castle and onto the street again.

WE SPENT about a half-hour navigating the city in unsteady silence searching for a good place to sit and watch the great caravan pass. Soya bought a skin of wine and a bag of dried dates, and by the time we found a suitable rooftop – a two-story tailor's shop near the main gates of the city – the sun was setting over the water. On the horizon, we could see a dark line of camels and carts moving slowly toward Ellorian.

We sat on the edge of the roof for a time. I drew my legs up to my chest, and Soya looked at me in silence as she fussed open the bag of dates.

"So," she said. "Greatmother Amira. Godspeaker to the Worldmother."

When she offered me the bag of dates, I took one without answering.

"I always thought being a Godspeaker would be sort of terrible," she continued. "Walking around all the time with a god in your head, telling you who knows what. That's got to get annoying after a while."

Not that I didn't appreciate her effort, but after learning of my family's treachery, I wasn't in much of a mood for talking.

She sighed, nudged me with her elbow.

"Don't let them ruin your coming-of-age."

I rolled the date between my fingers. "It w-w-was ruined the m-minute they t-t-told me about the p-party." Granted, there had been parts that had made it worse.

"Look!"

I looked.

The great golden gates of Ellorian were being drawn open with the grinding of metal on metal. A cheer was rising from the crowds lined up along the main artery of the city. The procession had arrived.

"*Sol! Sol! Sol!*" came the low, rhythmic chanting of the crowds, the Worldmother's name like the heartbeat of the living rock beneath us. The first flank of guards passed under the gate on camels, and even from a distance, I could make out their sun-darkened skin, the metal beads woven into their hear. They were Ansu, like their Godspeaker, hailing from the jungles of Onansu. I was only a child during the previous Queensday Tournaments, and had never seen an Ansu before. I hadn't even had any expectations, but they somehow surpassed them anyway. They were strange and exotic and beautiful.

"Do you think the legend is true?" Soya asked. "About how she was kissed by the Worldmother?"

I didn't know, but at that moment I was willing to think it might be.

"Sol's Light," she said, "look at their armor—!"

"I s-see it." It was ring mail on boiled leather, all shades of gold and copper and bronze, gleaming in the sunset. I'd never seen anything quite like it.

"That must be her carriage."

It had just passed under the gates, large and wooden and oblong with gold leaf inlay that gleamed brightly. We were too far to see into the windows, but many of the onlookers were tossing flowers as it rolled past.

"I w-w-w-wonder what she's l-l-like," I said, mostly to myself.

"I hear that her eyes are silver-white like the sun," Soya said. I'd never seen anyone with silver eyes, but it didn't seem out of the purview of a Godspeaker.

And after such a disastrous day, this was good. I dreaded tomorrow, when I would have to face my family about their subversive attempt at betrothing me, but for now, it was good.

We watched the caravan move through the city and make its way toward the Temple of Sol. We finished off the bag of dates, drank the wine, and speculated about Greatmother Amira until the stars came out.

I fell asleep on that roof long after Soya had left, once again watching the stars, and when I woke up, it was, as always, in my own bed, with a nightlily in my hand.

AS SOON AS I CLEANED UP and went downstairs for breakfast that next morning, I was met with the stony face of my grandmother, sitting alone at the dining table and leveling me with a dreadful stare.

I'd steeled myself for this moment, of course, but it was so easy to shrink away from her silent fury. As it always did, her anger reduced me to a child, and I faltered in the doorway, seriously considering the possibility of turning right around and leaving. But then, that would only be postponing the inevitable.

"You must have come in quite late last night," she said, breaking the uneasy silence.

Slowly, I crossed the dining room and took a seat in my usual chair.

"We stayed up waiting for you, but you never showed."

Her tone was already scolding, and I felt awash in a sense of profound shame – so profound that it took several seconds for me to remind myself that I had nothing to be ashamed of. I hadn't done anything wrong. I hadn't done *anything* wrong.

"I s-s-stayed out to w-watch the Godspeaker's ar-r-rival."

Grandmother hummed once, unimpressed.

"Dorran of House Valnon tells me you left the party nearly before it began."

"After hearing wh-what he had to say," I answered softly, "I f-f-found myself feeling r-r-rather nauseous. I d-d-d-decided to leave early."

My grandmother's eyes narrowed, but I refused to shrink under her glare. *I have done nothing wrong*, I chanted to myself. *I have done nothing wrong.*

Our servant, Ferra, was at my side a moment later, filling the empty plate in front of me with the morning's breakfast – fish, roasted pear, olives, and poached egg. It smelled wonderful, and despite my rapidly waning appetite, I forced myself to pick up my fork and knife.

"Are you really so ungrateful?"

My hands fumbled for a moment; my knife scraped loudly against the rim of my plate.

"Was it g-g-grateful I was m-meant to be?" I returned. "Whatever f-f-for?"

"Dorran of House Valnon is a good match for you," Grandmother growled. "And finding any match for you at all was no easy feat. Do you have any idea how *hard* it is to find a respectable family with the remotest interest in *you?* In case no one's told you, you're hardly marriageable material."

"I c-c-could have t-told you that from the outset," I answered. "B-b-b-but then, to do th-that you w-would have had to tell m-me of your m-machinations, and c-c-clearly *that* n-never occurred to you—"

"Oh, *told you?* Is that why you look like a babe plucked from the bottle? Because we didn't tell you?"

"D-d-don't try to act as th-though I have n-no right to be involved in m-m-my own b-b-b-b—!"

"We involved you the moment your opinion became relevant," she said, and my hand tightened around my knife in frustration. I *hated* it when she wouldn't wait for me to finish my own cursed sentences. "We involved you when we had straightened out with the family."

"The v-v-very l-least you could have d-d-done was given me w-w-warning! You kn-kn-know how I am ar-r-round strangers!"

Ferra finished filling my mother's plate, then went to fetch our tea.

"Yes," Grandmother answered icily. "I know."

I hated her at that moment. Would she ever stop punishing me for anxieties, for my stutter? Why was empathy so impossible for her?

"Well, it hardly matters now." Grandmother speared her fish with undue force, sawed it in half. "You've likely ruined one of the few options available to you. I would accuse you of sabotage if I were not already painfully familiar with your complete inability to behave like a rational person in a public setting."

"If you kn-kn-knew, then the only s-s-sabotage could have b-b-been on your end!"

"You should be *so lucky* as to marry into House Valnon, Silas!"

I was ready to shout back, but the shout knotted in my throat and choked the sentence out. Ferra returned, filled our cups with steaming golden tea. The only thing I could say to that, the only thing I could think, was, "M-m-m-marry in?"

"Don't tell me you're surprised," Grandmother answered, tearing a bite of fish off the end of her fork. "Do you really think we'd ever have *your* spouse married in?"

My lips were moving, I could feel them, but no sound came. I stared at her in open-mouthed silence. I was shocked, of course, but beyond the shock, there was a slowly growing pain gnawing at the pit of my stomach.

"You w-w-want to r-r-remove m-m-m-me f-from my house?"

"What can House Olen offer you, Silas?" Grandmother barked. "Nothing! We're a family of lawmakers and councilors and diplomats – what use does it have of *you?* You, who can barely speak, let alone orate? Who cares more for the stars than for the state, who becomes *useless* in a room with more than ten people in it? Of *course* we want to marry you out of the family!"

The pain in me had sharpened, deepened. I found myself hunched slightly, as though her words had physically struck me. My hands wrung around my fork and knife. They wanted to marry me out of the family? Families on the Queenscourt, families of standing, did not marry the children *out* – not unless they were a grave embarrassment.

"You r-r-r-raised me on our f-f-f-f-family w-w-words." My stutter was getting worse. I did not know why at first, until I realized, quite abruptly, that I was on the verge of tears. "B-b-b-b-b-blood ab-b-bove all."

"Silas—"

"All m-m-m-m-my l-l-life you p-p-preached ab-b-bout the l-l-l-loyalty of b-b-b-b—"

"I don't have time for this."

Grandmother threw down her silverware; the clattering sound made me jump in my seat. She rose and said to Ferra, in the corner of the room, "I'll take my tea in the solarium."

"Yes, ma'am."

"And as for you."

Grandmother rounded on me. I willed my tears back; I would not cry in front of her.

"Someday, Silas, you may learn that true loyalty often severs as much as it binds," she said, and I hated her, *gods*, I hated her, and I hated myself. "But until that day comes, I fear you shall always remain a child, coming-of-age or no."

She stormed from the dining room, and the deafening silence of her presence was all that remained. I sat still like ice in my chair, staring at my food but nauseated by the sight of it.

So this was why they hid it from me. Because they did not want me anymore, and they could not bear to say so to my face.

Slowly, slowly, I rose from my seat, weak with some combination of heartache and anger and impotent frustration, and I stumbled out of the dining room, and I left the city.

THERE WAS A SPOT not far from the bluff that no one knew of but me.

East along the edge of the cliff, down the path leading to the shore, and through a labyrinth of shale rocks jutting up from the black sand at strange angles, there was a little alcove with a few palms, a cave, and a collection of great, mossy stones. At high tide, the water would snake through the tallgrass and fill the cave with a shallow pool of seawater. At night, it was blanketed with impenetrable darkness.

I went there, sometimes, when even the company of my best friend seemed unpalatable, when the world felt entirely too cruel and too close, when I was drowning in myself, when I needed solitude more than I needed my next breath of air.

After breakfast, I went down to the alcove and stayed all day.

I sharpened a piece of driftwood to a point and used it to catch a fish trapped in the nearby tide pool. I gathered bramble and built a fire. I ate.

I thought a lot – about my family, about my shortcomings, about my comforting hatred for myself – but I did not sleep. I dared not sleep. I did not want to wake up in my bed again, in the throng of that house that so hated me, perhaps not ever again. Perhaps it would be better for everyone if I left and never came back.

When night came, I sat down, legs drawn up to my chest, and I watched the sky.

The flying star was still there, still low on the horizon but higher than last time, its long white tail flickering against the sky. I wished I could go back, if only to get my spyglass, but it wasn't worth the trip.

Your friend was right.

Even after all this time, I still hesitate to describe what exactly it was like, hearing his voice – and I use the term "hearing" loosely, since it was not an actual sound. It wasn't even really a voice, as the word implies some sort of physical system of air and muscle movements, and it involved none of that.

If nothing else, I can say that it was startling – so startling that I nearly fell off the rock upon which I was sitting. I spun around to look for the source, even though it had rung directly inside my own head. There was no one and nothing there.

"Wh-wh-wh-wh-wh—"

It is indeed an omen.

And then there he was, standing just across from me. That first image of him has been burned indelibly into my mind.

By all rights he *seemed* an Andel – that is to say, he had a head, a torso, two arms, two legs – but there was a part of me, deep down and instinctual, that knew he was most decidedly not an Andel. He did not *feel* like an Andel, though I could not rightly tell what it was he did feel like. But whatever he was, there was no denying the fact that he was striking.

What I noticed first was his skin, luminously and unnaturally pale, pulled taut over thin, fine bones. Then I noticed his face, sharp and handsome, though not in the classical way – he was more angular than that, more severe. His eyes were so dark that they seemed to absorb the light around them, and he was dressed in what looked like raw, undulating twilight – swirls of black and deep blue and green, freckled with glimmering stars.

"Wh-wh-wh—"

He smiled, and it was a strange thing to see, sort of serene and otherworldly.

I put it there myself.

My mind was finally catching up with me. But surely that was impossible. Surely I was mistaken, because the only explanation for all of the facts—

So jittery, he remarked. *Like a little bird.*

—and then he was moving, smooth and imperceptible as water, toward me. My heart was beating in my throat, and despite a lifetime of fear, I was forced to reassess everything I thought I knew about terror.

You know who I am, don't you, little bird?

I could not answer. My voice had abandoned me entirely, and my body was frozen from fear. Still, there must have been some answer in my eyes, because it drew his strange and otherworldly smile ever wider.

I did know who he was. He was Umbrion, the Night Father, the eldest child of the Worldmother, the god of night. And he was so close to me that if I reached out my hand, I could touch his robe of twilight. But of course, I did not dare.

Granted, the image that you're seeing isn't my genuine physical manifestation, he explained, spreading his arms and looking down at himself appraisingly, causing little twists and ripples in his starry shroud. *This is just an avatar. No sense in causing any undue stir with my true form.*

I made what must have been an entirely undignified sound, low and strangled in the back of my throat. All at once, his words made me painfully aware of the extreme power disparity between us. He was to me as I was to mayflies: so utterly beyond any hope of comprehension, so tremendous where I was so insignificant, and it would take him no effort at all to swat me—

There's nothing you need fear from me.

My mind stuttered to a halt. That otherworldly smile of his had tempered with sincerity, and with something like warmth.

I would never bring harm to you. I have been waiting for you for an age, Silas of House Olen.

I understood his words, but within the context of a sentence they might as well have been gibberish. Because what in Sol's name would a god want with *me?*

You seem so surprised, he said, and for some reason that seemed to amuse him. *Has it not been obvious from the outset? Why were you always drawn to the night while the whole world disparaged you for it? Who do you think brought you back home every time you fell asleep under my stars?*

Something twisted tightly in my throat. A strong wind brought a gust of ocean spray, peppering me with tiny droplets of water that made me shiver.

We're connected, you and I. I felt it at the instant of your conception. I have been with you ever since.

Perhaps the idea of a godly shadow should have been unnerving, but it wasn't. After all, what was three hundred seasons to a creature whose age put the foundations of the earth to shame?

You don't yet see it, he said, *but you and I are very much alike. You don't yet know it, but this is the first day of a new age of Andelan. I have many plans for you, my little bird.*

He lifted one hand and pressed it to my chest, and before I could react, I could feel it, even through the linen of my tunic: cool and smooth and soft, shivering up and down my spine.

You are my Godspeaker, he said, and I was undone. I felt his dark and strange Craft surging through me like cool water in my veins, growing stronger, stealing my breath and my vision, pulling me apart at the seams. I knew nothing of Craft, but I could tell from the sensation alone that this was a binding.

I could feel his presence inside of me, and it was intrusive to the point of pain, horrible and wonderful. It deadened all sensation while simultaneously making me aware of every nerve and muscle and sinew in my body. I somehow wanted it to stop and once and to never go away.

You are my Godspeaker, he said again, *my voice on this plane. You will be the harbinger of a new era. We will change this world together, little bird.*

The binding Craft had gone from cool to boiling hot, burning in my blood, and my legs were close to giving out. I couldn't handle much more of this, whatever it was.

Sleep now, he said. *Let my Craft settle in you. When you wake up, let spread the word. Let slip the tides of change.*

Sleep, he said, *sleep.*

The last thing I felt was a steady grip into which I fell, before there was nothing.

I LOOK OVER everything I've written thus far, and all I can feel is dread.

Outside my cell, I hear the clash and clatter and cries of battle. The line is holding, but for how long? Is there nothing to be done? What will become of this city, of our civilization? Will anything I write here even matter when the monsoon ends? Will there be anything left *to* matter?

Despair is such an easy trap to fall into in these dark times. It takes everything in me to resist the temptation to drown in it.

I must keep writing. If this world ends, nothing will matter. If it does not, and the world forgets, then all of this pain and darkness will have been for nothing.

I must keep writing. I must keep writing.

I AWOKE GRADUALLY at first, and then all at once.

Memories battered down the walls of my mind, and I shot upright in my bed - back in my bed, back at home—

—had it been a dream? I found it comforting to think so, but it seemed too vivid, the images too clear. But the alternative - the idea that it had *actually happened* - seemed too ludicrous to entertain as possible. It couldn't have - surely *I* of all people couldn't—

I turned my head away from the sunlight streaming in through the window and looked down at my lap. Lying tightly-clutched in my hand was a single nightlily, its stalk bent in my vise-like grip.

Somehow the sight of it was both intensely comforting and profoundly terrifying all at once.

A moment later, I noticed a sensation that I was sure hadn't been there the night before.

Of course, "sensation" isn't the ideal term, but there's really no other word for it. Andelish hadn't evolve to describe it. It was closer to a physical sense like sight or touch, something that was woven into my biology, but instead of interpreting the world around me, it linked me directly to *him*.

There was no mistaking it. In the same way I knew myself, I knew *him*. I could feel him, undetectable yet omnipresent, cool and dark like night and still water, calm and thoughtful and vastly, hugely unknowable. It was such a simple and obvious feeling that it would have been an exercise in willful ignorance to deny it:

It had not been a dream. As impossible as it felt, I was Umbrion's Godspeaker.

This understanding raised a few rather alarming questions, not the last of which was *what in Sol's name am I supposed to do now?* What was the proper way of handling this information? Godspeakers were holy people, advisors to the Queen, leaders of the Temple, scholars and diplomats – how could I possibly insert myself into such a role? How would I even begin?

I rose from my bed and found myself unsteady on my feet. It might have been from hunger – I hadn't eaten much the day before – but more likely, it was from fear.

I padded barefoot out of my room and down the hallway, clutching the nightlily to my chest. The house was quiet, but from below me I could hear soft, muted voices. I followed the sound down the steps, and they became clearer and sharper.

"... would think that he'd be glad – proud, even." I recognized the voice as Mother's.

"You'd think so," answered a voice I knew to be Perenor's, "but you'd be wrong. Scholar Jeron is quite a purist about these things."

"Surely he could set that aside and help his own acolyte prepare for the Queensday Tournaments." It was my father this time.

I saw them through the sheer drape of silk that separated the atrium from the salon. Perenor was standing by the window, my mother and father seated on the whicker settee, and my grandmother perched on the armchair by the unlit hearth.

"He doesn't like the whole concept of combat Craft," Perenor said. "He thinks it an undignified and improper use of the gift. Besides, I'm confident in my own abilities; I don't need my master's hand to hold."

"You won't be competing against other acolytes, Perenor," my mother reminded him. "These are the greatest fighters from across Andelan."

Before Perenor could answer, I ducked under the silk curtain. The conversation abruptly stuttered to a stop, and remained silent for several unbearable seconds.

My mother was the first to break it: "Silas," she said, sounding surprised. "Your grandmother said..."

"Well, well, well," interjected Grandmother on cue. "He returns after all. I trust you're done throwing your little temper tantrum."

The words curled low in my belly, boiling in a volatile mixture of shame and anger. I wanted to make her eat her words, but when I tried to start the story of last night's events, they caught in my throat.

"I..." I swallowed. "I-I..."

My stutter was always worse when I was nervous, and I didn't realize just how nervous I was until I was at the edge of saying what I needed to say. The words were stuck in my throat, and I hated myself for it. This was so *important*, so unbelievably important; I *had* to say it, why couldn't I just *say it?*

"Where did you go?" Perenor asked, though by his tone he scarcely seemed interested. "Swan off with that noble girl?"

"I-I... I..."

"Oh, for Sol's sake," my grandmother sighed, and my throat tightened even further. *Just say it,* I chanted to myself, *just say it, you have to say it.*

"Can't be that important if he can't get the words out," Perenor said, and he turned back to our parents. "I know the competition will be harsher, but that's rather the point of the qualifying rounds."

It was infuriating. It was always infuriating, but now a thousand times more. I took several deep breaths, because I had to *say it, just say it, Silas, you have to say it.*

"I have nothing but confidence in your abilities, Perenor," Father said, smiling in a way he'd never smiled for me. "My son will be the youngest Queensday Champion in history."

Say it, say it, say it, say it, say it.

"I..."

"I just hope it remains a hobby," Grandmother intoned. "We certainly can't have you making a career out of it. A scion of House Olen needs his focus to be on matters of the state."

Were they not even paying attention? Why wouldn't they just *listen?*

I gripped my nightlily tighter, furious, exasperated. Why couldn't I just speak clearly for one instant, for one sentence?

"G-g-g-g—"

"I'd much rather become a scholar of Craft than a diplomat," said Perenor with a frown.

If I could just get the word out, I told myself, if I could just manage the one word, perhaps the rest would tumble out with it.

"G-g-g-g—"

"Don't be ridiculous, Perenor," Grandmother said. They weren't even pretending to care about me, standing there and stuttering like a fool. "Craft is a splendid hobby, but don't entertain the idea that you can build your life around it. Your place is on the Queenscourt, with your mother and—"

"*Godspeaker.*"

The word was victory on my tongue. The conversation, once again, abruptly stopped. They all looked back at me, and I swallowed what was left of my fear.

"G-Godspeaker," I said again, more sedately. "I-I-I am Umbrion's G-Godspeaker."

And then, further silence. I watched their faces. They seemed astonished, staring at me as though I'd grown an extra head right before their eyes.

"L-l-last night," I began, my breath and my words blessedly steadier, "I w-w-went down to the b-b-bluff, and he c-c-came to me as a s-s-specter."

"Excuse me?"

Grandmother's voice was quiet, drawn.

"He n-n-named me his G-G-Godspeaker," I said, coming forward. "He g-g-g-gave me..."

I held out the black nightlily to my grandmother. For a time, all she did was stare at it.

"A nightlily?"

"His f-f-f-favored flower."

"I know what the Night Father's favored flower is," she said lowly. "I also know that we grow them in the back garden."

She ripped the flower from my hands. Startled, I took several steps back. She vaulted from her chair and loomed down over me.

"I will not have my grandson speaking heresy in my house."

I reeled back a step further. "H-h-*heresy?*"

"*Godspeakers*, Silas," she snarled, advancing, and I stumbled away in equal pace, "are Andels of strength and grace and virtue. They are *not* secondborn recluses with stutters."

"G-g-grandmother—!"

"Is this about your brother?" she demanded. "Are you jealous? He succeeds where you fail in every dimension, and the night I tell you

you're to be married out of the family, the night your brother graduates as a sorcerer and enrolls in the Queensday Tournaments, you *vanish* and come back with this ridiculous, heretical *lie?*"

"I'm n-n-n-n-not *lying!*"

"Why would the Night Father speak through *you*, Silas?" she bellowed. "You can barely speak at all!"

In my life, I've endured quite a lot of cruelty, dismissal. But to hear something so profoundly cold from my own grandmother felt like a physical blow. I wanted to challenge her, I did, but all I could do was stare at her and ache. I was so unworthy in her eyes that the mere idea of my life having greater meaning rose anger in her.

"I have looked up on his *face*, child!" she roared, waving the nightlily in wild gesticulation. "I was there at the Manifest and I heard his voice! He would *never* grace his presence on a foolish, jealous, useless boy – I have half a mind to force you down to Umbrion's temple and make you pray for his *mercy—!*"

"Mother, please!"

"*Talk some sense into him, Viera!*"

Mother had risen to her feet at some point; I had been so transfixed on my grandmother's theatrics that I had not even noticed. I stared at her retreating form. The shaking began in my fingertips and climbed like spiders up my arms. Perenor, behind her, ducked down and plucked the nightlily up from where it had fallen on the floor.

"Silas," Mother said, suddenly in front of me with her hand on my face, "is it not possible that you dreamt this encounter? You've always had such vivid dreams."

I slapped her wrist away. Her comfort was salt in my wounds. My eyes burned with a dark combination of incredible sadness and black rage.

"I apologize for s-s-s-so insulting y-your sensibilities w-w-w-with the t-truth," I hissed. "I'll b-b-burden you no f-further."

"Silas!"

I stormed from the room, and as I made my way to the door, I heard my father say, "Let him go. Whatever the truth is, I don't think it would do to follow him."

THERE WAS A GREAT DEAL OF COMFORT, I found, in this new sense I had – this perpetual awareness of Umbrion's existence. It was as though there was an ocean in the corner of my mind, soft and cool and temperate, and anytime I felt frayed or frightened, I could sink into it.

It did not erase pain, but it did ease it. I could immerse my consciousness into an all-encompassing calmness, and I wondered how I had ever gone without.

"Godspeaker," Soya said, for what must have been the fifth time since the conversation began. "You're sure?"

The question was starting to grate my nerves.

"Yes," I hissed. "F-f-for Sol's sake, y-y-yes, Soya, I'm s-*sure*."

She leaned back in her chair, its weathered wood groaning in answer. The Blue Star Tavern was not an upscale establishment by any stretch of the imagination and likely couldn't afford anything better than old, creaky furniture. But then, we weren't patronizing it for its quality, rather for its reliable emptiness.

"It's just..." She hesitated. "It seems..."

"Y-y-y-you don't b-believe me."

"Look, Silas, you've got a lot of virtues—"

I groaned and fell forward over the table. This was *unbearable*. My family didn't believe me, my friend didn't believe me. And how could I prove it to them? I couldn't let them into my mind. What if the Queen herself called me liar?

"Silas, let me finish! You've got a lot of virtues! You're smarter than you have any right to be and you're funny and sweet, but those aren't the *qualities* of a Godspeaker."

"Oh, b-b-because you've m-met so many!"

"You're not the only one between us who reads!" she said

defensively. "They write poems about Godspeakers for a reason, you know."

"If you th-th-think I don't know how w-w-wildly unqualified I am for this, S-Soya, you've lost your mind," I said.

"Godspeakers are more... they're more..."

"N-n-not me."

Soya sighed. "I wasn't going to say it like that, but yes," she said. "Godspeakers aren't people like you, Si."

"L-l-l-look," I said, "I kn-kn-know it sounds impossible, b-but I'm n-n-not lying and it w-w-wasn't a dream. I c-c-can *feel* him, Soya, in m-m-m-my *head*, I can f-*feel* him."

The admission caught her attention, and she sat up a little straighter. "Right now?"

"Y-y-*yes*. Right n-now, in m-m-my head."

"Is he talking to you?"

I shook my head. "N-no, n-n-not talking, j-just – I can j-j-just feel him, it's hard t-t-t-to explain."

She sat back again. She was looking at me with a peculiar sort of intensify, as if trying to find the answer to her questions hidden in the lines of my face.

"M-m-my family d-doesn't b-b-believe me, either," I said. "I d-d-don't know wh-what to do. A g-g-g-god has ordered me to s-spread the w-w-word that n-no one believes."

She sighed then, looked away, drummed her fingers on the tabletop.

"You could try the vizier," she said, after a lapse of silence.

I frowned. "The Q-Q-Queen's? C-can you get m-m-me in to-to talk to him?"

"I barely know him," she answered. "I'm not on the Queenscourt yet, much to my father's chagrin."

The only other people I knew who could give me audience with the Queen's vizier were my mother and grandmother, and, "Th-there's no w-w-w-way my f-family would help. Not after G-G-Grandmother's theatrics this m-m-morning."

"He's going to serving as judge for the qualifying rounds of the Queensday Tournaments the day after next," she said. "Perhaps you could pull him aside."

"M-m-maybe." I scraped the heels of my palms across my eyes. "N-n-not that it will m-m-matter, if he r-reacts like everyone else."

We sat in silence for a while. I looked out the dirt-streaked window onto the alley. It would be sunset soon. I patted myself down, wondering if I had enough coin for one of the Blue Star Tavern's sub-par ales.

"What's it like?" Soya asked suddenly.

"Wh-what?"

She gave me her best *don't be thick, Silas* look. "Having a god in your head, stupid."

"Oh." I thought about it for a while. "It's all right, I g-g-guess."

The answer didn't seem to impress her. "It's 'all right?'"

"It's n-n-nice," I continued. I wasn't really sure how to describe it. "C-calm. Sort of l-l-like ocean and s-s-starlight."

"I thought Umbrion just didn't want a Godspeaker," she said. I finally managed to fish the coins from my tunic pocket. "I mean, he's had ten thousand seasons to pick someone. Why now?"

"B-b-b-beats the fuck out of me," I answered, which was true. "Ale? I'm b-b-buying." I slid the coins across the table.

"Ale, please!" Soya called, and the bartender across the room grunted back at her. "Maybe you can ask him why. He's in your head now."

"I'm p-p-pretty sure it d-doesn't work l-l-like that," I muttered. "B-besides, I c-c-couldn't even speak to him when he m-m-manifested, I was s-s-so scared."

Soya released a sudden, startled laugh. "Sol's Light," she said, "of course you couldn't. Gods, that had to be embarrassing."

As I recalled, I was a bit too busy being terrified to be embarrassed. "C-c-can I s-stay at your place t-t-tonight?" I asked. "I l-l-loathe the idea of g-g-g-going b-back home."

Soya smiled. "You're always welcome, Godspeaker or not," she said, and I smiled back at her. She was more relaxed, but I knew her well enough to know that she still couldn't quite believe me. And that knowledge did upset me, but at the very least it didn't surprise me. Apparently the mere idea that I was chosen for a position of such import was entirely unbelievable.

And for a moment, I entertained the notion that perhaps my mother had been right. Perhaps it *had* been a dream. An extremely strange, incredibly vivid dream. But then, that vast, calm, cool ocean was still there in the corner of my mind, and it left no room for doubt.

IN THE DAYS since the arrival of Greatmother Amira, Godspeaker to Sol, Ellorian had become steadily and increasingly crowded. The inns filled up first, then the tents started springing up around the grounds outside the city walls. It was as though the Queensday Tournaments had drawn the whole of Andelan to the city's gates, and everyone in the capitol was feeling its effects.

For my part, I tried to bide my time and avoid the crowds. I slept in Soya's spare bedroom, in the house her father rented for her, and spent most of my days going through piles of scrolls in the Capitol Library. It had occurred to me that we knew so very little about Umbrion (due in large part, my mind supplied mirthfully, to the fact that he did not have a Godspeaker), and it seemed like good sense to find out as much as I could.

There wasn't much information to be found. He had temples, of course, and a small number of priests and devotees, and was often prayed to for the interpretation of dreams – but there was hardly a wealth of knowledge to be found compared to those of his siblings and mother.

I would have dove into some of the more obscure texts, or even taken the day-long journey to his temple outside Ellorian, but for the fact that I simply didn't have time. Two days later, the qualifying rounds of the Queensday Tournaments were underway, and I woke up early to go down to the arena and find the Queen's vizier.

The Capitol Arena, or the Queen's Ring, as it was known to locals, was a great circular building in the northern district – three stories of sandstone arches, open to the air, strung with the blue-and-silver banners emblazoned with the Royal Crest. Though the qualifying rounds were not, strictly speaking, open to the public, that didn't seem to stop anyone. Nearly three thousand people had come out and were flooding through the wide arena doors to find a seat and watch.

Five days ago, going anywhere near such a crowd would have had me nauseous from fear. But now I had Umbrion's ocean in my mind, and I found that it was not only possible, but relatively painless. I still felt the little tremors and flutters of nervousness in my chest as I came upon the massive crowd surrounding the building, but it was more residual than it was active. The vast coolness of the Night Father seemed to wash away all my anxiety.

My objectives were twofold: first, find the vizier and talk to him. Second, avoid Perenor at all costs.

As it turned out, avoiding my brother proved rather simple, because as soon as I came through to the arena floor, he announced his presence with a sudden clap of thunder.

I had to admit, despite my reluctance to do so, that he did look very impressive in his combat leathers with his long, runed staff. He was sparring with an equally impressive-looking woman in combat leathers of her own, who had instead of a staff a fearsome pike with runes carved along its shaft.

Of course, I use the term "sparring" loosely, and anyone who's seen any demonstration of combat Craft will know why.

He came into my line of sight just as he was spinning on his heel, thrusting his staff out toward his partner, and *CRACK*, blue-white lightning came rocketing out toward her, which she deflected a blazing white shield. Then she countered with a downward thrust of her pike into the ground, and *BOOM*, the living rock buckled and broke under Perenor's feet. He rolled out of its path and *CRASH*, with a swing of his staff, a burst of red light.

It was actually quite awe-inspiring, to my aggravation, and I dutifully set to ignoring it entirely, making a wide circle around the duel and moving further towards the center of the Ring.

Past all the sparring partners and hopefuls, there was a large, cleared-out area with a few official-looking tables. Two people were dueling in the very center of the arena, and I noticed a man in rich silks looking on as a page took notes beside him. A golden brooch pinned to his tunic flashed in the sunlight – the Royal Crest. It could only have been the vizier.

At that point, the question became which was the best way to approach him. He seemed quite busy – would he be upset if I interrupted? Should I wait until the next pair came forward?

Before I could come up with my plan of attack, a large hand clapped on my back, and I nearly fell over from the force of it.

"I suppose I can add this to a list of things I never thought I'd say," said an all-too-familiar voice. "My brother, out in public!"

I grit my teeth. My plan of avoiding him had been going so well.

"N-n-n-not n-now, Perenor."

"What is it you're doing here, if I may ask?"

"You m-m-may not ask," I answered shortly.

He sneered at me, thumped the end of his staff against the dusty arena floor. "You're always so clever, aren't you?"

"C-c-c-cleverer than y-you."

He rolled his eyes and reached for a flask of water on his hip. As he emptied the contents liberally over his sweat-streaked hair, there came a large, collective sigh from the side of the arena. I followed the sound to a section of seats in the lowest row of the arena, from a group huddled against the balustrade.

"G-go easy on the w-w-water," I said. "Your f-f-fan club is going to w-wet themselves."

That was just the sort of effect Perenor had on people, ever since he'd reached young adulthood. When he did not make friends, he made fans, all of them swooning and sighing at his every motion. I'd always wondered why he'd never courted anyone – he certainly would have had his pick.

Perenor flinched and glanced black at them, which turned out to be a mistake, because the moment they saw him look, they all stared giggling and waving enthusiastically. Many were young, but there were more than a few that were old enough to know better.

"Don't engage them," he said sharply, grabbing me by the arm and turning me away from them. I jerked out of his grip.

"I have n-n-no business w-with you," I said.

"I disagree," he answered. "What is it you've come here to do?"

"That's n-n-not your c-concern."

Perenor glared at me and I glared right back at him. Ours was an old enmity, but at least it was comfortably familiar.

"You're here for the vizier, aren't you?"

"Perenor of House Olen!"

At some point, the duel in the center of the arena had ended and the combatants cleared from the ring. A large Ansu woman was leaving victorious, by the way her opponent was limping away.

"You still claim to be Godspeaker to Umbrion?" Perenor asked me.

"Wh-wh-why would I l-l-*lie?*" I asked. "M-more to the p-p-point, how c-c-could I ever get aw-w-way with it?"

Perenor's eyes searched mine a moment. "That's what I've been wondering," he said after a moment. "That nightlily you presented to grandmother..."

"Perenor of House Olen?" The crier on the far side of the ring was scanning the crowd for him, but Perenor hadn't looked away from me.

"Wh-wh-wh-what about it?"

"It's black," he said.

I drew no meaning from his words. It must have been obvious on my face.

"Grandmother accused you of taking it from the back garden," he said. "But the nightlilies in our garden are blue."

I set my face. "Th-th-then I m-must not have g-g-gotten it from the g-garden."

"Perenor – is Perenor of House Olen present?"

"You sh-should go b-b-before you name is s-skipped," I said.

Perenor glanced over his shoulder, then back to me. "Whatever it is you're planning to do," he said, "try to do it without embarrassing our family."

With that, he jogged off. I glared at his retreating form. He came into the ring to the sound of vociferous cheering from his fan club. His opponent was a spry, muscular woman with short-cropped hair and a strong jaw. She greeted Perenor with a firm, businesslike grip to his forearm, which he returned. The referee gave a nod to the man who I could only imagine was the vizier, and the duel began.

In another situation, I would have been keen to watch, but at that particular moment I hated him a little too much. I moved around the ring as they fought, ignoring the great cracks and clatters of Craft, and up to the dais.

Now that I was closer, I could see the vizier with more clarity. The lines of his face were sharp and straight, making him look slightly birdlike, and he was watching the duel with an intensity that he hadn't had for the one before.

"... look at him fight," I heard him mutter to his page, who was scribbling notes furiously. "I hardly believed the rumors, but there it is... who'd have thought a house of politicians could breed such a competent sorcerer...?"

Speaking to strangers was never very easy for me, even when I was neck deep in Umbrion's ocean. I swallowed the sudden flare of nervousness in my throat. "S-s-sir?"

The vizier looked at me, but only briefly. His attention quickly returned to the battle.

"Yes," he said, looking off-put at the distraction, "what is it?"

"S-s-sorry," I said. "I d-d-don't mean to-to interrupt, but I have s-s-some rather important n-n-n-news..."

"Oh!" the vizier cried suddenly in reaction to a tremendous flash of light from the ring. "Did you see that, Lorwin? What a display! Make sure you note that."

I sighed. Even without making a concerted effort, Perenor was still making my life difficult.

"M-my name is Silas of-of-of House Olen."

That, at least, caught his attention. He looked back at me, dark eyes widening in surprise.

"House Olen?" he repeated. "So you're—?"

"His b-b-brother," I answered, "y-yes."

"Your brother, then, is quite a talent," he said, looking back at the battle. "I've never seen anyone use Craft like him – and so young! He only recently came of age, did he not? To master such a difficult art having only lived for three hundred seasons – how long has he been studying at the monastery?"

He began his tutelage around the same time I'd built my first spyglass, so it must have been at least 120 seasons ago, but I knew better than to answer. "I n-n-need j-just a m-moment of y-your time," I said instead. "A f-f-few nights ago, I w-w-was confronted b-b-b—"

"I'd heard *rumors*, of course," the vizier continued as though he hadn't heard me. "*Everyone's* heard the rumors – an acolyte like him doesn't come along without turning some heads—"

I was starting to get a headache. "S-sir—"

"—but so often, the truth is hyperbolized. I think this may be the first time the truth actually exceeds the rumors—!" *CRACK*, from the ring, accompanied by another tremendous flash of light. "Sol's Light, did you see that—?"

"*Sir,*" I said, loudly this time, "the g-god Umbrion has ch-ch-chosen me as-as his G-G-Godspeaker!"

I once again managed to draw his attention, though this time for a more significant amount of time. I did my best to ignore the way that, from the raised dais, he loomed down at me from a position of not insignificant power. I would not let myself be intimidated. I must not.

Slowly, the vizier narrowed his eyes.

"What is your name?"

My mouth twisted. "S-S-Silas."

"Silas," he echoed. "I've heard of you, too."

The answer didn't bode well.

"Your mother and grandmother sit on the Queenscourt, after all. I know them well. They came to warn me..."

Anger latched tightly onto my throat. They *warned* him. Of *course* they warned him.

The ocean in the corner of my mind began to feel a bit warm. I was getting so very, *very* tired of other people deciding what I was capable of.

"How about we just go our separate ways, my boy," the vizier said, coolly, with just a hint of disdain, "and we'll forget this whole thing."

"I am afraid th-th-that is n-not possible," I answered, voice measured. "I am g-g-given order by the N-Night Father; his w-w-word far outranks y-yours. I s-seek audience with the Queen."

"Your grandmother already explained—"

"My g-g-grandmother does not know," I interjected. "When c-confronted with a t-t-truth that defies her expect-t-tations, she c-c-calls me liar. *I s-seek audience with the Queen.*"

The vizier sneered at me. Warmer and warmer and warmer; the ocean turned to a sun-warmed creek, then a hot bath, then a pot of boiling water.

"I'm not sure if you're deluded or just slow," the vizier said, "but it is obvious to anyone who's spent any time at all with the *true* Godspeakers – *and I have, boy* – that you are *not* among their number. To say otherwise is heresy."

"*Heresy.*" My ocean was boiling hot, and my vision was dark with fury. "You speak to-to *me* about heresy? Three d-days ago, the Night Father c-came to me an ordered me to l-let spread the w-word of my d-destiny. *You* are the one who st-stands in the way of his c-commands. *You* are the heretic, *not me.*"

The vizier sat up a little straighter, nearly more astonished than he was offended. Behind him, the page had stopped taking notes and was staring at the sky in open-mouthed astonishment. My vision grew even darker.

"Now – now see here—!"

"*I am the mouth and the hands and the will of the Night Father,*" I said, and my voice was booming, and my ocean was boiling me alive, but I had never felt so strong. "*I am the Godspeaker to Umbrion, and to defy me is to defy him!*"

BOOM, a tremendous, earth-rumbling clap of thunder. The whole arena had gone dark, and people were screaming, scattering, scrambling away, but my eyes were on the vizier, who was now ashen-faced and shaking.

"Sol's Light," he breathed, "how is that—?"

BOOM, another clap of thunder, louder than the first; the vizier sprang from his seat so abruptly that he knocked it over and off the dais. I could still hear the screaming, and my ocean was boiling all the hotter, and—

"Silas!"

There was a hand on my shoulder that wrenched me around, and suddenly I was staring at Perenor.

The first thing I noticed was the expression on his face – a curious combination of concern, alarm, suspicion, and fear. The second thing I noticed was that, at some point, it had turned to night.

Or, to be more specific, the sky above my head had stained with darkness as ink stains paper, and the wispy cirrus clouds had thickened, darkened, and turned to thunderheads.

It took a moment for the anger in me to settle, for me to realize what exactly had just happened. It took me even longer to realize that dark veins had appeared along the palms of my hands, spiderwebbing up the undersides of my arms.

"What the fuck was that?" Perenor asked.

The ocean was starting to cool again, and as time passed, my breath evened – had I been panting? – and the veins on my skin began to recede. I breathed and I centered myself, and I tried to come up with an answer to his question. Unfortunately, I had no idea.

"I... I..."

"Your Holiness..."

I turned. The vizier was on his knees, genuflecting before me. His face was white as ocean foam, and he was terrified, but with a devastating clarity carved deeply into every line of his face.

"I – I am so sorry," he stammered. "My words were hasty and out of turn, I just – I had no idea..."

I wetted my lips and looked around the arena. Those that had not fled were standing at a wide radius, primed as if ready to run, staring at me with big, frightened eyes.

Being feared wasn't a good feeling. For one maudlin moment, I wished they would go back to disdaining me. At least I was used to that.

"I will give you audience with the Queen, Your Holiness," the vizier said, head still bowed in genuflection. "I will return to the palace now and arrange for your meeting. There will be much to discuss."

I nodded, but the vizier did not move. He looked at me as though he was waiting for me to do something, but was too scared to say what.

"Protocol dictates those of lower rank may only leave when dismissed by the higher ranks," Perenor muttered.

I turned to him in confusion. "Am I—?"

"You're a Godspeaker," Perenor answered, face inscrutable. "You are the highest rank there is."

It seemed ridiculous, but when I looked back to the vizier, he lowered his eyes again. He was still genuflecting.

"Y-y-y-y-you may l-leave?" I hazarded.

And leave he did, though it was less like leaving and more like fleeing. He scrambled off the dais and past me, bowing shortly as he left my line of sight. His page was scrambling after him, and I was left standing in the center of a dusty arena, surrounded by a terrified, silent crowd.

I found my feet soon enough, and I moved to leave as well through the southern exit.

"Silas!"

It was Perenor, of course, but I didn't look back. The sky over the arena was clearing, and those still in the arena parted, scattering from my path like reeds in a strong current.

"*Silas!*" He grabbed my wrist and turned me around again; I deliberately yanked out of his grasp and turned to glare at him. "Do you want me to tell Grandmother?"

"T-t-tell her what you w-w-will," I mumbled. "I c-c-care not what she th-thinks."

Perenor stopped following me. The clouds were almost gone now, and the sun was shining as though the great shadow had never fallen at all, and I left the arena, head spinning.

I SPENT the rest of the day outside the city, at the bluff overlooking the ocean, with nothing but a small lunch bought at the market, my spyglass, and my star charts. After a day like that, the solitude was a blessing for which my gratefulness knew no bounds.

Though I had so much to think about, I willed it all away. My life, I knew, was about to change forever, and I wanted to take my little pleasures – my bluff, my stars – while I still could.

When I fell asleep, it was curled up on the moss bed, around my book of star charts. That night, I dreamt of cool water and starlight and Umbrion.

Quite a display you put on, he remarked to me. We were standing by the edge of an ocean of black water, edges hazy in the way only a dream can be. *You nearly called down a tempest over the arena.*

I didn't answer. Instead, I took the time to study Umbrion more closely. He was still handsome, in a sharp sort of way, still robed in twilight, still angular and lean and severe and pale. The wind off the sea was low and constant, making his dark hair twist and dance in strange and impossible ways.

Looking at him was like looking at art. He was night in Andel form, ethereal and majestic. I wondered what he would feel like under my fingertips.

Going to dare to speak to me this time, my little bird?

I smiled.

"Why not?" I answered. "This is a dream, after all."

Yes, he said, *it is. Dreams are a natural part of my domain, and an easy way to communicate.*

It took my sleeping mind a moment to discern the meaning of his words. I came toward him slowly, with a fearlessness only possible in dreams.

"Is this real?" I asked him.

That depends on your point of reference, he replied. *This conversation may not be happening in the traditional way, but it is still happening. Does that not mean it is real in the most essential respect?*

"You're right, Night Father. It was a question wrongly asked," I said. "So let me rephrase. Am I conversing with Umbrion, or with my own mind's projection of him?

There fell a lapse of silence. He was silent a moment, and he looked me over with starlight eyes. Eventually, he smiled.

I am no figment of your imagination, my little bird.

Perhaps the news should have made me nervousness, but in the easy, aimless haze of sleeping, all I felt was happy. I was happy to see him again, to talk to him again.

"What happened at the arena?" I asked him.

When I forged our connection, he explained, *it linked my essence to you, and likewise yours to me. When you felt that anger, my own Craft reacted accordingly. You became an extension of my wrath.*

It was an interesting answer, and it offered plenty worth thinking about. But the detail that stuck out to me the most was— "You're receptive to me?"

Of course, he said. *I sense you as an extension of my own consciousness, just as you do of me.*

It seemed silly. Of all the Andels in all the world, "Why me?"

Umbrion canted his head to one side. The ocean lapped at my bare feet. He did not seem to understand the premise of my question.

"Why did you choose me as your Godspeaker? Surely it was not some great cosmic dart that just happened to land on my name."

I chose you because we are kindred souls, he answered.

"I am unworthy of the comparison," I said. "I am nothing. I am a secondborn with a stutter and a fear of strangers."

Umbrion laughed, and it was a startling sound, deep and low and sonorous like temple bells and rushing water, and it set off little sparks all along my nerves.

My little bird, he said fondly, *what have they done to you?*

I wasn't sure what to say. He reached up and pressed his hand to my face, and any words I might have had left me in a shudder. His touch was lightning and velvet, and at once my mouth was dry.

That you can even hear my voice is a testament to the strength of your spirit and the acuity of your mind. But I suppose, after a lifetime of being called strange and useless and wrong, even a soul like yours would be tricked into thinking it's true.

I was trying very hard to listen to his words, but his hands – gods, his hands – they were fire and ice and electricity on my skin, and through the haze of dreaming I could feel myself shuddering.

But then, that's also why it's you, he said. *Why it was always going to be you. You struggle like I struggle. You know my pain more completely than you yet understand. And I know yours.*

Was this some sort of Craft? This intoxicating touch that lit my skin afire and thrummed in every sinew of my body? Was he doing this intentionally?

"You..."

My words fell from my tongue and dropped away, which was just as well, because I did not know where I'd wanted that sentence to go. The Night Father was very close to me, and there was starlight gleaming in his eyes.

I chose you because, beyond the Craft that now binds us, we are connected by a shared suffering. That more than anything is the necessary quality of my Godspeaker – and that is why we will change this world together, little bird.

Any part of me that might have been curious as to how we were going to change the world was drowned by the much larger part of me that was intoxicated by the fact that this being – this immensely, unfathomably powerful creature, this *god* – was cradling my face with such incredible tenderness, as though I was made of glass and he was worried I might break.

And I was a little bird, I realized, cupped gently in the hands of the giant, and I felt safe.

We will speak again very soon, he said, and his hands moved downwards, those electric fingertips ghosting across the lines of my throat. *But for now, I'm afraid you must—*

"Wake up."

"SILAS? Wake up."

And I did, shaking and panting with the echo of those fingers on my throat and the memory of starlight eyes fresh and vivid in my head.

"Bad dream?"

I swallowed and willed my mind to rise up through the various levels of consciousness, to forget the fingertips on my skin. With effort, they fell from my mind like water through cupped hands. There was sunlight on my face that made me squint, and I forced myself to sit up in bed.

Bed - so I was back at home. At some point during the dream, Umbrion must have spirited me back into my room.

"You always had such colorful dreams."

I looked over. My mother was crouched at my bedside, her sand-colored hair pulled into a long braid. She was still wearing her linen dressing gown. It must have been quite early.

"Wh-wh-wh—?"

"Amon of House Cyrine is here for you."

I frowned. "Wh-who?"

"The Queen's vizier."

"Oh." I hadn't expected him so early. I threw off the blankets and stood, making my way to the dressing screen near the door, still fighting away the image of starlight and the touch of lightning.

"Is that—?"

I looked back at her. She was staring at my hand, where a nightlily was loosely clutched in my fingers. I hadn't even noticed it.

Wordlessly, I dropped it in a vase on a table by the window, where I usually put them. Then I ducked behind the dressing screen and opened the wardrobe, suddenly confronted with the question of what I should wear while meeting the Queen of Andelan. It wasn't a problem I'd ever anticipated dealing with.

On the other side of the screen, I heard Mother approach the vase, hear her fingertips scrape lightly along the glass.

"Does..." Her voice was wan. "Does he give you flowers?"

"He alw-w-ways has," I answered. "S-s-since I was l-little."

"Why did you never say?"

"I n-n-never knew it w-w-was him till he t-t-told me."

I picked out a nice, wrapping linen tunic, white with gold embroidery and loose cotton trousers, in the absence of knowing dress protocol for meeting the Queen. I started to dress.

"S-s-s-so I gather y-y-you finally t-take me s-s-seriously?"

"Perenor told us what happened at the arena," she said softly.

I drew tight the laces of my trousers. "S-s-such a shame that I n-need to draw d-d-down a god's thunder to-to-to win my f-f-family's trust."

I could see Mother's reflection in the mirror, facing away from the dressing screen. She flinched at my words.

"Your grandmother has requested your presence at dinner tonight," she said.

"I n-n-n-need invitation to-to-to dinner at m-my own home?"

"Of course not. But she thought it might be a good idea to extend it anyway. She wasn't sure you'd show up otherwise – you've been sleeping at Soya's, as we've come to understand."

"S-Soya hasn't b-b-been plotting s-s-secret betrothals b-behind my back or accusing m-m-me of heresy," I said.

I could see her flinch again. "Yes, I imagine that would be no small comfort."

I kicked on a pair of sandals and grabbed a comb to work out a few knots in my hair.

"For what it's worth, Silas," Mother said, "I was opposed to your grandmother's decision to hide the discussions of betrothal from you. And I thought she was unduly cruel to you when you told us of – of Umbrion's manifest to you. But if anyone could talk our dear matriarch out of anything, all our lives would be very different. I just hope you know that we only had your best interests at heart."

I came out from behind the screen. "And if m-m-my best interests j-just happen to c-c-coincide with y-y-your desire to marry your sh-sh-shame out of the family, all the b-b-better."

"Silas," she said, approaching me, brushing her hands over my hair, "House Olen is a family of councilors and diplomats – people who spend their lives in the public eye. Do you really think you could really be happy in such a situation?"

"I th-th-think you're t-trying v-very hard to-to rationalize f-f-foul behavior," I answered neutrally, "wh-when you kn-know there's n-n-no excuse."

She was silent a moment, staring at me in a strange, tragic combination of heartache and resignation. She smoothed my tunic for me, and I found that I felt very little sympathy for her.

"When did you get so smart, Silas?" she asked.

"I've al-al-always been s-smart," I answered shortly. "Y-y-you've just n-never cared to n-n-notice."

The answer must have stung, because she did not answer. I crossed past her and toward my bedroom door.

"Do you want breakfast?" she asked halfheartedly as I exited into the hallway.

"N-n-not hungry," I answered.

Luckily, there were no other family members to deal with on the way downstairs and into the salon, where the vizier – Amon, apparently – was waiting on the whicker settee.

When he saw me, he scrambled to his feet so quickly that he nearly dropped the cup of tea I could only presume Ferra had given him.

"S-s-s-sorry to k-keep you, I —"

"No, no, no, it's fine, it's fine," he assured me, speaking a bit too quickly, bowing very low. "Your Holiness need not worry I – I brought a carriage; it's waiting just outside – if you're ready to go?"

I was still not used to the bowing. "I'm r-r-ready." It was best to leave now, before anyone woke up. "Just l-leave your cup; Ferra w-w-will take c-care of it."

Amon nodded, rose from his bow, and took off out of the salon. I could tell by his gait that he was trying very hard to conceal his nervousness.

As he'd said, there was a carriage waiting outside – a large, stately thing, drawn by two camels – and I found myself quite surprised that they'd spare such an expense for me before I remembered that these things would be expected for a Godspeaker. When the driver opened the door for me, I tried to hide my surprise and climbed inside.

THE RIDE TO THE PALACE was intensely awkward. It was for the most part silent, punctuated only by occasional looks of uneasy curiosity from Amon, who seemed to perpetually be on the edge of asking me a question before thinking better of it.

I certainly felt no inclination to strike up a conversation. Even when my mind wasn't preoccupied, I was nothing resembling a stimulating conversationalist. So I sat back and I thought of my family, of the queen, and of course those all-too-insistent thoughts of starlight eyes and electric fingertips on my throat.

By carriage, the journey was quite brief. So early in the morning, the city was still waking, and the market was muted as we passed. I could tell when we arrived, because the rumbling thrum of cobblestone under the wheels gave way to smooth flagstone.

We rolled to a stop, and when the carriage door opened, it was to a bright courtyard lined with palms and bushes flowering in bright red and gold and blue. In the center was an immense marble fountain that filled the area with the sound of laughing water. Peacocks strutted across the stone, blue-and-gold feathers extended.

"Have you been to the palace before?" Amon asked me, once again trying too hard to sound casual.

"A f-f-few times," I said. It was inevitable, being raised in a family of politicians, though it had never earned any pleasant memories.

"Ever had audience with the Queen?"

I shook my head. I had seen her once or twice across the room when I was little – I still recall the beautiful silvery ribbons braided into her dark hair – but I had never spoken to her.

"Well, in case you're not familiar," Amon said, moving towards a tall set of doors on the far end of the courtyard, which two guards opened for us, "the proper form of address is 'Your Grace.' It's considered impolite to sit down in her presence unless she is also sitting. And when she first arrives, bow until she bids you rise."

We crossed down a long corridor of a wing I'd never seen before, full of elaborate frescoes and windows of patterned, colored glass.

And suddenly, after all the rush to get here, my anxiety caught up with me.

I was about to meet the *Queen*. Why had this not occurred to be me before? What if I made a fool of myself in front of her? What if I became so nervous that I couldn't even speak? That had happened to me before.

"She's hardly a stickler for propriety, though, so don't be too concerned," Amon said, laughing nervously. "On a personal level, she's very gracious."

I threw myself into Umbrion's ocean. If I could just get through this with my dignity intact – if I could just keep my stutter under control—

"Here we are."

Amon had pulled open a door to what looked like some kind of gallery. The windows in the ceiling were colored glass, illuminating the room in red and blue and green and gold. There were tapestries, paintings, statues, pottery – I had never seen such a concentration of beauty in all my life.

"She bid me to have you wait here," he said. "I'll go and let her know that you arrived."

I nodded, and he bowed, and he left. And I was alone with my thoughts. The churning anxiety was still there, but immersed in Umbrion's ocean, I was able to keep a rein on it. I flexed my hands to keep them from trembling, set my face, and went slowly into the gallery.

There was one immense tapestry woven in red and gold that took up the bulk of the northern wall. It depicted a beautiful woman with long, dark hair and skin like copper above the canopy of a rainforest, silhouetted against the sun. I knew at once that it must have been Sol. The way she was drawn, all long lines and ethereal golds and whites – she just gave the impression of godliness.

"It's nice, of course," said a voice from the side of the room, and I spun on a heel, "but it rather makes you wonder if gods are the only thing artists can depict."

It wasn't the Queen, to my relief. The woman had emerged from one of the hallways extending out from the gallery, fair of hair and skin, dressed in a robe of rich, vibrant blue silk. Her hair was pinned up with golden clips and her eyes were lined with dark kohl, making the pale gray of her irises all the more striking.

I wet my lips. My anxiety had not gone away – Umbrion's ocean could not entirely save me from my pathological fear of strangers – but it did ease me enough to manage a response.

"R-r-r-religious history m-m-must b-be a p-p-p-popular subject."

She stooped a few feet away from me and canted her head to the side, smiling thoughtfully.

"Sometimes it feels like the only topic," she said. "Wouldn't it be refreshing to see a great mosaic or fresco of someone eating breakfast or milking a goat?"

I laughed, startled, and her smile widened.

"You must be the newly chosen Godspeaker," she said. "Amon mentioned that you spoke with a stutter."

The laugh faded. I lowered my eyes.

"Y-y-yes. Silas. H-H-House Olen."

She strengthened her smile further, as if to reassure me. "It's good to meet you, Silas." She crossed the remaining distance between us and placed her hand gently on my shoulder. "My name is Roslin."

The words may not have physically struck me in the face, but it certainly felt like they had. At once I staggered back and sank into a deep bow.

"M-m-m-m-m-m—"

"Oh, goodness," she laughed, "please, it's all right. You don't have to bow. I'm not the Queen; I just had the bad luck of falling in love with her."

I didn't feel reassured. The Lady Queen Roslin Tarmin may not have been a comparable political figure, but as her spouse she was in all respects besides equal to Queen Nerisa, herself. I took a few calming breaths and immersed myself deeper into the ocean, doing everything I could to keep myself in check.

"Don't be nervous," she said, the hand on my shoulder squeezing lightly. I looked up at her. "I promise you, my wife is kind and courteous. She didn't get to be queen on luck alone."

I wetted my lips and took a few more breaths before I dared to hazard a response.

"D-d-d-does sh-she kn-know th-th-that I...?"

The Lady Queen gripped my shoulder all the tighter. "Does she know that you stutter?" she guessed. "Yes, she does. Amon informed us both. I wouldn't worry about it; it's not in my wife's nature to be callous or impatient."

"I see you got to him first!"

I told myself that the intense sensation of twisting, churning fear in the pit of my stomach was only natural, that any Andel who turned around and saw the Queen of Andelan gliding toward them would feel just the same.

She was every inch a queen, from her golden crown to her long waves of inky hair to her skin like tea with too much milk to her rich cerulean robe hemmed with silver – she was tall and lean and striking, walking with unerring purpose out from the hallway on the far side of the gallery and over toward us. I had stared into the eyes of the Night Father, and somehow this woman's effortless grace and nobility was more nerve-wracking to behold.

"I'm sorry if I kept you waiting," she said, and as she came closer I could make out all the details of her face – the patrician nose, the pointed jaw, the dark eyes. She crossed to her wife's side; they exchanged a smile and a brief kiss before the Queen returned her attention to me. "With the Tournaments coming up, I find there is never enough time in my day. You must be Silas."

I swallowed, inclined my head. Then my mind kicked back into motion and I bowed instead.

"Please," she said, "rise. You are a Godspeaker; you bow to no one."

The mere suggestion that I was on equal footing with the Queen of Andelan would be laughable if it weren't so desperately serious. I stood upright and keep my face studiously blank.

"Your mother and grandmother are valued members of my Queenscourt," she said. "You have quite a pedigree."

There was quite a bit I could say to that, but even if I trusted my words to say them, it seemed improper to bring it up. Instead I only smiled briefly.

"It seems strange, though," she continued. "I've met your brother – your grandmother was eager to introduce him to me the moment he was accepted as an acolyte at the monastery – but I don't think she ever mentioned having another grandson."

I wetted my lips, wondering the best way to be both delicate and brief.

"Sh-sh-she w-w-wouldn't have," I said, slowly and deliberately. "Without g-g-g-going into d-d-detail, I've n-n-never been an-an-an ideal s-son."

The Lady Queen gave her wife a knowing look. Queen Nerisa caught the expression, then smiled and changed the subject.

"I had Amon leave you here for a reason," she said. "Come look at this."

I followed her to the far end of the room, up to the large mosaic that dominated the southern wall. In all shades of crimson and violet and blue and gold were depicted five figures, haloed in light, approaching a crowd of astonished onlookers.

"Do you know what this moment is depicting?" the Queen asked.

I didn't know for sure, but if I had to guess—"Th-th-the M-Manifest?"

She smiled at me. "Just so. The very first time the gods made themselves known to us."

"S-s-so that's y-you?" I couldn't help but ask, gesturing to the dark-haired woman at the front of the crowd of onlookers, whose arms were extended toward the haloed figures.

She laughed. "Good likeness, don't you think? Yes, that's me. And that—" (she gestured to another dark-haired woman in the middle of the pack) "—is your grandmother, Cisera."

"Wow..." It was a tiny bit alarming to see my grandmother on a mosaic. She so rarely talked about the Manifest.

"It was so many thousands of seasons ago, but I remember it well," the Queen said, sounding maudlin. "I was the only one foolish enough to approach them, talk to them – and for that, they made me queen. I remain unconvinced that it wasn't a bit more than I deserved."

"You were made queen for a bit more than *that*, my love," the Lady Queen laughed. "You're rather leaving out the way you fell into natural step as leader, spread the Worldmother's word, united the tribes—"

"All of that would have been impossible without my council," she said dismissively. "One woman does not a kingdom make. My point stands."

"If you say so," the Lady Queen said slyly.

"Anyway, Silas, I bring it up because this mosaic is remarkable for one particular reason."

I looked at her uncomprehendingly. She stepped closer and gestured to one of the haloed figures, robed in black and illuminated with bluish-violet light.

"Umbrion," I said at once.

"So far as I've been able to tell," she said, "this is the only depiction of the Night Father that exists."

I took a few hesitant steps forward to examine it more closely. He was slightly in the background and partially obscured by a golden-haired man that I could only assume was Aemor, god of love, but I could make out the pale skin and dark eyes.

"What do you think?" she asked. "Good likeness?"

"Y-yes," I answered. "W-w-well, sort of. I m-mean, it's c-c-close."

She laughed, and I smiled, and I felt more at ease. I still couldn't quite get past the fact that I was talking to the Queen of Andelan, but the vizier and the Lady Queen hadn't been wrong – she was very gracious and forthcoming and easy to talk to, much to my relief.

"Umbrion has always been such an anomaly," she said, folding her hands behind her back and studying the mosaic with me. "Since the Manifest, he's never once made himself or his will known to us. All of his siblings chose their Godspeakers, involving themselves in the lives of Andels, but not Umbrion." She hummed thoughtfully. "Never Umbrion."

I hoped she wouldn't ask me why, because I had no idea. Luckily, she didn't.

"We're all hoping that his selection of a Godspeaker means he is opening himself up to us. There are already scholars chomping at the bit to talk to you, to fill in the gaps in our understanding of the Night Father."

"Oh."

My tone must have conveyed how unenthusiastic I was about the idea, because Queen Nerisa smiled and patted my shoulder.

"They can wait," she said. "There's much to talk about in the interim, after all."

"We'll have to plan for the confirmation ceremony," the Lady Queen said. "We haven't had one of those in nearly eight thousand seasons – not since Arana was chosen as Godspeaker by Lilline."

"Wh-wh-what's a c-c-c-confirmation ceremony?"

"Just what it sounds like," Queen Nerisa said, "a public confirmation of your status as Godspeaker, a sort of announcement for all of Andelan. You're given your crown, confirmed as a member of the Queenscourt, and then Umbrion uses you as an avatar to address the people."

"It's important," the Lady Queen interjected. "It's a rare opportunity for the gods to address us directly. And it's as good a reason as any to throw a party."

I couldn't say that I was looking forward to a party, let alone standing in front of a large crowd of people, but it was easy to smile anyway.

"Of course, with the Tournaments about to begin, we'll have to postpone it," the Queen sighed. "When it rains, it pours."

"It's just as well," the Lady Queen said. "These things take a lot of planning. But I'm sure we can have everything set in motion by the end of the Tournaments."

"I hear that your brother passed the qualifying round!"

Had he? I hadn't heard – but then, I wouldn't have been one of the people he'd be most likely to tell.

"What an illustrious house yours is turning out to be," the Lady Queen said to me, and the warmth of her smile softened all my edges. "You both bring great pride to your family."

Pride – *that* was a new sensation. Up till that point in my life, the best I'd ever managed was not being a complete embarrassment. But *pride?*

I looked back at the mosaic, at the depiction of Umbrion, and thought of every bitter disappointment and cruel irony that had brought me to this point, every moment I had been made powerless to my stutter, my anxiety, my strangeness.

And I thought perhaps that this little twist of something, the little spark in my heart – perhaps it was pride, after all.

"SOL'S LIGHT."

I took a sip of my wine. Soya turned the crown over in her hands.

"Don't be alarmed, Si," she said, "but I think this thing might be worth more than your house."

"P-p-probably."

"I think it might be worth more than both our houses *put together.*"

She held it up to the light that streamed in through her bedroom window. It was silver – Mryian silver, if I had to guess – and inlaid with so many diamonds that the whole front of it gleamed brightly.

"Have you put it on yet?"

"T-too nervous," I answered, which was true. It had been an emotional struggle just to let Soya take it out of its box for fear it might break.

"Do all the Godspeakers get one?"

"They each g-g-get a c-custom one, according to-to-to the royal j-jeweler."

She looked up at me, astonished. "He whipped this up for you special? In the *five days* since you went to the palace?"

I laughed. "I'm sure he m-m-made it ages ago."

Soya's eyes lit up. "You should put it on."

"Oh – n-n-no, Soya, I d-don't th-think—"

But I was never really able to talk Soya out of anything. She grabbed me by the wrist and yanked me up out of my chair toward the mirror hanging on her bedroom wall.

"—r-r-really, I d-don't want to-to-to—"

"It's solid Myrian silver!" she said. "What are you going to do to it?

Hold still."

She arranged me in front of the mirror, and I was left staring awkwardly at my reflection, fidgeting and fussing with the sleeve of my tunic.

"Silver was always a good color on you," she said as she returned to my side and set it down on my head. It draped perfectly across my brow, coming to a point about an inch above the bridge of my nose. "See?"

I didn't see, but Soya must have, because she draped herself over my shoulders and grinned at my reflection.

"You look like a king," she said.

"I'm n-n-not a king."

"No," she agreed, "you're a *Godspeaker*."

I kept fussing with the sleeve of my tunic. The silver of the crown was cool on my forehead.

"I'm g-g-going to have d-d-diner with the-the others," I said.

Soya straightened. "The other Godspeakers?"

"Queen N-N-Nerisa said it's n-not a c-c-custom, b-but since th-they're all in t-t-town for the Tournaments, we m-m-might as well." I said. "Aemor's G-Godspeaker is arriving t-t-t-tonight, and I'll m-m-meet them t-tomorrow."

"All five Godspeakers in the same room," Soya said wonderingly, dropping to a sit at the end of her bed. "Nervous?"

I laughed humorlessly. "Y-yeah." I plucked the crown from my head and put it back in the heavy wooden box in which I'd received it.

"It might be good," she said. "Gives you a chance to make friends. Commiserate. Swap fun stories about times you've talked to gods."

"I've only t-t-talked to him twice."

"That's two more times than most people," she returned. "What's he like?"

I paused. It was such a simple question, but it had such a complicated answer. What was Umbrion like? Was there any combination of words that could really give an accurate description?

"He's..." I hunted for the right adjectives. "Q-quiet. Sort of – s-sort of intense. His p-p-presence is overb-b-bearing, but n-n-not in a b-bad way. His eyes are l-l-like starlight."

And his touch was like electricity. I decided to leave that part out.

"Eyes like starlight," she repeated. "Poetic. If I didn't know any better, I'd say you had a crush."

I laughed, and she laughed, and I pretended that I wasn't thinking about the way the Night Father's fingertips were lightning on my skin. I sat back down and took another swallow from my cup of wine.

"So are you excited?"

I laughed until I realized that I didn't really know if I was.

After a while, I decided, "Y-y-yes." I dared a small smile. "I'm excited. D-d-despite it all, I'm v-v-very excited."

I looked up. Soya was beaming at me.

"And th-th-thank the g-g-gods for it, t-t-too," I laughed, "because I d-d-don't think I c-could have m-m-made a career out of s-s-stargazing."

She laughed right along with me. "Are you trying to tell me that there's no market for getting drunk and staring at the night sky?"

"Astonishing, I kn-kn-know."

"I'm glad you're happy, Si," she said.

"I am," I answered, finding that it was true. "Umbrion is w-w-w-wise and k-kind, and even th-th-though we've only s-spoken twice..."

Soya did not interrupt. In fact, she hung on my every word.

"I f-feel like he understands m-m-me, in w-w-ways I don't even understand m-myself." I thought back to his kind words of reassurance, his hands on my skin, and I smiled to myself. "He s-s-says we will ch-ch-change the w-world. I think we w-w-w-will."

"Change the world, huh?"

I grinned and looked up at her, only to notice that her expression had shifted into one of thoughtfulness.

"Wh-wh-what's with the-the look?"

"Nothing," she said, even though it was obviously not nothing. "It's just – you know I'm sorry, right?"

I raised my eyebrows without responding. She continued.

"About not believing you."

I sighed and slumped in my seat.

"W-w-well," I said, "it's n-not as if y-you were alone in th-the assumption."

"I'm your best friend," she answered. "I should take what you say seriously."

"Yeah, you w-w-were a b-bit of an ass."

Soya laughed and I laughed with her, and that was that. "A bit."

Which reminded me— "C-c-can I stay h-here again t-tonight?"

"Are you just going to keep your family hanging forever?" she asked, leaning back on her palms. "Not that I don't enjoy their suffering, but it has been a few days."

"I kn-kn-know I'll have to-to-to confront it ev-v-ventually," I said, "I j-j-just don't w-want to. And I w-w-want them to know how m-m-much I don't want to."

"If it were me, I'd be lording it over them," she said, collapsing backward onto the bed. "All the shit they gave you all your life, and now you're one of the most powerful people in Andelan? I'd be gloating for the rest of my life."

"I'm n-n-not good at g-gloating," I said. "No experience."

"Well, when you do finally decide to rake them over hot coals," Soya said, "make sure you let me know so I can watch."

I plucked the crown off my head and put it back in the box. I smoothed my hand over the polished wood, and hoped for the only thing I could hope for: that when the inevitable conversation did come, it wasn't too painful.

DINNER AT THE PALACE, like most things at the palace were turning out to be, was something for which I was woefully unprepared.

The fact that it was dinner with the four other Godspeakers did not make it any easier.

Nor indeed did the fact that the moment I arrived, it was to fleets of servants and dignitaries and diplomats all bowing their heads to me as I passed and calling me *Your Holiness.* I found it strange and alarming that this was to be my new reality: a world in which I was given unquestioned respect and sycophancy. It was so utterly beyond the world in which I'd been raised, where those who did not fail to notice me entirely sneered at my stutter.

It was surreal and disorienting. Were all these people really bowing to *me?* Was *I* the one who drew worshipful stares and frantic whispering? Hadn't anyone told them that I was just Silas, just some secondborn with strange hobbies and a stutter?

I didn't have very much time to consider these questions (which was probably for the best), because the moment the servant escorting me to the dining room came to the large double doors, I could think of little else but the fact that the four other people standing by the window were Godspeakers. They turned to me and I was lost for breath.

They were Godspeakers, not me. They were regal and holy in their long silk robes and crowns and effortless poise, and it seemed ridiculous for me to even be in the same room with them. I couldn't possibly belong to this collective of the most powerful people in Andelan, with their dignity and pedigree. I was nothing next to them, *less* than nothing, I was just—

"Silas!"

One of them, a woman with long red hair and bright eyes, smiled widely and darted across the room toward me. She gripped me tightly by both arms.

"Lilline extends her sincerest congratulations," she told me, and I tried not to be disoriented by the fact that the goddess of art and beauty was extending anything at all to me. The woman in front of me was short but willowy, beautiful in a very classical way. "She is pleased that her older brother is finally reaching out and making an effort to be heard."

"I... I..."

"Don't be nervous!" she said, smiling all the wider. "My name is Arana, Godspeaker to Lilline. I'm eager to get to know you! Everyone is."

My head was spinning. The news made perfect sense and no sense at all.

"Come," she said, tugging me gently by the wrist toward the other three. "Introductions all around. Silas, this is Grand Scholar Fiyera, Godspeaker to Elwen."

She was robed in rich but practical black silk, dark of hair and eye. She smiled at me, looking tired. "The goddess of knowledge and wisdom offers her greetings and congratulations to the new Godspeaker," she said. "And so do I."

I swallowed and bowed my head shallowly.

"And this is Rolen of House Chastain, Godspeaker to Aemor."

Robed in scarlet and gold with eyes twice as blue as they had any right to be, he smiled at me with a warmth that took me entirely off-guard. "Hello, Silas."

"And this, of course, is Greatmother Amira, Godspeaker to Sol."

I had been trying so very hard to keep my eyes off her. The whole situation was nerve-wracking enough, but *her*—

She was tall and well-proportioned, beautiful, and with strength in her eyes and in the lines of her face. Her dark hair was braided intricately with beads of white and silver that gleamed all the brighter against her coppery skin. Unlike the others, she was dressed more practically, in fitted leathers with quality in every stitch.

Her eyes, I noticed, were not silver-white like the sun, but rather rich and dark brown like soft earth. They regarded me with a dispassionate sort of intensity.

I swallowed and bowed my head low.

"I am pleased to meet you," Greatmother Amira said. She had a thick Ansu accent, exotic but not impenetrable, and her voice was strong but not unkind. "The Worldmother was surprised to hear that her eldest son finally chose a Godspeaker. It appears he did not see fit to warn his mother of his plans. I don't suppose he mentioned why that might be?"

The chances of my managing a response while staring up at the most holy woman in Andelan were low. I shook my head rather than hazard speaking.

"You mustn't blame him," Arana said. "He's a servant, like us; not a confidante."

A moment passed, and then Greatmother Amira smiled.

"I don't blame him," she said.

"I think dinner's arrived," said Rolen, and when I looked over my shoulder, I saw a fleet of servants bringing in more trays of food than could possibly be used to feed only five people.

"Queen Nerisa tells me that you come from a family of politicians," Arana said, suddenly at my arm and smiling brightly. I nodded again. "Your mother and grandmother sit on the Queenscourt?"

It would have been nice to just keep nodding, but if I didn't say something soon they'd likely get suspicious. I took a quick breath. "Y-y-yes."

Either they had been warned in advance or they were being very charitable, because none of them seemed to acknowledge my stutter. Arana just smiled all the brighter. "Then you'll soon be joining their ranks. They must be very proud of you."

"Th-th-they m-must be..."

The servants had finished placing the dishes. Just as I was wondering if there was any sort of protocol to who sat down first – would it be Greatmother Amira, since her goddess was senior? – they all sat down at the same time. I followed suit.

"Of course, if serving as councilors on the Queenscourt were a Godspeaker's only duty, our lives would be much easier," Grand Scholar Fiyera said as she pulled in her chair. "You'll have to take over as the head of Umbrion's Temple. It may take you a while to learn the subtleties of the job."

The servants uncovered the dishes all at once. Roast pork, fillet of fish, kale, sliced pears in honey, poached eggs, wine – I suddenly realized that I was extremely hungry.

"Wh-wh-what will th-that include?" I asked as a nearby servant filled my plate.

"It depends on what Umbrion wills," Rolen answers. "You'll take direction from him and shape his Temple in the way he wants you to. Just as all the gods' temples differ in purpose and function, so too will Umbrion's."

I suppose that answer should have been obvious. I nodded, wondering what sort of role the Temple of Umbrion would fulfill.

"Don't worry about it just yet," Arana said as she took a bit of pork. "He's only spoken to you once; you can't be expected to build a temple with pebbles."

"W-w-well, twice," I said, taking a serving of pears in honey.

They all seemed very surprised. I looked between them, suddenly afraid I'd said something wrong. Should I not correct a Godspeaker?

"Twice?" repeated Greatmother Amira. Her surprise was tempered with a smirk. "In so short a time? He must like you."

"I..." A servant filled my cup with wine. "It's b-b-been d-days," I said. "I'm s-s-sure it's n-not so unusual..."

"Time doesn't pass the same way for gods as it does for us," Grand Scholar Fiyera answered. "Our ten thousand seasons on Andelan is a drop in the bucket for a god. What's felt like days to you has been mere moments for Umbrion. It means he's spent the time at your side, even if you haven't perceived it."

It made sense to think of it, but the idea still lit little sparks along my nerves, bringing to mind memories of fingertips on my throat and starlight eyes. I swallowed and served myself some pork. "I j-j-just pray I w-w-won't m-muck anything up too-too-too badly," I said.

"Umbrion chose you for a reason," Arana assured me, patting my arm and smiling. "The gods are wise. They wouldn't give us a destiny of which we were not capable."

In any other situation, it would have been a meaningless platitude. In this context, however, I found it strangely reassuring in how very literal it was.

"Why don't you shadow me for a while, as long as I'm in Ellorian?" Greatmother Amira said suddenly, and I looked up from a bite of kale. "I'm going to be making visits to Sol's temple. If you're nervous about taking up your new mantle, come watch me handle mine. My duties won't be identical to yours, but you'll get a rough idea."

I straightened in my seat. It seemed impossibly generous, though I knew it wouldn't be a great sacrifice. Still, I bowed my head reverently.

"Th-th-th-that w-would be…"

I couldn't finish the sentence – not because the word wouldn't come, but because I wasn't sure what word to use. There was something unfamiliar warming me from the inside out, one I couldn't quite name.

"Come find me the day before the Tournaments begin," Greatmother Amira continued. "Just after sunup. Hopefully you'll find it edifying."

"You'll fit in just fine, Silas," Arana intoned, and that warm sensation suddenly had a name: I was *fitting in*. I could not recall a time in my life up till that point when I had fit in anywhere or with anyone, barring my single friend in Soya. My life had been a never-ending string being too strange, too quiet, too full of shortcomings, and all of a sudden people were forthcoming, friendly, helpful – they even seemed to like me.

I hoped that the sudden rush of emotion didn't register on my face. It seemed like such a silly thing to put me on the verge of joyful tears.

WHEN I HEARD the rustle of fabric, I said, "I th-th-thinks it's g-getting bigger," without looking away from my notes.

There was no answer, so I kept going.

"Its angular d-d-d-diameter has increased by-by a factor of three," I continued. "P-p-perhaps the star is f-flying, after all."

I looked back at what I assumed was Soya – after all, it was her house – but was rather disappointed and alarmed to instead find—

"P-Perenor?"

The first thing I noticed was that he looked intensely uncomfortable and a little bit upset – not at me, but at the situation, like he didn't want to be here.

"What's an angular diameter?" he asked.

Doubting he cared about the answer, or that he'd understand it if I explained it, I instead responded, "What are y-y-you doing here?"

"Grandmother has sent me as an envoy," he answered. He crossed the salon slowly to where I had set up the spyglass by the window, his hands buried deep in the pockets of his plain, black tunic. "When Mother invited you to dinner, it didn't work. So now they're sending me instead."

I fought back the urge to snarl. I snapped shut my book of star charts and set to collapsing my spyglass.

"Silas," Perenor said, "you're going to have to face us eventually."

"F-f-forgive me for n-not jumping at the ch-chance," I growled, stuffing the collapsed spyglass into its carrying case.

"Aren't you even interested in what Grandmother has to say?"

"N-n-n-not particularly."

Perenor sighed heavily, like I was being childish. It made the skin at the back of my neck prickle with anger.

"Look, what do you want? I'm sorry I didn't believe you at first. Forgive me for finding the idea a little unbelievable."

I scoffed. "Is that y-y-your idea of an-an apology?"

"Are you really going to hold our skepticism against us?" he asked, throwing his hands over his head in exasperation. "In case you haven't noticed, Silas, you're not what anyone would consider a Godspeaker!"

"Except for-for-for Umbrion, apparently," I snapped.

"Silas—"

"I c-c-could have handled j-just *skepticism*," I said, "but you were c-c-*cruel*. I n-needed help, and y-y-you called me liar—!"

"Come to dinner, then!" he interjected. "Air your grievances! I think it's fair to say that this will be a topic of conversation!"

I stared at him, my hands flexing at my sides, and I felt nothing but anger. All my life, he had outstripped me in every capacity, and now that there was finally something – one thing, one massive way in which I had advantage over him – I couldn't even feel *good* about it because of how angry he made me.

He seemed to detect my anger and sighed.

"Look," he continued, "Mother and Father are really worried about you."

I scoffed.

"They are," he insisted. "And I am, too, a little bit. And Grandfather was upset the moment you left. Just come to dinner for his sake."

And gods, but I would have liked to say no – just on principle, just because of how badly they'd hurt me – but I knew I couldn't. This was a conversation that had to happen, despite how every fiber of my body screamed in protest against it. Avoiding this would just prolong the inevitable.

So I sighed, and I shut my eyes, and I resigned myself to a very unpleasant evening.

"Fine," I said. "L-l-let me l-leave a note for Soya."

SOYA'S HOUSE wasn't far from ours, which was good, because the walk back was awkward and silent. When we made it back, Ferra met us at the door and informed us that dinner would be out in the back garden. And though I was looking forward to her honeyed pork and yams, I was most certainly not looking forward to the silence that fell, harsh and inevitable, the moment. We stepped out through the solarium and into the garden.

The dinner had already been set up, but it must have been early yet because the food had barely been touched. When we came through the door, Grandfather was the first one to stand, eyes alight with sudden relief.

"Silas," he said. Mother was smiling, as well, and even Father seemed allayed. The only one who remained stiff and still in her high-backed chair at the head of the table was Grandmother.

Perenor sat. Slowly, I sat down next to him, across from Mother, whose tight-lipped smile was gaining a subtle pain to it. Our plates had been left empty, and I moved to fill mine.

"It's good to have you home," my grandfather said, and I offered him a hesitant smile. "There's so much we need to catch up on. Rumor has it that you were able to meet the other Godspeakers, is that right?"

I hesitated, but eventually nodded. "I'll b-b-be spending a d-day with G-Greatmother Amira," I answered. "She's al-l-l-llowing me to sh-shadow her, f-familiarize myself with the-the duties of a Godspeaker."

"That's very generous of her," Mother said.

Despite my better judgment, I looked sideways at Grandmother. Her eyes were focused on me with an intensity that should have made me nervous - that *would* have made me nervous but for Umbrion's ocean in my mind. As it stood, I found her scrutiny not so much frightening as irritating. This was the same glare she'd given me all through my childhood, whenever I'd shied away from talking to a stranger or stuttered at whatever diplomat to whom she'd introduced me.

I refused to let it intimidate me anymore.

"It seems rather childish of you," she said suddenly, "swanning off like you did, no warning or explanation."

Privately, I was amazed that, after everything, she still wanted to antagonize me. But for the first time, I was ready to antagonize her right back. I was a Godspeaker now, and for the first time, I felt like it.

"I agree," I answered, cutting neatly into my pork. "Wh-what sort of person would d-d-do something so m-m-monumental without even c-consulting relevant parties?"

Darkness fell over my grandmother's eyes.

"Dorran of House Valnon is a good match for you," she said, voice low. "Or at least he was."

"That w-w-would have been g-good to know b-b-before I met him."

"The situation was handled poorly," Mother said.

"The situation was *handled* precisely as it needed to be handled," Grandmother bit back. "Silas, if you're expecting some simpering apology, you're in for a disappointment."

"I'm s-s-sure I'm in for m-many," I said lowly.

"Let's try to keep things light," Grandfather said uneasily.

"T-t-tell me, Grandmother," I said, "wh-what is the s-s-slight for which I d-do not require an apology? For the horrifying d-d-duplicitousness of hiding p-plans of b-b-betrothal, or f-f-for false accusations of h-h-heresy?"

"Silas, bite your tongue," Grandmother growls. "This is no way to talk to your matriarch."

"Or d-d-do I not require an apology f-f-for the years of c-c-callous resentment and c-c-c-cruelty over th-things I can't control?" I ask. "D-d-do I require n-no apology for that, as w-well?"

"Please," my father says suddenly, "let's not do this now. This should be a time of celebration—"

"No, Oderon, the boy has grievances," Grandmother says. "Let him air them, by all means. Do you have complaint over the years we spent raising you, feeding you, clothing you, sheltering you?"

"Is th-th-that all it takes to raise a child!" I said. "I w-w-wonder, then, wh-why you wasted s-s-so much love and appr-r-roval on Perenor, wh-when I received so l-l-little."

"I'd thank you not to drag me into this, brother," Perenor said.

"This insolence is a new trait in you," Grandmother said. Her voice was dangerous. "It must be true what they say about the corruptive properties of power."

The ocean around me began to feel a fair bit warmer. "It m-m-must be," I said, "if y-y-you're any example."

"Please stop this," Mother interjected, "both of you."

"S-s-s-so no apology f-for the betrothal," I continued, "n-n-no apology for c-c-c-calling me a heretic, no apology f-f-for a l-lifetime of resentment. Wh-wh-why then am I here, pray tell?"

"Because this is the Seat of Olen," Grandmother growled at me. "This is where you belong."

All at once the tepid water of my ocean was at a full, rapid boil.

"Oh, *is it!*"

I stood up so sharply that I knocked over my chair; the metal frame clattered down on the flagstone. *BOOM*, from above; I took great and dark pleasure in seeing everyone at the table jump, including my grandmother. The sky above us had darkened considerably.

"Is it r-r-r-*really?* Because less than a f-fortnight ago, I was to b-be *married into House Valnon.*"

It would have been easier if Grandmother had matched my fury; unfortunately, she sat still as stone in her seat at the head of the table, eyes cold and fixed.

"Things have changed now," was all she said.

"Oh, of c-*course* they have, n-now that I'm a Godspeaker, you c-can finally stomach m-my presence in your most illustrious house!

"House Olen, *blood above all!*" I bellowed. "All those heavy-handed lessons of loyalty to the house, to the family, *meaningless!* Is our blood only thicker than water when the weather's fair?"

"Silas," Mother whispered, "you're frightening me."

I spared a glance at the sky; a warm midseason evening had turned dark and overcast, and I screwed my eyes shut and breathed deeply. Satisfying as it would have felt, calling down a tempest over dinner likely would have only caused more problems.

"It's Um-m-mbrion's magic," I muttered. "It comes out wh-wh-when I'm angry."

The sky slowly began to clear; the ocean around me began to cool. The anger dissipated, but at the core of all that rage was still that tiny knot of sadness, the same part of me that wept in my room every time I disappointed my grandmother – and I'd done that so many, many times.

"S-s-s-since your desperate d-desire to b-be rid of me is so at odds with y-y-your thirst for the p-political sway of a G-Godspeaker, I-let me make the d-d-decision easy for you." I kicked aside my overturned chair. "I w-w-would sooner renounce my house than s-s-spend another m-moment under the r-roof of a w-w-woman who can b-*barely tolerate me.*"

"Silas!" Father said, rising to his feet.

"I'll s-s-s-send for my th-things in the morning," I said, and I left over their shouted protestations. There was nothing in the world that could have made me look back.

SEVERAL LEAGUES past the city walls, tucked into the rolling sand dunes of the Wastes, Ellorian's temple to Umbrion stood tall and narrow on the horizon. I walked all night to reach it, ignoring my own hunger, the soreness that quickly spread through my legs, and the ever-encroaching darkness of my own thoughts.

It was not the first time I'd been to a temple – I'd attended weddings at Aemor's temple on the coast and seen Perenor's monastery in Elwen's temple on the hill – but it was the first time I'd ever seen Umbrion's. His was not a popular destination in terms of temples; he offered little to and interacted rarely with Andels, and his temples reflected that. Most temples built in his honor were done perfunctorily, for no other reason than all the other gods had one, so he should, too.

Still, it *was* a temple, and even at night when the only like came from the stars and the sky-river, it was open to everyone. I couldn't make out the major identifying features of it through the darkness, past the fact that it was tall and pointy and narrow and assembled of what looked like limestone.

The doors gave way when I pushed at them, and I stumbled inside, legs weak from the three leagues worth of walking, nerves ragged. The interior of the main room was sparsely lit, with plain stone floors and a vaulted ceiling full of bas-relief carvings. There were stone pews, all of them facing the apse where Umbrion's sigil was carved into the rock.

I sank down on the nearest pew and immediately doubled over, knotting my hands in my hair.

And slowly, slowly, all the emotions that I'd crossed three leagues of desert to escape caught up with me. The trembling came first, then the wheezing, then the desperate tears.

Perhaps I shouldn't have been surprised that I was still, after everything, not wanted, not really. The writing had been on the wall since I was a child, and it was foolish of me to think that anything could ever really change it. With my newly minted status as Godspeaker, they were willing to keep me in the family, but it had nothing to do with any love of me.

Had they ever loved me, some small and vulnerable part of my mind whispered. Had I ever been worth loving?

Oh, my little bird...

I gave a start and lifted my tear-blurred eyes. Standing on the far end of the middle aisle, robed in undulating twilight—

"Umbrion..."

It is a hard-learned lesson, he said gently, gliding down the aisle in ebbs and ripples like the tide, *but one that you were always fated to learn. Still, it hurts me to see you in such pain.*

My throat tightened. Some part of me felt ashamed for weeping openly in front of the Night Father, but I couldn't stop even if I wanted to.

When he was in front of me, he dropped to his knees and pressed his hand to my cheek. My eyes fell shut and *oh,* that electricity had not been a product of my dream. It was real, and it was racing along my skin in little arcs and jolts. I leaned into his touch quite without meaning to, and his thumb smoothed across my tears. He smelled of ocean and smiled like twilight, soft and strangely sad.

"Wh-wh-wh-why am I n-n-never enough f-f-for them?"

It seemed strange to ask him, but clearly he had some insight. And it wasn't as if this pain in my chest could get any worse.

Because you are different, little bird, he answered. *Because you can never be like them, like anyone. You defy their expectations, their only metric of worthiness, and they fall back on the assumption that it means you are not good enough.*

His cool fingertips threaded through my hair, and a powerful shudder ran up the length of my spine. My eyes fell shut, and though the pain was still there, still raw, his touch softened all its hard edges, and my heart beat faster against my ribs.

But you are good enough. You are far better, far worthier, far stronger than they can possibly imagine.

How easy, how frighteningly easy it was to let all that heartache drain away from the tips of his fingers, falling away like so much water through a sieve, until all that was left was him and the lightning in my nerves. I would have liked to think that this was some godly Craft, some small act of deliberate mercy that melted my pain, but the truth was bearing down on me.

That is our lot, little bird. We're different. We'll never walk in their sunlight, never be what they want us to be. Why should we even try?

Down and down and down those fingertips trailed, slipping through my hair and again over my throat. I made a low and desperate sound, and the truth I had been trying so hard to ignore became all-eclipsing and unmistakable:

This was, beyond any doubt, attraction.

It wasn't even the easy kind of attraction, flighty and silly and ignorable – this was intense, crippling, mind-bending attraction. I wanted him so badly it was physically painful. I was drunk off the touch of him, addicted. And wasn't that preposterous? Wasn't that insane, impossible, ludicrous?

That is the hard-learned lesson, little bird, he said. *The lesson that you must forsake your family to truly flourish. But if I can do it, you can do it.*

I opened my eyes with the intention of asking him what he meant by him having forsaken his family, but all my words evaporated the moment I saw him, saw how close he was, felt the thrum of his starlight on my skin. And I was mad, and this was ridiculous, and what sort of lunacy could ever possess me to feel this drawn to a creature so completely beyond my comprehension?

But he was so close, so incredibly close – was that his breath I felt on my mouth? Did the gods even have breath? When had he leaned in so near? If I were to lift my chin just the merest fraction—

"Oh! A visitor!"

I nearly swallowed my tongue.

I wrenched around in time to see a man in black temple robes emerging from a side door. When I looked back around, Umbrion was gone.

"Sorry, we're not quite accustomed to visitors here, let alone so late..."

My head was still spinning. It seemed too outrageous to even consider the possibility – but was that – had I nearly just—?

"Mostly it's just travelers looking for a bed before they reach the capitol – not that there's anything wrong with that, of course! Is that what you need?"

I blinked a few times, rubbed my neck. I could still feel his fingertips there, still detect the echoes of electricity on my skin.

"You don't much look like a traveller, not in that tunic."

"I'm n... I'm n..."

I forced my eyes to refocus and looked over at the man attending me. He was likely some kind of lower priest, by the look of him – I couldn't imagine that Umbrion had many priests at all, and so I wasn't surprised that a lower-ranking one had been trusted with a temple.

And though I was cognitively aware of the fact that this was a person who would soon be my subservient, all I could think about was the Night Father and how close he had been, and the implications of that closeness.

"Are you all right?" the priest asked. He was dark-haired, skin bronzed. "You look as though you've seen a shade."

No, I decided – that was simply not possible. And beyond that, it was probably heretical to even consider it, somehow. Surely I'd misinterpreted it. Surely...

"I'm f-f-fine," I said, willing myself to believe it, even though I could still feel those fingertips, even though the fading pulses of lightning still thrummed under my skin, even though my mind was still full of starlight. "I'd th-thank you for a b-b-bed tonight."

The priest nodded slowly. "Certainly," he said, not without some skepticism. "This way."

I rose to my still-aching feet and followed him down the aisle, forcefully willing away all those lingering sensations. Unfortunately, past the Night Father, the only thing left to think about was my family.

Umbrion had told me that I had to forsake my family to flourish. It seemed like a strange and somehow ungodly command, but as I followed the priest through to the small barracks along the western wall of the temple, I could not help but think that perhaps he was right. Perhaps that dinner had proven as much.

And in her own way, perhaps Grandmother had also been right. Perhaps I had nothing to offer House Olen, nor House Olen anything to offer me.

"What's your name?" the priest asked as we walked.

I was so deep in my own thoughts that it took me a while to climb back out of them.

"S-Silas," I said shortly.

"Night Father's blessings upon you," he answered cheerfully. He opened up a small closet and produced a bundle of blankets, which he handed to me. "You know, our new Godspeaker's name is Silas."

After some consideration, I decided not to respond. I took the bundle. My silence seemed to make him nervous.

"Just pick whatever bed you like," he said, gesturing to a nearby doorway leading to a room full of barracks. "You look like you need the rest."

And I did. There was an exhaustion in me that ran bone-deep. The day had been too eventful, too full of heartache – too much.

And though there were so many more important things to consider as I fell asleep, I found myself going back again and again to the memories of Umbrion's fingertips. The images carried with me into sleep, and I dreamed that night of starlight and lightning and the touch of his skin.

"GOOD TO SEE YOU, Silas," Greatmother Amira said when she came gliding out from the main door of the palace. She was once again decidedly not dressed to her station, this time wearing only a fitted, practical tunic, though she more than made up for her plain clothes with careful poise and effortless authority. The guards at the door bowed as she stepped into the sunlight of the courtyard. "Ready to go?"

I inclined my head. The camel-drawn carriage was waiting for us, not quite as stately as the massive, gilded one in which she had arrived, but still perfectly serviceable. I was about to open the carriage door when a footman did it for me, bowing deeply. I climbed inside, trying to act as though I wasn't startled by such simple things.

"It's all right," she told me after she had climbed in next to me. "It will take you a while to get used to it."

"Th-th-th-they treat m-me like I'm s-s-something special," I said doubtfully. The same footman shut the carriage door, and I peered out the window just before he thumped the side of the carriage and it slowly pulled out of the courtyard.

"You are special," she said, and I looked back at her with a frown. "I know it's a difficult thing to accept – ugly, even. It's hard to wrap your head around the idea that you are more special than the people you called equal a season ago. But ugly truths don't age well unacknowledged. You are the voice of a god now, Silas. No one is going to forget that, so you shouldn't, either."

I supposed she was right, although it didn't make it any easier to accept.

The carriage wheels started to rumble in earnest when we made it onto the aging, bumpy cobblestone of Ellorian. The walls muted the sound of the market to a dull, indistinct rumble.

There was a question hanging heavy in the back of my mind. Several questions, actually – ones that I didn't know how to ask, or even how to approach.

"Wh-wh-what will we be d-doing today?" I asked instead. "S-s-specifically."

"I'll be checking up on the local hospice, for a start," she answered, "and I'll be meeting with the High Priest of Ellorian to receive an update on new recruits and other notable events. And I can never visit any of Sol's temples without being roped into giving a sermon."

The mere idea that I would have to give a sermon made me nauseous. "W-w-will I have to-to do that, t-too?"

"If Umbrion wills it," she answered, smiling patiently. "But if I had to guess, I'd say no. The function of each Temple is determined by its patron god's will. Sol willed her temples to be places of contemplation, worship, healing, therefore sermons occasionally fall under my purview. Elwen wanted monasteries and libraries, so Fiyera's duties are scholarly and managerial; Aemor asked for temple courtesans and marriage registries, so Rolen functions as a chaperone; Lilline wanted the museums and art patronages, so Arana serves as a curator. Our duties as Godspeaker are as diverse as our gods.

"I'm happy to have you shadow me, but to really know what your duties will entail, you must think in terms of what Umbrion would want his Temple to be."

It was certainly an interesting question, and one that had no answer at the moment. What would Umbrion will his legacy to be on Andelan? Perhaps I'd simply have to wait for more guidance, because I could not fathom it.

"Have you spoken to him again?"

I hesitated, but nodded.

"My goodness," she said. "He really does like you."

"He s-s-said..." But again I hesitated. Ever since it had happen, my mind had been a tangle. Umbrion had said and done quite a few things, a mess of thoughts and deeds and sentiments that left me unsure of what to bring up.

"What did he say? Greatmother Amira prompted when the silence grew too long.

"Has... h-has Sol ever m-m-mentioned – and I'm s-s-sorry if this is impolitic—"

"Oh, I'll thank you not to care about that," she said, giving the universal *never mind it* gesture. "Please."

"—b-b-but has Sol ever m-mentioned her r-relationship with Umbrion?"

She raised both eyebrows at me. Clearly, that hadn't been the direction she'd been expecting me to take. "Her relationship?" She asked the question as though she found it peculiar to consider that the gods had relationships at all with each other, and I couldn't blame her. It was peculiar for me to consider, as well.

"He said..."

That is the hard-learned lesson, little bird. His words rang in my head, fresh and clear as though he was still present. *The lesson that you must forsake your family to truly flourish. But if I can do it, you can do it.*

"... s-something strange," I concluded, rather anticlimactically.

"Well," Greatmother Amira said slowly, "she loves all her children, which I can only assume includes the other gods."

She paused suddenly, frowning as though remembering something.

"Now that I think of it," she continued, "over the years, she has always sounded... sad, when she talks about Umbrion."

"Sad?"

"That's always how it came across to me," she answered. "Then again, it's not really our place to understand such things. Ours is just to communicate their message, not to know the deepest parts of them."

Perhaps that was true. Perhaps it had always been presumptuous of me to think that I - that any Andel, Godspeaker or otherwise - could ever truly know the mind of a god.

But on the other hand, Umbrion seemed to think different. He saw a deeper connection and empathy between us.

That is our lot, little bird. We are different. We will never walk in their sunlight, never be what they want us to be. Why should we even try?

I felt the echo of his fingertips on my throat and shuddered.

"Why do you ask?"

Should I bring up Umbrion's words? Should I try to divine some meaning or implication in them? Would Greatmother Amira be able to offer any insight? Would there even be any insight to gain?

After a moment, it occurred to me—

"Y-y-y-you were k-k-kissed by the W-W-Worldmother," I said.

I'd managed to surprise her again.

"I m-m-m-mean," I added, somewhat overhastily, "if the l-l-legend is t-true."

"It's true. Most legends have some basis in fact." And she repeated, "Why do you ask?"

It was suddenly quite important for me to come up with a plausible reason, or at the very least a suitable distraction, so as to keep her from trying to guess. "The b-b-b-books always c-c-call it the B-B-Benediction."

"Aye," Greatmother Amira said, "a better descriptor than kiss. Don't mistake me, it had all the mechanics of a kiss, and it was certainly meant to convey love, but it had less to do with me and more to do with all the Ansu people. It was her way of ending our suffering."

I wondered if that was what Umbrion had intended – to end my suffering. And, for the thousandth time, I wondered if I had misinterpreted the entire thing, because why on earth would he ever want to kiss *any* Andel, let alone *me?*

"I'm still not sure what this is about," she said, pulling me back out of my thoughts. "If I can help you, I will. But you'll quickly come to discover that many of your questions will go unanswered by virtue of their nature."

I frowned at her, and the question must have been in my eyes, because she kept going a moment later:

"Theirs is an experience far removed from our own," she said. "In the same way a bird could not understand the depth and complexity of your inner life, so too are we ignorant to theirs. I've found that it is best to trust them, even when it's difficult. *Especially* when it's difficult. They've not yet led us astray."

I turned her words over in my head for a while as the conversation lapsed into a comfortable silence.

It was a comforting notion, and – I hoped – a correct one. I found that I did quite desperately want to trust Umbrion. Surely it was the very least I owed him after he provided me with such a tremendous privilege.

And as our carriage rolled out of the city and towards Sol's temple nestled in the heart of the jungle, I decided that I would. Surely, I thought, surely there was nothing to fear.

Never in my life before had I been, nor ever in my life forthwith would I be, so desperately, completely, and eclipsingly wrong.

THE REASON, I was beginning to suspect, that all of the Godspeakers came to Ellorian for the Queensday Tournaments, despite what must have been long and exhausting treks from all corners of Andelan, was not so much any real desire to observe as it was the forceful compunction of custom.

I hadn't had any intention of actually going until I shared this news with Amon upon my return from Sol's temple the evening before they were set to begin. He gave me a look of such abject horror that one would have thought he'd been slapped. Any hope I'd had of sleeping in after such a long journey to and from Sol's temple was swiftly and ruthlessly dashed.

And so, still tired and more than a bit irritable, I woke up with the sun, dressed, and went down to the Queen's Ring for the opening day of the Tournaments.

The whole experience was made so much worse by the fact that Soya, as my official plus-one, insisted on being so *chipper* about the whole thing.

"Which events are going on today?" she asked the moment she climbed into my carriage.

I rubbed my knuckles into my eyes. "I d-d-don't know."

"Are we going to be sitting with the other Godspeakers?"

"I d-don't *know.*"

"You'll introduce me, won't you?"

"I w-want to go b-b-back to bed."

"Come on, you must be at least a little excited!"

Somehow, startlingly, I couldn't muster a single iota of excitement.

There wasn't even enough time for me to nap in the carriage. I had spent the night before at the palace at the behest of Greatmother Amira when we arrived back later than expected, and the trip between the palace and the Queen's Ring was a short one, just across the city.

The closer we got to the arena, the denser the noise became. Through the walls of the carriage, I could hear vendors shouting, children laughing, and the thrum and buzz of a city close to bursting with people. And somewhere, amidst all the noise, I could hear a low, rhythmic chanting – "*Umbrion! Umbrion! Umbrion!*"

"They're chanting for you," Soya said. She had drawn back the curtain over the window of the carriage and was staring out at the crowd, so close, mere feet away, throwing nightlilies.

"They're ch-chanting for Umbrion," I answered, looking away from the window.

By the time the carriage rattled to a halt, the volume was almost unbearable. The moment the door was pulled open, it sharped steeply upward to near-deafening levels.

"*Umbrion! Umbrion! Umbrion!*" The crowd seemed ecstatic, and I did my best not to panic at the sight of them, which I only accomplished neck deep in Umbrion's ocean.

I climbed out onto the road, which was strewn with flowers, and the crowd gathered at the edge of the arena cheered even louder. I quavered under the intensity of their enthusiasm. I did my best to be grateful, but it was no easy thing. I hated strangers and I hated crowds. It was an intense and cruel irony that I'd likely have to spend much of my life around both.

Behind me, Soya climbed from the carriage and thumped me heartily on the back.

"You're all right," she said. "They love you!"

That fact comforted me less than she would have liked. I grabbed her arm and pulled her away, into the large passageway leading through to the vomitorium. The guards lining the walls came to sharp salutes as we passed.

The Queen's Ring was already full when we came out into the sunlight in the middle tier of the arena. There was more cheering, but at least this time it was from a distance.

We made our way to the side of the arena, past rows and rows of spectators all gathered for the Tournaments, up toward the seats of honor. Greatmother Amira was already seated.

"Hello, Silas," she said as I came into earshot.

"Good m-m-morning."

"Who's this?"

I looked back at Soya. It was pleasing, in a dark sort of way, to see *her* looking nervous and flustered for a change.

"This is m-my friend, Soya, f-f-f-firstborn scion of House Rhodan," I said. "S-Soya, this is G-G-Greatmother Amira, Godspeaker to S-S-Sol."

"Worldmother's blessings, Soya," said Greatmother Amira, and in answer, Soya made an extremely undignified squeaking sound. She bowed low. "I think I recognize your house. Is your patriarch, by any chance, Lord of Avenos?"

Soya nodded mutely. I wasn't used to seeing her look so nervous. It was a tiny bit hilarious.

"I've had occasion to meet your Lord Father," Greatmother Amira said. "Quite a man, and quite a Lord."

"So I've been told, Your Holiness," Soya answered, barely.

I sat down on one of the handsome pine benches next to Greatmother Amira. Soya sat beside me and at once leaned in to whisper—

"I can't believe we're just sitting next to her!"

"She's j-just a p-p-person," I said, taking more enjoyment from her nervousness than I probably should have.

"She's the mouth and the hands and the will of the Worldmother!"

"Are you excited for the Tournaments?" Greatmother Amira asked, and if she'd heard Soya's frantic whispering, she was doing a good job of pretending she hadn't.

"I'd r-rather be sleeping," I confessed.

"So would I," said a voice from behind – Rolen, as it turned out, Aemor's Godspeaker, with a woman who I was willing to bet was his wife. "I personally don't see much appeal in the entire concept of the Tournaments. What does being the fastest or the strongest prove?"

Soya gawked, and then elbowed me in the ribcage as if to ask *is that who I think it is?* I glared at her and rubbed the sore spot

"It proves nothing," Greatmother Amira conceded, "but it does wonders to stimulate Ellorian's economy. And it gives the citizens something to enjoy."

"Ever the pragmatist, Greatmother," Rolen said, sitting down next to Soya. "Who's this?"

Introductions continued over the next few minutes as all the other Godspeakers arrived, all with accompaniment. Fiyera arrived with her wife, Arana with her sister, and then the cheering suddenly got much louder.

Just below us, I could see her enter – robed in gold with her crown gleaming in the sunlight, stately and powerful and proud: Queen Nerisa, her Lady Queen on her arm.

She had a special seat on the tier just below us, on a throne of polished brass and blue velvet cushions. When she moved to the edge of the balustrade overlooking the arena, she raised both her hands, and a hush fell over the crowd.

"Friends, subjects, countrymen – I bid you welcome to the twenty-ninth Queensday Tournaments!"

The cheer rose up at once, so loud that the rock of the arena rumbled as if cheering with them. It wasn't until Queen Nerisa lifted her hands again that it settled down.

"It's a tradition that began with a celebration of my coronation," she called, the acoustics of the arena carrying her voice all across the ring, "but it would be presumptuous of me to pretend that these Tournaments have anything to do with my rule.

"Seasons pass, children of the fourth and fifth and even sixth generations are born, and these Tournaments continue – not only as a test of mettle and physical prowess, but as a standard by which we measure ourselves and how we have used the gifts the gods have given us.

"It is my pleasure and my privilege, here in the sight of our gods and our Godspeakers—" (here she gestured briefly up to us) "—to declare that the twenty-ninth Queensday Tournaments are officially begun!"

More cheering, even more impossibly loud, and the great wooden doors on the far end of the arena floor groaned open. The athletes for the first event came out on chariots to the sound of thundering drums.

"The first event is archery," Greatmother Amira said to me, though she had to shout to be heard over the fanfare "I don't think anyone would notice if you took a nap."

I grinned at her.

I HAD THOUGHT that my presence would only be required during the opening day of the Queensday Tournaments, but as it turned out, such was not the case – I was expected to be at every one. So in addition to my upcoming confirmation ceremony and coordinating with the High Priestess of Umbrion (the *only* High Priestess of Umbrion, as it turned out) about my upcoming duties as the head of her Temple, I had to take six hours out of each day to watch the games.

On the third day, the first event to take place was combat Craft, Perenor's event. I wasn't particularly eager to see him, even from a distance. Long before I'd made it into the Queen's Ring, my mind was turning over the painful, troublesome problem that was my family and what to do about them.

But thinking about it turned out to be a mistake, because when I made it up to the special section of seats on that third day, there she was – my grandmother, as though manifested directly from my desire not to talk to her.

She was sour-faced as ever, looking particularly pale in the bright sunlight, and I could tell from her gait alone that she had been waiting for me.

"Grandson," she said, voice flat.

I stopped a few feet away from her. For a moment, I seriously considered just leaving from whence I came, but I doubted I could get out unnoticed. Maybe I could get a guard to throw her out? Then again, she *was* a member of the Queenscourt, so the chances of that working were very slim.

"How much longer, may I ask, are you planning on avoiding your family?"

Well, it could never be said that my grandmother was one to mince words.

"Only as l-l-long as you are its m-matriarch, I suppose."

The glibness of my answer did not land well with her at all, which, quite to my surprise, did not bother me in the least. Time was, that smoldering glare of hers would eat the heart out of my chest, but as I met her eyes, I felt no fear.

Perhaps she didn't have power over me anymore. Perhaps, as Umbrion had asked of me, I had already forsaken her.

"You do not wear this new power well," she said coldly.

"W-well it's a good thing that I d-don't care about y-your opinion, then."

I sat down neatly on the bench. Grandmother straightened, bristled, narrowed her eyes. I must have struck a nerve.

"Then perhaps you'll care about common sense and propriety," Grandmother said. "Perhaps, in the absence of any formal declaration from you, you have realized the very serious and far-reaching implications of formally renouncing your house."

I could already tell this was going to be a tedious conversation. I looked down at the arena where the contestants were gathering.

"Silas, if you actually renounce House Olen, there will be very real political and economic consequences," Grandmother said severely. "We have important diplomatic ties all over Andelan that would be put under considerable strain if word got out that you renounced it."

Struck by the sudden dark irony, I laughed. The reaction seemed to bother her quite profoundly, which only made me laugh harder.

"Do you think this is funny?" she demanded. "Do you have no concept of the trade deals we keep in place, the delicate diplomacy House Olen facilitates? This would cast a very real shadow—"

"Grandmother," I interrupted, still laughing, "if y-y-you think I haven't c-considered the political and econ-n-nomic ramifications of renouncing m-m-my house, you underestimate m-me more than usual."

"Silas—"

"Of c-c-c-*course* I know the ramifications," I said. "I'm n-n-no fool. If I have not y-y-yet made my d-d-declaration, it's only b-because I know how b-b-badly the s-s-scandal would strain important d-d-diplomatic ties."

"Then why in the name of *all the gods* would you even *threaten* something so grave?" she demanded.

"B-b-because it s-s-seemed like the quickest w-w-way to what we b-b-both want," I answered honestly. "Or will you d-d-deny that you w-want to be r-r-rid of me?"

"That's..." Her expression soured. "Silas—"

"D-don't trouble y-yourself with m-m-my heart, Grandmother," I answered. "You n-n-never have b-before."

Oh, yes, *that* had hit a nerve. Good.

"B-b-besides," I continued, "the N-Night Father all but g-g-gave me holy order to-to-to forsake you."

Grandmother reacted as though my words had struck her across the face. I kept going, taking a dark and intense pleasure in her sudden alarm.

"He's b-b-been with me all m-m-my life," I continued, "w-watching over me s-s-since conception, and his advice w-w-was to forsake you."

She did not have a response, so I kept talking.

"I was sh-shocked at first – it d-d-didn't seem like advice th-that a g-god would give – but I've had t-t-time to think about it and n-n-now I th-think I understand. I am st-stronger without you, w-w-w-without your poison."

"Silas," she said. Her voice was softer this time, but I was no longer interested in hearing what she had to say.

"You d-d-don't even know how b-badly you hurt me – or if y-y-you do, you don't s-seem to care," I said. "You t-t-tried to betroth me behind m-my back, you c-called me a heretic wh-when I needed you m-m-most—"

"Silas," she said a second time, but it was not her turn to talk.

"All th-th-this, after a l-life time of c-contempt, derision, cruelty. If y-y-you have ever l-loved me, you've c-c-c-certainly n-never taken pains to sh-show it.

"So wh-wh-why shouldn't I f-forsake you?" I asked. I did not take my eyes off her. I drank in every line and subtlety of her face, every twitch, every restrained grimace. "Why sh-shouldn't I renounce House Olen? Wh-wh-what loyalty do-do I owe it, after everything? What l-loyalty has it ever sh-sh-shown me?"

She opened her mouth as if to respond, but no words came. All the times her cruelty had left me stuttering in heartbroken impotence, all the times she'd let me hate myself, this felt like justice, or at least something like it.

And then there was the sound of screaming.

It took me a moment to refocus, to pull myself up and out of the conversation and identify the source. On the far side of the arena, the spectators that were not scrambling towards the exits were staring up at the sky in open-mouthed shock. I turned over my shoulder, and it did not take long for me to find the source of their fear.

Screaming out from and ripping apart a large fair-weather cloud was an immense, silver-white light with a long tail. It was hurtling down for the sky, aimed straight at the arena.

"What in Sol's name is that?" I heard Grandmother breathe.

I had no answer. I did not know. Whatever it was, it was huge and it was barreling down toward us faster than the sound of it could catch up.

"Silas—" Her hand found my shoulder. "Silas, we have to run—"

"There's n-n-not enough time." It was moving far too quickly. "W-w-we need cover—"

The screaming was getting louder, more frantic. People were clogging the vomitoria, scrambling over each other to get out—

"*Perenor!*" Grandmother cried, bracing both hands on the balustrade that overlooked the arena. "*Perenor!*"

Down in the middle of the ring, the battle had stopped. I could see Perenor - or at least, the indistinct outline of Perenor - standing on the dirt, shoulders heaving, looking up at Grandmother, then the crowds, then the sky.

"*Run, Perenor!*" she shouted. "*Find cover!*"

But he didn't run. He stood and stared up at the sky. I could see his hands wringing around his staff. And suddenly, he was holding it over his head, and was glowing with a brilliant white light—

"Wh-wh-what's he d-doing?"

She swore colorfully in the Old Tongue. "That foolish boy!"

I felt arms around me a moment later, and I was pulled down, behind the balustrade.

"Grandmother—!"

"Stay down!"

I did not have time to protest. One after the other, several things happened very quickly:

First, there was a rumbling, low and sonorous, as though springing up from the depths of the living rock under our feet. It was accompanied by a sudden burst of white light – not from the sky, but from the center of the arena. It domed outward, a thick layer of Craft that was hot to the touch, that expanded across the entirety of the Queen's Ring.

Then, there came a sound so deafening, so impossibly loud, that for a moment I thought my head might split open from the force of it. It darkened my vision and the shockwave knocked me flat, my grandmother on top of me.

Finally, there was a light, and a tremendous shaking, and the smell of ozone and rising dust. Then there was the sensation of falling, as though the ground had given out beneath my feet, and we fell, Grandmother and I, tumbling over what felt like broken rock and splintered wood and debris.

We tumbled through the sound and the chaos and the roaring fury, until we stopped.

I was immersed in a terrible, numb silence. I blinked open my eyes but could see little past smudges of yellow sand and white limestone.

My ears began ringing, softly at first, and then louder. The world came gradually back into focus.

I could hear my grandmother – or rather, I could hear a muted, foggy blur of sound that resembled something like my grandmother's voice – but I could not make out the words. There was ash raining from the sky, black and hot, and it burned my skin.

"Silas," I could hear Grandmother say as the ringing in my ears began to subside. Her voice was hoarse, and she was coughing, and there was distant screaming. "Silas – Perenor—?"

"Your Holiness!" came another voice, but I was being swallowed by an ever-encroaching darkness. "Your Holiness, Your Holiness, are you all right? Stay awake! Stay awake!"

But I did not stay awake. I fell into the swallowing dark, and then there was nothing.

ARE YOU HURT, little bird?

We were once again back at the beach, awash in water and starlight.

I knew that this was a dream, and though I had dreamt *of* him many times, I had no doubt that this was a true manifestation.

He moved toward me in subtle, rippling movements, until he was close enough to lay his hands on my face. I shivered at his touch, and all the terrible-wonderful sacrilegious wanting came surging back to life in my chest and on my throat.

I must be more vigilant, he said. *I can't have my little bird breaking a wing.*

I wetted my lips, tried to focus. It was always so hard to concentrate when he was close like this, and it took everything in me to come up with a response, even in the sleepy, hazy, uncoordinated fog of a dream.

"What happened?" I asked him. "Do you know?"

The corner of his mouth quirked upward into a strange, ethereal smile. His hands did not move from my face.

A large chunk of rock fell from the sky, he answered.

"A rock?" I repeated. "But it was on fire. Stone can't burn."

An artifact of high velocity, he said, which was a fascinating answer, and I would have liked more time to think about it, but unfortunately he didn't give me the time. *These are not the interesting questions you're asking, little bird.*

Despite myself, I smiled. Somehow the fact that he was speaking in riddles struck me as oddly charming. I'd always loved riddles. "And what are the interesting questions?"

The most interesting question, I should think, is where it came from.

It seemed strange to consider that such a massive, cataclysmic event could have come from anywhere. I frowned and thought about it, but my mind could come up with no answers.

You'll understand in time, the Night Father assured me. He lifted one hand and brushed it through my hair, and all at once I fell apart underneath his fingertips. I wondered if he knew what he did to me, the reactions he evoked in me. *In fact, I imagine that when we next meet, everything will be made quite clear to you. How is your family, my little bird?*

The abrupt change in the conversation was surprising, though only for a moment. I looked down at my feet as I thought. The dream-blackened waters were lapping at my feet, though I could not feel the.

"I think I will renounce my house," I answered eventually.

A weighted action in your culture, in my admittedly limited understanding. I cannot say that I'm surprised. It was always going to end this way.

"Was it?" I asked him, looking back up.

His hands travelled lower, closer to my throat. My heartbeat hastened.

You are stronger without them, he said. He was nearer now, so close that his starlight hummed against my skin. *We both are. Our destiny is beyond anything they could possibly hope to comprehend.*

The only explanation I have for what I sad next is, despite knowing that I was addressing a deity whose power and ineffability could chew me up in an instant, the strange feeling of invincibility unique to dreaming had not gone away.

I was not thinking of his godliness at that moment. I was thinking of his fingertips and of how badly I wanted him. I felt ethereal, windswept, fearless, and I asked—

"Are you going to kiss me?"

It seemed like a perfectly fair question at the time. After all, he was so very close to me, and his touches were intoxicating.

But his response was not immediate. For a moment, all he did was study me, his eyes like auroras and his fingertips like lightning, until the corner of his mouth twitched upward into a half-smile.

Would you like me to kiss you?

I tried to swallow down the heart in my throat to little success.

"Yes," I answered. What point was there in lying to a god, after all?

Then I will kiss you, he said, and that was precisely what he did.

There was a moment quite some time after the fact that I realized the last time a god had kissed an Andel, an entire culture had sprung up around her.

I doubt that any songs will be sung or legends passed down about this kiss – or at least not any that I should like to hear – but some selfish part of me thought it deserved some fanfare.

Calling it a kiss at all was a bit of a misnomer. It was a kiss in the same way the ocean was water – correct, but vastly oversimplifying. Far more than a kiss, it was an *event,* one that ripped me open and dissolved me into stardust.

There are no words that can really do it justice. The best I can say is that being enfolded in his arms was like being submerged in liquid twilight, and that whatever your mind could come up with as to what it is like to be kissed by a god, I can assure you that you are underestimating it.

But all dreams end, and though I would not have minded spending the rest of my life pressed into him, I was pulled away—

"SILAS...?"

I smelled tea, heard birdsong, felt sunlight. Perhaps it was my imagination, but I could still feel him on my lips, and my skin was still electrified.

"You're sweating. Are you feverish?"

A hand pressed to my head. I opened my eyes but found myself squinting against the light reflecting off the bright limestone walls. I knew at once that I must have been in the palace.

"Soya?" My voice came out as a rasp.

"The very same. You don't seem to have a fever."

Underneath her hand, which I could now perceive as being on my forehead, there was cold sweat beading. I had neither the faculties nor the impetus to tell her why.

"Wh-wh-wh-what happened?" I asked, coming up through my own consciousness one stage a time.

"No one's sure." I blinked a few times, willing my eyes to refocus. Soya had withdrawn her hand and was sitting on a chair at my bedside. "The scholars are still arguing about it, in fact."

I sat up slowly. There was a tray of food at the foot of my bed – fresh bread, ham steak, and tea, the sort of meal you'd give to someone who was recovering from something, which I suppose I must have been.

"It was a ch-chunk of rock that f-f-fell from the s-sky," I said, realizing as I stared at the food that I was ravenous. I tugged the tray over and went straight for the fragrant, floral tea.

"Well, no one knows for sure," Soya said, dragging a chair over from the wall and sitting down. "Perenor's shield apparently evaporated it."

I took several gulps of tea. I had nearly forgotten that detail – the bright dome of Craft from the center of the arena, the deafening roar.

"Perenor s-s-s-saved Ellorian." It would have found it more impressive if I didn't already find it incredibly obnoxious.

"Yeah," she said, nudging the ham steak toward me. There wasn't any silverware – though I was hungry enough not to mind that much – and I tore a large chunk from it. "It wiped him out, though. I guess Craft that strong will really run you ragged."

I frowned as I chewed. Even though I told myself I didn't care, I asked, "He's okay?"

She grinned at me. "He's fine," she said, "just tired. He's a hero of Ellorian now; he's being given the best care in the capitol."

Perenor despised the hero worship his fan club gave him, so the idea of him being subjected to more of such treatment made me a little bit happy.

"They told me not to wake you, that you had to sleep it off, but when I saw you sweating, I got worried. Bad dream?"

The images had slipped so easy from my mind, like water through cupped hands, but when they came back, it was with full force. My chewing slowed and I licked my lips as the gravity of what had just happened settled in my mind.

Because had I really just been kissed by a god? It seemed too preposterous a notion to entertain, and yet...

"*Good* dream?" Soya amended, and when I looked up at her, she was grinning coquettishly. I hit her with my pillow and she laughed.

"D-d-d-did they c-cancel the T-Tournaments?" I asked.

"They have not," she answered. "Remarkably, injuries and damages were very few. Perenor really saved the day, apparently. I don't know if they'll just declare him the winner of the tournaments outright, but they'll definitely award him *something*."

I frowned. If they weren't cancelling the Queensday Tournaments, that likely meant that they wouldn't reschedule my confirmation ceremony, either, which was a shame for no other reason than I would have liked a reason to postpone it.

"I'm glad you're all right," Soya said. I looked up at her. "Scared the fuck out of me, you know. I saw that fireball streaking down from the sky, headed right for the arena..."

I smiled. Not for the first time, I counted myself lucky to have a friend like Soya.

"I'll m-m-make sure n-not to tell anyone th-that you l-l-like me so much."

"Good," she said. "Can't let word slip that I'm getting soft."

I laughed and I let her steal a piece of my ham steak.

I WAS PERMITTED to skip the last four days of the Queensday Tournaments, both to accommodate my speedy recovery – which I didn't really need, because the injuries I sustained were very minor – and to continue preparing for my confirmation ceremony, which had been officially scheduled for the day after the Tournaments ended.

And despite how frequently and feverishly I told myself I did not care, after a few days I went to check up on Perenor.

It was no hard thing to find him. No one thought twice about a Godspeaker wanting to visit his brother, which made me glad they didn't have the context necessary to realize how strange it actually was. A guard directed me to a room in the east wing of the palace, a luxury presumably afforded a newly-minted hero.

I knocked twice and waited for an answer, but none came. I leaned forward to listen to the door, and could hear loud and animated talking – but the voice was not Perenor's. I knocked again, louder, and pushed the door open.

"—could hardly *believe* when I saw – oh!"

I noticed several things all at once – the mountainous pile of get-well flowers in vases all over the room; my brother sitting cross-legged and profoundly uncomfortable on the bed; and a tall, attractive young man with bright mahogany hair.

"Oh," the stranger said. Then, "*Oh!* Your Holiness!"

He bowed low. I still wasn't used to it. I looked to Perenor. I knew most of his friends, and this was certainly not one of them. Perenor gave me a pleading look, the meaning of which I couldn't quite discern.

"I'm so sorry, I must not have heard you knock!" the stranger said. "I was just visiting your brother, thanking him for what he did!"

I remained ungraceful at talking to strangers, but I inclined my head politely in the universal gesture of acknowledgment. I don't think he noticed; he turned right back around and looked again at Perenor, twisting his hands together anxiously.

"The whole *city* is talking about his bravery," the stranger said worshipfully, taking a half-step toward his bed. "And his strength! I could never have imagined that Craft could be so strong! To protect an entire arena and to dissolve that great fireball into dust like you did! Masterful – and so, *so* powerful."

Oh, I realized with a sudden and intense mirth, this was one of Perenor's *groupies*. I did my best to choke back on the bark of laughter trying to fight its way up my throat, to middling success. It came out as a sort of snort, though Perenor's fan didn't notice.

"I don't know if they'll name you the victor of the combat Craft tournament, but I think they *should*," his groupie said. "You're a hero of Ellorian, Perenor! Did you get the flowers I sent—?"

Hilarious though it was, if only because I enjoyed seeing my brother in discomfort, I felt as though I should probably save him from it. I cleared my throat pointedly, and the groupie looked back at me.

"Oh," he said. "Oh, you probably want to…"

I inclined m head again. He looked crestfallen, and he gave one last, longing look to Perenor.

"Brothers," Perenor said. "They can be so protective."

I choked down a second laugh.

"Right," the groupie said. "Well, enjoy the flowers."

"I hardly have a choice," Perenor answered, gesturing to the western wall, which was mostly dominated by them.

"Of course. Ah. Goodbye, then." He looked to Perenor, then to me. "Your Holiness." He bowed and left.

The moment the door shut behind him—

"*Sol's Light*," he said, collapsing back on the bed, and I finally stopped stifling my laughter. "That's *five in one day*."

"Enjoy the f-f-flowers!" I crooned at him through my laughter. "How m-m-many did you *get?*"

"Shut up," Perenor answered, covering his face.

"I im-m-magine your f-fanbase is bigger than ever," I said, moving to the nearest bunch of flowers and plucking a note tucked behind a nightlily.

"*They won't leave me alone,*" he groaned. "And shut up! I said, shut up, didn't I? What do you want?"

"To r-r-revel in your m-misery, of course."

"You're the worst."

"And y-y-*you,* brother-mine, are a b-b-*brave and handsome sorcerer!*" I read aloud from the card, laughing.

"Give me that!"

He climbed across the bed and tore the note from my hand, crumpling it up and throwing it across the room. His indignation, of course, only made the whole thing more hilarious.

"G-G-Gods know why you're s-s-s-so fussy about it," I laughed.

"I don't want suitors!" Perenor said, voice a touch shrill. "And I certainly don't want eight of them following me around like lovesick school children—"

"P-p-p-poor Perenor," I warbled, "subjected to the b-b-blind adoration of st-st-strangers! Fate has t-t-truly been c-cruel to you."

"I don't want their adoration! And I especially don't want the stupid love notes – what do you *want,* Silas?"

I laughed again and plucked a nightlily from one of the bouquets, inhaling deeply. "I j-j-just wanted to ch-check up on you," I said. "You know, m-m-make sure you're still st-st-standing."

"I *can* stand, I just *won't,*" Perenor said huffily. "That Craft took a lot out of me. And since when do you care about whether or not I can stand?"

I rolled my eyes. "F-f-fine. Gods f-forgive me for c-c-caring about my b-b-brother. I'll l-l-leave you to it."

I turned for the door. Coming at all had been stupid, of course, and now that I knew Perenor was fine, I could let him stew in his fatigue and groupies with a clear conscience. Before I could reach the door handle, I heard him say—

"Wait."

I stopped and looked back. Perenor was frowning, arms crossed.

"Grandmother said..."

I frowned back at him. I had a feeling I knew where this was going.

"Are you going to renounce House Olen?" he asked. His voice was surprisingly neutral – or at least, more neutral than I would have expected it to be.

"D-d-d-did she t-tell you to talk m-me out of it?" It certainly wouldn't have been out of her purview.

"No," he answered, and strangely, I believed him.

"Then wh-wh-what does it m-matter to you?"

"It matters to me like whether or not I'm still standing matters to you," he replied.

I kicked my feet on the flagstone floor self-consciously.

"I th-th-think I will," I said reluctantly. "Once m-m-my confirmation ceremony's c-c-come and gone."

I watched for his reaction. I wasn't really sure what to expect, which turned out not to be a problem, because Perenor didn't seem to know how to react.

"Will that make you happy?" he asked.

What a strange thing to hear, coming from him.

"M-my happiness is r-r-rather beside the p-point. And since wh-wh-when do you c-c-care about my happin-n-ness?"

Silence lapsed between us. It was deafening, heavy with a lifetime of mutual resentment and a million unsaid words. I regretted coming. I should have just had a servant check up on him for me.

"Enjoy your f-f-flowers," I said, and left.

SO FAR AS I COULD TELL, the only good thing about the upcoming confirmation was that I wouldn't have to do any public speaking. Umbrion would have to do some speaking through me, but I wouldn't be in control of my own body while it happened, so presumably I wouldn't do anything embarrassing like pass out from fear.

Still, my nerves weren't what you'd call soothed. Public speaking or no, I would still have to deal with the terrifying reality of being stared at by so many people, take up my mantle as Godspeaker officially, and pray to all the gods that I wouldn't trip in front of the entire population of Ellorian and thousands besides.

"Get plenty of sleep tonight, Silas," Greatmother Amira had advised me the night before the ceremony. "You'll need it."

So, in the spirit of how these things often go, I did not sleep at all.

I did try, in my defense. I tried for hours, tossing and turning in my bed at the Palace, staring at the darkened ceiling, mind caught in an endless loop of the millions of things that could go disastrously wrong.

It wasn't until near pre-dawn that I gave up on the idea of sleep entirely. By my estimation, there was less than an hour before someone would come to wake me up, anyway, so I climbed from my bed and went to the large picture window on the western wall of my room.

I knelt down at the foot of the window and stared out at the sky. The view was exquisite – a perfect division of land and sea, lit by the impossible colors and lights of the sky-river.

I wondered if it would be untoward for me to pray to Umbrion for his blessings. Underneath his breathtaking night sky, I certainly felt an impetus to. As I was considering whether or not he would hear my prayer above anyone else's, my eyes moved toward the horizon, and it was at that moment I noticed something – or, to be more precise, I noticed something was missing:

The flying star was gone.

For those of you confused as to why this realization frightened me to my core, allow me to explain the connections I made when I noticed its absence.

First: Umbrion had told me explicitly that the falling star was an omen that he had made, a sign of things to come.

Second: I had noticed before the Queensday Tournaments that the falling star's angular diameter had increased, implying that it had gotten closer.

Third: a fireball had nearly destroyed Ellorian five days ago.

In Umbrion's own words, the most interesting question I could ask about that fireball was where it had come from. The only conclusion I could reach, the only possible explanation for all of the facts, was that *Umbrion had brought down that fireball.*

But surely, my frantic mind supplied, *surely* that was not possible. *Surely* the Night Father would never bring down such destruction.

But as my mind went over all the conversations we'd had—

"Your Holiness?"

—hadn't Umbrion said something about a great change? Hadn't he mentioned the dawn of a new era? I hadn't thought about it at the time, but—

"Your Holiness, I've brought your breakfast."

—he *had*, I remembered, with rapidly spreading dread. He had called me a harbinger of a new age. If Umbrion had brought down that fireball, if he had the intent to cause so much destruction—

"You should eat quickly; you're needed downstairs for rehearsals in a quarter-hour."

There was a hand on my shoulder, and I wrenched around so abruptly that I startled the servant who'd arrived with my tray of food.

"I n-n-n— I n-n-n-n—"

The cursed words wouldn't come, and I suddenly realized that I was so scared my hands were shaking.

Was I misinterpreting this? Could there be some other explanation?

I had to talk to Greatmother Amira. If I was wrong, I'd do nothing but make a fool of myself – and Gods know I was used to that.

But if I was *right*...

"I n-n-n—" I tried again, but the words still refused to come. "I n-n-n—"

The servant, like most, was unaccustomed to my stutter, and though she did her best to be patient, I could tell she was in a hurry.

"Your Holiness, you need to get ready," she urged me. "The rehearsals will be starting soon."

"I n-n-n-n-*need* to t-talk to G-G-Greatmother Amira."

"I'll try to arrange for something, Your Holiness, but for now, you must eat. The rehearsals?"

I tried to calm myself down, through the shaking that was now pervading most of my body. I would talk to Greatmother Amira. I would talk to Greatmother Amira. She would know what to do. Surely she did.

If I was right – if I was right—

I SPENT THE ENTIRE MORNING in rehearsals with several royal functionaries, who had me run through everything I would have to do come the confirmation ceremony that evening – where to stand, when to move, what to do and when. It would have been an exhausting day in its own right, but it was made all the worse by my lack of sleep and the fact that I couldn't get my mind of that morning's realization.

The break for lunch could not have been more welcome. The moment I was released, I hurried toward the wing where I knew Greatmother Amira's room was, but was startled to find her already heading down the hallway.

"Silas!" she said. "Your servant mentioned you were looking for me."

I nodded frantically. All the nervous tension and fear that I'd been crushing for the past several hours was boiling up again. "C-c— c-c-c—"

The words were stuck, and she raised her eyebrows in apparent acknowledgement of the seriousness of the matter. "Easy does it," she said. "It can't be as bad as all that."

"C-c-c-c-c-can I t-t-talk to y-you alone?" I stammered out at last.

"Of course, of course." She gestured behind me, toward the communal dining hall in the wing. I hurried inside, rubbing my hands together, and the moment I heard the door close behind us, I spun on a heel to face her.

"I th-th-think that Umbrion b-b-brought down th-that fireball," I said, because what point was there in not cutting to the chase?

Her reaction was somewhat delayed. She turned around very slowly, eyes narrowed in some combination of skepticism and confusion. For several long, drawn-out moments, she did not respond. When she did, it was slowly and carefully.

"I beg your pardon?"

I swallowed the lump in my throat and set off on my stuttering, rambling explanation – the falling star, Umbrion's claim it was an omen, the angular diameter. Throughout the process, neither of us moved. By the time I came to the end of my explanation, the only discernible difference I could see in her was the fact that she had straightened in her spot, that her shoulders were set, that her dark eyes had become impossibly, unnaturally steady.

For a while, I stared at her in silence, hoping beyond hope that she could provide me with some simple explanation, that with just a few words and a burst of logic she could assuage my fears.

That did not happen.

Her silence stretched even longer, raising hairs on the back of my neck, a process of shivering that would only grow in intensity.

Eventually, she slowly wet her lips.

"Listen to me very carefully, Silas, because I am about to say words that I dare not repeat."

The fear in me only grew. I nodded.

"We are Godspeakers, and as such, we cannot assume that our words are ever truly said in confidence. Do you understand?"

And I did, with a horrible, sinking clarity, I did. Umbrion may already know of my suspicions.

"Are... are th-th-they always—?"

"Not *always*," she answered, "but we must not let that make us complacent."

I nodded again, dread making my head light and my stomach heavy.

"The gods are ineffable," she began, at long last moving toward me in slow strides, "and it is not impossible that you have in some way misinterpreted all this. That said, I admit that if what you've said is true..."

"It's t-t-t-true."

"Then that is—" (she hesitated on the word) "—highly suggestive."

There came a wave of dizzy nausea wrapped in fear. What other way was there to feel, when it had been made clear that a god was trying to destroy Andelan? "Wh-wh-what do we d-d-do now?"

"There's very little we *can* do," she said slowly. "One of the things that a Godspeaker must learn is that, for all the power their station affords them, they have *no* power over the gods. We are their consorts and servants, *not* their masters."

"W-w-w-we can't j-just d-do nothing!" I said shrilly.

"I'll pray to Sol," she said. "She is his mother. She'll know what to do with this information. I just hope she answers in time."

The fear begins to grow into panic. "S-s-so that's it? Th-that's all w-w-we can do? J-j-just wait and p-pray? We have to-to-to at least t-tell Queen Nerisa—"

"What good would that do?" she asked me. "What would be in her power that wouldn't be in ours? How would we stop the Night Father from anything? And even if we had some idea, how would we find him?"

Good questions, all. I gripped my stomach and tried to smother my own panic.

"For now," Greatmother Amira said, "we must go on. We must not arouse suspicion or alarm. We will wait for Sol's answer and go from there. Let's focus on not causing any undue alarm. All right?"

I nodded and pushed my hands through my hair. I still felt frantic, jittery – and now, more than ever before, deeply and profoundly scared.

A moment later, I felt Greatmother Amira's hands on my shoulders. I looked up at her; she was staring down at me with a calm and collectedness that I found myself deeply envying.

"Peace," she said. "Peace, Silas. The only benefit to helplessness is that there's no cause for doubt or guilt. There is nothing anyone could have done to change things. What will be will be."

I wondered if she was right. I certainly wanted her to be, because despite my best efforts I could not talk myself out of this growing sense of doom and dread. Could I have talked him out of this, somehow, if I'd noticed earlier? Could I have done something, anything at all?

"I'll go now and pray to her," she said. "Until we hear from her, it's best that neither of us speak of this again or behave any differently."

That seemed impossible, but I nodded anyway.

"Peace," she said again, placing an affectionate, motherly hand on my cheek before she disappeared from whence we'd arrived.

I THINK IT'S FAIR TO SAY that I never really would have enjoyed the confirmation ceremony, but the process was made all the worse by the weight of my recent conversation with Greatmother Amira. The exchange was weighing heavy in my mind as I was fed, washed, dressed, coiffed, made-up, as I was run through all the last-minute preparations.

The only good thing to come from the situation, really, was the fact that I was so nervous about Umbrion's plot that I had completely forgotten to be nervous about the ceremony. By the time the doors of the Palace opened and the cheer went up at the sight of me, I was so deeply in my own thoughts that the sudden awareness that the ceremony had begun managed to startle me.

The crowd was *massive*. Even after the Tournaments, I had never seen so many people in one place before. They were packed tightly into the main street leading away from the palace, on roofs, craning over vendor stands, throwing nightlilies in the air and chanting – "*Umbrion! Umbrion! Umbrion!*"

The other Godspeakers, along with Queen Nerisa and Lady Queen Roslin, were standing along the steps leading up to the main doors. My heavy silk robes, luxurious as they were, proved suffocatingly hot in the dry heat of the evening. My heartbeat was thrumming in the side of my neck from fear – though fear of what, I couldn't say.

My legs felt stiff and awkward. I climbed down the steps toward the gently smiling Queen Nerisa, her golden crown gleaming in the sunlight, and tried to keep myself upright. I just had to make it to the end of the ceremony.

I looked across to Greatmother Amira, who was smiling at me with traces of worry so subtle that they were invisible to anyone not looking for them. I took a breath and moved down the long steps.

Queen Nerisa met me halfway down. A young page approached

fro the side, carrying the box with my crown. We stood face to face, and she recited the now-familiar script:

"You are chosen as the mouth and the hands and the will of Umbrion. Praise unto Umbrion and praise unto the night."

"*Praise*," echoed the crowd, though their voices were uneven, starting in the front from those who were close enough to hear and moving its way backward in a wave.

The last stains of sunset were fading from the sky, and the stars were coming out. I tried to draw that familiar comfort from the stars, but found I could not. My heart was beating too fast.

"We honor Umbrion's choice and his mercy and his wisdom. We name you Godspeaker and beg your counsel. Praise unto Umbrion and praise unto the night."

"*Praise*," echoed the crowd again, more loudly.

I took several swallows of air and willed myself calm enough to answer, though the words still came out in fits and starts:

"I accept y-y-y-your naming and-and offer Umbrion's c-c-counsel to... to m-m-my queen and c-country, to all of An-n-ndelan." I was glad that most of the spectators weren't close enough to hear me.

"Praise unto Umbrion," Queen Nerisa said with a smile, "and praise unto the night."

"*Praise*," the crowd echoed a third time.

I ducked my head. The page offered up the box, which the queen opened to produce my crown. She plucked it from the bed of silk and placed it delicately on my head. The cool metal all but made my fevered brow sizzle.

"The Godspeaker is arrived!" Queen Nerisa called, turning to the crowd and outstretching her arms. "Praise unto Umbrion and praise unto the night!"

There may have been the answering call from the onlookers, but it was lost in the uproar that followed. Nightlilies went flying into the air, and the sound of their adulation thundered through the living rock. Queen Nerisa turned again and bowed, and I tried to pretend I wasn't dumbstruck at the sight of the Queen of Andelan bowing to *me*.

She stepped aside and I walked further down the stairs. That I was able to move at all was a small miracle in itself, considering the fact that I was so nervous I could barely feel my legs. All at once, the crowd went quiet. They knew what was coming as well as I did.

"Umbrion w-w-would speak to y-you," I stammered, hands clenching and unclenching at my sides. Another cheer went up, briefer.

I was halfway to wondering if I would have to do something to summon him – was there some Godspeaker-specific trick they were expecting me to know? – but before I could, he was there. In an abrupt, unignorable, all-encompassing way, he was there.

There's really no easy way to describe what it feels like to be possessed by a god, past saying that I'm very glad I'll never have to do it again. It was an impossible feeling, so intense that it was nearly painful, as though the essence of him inside my head stretched my physical body to its absolute limits, threatening to rip me open. An Andel body was not meant to play host to such things, and I would have grimaced or cried out or fell to my knees but for the fact that my body was no longer in my control. I was just a passenger, sequestered in my own mind, observing myself as I'd observe anyone else.

Umbrion was still for a moment, looking out into the crowd. I felt him flex my fingers, slowly and deliberately, and he scanned the crowd with my eyes. Then he curled my lips into a sneer.

For several moments, he did not speak. The crowd waited in eager, anticipatory silence.

Then, quite abruptly, he said, "*Pathetic.*"

His voice boomed from all corners of the capitol, deep and tremendous and omnipresent. It shook the ground and sent those too close stumbling back in shock at the sheer force of it.

That single word filled me with fear all over again. *No,* I thought, not sure if he could hear me, *no, please no, not now* – but my body was not my own.

"*Look at you,*" Umbrion said with my mouth, "*chanting and praising and echoing words that possess no meaning to you – praise unto the night? When have any of you truly praised my night? Your words are hollow.*"

He made my eyes swivel toward the other Godspeakers. They were uniformly alarmed and confused, save for Greatmother Amira, who gazed back at me with cold clarity.

"*You luxuriate in my mother's Light,*" he said through my mouth. "*You take her innumerable gifts so thoughtlessly, so thanklessly, never truly understanding, never appreciating. You bask in and abuse the gifts that I can never have. You writhe in the dirt of this loathsome little world, stupid, ungrateful, disgusting, and still she loves you.*"

I could hear the whispering at that point, soft at first, but getting louder. If I had any control over my body, I'm sure my heart would have been beating madly. My eyes scanned the crowd. I could feel his disgust.

"*I do not share her love,*" he had me say. "*I cannot share her love. The gifts you so readily abuse were not extended to me. I can only see you for precisely what you are: unworthy.*"

Those closest to the palace palisade were backing away. He trained my eyes on them, and they froze in fear.

"*The sun sets on this day and on this miserable planet. A new age begins. All those who denied me the Light will choke on the Shadow. Tremble, you vile little creatures, because the Light will not long protect you.*

"*Night falls.*"

He extended my hand out. There came the sound of screaming.

He turns my head so I can see – Queen Nerisa was being lifted into the air, thrashing and kicking against an invisible force holding her aloft.

"*I rise.*"

I could hear Lady Queen Roslin screaming, the shrieking of her subjects. Some were scattering, scrambling away. Others stood transfixed, paralyzed by terror.

"*My vengeance will swallow the sun!*"

I watched, powerless, as Queen Nerisa was ripped to pieces.

I'M SORRY, I'm sorry, I'm sorry, I'm sorry, I'm so sorry.

I should have called off the ceremony the moment I worked it out. I didn't think at the time – I never could have imagined – but I should have.

I was not the Queenslayer, but her blood was on my hands, figuratively as much as literally. I should have done something. *Anything.* I should have seen, should have known. Instead my foolishness and fear had killed the Queen.

My hands are shaking and my words are barely legible. I can't write anymore tonight.

I'm sorry I'm sorry I'm so sorry

IT OCCURS TO ME that this manuscript, if it is read at all, may not be seen for many thousands of seasons. Distant generations may have lost the cultural context and the implications surrounding the death of Queen Nerisa. I'll do my best to explain.

Death, for an Andel of the First Age, was not so much a state as it was a nebulous, indistinct idea. We had some understanding of mortality - we hunted, we slaughtered livestock, we cut down trees - and as a society, we had a general idea of life's impermanence, but we had no practical knowledge of the matter. Combat was a sport, not a necessity; death was a thing that happened to other creatures, not to us.

On the day of my confirmation, when Queen Nerisa was lifted into the sky and torn limb from limb, it was the first time any Andel had ever died. Up until that point, we had been protected and made longevous by the Worldmother's Light. It was the first gift of hers that Umbrion took from us.

So try to understand the context: after tens of thousands of seasons of life without end or age, you watched your beloved Queen die. You barely understand death at all, and to make matters words, a god had just sworn vengeance on you.

To say that panic spread through the city would be a shameful understatement.

The first thing I remember after Umbrion left my body was the sound of screaming from every direction and great clatters of wood on stone as carts and vendor stalls were overturned in the street. As my eyes refocused, I saw people running, *fleeing*, scrambling down the main artery of Ellorian as though pursued.

The Godspeakers were gone. Not fleeing, but genuinely gone, as though they hadn't been there at all - I didn't think of it at the time, but in hindsight I know that their respective gods must have spirited them to safety.

And there I stood, splattered with the blood of Queen Nerisa, no longer possessed, but still utterly incapable of movement. Every part of my body was trembling with a greater intensity as the moments ticked by. What had just happened? How was that possible? My mind could make no sense of it.

A few seconds or perhaps several minutes later, there was a hand on my shoulder that wrenched me around.

Soya – she was frightened, ashen white, but resolute.

"We need to leave," she said.

"I—"

"*Now!*"

She used her grip on me to tug, and I went stumbling forward, nearly falling, and she took off in a dead sprint.

People were fleeing in every direction, screaming, scrambling through the streets. If any of them noticed me, they had better things to do than acknowledge it.

And beneath my feet, I could feel a dreadful rumbling. The veins of the hot spring underneath the city were rolling, growling, and the volume of it was only getting louder.

Before long, we made it through the ever-thickening crowds and burst through the door of Soya's rented house.

At once, she spun to face me.

"What did he *do to her?*"

I almost swallowed my tongue from fear. "I d-d-d-d— I d-d-d—"

"Silas!" She was frantic, and the terror she'd been trying so desperately to keep in check was seeping through the cracks. "What did he do to Queen Nerisa?"

I couldn't blame her for not knowing; I didn't know, myself. All I could do was shake my head, because the words would certainly never come. I hoped she could read the answer on my face. "I d-d-d— I d-d-d-d—!"

Soya let out a furious sound that was equal parts fear and frustration. She began to pace the floor, wringing her hands together. "How could he kill her?" she asked. "He couldn't, right? The Worldmother's Light protects us from death, how—"

The ground lurched underneath our feat; the entire building

rumbled. This city was breaking.

She steadied herself with a hand on the wall. She looked to me, desperate. "Silas, do you think he took away her Light—?"

I did not have time for theology. I pushed past her into the kitchen and grabbed a bag from the wall, shoveling food into it - pears, potatoes, salted pork, wine—

"What are you doing—?"

Another great rumble and lurch; I had to steady myself on the wall, Soya on the door frame.

"W-w-w-w-w—" Curse my tongue; I had no time for it. I grabbed a second bag and threw it at her, then pointed toward the front door urgently.

It took her a moment, but only a moment. "Right," she said. "Right, we can't stay - we have to—"

I kept shoveling food into the sack. Soya muttered something about clothes and took the bag with her out of the kitchen and onto the upper floor.

Bread, kale, peaches, cheese - it would have to do. We might be able to pick up more provisions later, but right now we had to get out of this city before it broke in half.

I sprinted out of the kitchen just as Soya was scrambling down the steps, her pack stuffed with clothes.

"You can't go outside without disguise; who knows what they'd do to you," Soya said, urgently handing me a black cloak over her arm. "Put this on."

I flinched, but shrugged it on anyway.

"We can make for Avenos," Soya said, fastening the bag closed as I pulled up the hood. "My father will protect us - we have scholars, diplomats, we can—"

"L-l-l-l-l-let's go—"

She bolted for the door; I followed hot on her heels.

The streets of Ellorian were madness given form. People ran in every direction, screaming for loved ones, hurrying to load up their carts with provisions. From somewhere, a man screamed, "*We are betrayed by the Night Father! His vengeance is upon us!*"

I did not have time for the crushing guilt I felt at that moment. I took Soya by the arm and we ran straight for the main gates of the city.

There were great cracks forming along the streets, jets of steam shooting into the sky. In the process of dodging them, and other people, and overturned vendor stalls and carts, I did not notice at all that we were being pursued until—

"*Silas!*"

—I was grabbed by the shoulder and spun around, slammed into a nearby wall.

"*What did you do!*"

Before I could determine whose voice it was, before I even knew the words being screamed at me, I felt something pressed into my neck - wood, I recognized, carved elaborately. It was Perenor's runed staff, pressing so hard into my throat that it choked my breathing. Reflexively, I grabbed the staff and tried to wrestle it away, but Perenor always was stronger than me—

"Get off him!" Soya cried from behind. "Perenor, you brute, get off him—!"

"How far does this treachery extend?" Perenor roared at me, face so close to mine that I could feel his breath on my cheek. "You *traitor*, were you *in on it?* What did you do the Queen—?"

I kneed him hard in the gut. He doubled over and I used the opportunity to punch him in the nose. As soon as he tumbled, I grabbed Soya's arm and took off running again. I was nearly back onto the street when I felt tendrils of magic snarl around my ankles, and I went crashing to the ground.

"Silas!"

"How dare you *protect him!*"

"Perenor, stop! Stop it!"

"*Stay out of this, Rhodan!*"

The Craft around me was dragging me back into the alley, despite my fingers scrabbling for purchase on the cobblestone. I wrenched around and saw Perenor standing up, hands and staff glowing hot with Craft, blood streaming out from his nose down toward his chin.

"What would you *do to him, Perenor?* He's your brother - *your brother, the Godspeaker!* Do you honestly think Umbrion will let you fell a single blow?"

"Let the traitor-god come! Let him answer for what he did—!"

"He's the only link to Umbrion!" she said, grabbing Perenor's arm and pulling so sharply that at last, the Craft around my ankles was dislodged; I scrambled back, heart thundering in my ear. "He's the only person alive who can give us any insight into what his planning, so either you honestly think you can best a god on your own, or you *need him!* We all need him, Perenor!"

His breath was hot and ragged. He looked wild with fury, dangerous, and I braced my hand on the nearby wall, ready, if necessary, to run. Perenor's eyes were darkly burning, but he must have heard some truth in Soya's words, because they had stilled him.

"Look at him," Soya said. "What kind of evil mastermind do you imagine him to be? He's an academic, not a war criminal! You've known him your entire life – he is so many things, but has he ever been malicious?"

Perenor was grinding his teeth, fingers flexing around the shaft of his staff. Slowly, slowly, the burning left his eyes and his shoulders slumped.

Then, *CRACK!* A sound like thunder but deeper, from below rather than above, followed by a deafening hissing sound. I wrenched around – the main artery of Ellorian had split open down the center, and the hot spring underneath was spitting white steam high into the air.

"This city is breaking!" Soya cried over the sound. "We don't have time to stand here and argue. Make yourself useful, Perenor, and get us out of here!"

Perenor stepped around me, staring into the ever-widening chasm opening up on the street. People were screaming – some even fell into it, along with their carts and camels and large chunks of debris.

"We can't outrun this," Perenor said. "Grab hold of me."

"Grab hold—?"

Perenor grabbed me by the shoulder and hauled me to my feet. "Like you asked, Rhodan, I'm getting us out of here!"

He didn't wait. With one hand on me and another on Soya, he glowed white-hot with Craft, and then there was a sudden pressure that started in my gut and *ripped—*

"... CAN'T POSSIBLY think this..."

Voices, fading in and out. A disorienting, churning, rocking sensation.

"... no other way, the city..."

I forced my eyes open and found myself staring into firelight. I was on something soft.

"... raze this temple to the ground if word got out!"

My senses slowly came into focus. I took stock of my body. I didn't seem to be in any pain, though I did feel strangely nauseous, sort of seasick.

"It won't be for long." It was Perenor's voice, I recognized as my mind began to clear. "Please, Scholar, you must understand the urgency."

"Of course I do, but that doesn't change that fact that what you're asking—"

"He's waking up."

It was Soya's voice this time, closer than the others. I gathered my strength and sat up slowly. The room was bare, spartan stone with a single window open to the air. The sound of the fire mingled with the rushing of waves in the distance. It was hard to say for sure where I was.

There were three others in the room: Soya, Perenor, and a man whose face I couldn't quite recognize, although he did seem familiar.

They were all three staring at me as though concerned that, at any moment, I might physically explode and take the building down with me. Soya even inched away from where she'd been kneeling at the foot of the cot on which I was lying.

"Sleep well?" Soya asked, daring to break the sudden silence.

"I w-w-was asleep?" I couldn't recall how that had happened. Although now that I thought about it—

"You weren't asleep," Perenor said, "you were unconscious. That can happen when you're translocated via Craft."

I'd never heard the word "translocated" before, but I could glean enough by the context.

"Is he...?" Soya began, but didn't finish.

I looked sideways at her, frowning in confusion.

When I didn't respond, she continued: "... I don't know... here?"

"Is wh-who – oh."

I suppose I should have known immediately who she meant, but it took the question to send memories flooding back, and when they did, they hit with a force so strong that it was almost physically painfully. The confirmation, the possession, the Queen—

I shut my eyes tightly.

"Y-y-you'd know if he w-was here," I answered softly.

"Is he listening?" Perenor asked, expression hard and unforgiving.

"I d-d-don't know. I c-can't know."

"Splendid," said the man I didn't recognize, looking angry. "So not only is this temple to play host to Umbrion's Godspeaker, it's to do so while the traitor-god may or may not be listening in on everything that happens."

"You know I wouldn't come to you, Scholar, if I had any other option," Perenor said.

The man – the scholar, presumably – pointed a long, accusatory finger toward Soya. "She said he'll be protected in Avenos. Why don't you go there?"

"If they make that journey without protection, they'll be found before long. Once people stop being frightened, they'll be angry, and they'll come for Silas long before they make it to Avenos."

"They *have* adequate protection," the scholar said, leveling Perenor with a pointed stare. "You're the finest sorcerer this monastery has ever produced; I'm sure you're perfectly capable of protecting them!"

"I appreciate the vote of confidence," Perenor answered, "but I just translocated three people fifteen leagues. I need at least a few hours to rest."

Now that I was looking properly, and now that Perenor had pointed it out, I noticed that Perenor's hands were trembling and his skin was ashen white. He looked awful.

I could see the scholar's tongue rolling behind his teeth. He folded his arms and visibly weighed his options.

"Please, Jeron," Perenor said, voice suddenly soft. "Just a few hours."

Another moment of silence, and then the scholar sighed.

"Until dawn, then," said Scholar Jeron, and suddenly I knew who he was. Scholar Jeron was the master of Craft at Perenor's temple, who taught Perenor and his fellow acolytes. "But I can't let him stay any longer than that, Perenor. I will not risk this temple or anyone in it."

"I understand," Perenor answered solemnly. "Thank you, Scholar."

Scholar Jeron strode from the room, ducking under the heavy curtain draped over the doorway. The moment he was gone, Perenor seemed to physically deflate, and he staggered under his own weight as though he might collapse. I jumped from my cot and caught his wrist to hold him steady.

"I'm fine," Perenor snapped at me, pulling himself away. "I'm fine, I just—"

Perenor sat down heavily, rubbing his shaking hands into his face.

"You look like shit," Soya said. "No offense."

"How could I possibly take offense to that?" Perenor grumbled.

"Will you even be ready to leave by dawn?"

"Not much of an option, is there?" He lowered his hands. I slowly sat down on the cot across from him. "How long is the Long Road?"

Soya frowned. "At the risk of redundancy, long," she said. "We'll be lucky if we get there before the monsoon starts."

Perenor looked up at her. "*Forty days?*"

"I didn't make the cursed maps," she returned. "Why can't you just translocate us once you've got your strength back?"

"I can only translocate to places I've been," he said. "Besides, forty days' travel is way too far. That would take an amount of strength I just don't have."

She sighed. "There's always a catch with Craft." She rose to her feet and crossed to the window, just as the breeze off the ocean caught the long strands of her mahogany hair.

For several moments we each sat in silence, each preoccupied with our own thoughts. The weight of everything we weren't saying was heavy, weighing down on the room like fog.

"Y-y-you've got a little..."

I reached up and pressed my thumb over Perenor's upper lip, which was coated in dry, brownish blood. He jerked away from me.

"No shit I've got a little," Perenor growled at me, "I think you broke my nose."

"Oh," I said. "S-s-sorry."

"No, you're not."

"No, n-n-not really. You d-d-d-did have your s-staff to my throat—"

"It's taking a long time to heal," Soya interjected. "It's been nearly an hour now. Does it still hurt?"

"Yes," Perenor answered, glaring at me. I refused to feel bad, of course. If he didn't want to get punched he shouldn't have pinned me to a wall.

"Do you think—" Soya hesitated a moment. "Is it possible – what he said during the confirmation, and the Queen—"

The image brought a fresh surge of nausea. I willed away the images of ripping flesh and spurting blood, screwing shut my eyes.

"He killed her," Soya said, slowly. "And he said the Light won't protect us. Do you think he was talking about the Worldmother's Light? Is it possible he made us..."

I hadn't really considered it before, but now that Soya brought it up...

I looked up at her. Soya was hunting for the right word; it wasn't one that was in common parlance.

"... mortal?" she finished, anticlimactically.

"I'd say it's not possible," Perenor answered slowly, "but if it is, it would only be possible through the will of a god."

"Perenor, you studied religious history, didn't you? Isn't it required as part of a sorcerer's curriculum?"

"I did," he said, pressing his fingertip against his nose and flinching.

"What is it that the Worldmother's Light does, specifically?"

"It's kind of nebulous," he answers. "People often mistake it for the physical sunlight, but it's more like an energy. It burns away creeping age and shields us from damage and disease. The Worldmother's Light comes from the Worldmother's Flame, which people usually mistake for the sun but which is actually the flame of courage, another gift of hers to us."

"Priestly knowledge is always so wishy-washy," Soya sighed. "What even happens to a thing when it dies?"

"I don't think Sol ever intended us to find out," Perenor answered.

There fell a lapse of silence. I spent a while worrying my lower lip.

"We'll make for Oberine as soon as the sun rises," Soya said. "We'll all be safe in Avenos; my father can protect us."

"We can make the first leg at dawn," Perenor added, "but then we really should only travel at night. Someone will recognize him, and since we're apparently mortal now…"

"I'm s-s-s-sorry," I said suddenly.

The conversation stuttered to a halt; they both looked at me, but I kept my eyes low.

"B-b-b-before the confirm-m-mation, I w-worked it out," I said. "I told G-G-Greatmother Amira, b-b-but I sh-should have d-d-done more."

"What more could you have done?" Soya asked. "What could you have possibly done against a god's will?"

"Something, perhaps," Perenor answered, voice deathly quiet.

"Perenor," Soya snapped at him.

"I don't claim to know the details," he continued, "and I know that true blame can only rest with Umbrion, but at the same time, I don't believe in fate or inevitability and I never have. There's nothing that has ever happened or ever will that couldn't have been changed. Perhaps this particular event could have been avoided."

"Watch your mouth," Soya growled, storming toward him to shove roughly at his shoulder. Perenor glared at her. "It's easy for you to be all high and mighty when it wasn't you. What could he, or you, or anyone, have possibly done to defy *a god?*"

His glare only intensified, but he had no answer.

"*I* don't blame you, Silas," Soya said then. "Others might, but I don't. I know you too well to think you'd ever be party to something like this."

"Th-th-thank you," I said, slowly, "b-but your words d-do little to assuage m-m-my guilt."

"There's no time for your *guilt*," Perenor snapped.

Soya rounded on him so abruptly that her long hair fanned as she spun. She shoved at him again, this time with both hands, and he would have fallen from the bed if he hadn't grabbed the wall just in time and staggered to his feet.

"How can you possibly be so *callous* to him after everything he's been through?" she demanded. "He's your *brother*, or do you only acknowledge that fact when it's convenient for you to do so?"

I looked over at Perenor, and Perenor looked back at me, and something like remorse was in his eyes.

But that expression, if it was there at all, only lasted a moment.

"I'm going to bed," he said. "Wake me at dawn."

He made for the door. There was no strength left in his stride; the weariness had weathered him down.

"Don't listen to him," Soya said, glaring at his retreating form. "He's a bully and a brute. Such a shame we need him, else I'd knock him out and drop him into the ocean.

"Don't b-b-begrudge him his f-feelings," I said.

"I'm not," she answered, "I begrudge him his behavior, which is at best callous and at worst despicably cruel."

"He's j-j-just angry and f-frightened," I said. "And I'm j-just a c-c-convenient outlet f-for it."

"You *didn't do anything wrong.*"

"M-maybe," I said, mostly to myself. I lied down and stretched out on the cot. "But I th-think I'll s-s-spend the r-rest of my life w-wondering if I c-c-could have s-stopped it."

Soya didn't seem to have an answer for that, which was fine, because I didn't really feel like discussing it any further. Eventually, she bent down and planted a benedictory kiss on the top of my head.

"Try to sleep," she said. "We leave at dawn."

WHEN DAWN CAME, Scholar Jeron all but pushed us out the door. We had a small, insufficient meal, which matched perfectly with our small, insufficient night's rest. I put on Soya's long black cloak, which was stiflingly hot in the dry and oppressive heat of the Wastes, and we set northwest along the Long Road.

Once we were sufficiently far from the temple – and everything else – it became rather hard to judge whether we actually made progress or if we were just walking in place. The Wastes were a massive stretch of identical, rolling sand dunes, with no markers to judge distance. To make matters worse, they were so insufferably quiet that all the stories I'd been told as a child about travellers getting lost in, and subsequently going mad in, the Wastes did not seem so impossible.

To say that I was the least active of the bunch would have been generous. Not one of my hobbies was anything close to physically demanding. Soya, on the other hand, was a talented and accomplished rider and archer, and Perenor lived a lifestyle that I could only accurately describe as nauseatingly active, the kind of active that makes you feel bad about yourself. I was sure that, between my own inexperience and the long black cloak I had to wear, that I would be the first one to ask for a rest.

But quite to my surprise, it was Perenor, around high noon.

"Wait," he said. "Stop. I need to stop."

Soya, several yards ahead, slowed to a stop and turned around. The long white shawl she'd tied over her face left long strands of her hair free and tangling in the wind. "It's another ten leagues to Oberine at least."

But Perenor was already sitting down, collapsing heavily along on the side of the road. Granted, calling it a road at all was a bit generous – it wasn't paved with anything, just marked every hundred yards with a large mound of stone. Perenor had collapsed against one of the mounds, folding himself into the narrow shadow it cast. Sweat was streaking his brow and he was panting.

I looked from him to Soya, giving her the *just a moment* gesture with one hand before I reached into my pack and produced a skin of water, which I offered to him.

"Here."

Perenor looked at me askance but was too tired for real skepticism. He took the skin with a grateful nod, thumbed open the cork, and took several long pulls.

I scanned the road. Since we'd left, we'd past several travellers bound in the opposite direction with camels and carts, but for now we were alone. I pulled down the hood of my cloak and sank down beside him on the opposite side of the pillar.

"D-d-didn't expect you to-to- be the f-f-first one to c-call for a rest," I said.

"I'm still recovering," he answered tersely between large gulps of water.

"From wh-wh-what?" I asked, a moment before I remembered. "C-Craft?"

"Don't sound so surprised," Perenor returned. "If Craft were easy, there wouldn't be temples dedicated to learning it." He dropped the water skin between his knees and leaned back against the sunbaked stone.

I shook my head. "I j-j-j-just hadn't expected th-th-the effects to b-b-be quite so physical," I said.

I heard the hollow sound of the water skin's stopper being replaced. "One of the first things you learn when you enroll as an acolyte is the First Fundamental Law."

I was surprised. "M-m-matter and energy c-cannot be created or d-d-destroyed."

"Only changed," Perenor finished.

"I d-d-didn't expect you to-to- know anything about the physical s-s-sciences."

"Well, you did take all the brains between us in the womb," he said, which drew a startled laugh out of me. "I got the good looks, though."

"And th-th-the ego, c-clearly."

"Anyway, we learn the First Fundamental Law because Craft is subject to it, like everything else," he said. "Your Craft is only as strong as what you're willing to sacrifice."

I frowned. "S-s-sacrifice?"

"Energy for energy," he answered, shrugging. "Matter for matter. Translocating the combined mass of three people several leagues required a huge sacrifice of energy. It's just not coming back as soon as I should like."

I'd never really thought of Craft in such practical terms before. Like most people, my only exposure to it had been in dry, scholarly lectures and the occasional bar fight. I'd never found it a particularly compelling field of study, but Perenor's explanation did make for some interesting thought.

"I never asked," Perenor began. "About the confirmation…"

I worried my bottom lip. I was glad we were facing opposite directions, even if it meant I had to squint against the sunlight and he had the shade.

"What happened?" he asked finally. "I mean, I know – I saw, I was there – he possessed you, fine, but *why?*"

"Wh-wh-why what?"

"Why did he do it?" Perenor pressed. I heard him half-turning behind me. "He's been in your head for weeks now; you must know something."

"You know as m-m-m-much as I d-do," I answered, keeping my eyes forward. "He's angry about s-s-something. He th-thinks we're ungrateful, as a s-s-species."

"He never said anything to you about what he planned to do?"

I turned around deliberately and met his eyes. "*No,*" I said to him, firmly. "What d-d-do you think a G-G-Godspeaker is? I'm n-n-n-not his cursed c-c-confidante, Perenor, I'm his s-servant."

"But he must have spoken to you."

"Of c-c-course he s-spoke to me, b-b-but *no*, Perenor, he n-n-never brought up th-the fact that he had p-p-p-plans to k-kill the Queen! The m-m-moment I worked it out, I w-w-went straight to G-Greatmother Amira, b-b-but by th-then…"

Perenor's head was turned just enough so he could watch me from one eye. Eventually, some combination of reluctant trust and exhaustion took over, and he turned around again, breathing out long and low. It was at that moment that I realized how incredibly shitty he looked. The Craft really had taken a lot out of him.

"M-m-maybe we sh-should have rested for-for an extra d-d-day," I said.

"No time," Perenor returned. "Besides, apparently you take not insignificant joy in seeing me suffer."

"Of c-c-course I do, but only wh-when I know y-y-y-you'll b-bounce back," I said. "It's n-not fun if you're r-r-really in d-danger."

Perenor was so surprised that he looked back at me again, and I hated it.

"Y-y-you're my b-brother," I continued. What more explanation could he possibly need?

He was silent a moment, slowly turning away. "Oh." He voice was somewhere between confused and concerned.

I knew the implication, of course. He didn't expect me to genuinely care about him because he'd never genuinely cared about me. He didn't say it out loud, of course – he didn't need to. A lifetime of resentment had proven it enough.

I swallowed down all the bitter memories of my lonely adolescence and turned away again. This really was not the time to be reopening old wounds.

So of course, his next question was, "You didn't see them get out, did you?"

It took me a moment to put together who he meant. I turned my head back to him. "Y-y-y-you didn't?"

"Mother and Grandmother weren't with me during the confirmation," Perenor said. "They were with the rest of the Queenscourt on the terrace. I was down on the street with Father and Grandfather, but I lost them in the chaos. Did you see...?"

I swallowed hard. "N-n-n-no. D-d-d-d y-you th-think th-th-they're—?"

"I don't know," Perenor said. "A lot of people were swallowed up by the spring."

"A l-l-lot of p-people weren't."

"Yeah," Perenor agreed, and neither of us felt better.

I'd never really liked my family – a sentiment mutually shared, of course – but I had certainly *loved* them, and I never wanted to see them hurt. The idea that they could be dead—

Of course, the word "dead" barely held any meaning to me at the time. I didn't quite comprehend the permanence of it, and I didn't know what to think of my own family being dead, if that was what they were.

"They'll find us if they can," Perenor said.

I nodded, unwilling to think on it any more closely for fear of where those thoughts might lead.

"We can't stay here," Soya called from up ahead. "Come on; the sooner we get to Oberine, the longer we'll have to rest."

I'd always had some trouble motivating myself with long-term goals, and the idea of standing up again seemed entirely unappealing. Perenor forced himself to his feet before I could protest.

"I'm fine," he called back. "Let's go."

And we went.

BY THE TIME we made it to Oberine, the sun had just started to set. We were all three of us sweaty and exhausted, and the little flecks of orange light still dappling over the sand dunes were beacons of hope and long-awaited respite.

Oberine was not a terribly remarkable city, notable only for being about a day's travel from Ellorian. Most of his buildings were inns and taverns catering to those travelling the Long Road. It was built on and around a large oasis, a freshwater pond circled by palms.

We set our sights on the nearest inn, which also happened to be the largest. When we made it inside, it was to a pervasive, disquieted rumble from all corners of the main room.

"Welcome to the Laughing Jackal," the innkeeper behind the bar said. "Renting a room?"

"Gods, yes," Soya said, collapsing onto her elbows over the counter.

"You're just in time," she said. "Only one room left. Huge crowd here tonight, all fleeing the capitol."

And here I'd almost pulled down my hood. I stilled my hand and shoved it away, keeping it up. That explained why there were so many people.

"Are they, indeed," Soya answered neutrally, reaching into the coin purse tethered to her belt.

"They say the city broke in two and collapsed into the hot springs," the innkeeper said. "Were you three there, too?"

"It was the traitor-god!" slurred a man on the far side of the bar, who sounded a bit drunker than was probably reasonable. "I was there!"

I pulled my hood down a little further.

"Is your last room big enough for three?" Soya asked.

"It should be," the innkeeper began, but the drunk was talking again, bellowing in the loud and boisterous way that only a drunk can:

"Our queen!" he caterwauled, swaying in his spot. "Gods' mercy, our queen – I saw her, with my own eyes, I saw her!"

"You're making a scene, Bernan," the innkeeper said gently.

"*Let me finish,*" the drunk, Bernan, insisted too loudly. "I saw her, do you hear? I watched her torn in twain! I saw the traitor-god's Craft lift her into the sky, saw her body rip—!"

"Fuck sake, Bernan, shut your mouth!" bellowed a woman in the back. "Do you think anyone here needs reminding? That anyone *wants* it?"

"Someone take him to dry out," the innkeeper said.

But Bernan only started talking louder, as if hoping to deafen his detractors into silence:

"The Godspeaker's body glowed black with the Night Father's Craft," he slurred, which had definitely not happened, "and he raised one hand into the sky and – and – and *blew everything up!*"

"That's not how it happened," one woman said to another.

"Yes, it was!" Bernan insisted.

"I was there, too, you prig," the woman in the back said. "That's now how it happened, now shut your drunk face about it!"

"Come on, Bernan," said a young woman who could only be the assistant innkeeper. "Let's get you up to your room."

"Here's your key," the innkeeper said, doing her best to ignore the goings-on behind us (*"I don't want to go to my room, I want to tell the world what happened!"*). "Third floor. I'm sorry about him. Once Tasha gets him up to his room, he'll pass out soon enough."

"It's fine," Soya answered. "Come on, Si—"

She stopped halfway through my name, wisely thinking better of using it.

"Come on," she finished, and we started for the staircase.

Bernan was frantically fighting off the assistant innkeeper, as though the veracity of his story was tied directly to how many people could hear him shout it. "It *is* how it happened!" he said to her, and before I even realized what was happening, I was grabbed by the shoulder and spun around. "*You* believe me, don't you—?"

The force of the spin sent my hood falling back.

I could tell from the expression on his face alone that he recognized me. It was a reaction that was delayed at first, so for a few moments I was hoping that perhaps he would be too drunk.

"Come on," Soya said again. Her voice was edged in panic. I pulled the hood back up.

Unfortunately, Bernan's mind caught up with him before she could pull me away:

"*Sol's Light!*"

In the same way an infant's scream is so viscerally different from its crying, so too was Bernan's sudden terror from his drunken theatrics. It was real and raw and all-consuming, and he went stumbling backward into a nearby table, which promptly capitulated and clattered loudly against the floor.

The room quieted. All eyes turned to me.

"It's you," Bernan said from the floor. His voice was no longer slurred; perhaps the drunk had been scared out of him. "It's you! The Godspeaker!"

It had all happened so quickly that I'd rather forgotten to be frightened, although my body had already tensed, ready for the fight-or-flight. I looked out at the tavern, now deathly quiet.

Not all of them recognized me, I could tell. Many seemed more confused or concerned. But a few of them – just a few, just one woman in the back, a man to the side – were slowly paling and rising up out of their chairs.

Just as the fear was starting to creep back into my blood, there was a loud, decisive, echoless *crack.*

Perenor had stepped in front of me, and his runed staff, which had up until that point been held unobtrusively at his side, was in full view. The runes carved along the neck were glowing bright silver-blue.

It was a threat, I could tell. A subtle threat, but a threat all the same. Any sorcerer skilled enough to use a runed weapon was a force to be reckoned with, one that no one was eager to confront.

"Come on, *brother*," he said, overemphasizing the final word. "Let's go."

Soya grabbed my arm again and pulled me away. I stumbled along behind her as we headed up the steps.

"Shit," I could hear her mutter. Whispers were breaking out behind us. "Shit, shit, shit. Maybe we should find another inn."

"There won't be anywhere else," Perenor said. He was looking over his shoulder, down into the main room of the tavern as it passed out of our sight. "You heard the innkeeper – the city is full of refugees. I'll ward the door with Craft, just in case."

I wanted to ask if that was really necessary, but I didn't, just in case the answer was yes.

Our room was at the top floor, at the end of a long hallway. As soon as it was unlocked, Soya pulled me inside. Perenor stood for a while just outside, giving the hallway a cursory look before he stepped inside, himself.

"I suppose this is a risk we should have anticipated," Soya said once the door shut.

I licked my lips. The room was plain, but comfortable enough, with a single window open to the Wastes. The wind off the dunes rattled the glass.

Perenor pressed his open palm to the flat of the door and shut his eyes. I could detect no change in it but for a subtle bluish glow that faded almost before it arrived. "I don't think it likely that they'll try anything," he said. "And if they do, they won't get through that door."

"It's bad enough that they'll speculate," Soya said.

"They would have speculated anyway."

"Yeah, but now they have a pretty good head start on it!"

"It's f-f-f-fine," I said at last. "It's f-fine. Nevermind it."

"Nevermind it?" Soya repeated. "They could start a riot! They could pull you out by the hair—!"

"And w-w-we'll deal w-with that as we n-n-need to," I said. I sat down heavily on the edge of the bed. My knees were trembling from some volatile combination of fatigue and adrenaline. "B-b-but for n-now, we're as p-p-protected as we c-can be."

I hadn't noticed it at first, but now that things had settled, I realized that, quite without thinking about it, I had thrown myself head-first into Umbrion's ocean in the corner of my mind. In such a short time, it had become an instinctual reaction to my anxiety.

Was it wrong for me to be tapping into his Craft like this? Would it make him aware of what I was doing or thinking? Even if it wouldn't, was there some ethical dilemma in taking comfort from a being that had just killed the Queen and broken my city in half?

But by those same reasons, what choice did I have? There was no time for my fear; I had to get to Ellorian, and this was the way to do it.

I shut my eyes and breathed in his ocean, calmed, but not truly comforted.

AFTER HOURS OF TOSSING AND TURNING and a startling inability to sleep despite a full day's worth of walking, I fell into something that was closer to unconsciousness than it was to sleep.

And despite everything, I dreamt of Umbrion.

I'd like to say that I felt guilty for the treachery of my sleeping mind, but in the hazy ether of dreaming, I wasn't thinking of his betrayal or all the death he'd wrought; there was nothing except the cool seduction of the Night Father's starlight. Without the context my conscious mind brought, it was easy – too easy, perhaps – to let myself slip away in the sensation.

It ended to the sound of rattling, echoing thumps and a high, thin wailing sound.

It was hard to say how long we'd been asleep – we'd all allowed ourselves to sleep in as late as possible to make the transition to travelling by night easier – past knowing that however long it had been, it had not been long enough. I wanted almost to the point of desperation to fall back asleep, to sink back into the Night Father's waiting embrace—

And then the thumping came again; the wailing growing even louder.

Beside me, Soya shifted.

"What...?" she began, fighting away sleep.

"Open up!" came a voice from the general direction of the door. The wail continued to rise in volume until it rattled my eardrums.

"The ward..." Perenor muttered on the other side of me. He rolled off the bed and I lifted my head in time to see him padding across the room.

The doorway now had a thin, lattice-like pattern of silvery-blue threads that pulsed each time it was pounded upon. This thought suddenly raised a rather alarming question—

"Who—?"

"Hush," Perenor answered, before stepping in front of the door. "Who is it?"

"Misra, the owner," came the answer from the other side. Her voice was gruff and businesslike, almost too much so, like she was trying to make a concerted effort to sound threatening. "Take down the Craft and come out."

Perenor glanced back at us. Soya sat upright and frowned at him. He hesitated a moment before pressing his hand into the door; the blue-silver lines vanished with a thin snap of Craft, and the wailing stopped.

When he pulled open the door, I could see not one but at least a dozen people crowded in the hallway. At once, Perenor groped for his runed staff.

"You're going to have to go," said the woman – Misra, presumably, the owner – at the front of the pack, folding her arms over her chest. Behind her, the group grunted and nodded and made efforts to appear threatening. "The innkeeper should have never rented a room out to you."

Unlike those making up the mob, Perenor did not have to make any particular effort to look threatening. He was plenty threatening enough on his own, with his fearsome runed staff in his hand. He leaned on it and frowned at them. A few drew away, but for the most part they held their ground.

"Is our money not good here?" he asked, eyeing them.

"We won't play host to the mouth and the hands and the will of the Traitor God," said one in the front. I swallowed and pushed my way out of bed, ducking out of sight and hurriedly dressing. "We know it's him. Don't try to lie."

"Do you really want to go on record with that? Perenor asked. I shrugged on a tunic and kicked on my boots. "You know he has a direct line to Umbrion, right? The Traitor God may not look too kindly on you if he knows you're turning him away—"

"D-d-don't antagonize them," I hissed at him.

"They're throwing us out!" he answered, glowering at them.

"We n-n-need to leave anyway, it's n-nearly nightfall." I secured my tunic and moved around Perenor. "We d-d-don't want any t-trouble—"

The moment I came into view, much of the crowd - eight or nine of the dozen or so - scrambled backward and away, gasping at the sight of me.

I still had not gotten used to the idea that people were afraid of me now. I was hyper-aware of the minutiae of their faces.

"It's al-l-l-llright," I said, "I m-mean you n-n-no harm—"

"What's the matter?" Soya asked sharply, barging in in front of me. "Never seen a Godspeaker before?"

"Soya," I said.

"What? They're *gawking*," she said. "It's *rude*."

"We just want him gone," said Misra, whose bravado had fallen off significantly since I'd come into view. She was holding up both hands. "We can't play host to him—"

"We heard you the first time," Perenor interjected sharply. "We need to leave anyway."

And with that, he slammed the door on her nose and turned around again.

"The depth of callousness of an Andelish heart never ceases to amaze," Soya growled. She was still half-dressed, and she pulled at the laces of her tunic like she wanted them to pay for the crimes of the inn's owner.

"They're just protecting their interests," Perenor muttered, heading over to the bag by the window to grab his clothes and boots.

She glared at his back. "Silas is no threat."

"Isn't he?"

Simultaneously, they both looked back to me. I shrunk somewhat under their gazes.

"He's got a direct link to a deity," Perenor said. "I'm not saying I'm going to let that scare me away, I'm just point out that you'd be stupid to think he isn't dangerous."

"You know, Perenor, you're really shitty at this brother thing," Soya told him.

Perenor frowned at her, as though he wasn't sure how to respond to such an accusation.

"L-l-l-let's just g-go," I said, moving to the dirty window and looking out over the small, rambling city of Oberine.

"We shouldn't stay much longer, now that they care enough to want us gone," Perenor agreed.

We packed swiftly and in silence. I did everything in my power to ignore the heavy, sinking dread in my stomach as I heard the commotion grow louder downstairs.

When we left our room and made our way down the steps, those who had gathered to throw us out were now lined up along the walls of the lower room, staring and silent all.

I could see Perenor's hand clench and unclench around his staff and Soya frowned. We slowed. As we moved, they parted around us, as reeds part for the current.

Their faces were so full of fear. Not anger, not hatred, just fear. A part of me wanted to reason with them, to assure them that I was no threat. Another part of me didn't want to frighten them further by saying anything at all.

But there was a guilt in me, low and roiling, that ate away at my voice. They were scared of me, and it didn't matter that their fear wasn't my fault. My presence was fearful to them, and I had no right to anything less.

So instead of saying anything, I kept my head down and I prayed that the heartbreak wasn't evident on my face.

WE WALKED ALL EVENING and through the night. We made camp come the morning, tucked into the little dells in the sand so as to be out of sight to anyone who might also be travelling the Long Road.

The Wastes seemed endless, and progress was a hard thing to judge. We stopped at little towns where we could, little ramshackle ones not so different from Oberine, and we picked up supplies where we needed them. But for the most part, the journey felt like the same three days on permanent loop.

On the seventh or eighth night, we were cooking a haunch of goat we'd bought the day before. We had set up a camp on a dune and had finished building the fire when I noticed something dart out of the corner of my eye, between the tallgrass that had just started to dapple the dunes. It only lasted a moment, and when I turned my head to look, it was gone, but I could have sworn—

"Is s-s-s-someone out there?"

"Yes," Perenor answered at once, and I looked back at him, startled. "I think so, at least. Hooded black cloak?"

I nodded slowly.

"They've been following us," he said as he rotated the haunch on the makeshift spit over the fire. "I think they've been following us for a while now, since we left Oberine."

I tried not to be nervous – there was plenty else that should have, by all rights, made me far more nervous – but I couldn't quite fight it down. "Wh-wh-who—?"

"Don't know," Perenor replied. "I've tried to confront them more than once, but they're always gone before I get there."

His answer certainly didn't sate my anxiety.

"I won't let them near you," Perenor said, which surprised me so much that, for a moment, I forgot to be afraid.

"Wh-what?"

"I won't," he said again. "I don't know what they're planning, but it doesn't matter. I'll protect you."

The surprise only intensified. "You w-w-will?"

He slowly turned the spit, not answering.

"You were r-r-ready to s-skewer me back in Ellorian," I said.

"I wouldn't have skewered you."

"You had y-y-your staff to m-m-my throat," I said. "I had to b-b-break your n-nose to get you off."

Instinctively, he reached up to touch his nose. It had been healing slowly.

"I wouldn't have skewered you," he repeated, sounding testier the second time around. "I was just upset, not thinking clearly. Now I know."

"And n-n-now you're m-my k-keeper?" I asked. "Now you s-s-suddenly feel a p-p-protective instinct wh-where none had b-b-been before?"

"Like you said," Perenor answered, "it's not fun if you're really in danger. You're my brother."

The answer surprised me. He looked up at me, I searched his face for some hint of sarcasm but found none.

"I s-s-suppose I'm just n-n-not used to s-seeing true b-b-brotherly affection," I said after a moment.

"Well, I've never really seen yours, either. I suppose we both know now that it doesn't mean it was never there at all."

Perenor looked back at the haunch of goat, giving it the sort of intense scrutiny one only gives roasting meat when one is avoiding giving scrutiny to other things. I rolled my tongue behind my lips.

"Is th-th-that wh-why you c-came?"

"Yes," he answered. "That brotherly affection never mattered quite so much."

I supposed that was true, although I couldn't help but feel some bitterness about all the nights I'd spent crying in my room over my grandmother's callousness or the cruelty of strangers. It wasn't life or death, but it would have been nice to have had a brother during those times, too.

"Besides," Perenor continued, "you need someone on your side besides a mass-murdering deity."

And that was vastly oversimplifying the matter, and it wasn't even really a joke, but for some reason I laughed anyway, and Perenor smirked and took the haunch off the fire.

"I'll keep an eye on our follower," he said as he started to carve. "You'll be fine."

IT WAS ABOUT ten days' travel from Ellorian to the next city of any substance, and it was ten days of wind and sand and not much else.

We travelled only by night, and when dawn came we set up camp and slept through the daylight. And when I dreamt, I dreamt of Umbrion – Umbrion and his starlight, his intensity, the echoes of his electric touch on my skin. I hated myself for finding respite in those dreams. He'd killed the queen and broken Ellorian, but in a life that had become screaming chaos and uncertainty, dreaming of him kept me grounded.

Still, I didn't tell Perenor or Soya of the dreams, which was just as well. I doubt it would have accomplished anything. They wouldn't really understand the context, anyway.

When we at last saw the end of those seemingly endless sand dunes, the weight it lifted from us was tremendous. A mind could only handle so many miles of uninterrupted desert, and when the sand finally gave way into hills and tallgrass and dappled forests, the simple fact that the scenery had changed did wonders to lift our spirits.

"We shouldn't be far from Annolum," Soya said, wiping her brow with her sleeve (night though it was, the dry season remained suffocatingly hot). "It should be right on the edge of the dunes."

"There," Perenor said suddenly, pointing to a low hill in the distance. I almost couldn't make it out through the shroud of trees – low and squat and wooden, flickering with dull orange lamplight, still necessary even in the light of near-dawn.

"That's it, thank the gods," Soya sighed. "That means we're a fourth of the way to Avenos."

"Sol's Light, a fourth," Perenor groaned, adjusting his grip on his staff – which had become more of a walking stick lately than anything else – and began walking toward the city. "It feels like we've been walking for ten seasons already."

"It's longer on foot," Soya agreed. "I've only ever made the journey by carriage."

I was looking forward to sleeping on something that wasn't sand, and that anticipation kept the last half-league from feeling too long.

Oberine hadn't been all that impressive – though perhaps I wasn't a good judge, having been born and raised in the capitol – but Annolum was somehow even less impressive. It was a proper city by size, but the buildings were all aging and rickety, made from weather-beaten wood; the roofs were dull tin, and even the ground was dry and cracked and thoroughly unspectacular.

I could tell that the weathered little city was only just waking up. The air was cool and still; the sun, not yet risen, had turned the sky a distinctive shade of dark blue; and behind the shuttered windows and doors, we heard the sounds of morning, of boiling tea and sizzling meats and sleepy, muted conversation.

"Wait outside, Si," Soya said as we came upon the only building that could have possibly been the inn (the Burning Book, by the sign). "Just until we pay for the room."

I nodded. After what had happened in Oberine, it was the only sound thing for us to do.

"I'll fetch you once we've paid," Perenor said, and they pushed through the door.

I breathed out long and low. There were no benches, so I leaned against the outer wall of the inn to placate my aching legs. As I waited, I looked up and down the street (such that it was; there was no paving, just a stripe of barren ground carved naturally out of the brush). I wiped a few beads of sweat from my brow. I drank a bit of water. I was halfway to shutting my eyes when I noticed them.

Three of them, hooded in black, sweeping down the street toward me in silence.

At first I couldn't even be sure where it was they were headed, but as they came closer, it grew apparent that there was nothing else besides me for them to move for. And by the time I realized that, it was too late.

The one in the middle unsheathed a blade with a soft sound of metal on a wooden scabbard. I took in a breath, and before my mind could tell me to run or shout or dive for the door, her hand was on my shoulder, and the tip of her blade was to my throat.

"Orina!" said the one on the left. "Her orders were for him to be taken alive!"

I knew at once that they must have been the ones following me, although any further deductions I might have arrived at were impeded slightly by the presence of a blade pressed into my throat. All at once, my heartbeat was stuttering against my ribcage.

"And what is it you think she means to do with him once she gets him?" the woman, Orina, countered. I could smell tea and honey on her breath. Before I could gain my bearings, she used her grip on my shoulder to drag me abruptly around the side of the inn, to the narrow alley between it and what looked like a smithy. My feet stumbled the whole way until I was slammed into the wall.

"She just wants him to herself," Orina continued, leaning in dangerously close, "but she's not the only one who'd taste vengeance."

The very tip of the blade pierced my skin and I grit my teeth in pain. Punching my brother in the nose was one thing, but this was a knife. If I was newly mortal, one wrong move could send it slashing open my throat, and who knows what would happen then? My mind raced for a way to extricate – if I screamed, would anyone hear? Would my face have them fighting against me?

"It's not yours to say what she wants," said the one to the left, as a hot line of blood sluiced down my throat. "And it's not yours to disobey her commands."

Perhaps I could reason with them – of course, that predicated me being able to speak, and I doubted I could under the circumstances. My heart beat faster and faster, and my fingertips tingled.

"My husband was in there, Godspeaker."

Her breath was hot on my face. The tingling in my fingertips moved up my hands, my wrists.

"My daughter," she continued, "scion to her house. She was barely a hundred seasons old."

It wasn't tingling anymore, it was a burning. And my vision was starting to darken – not from fear, or at least I didn't think so – and it wasn't until I saw – it wasn't my vision that was darkening, it was the sky. A great stain of swallowing darkness engulfing the sky over my head and – *oh, no. No, no, no.*

"What..." said the one on the left, also seeing the darkness rippling outward over his head.

I knew what this was. I'd felt it before. And it was far more dangerous than any sword to my throat.

"I saw her swallowed up in that great break," Orina snarled at me, and the blade pressed deeper, and my heels scrabbled at the dry earth. The tremendous black stain was growing ever larger. "She fell into jets of steam so hot that her *flesh melted off her bones.*"

"Orina," said her other cohort, seeing what the first saw.

"You bring *death* to these lands, *traitor,*" my attacker snarled. "Your evil brought so much loss. You stole the Worldmother's Light and left us breakable! You should have anticipated that someone would try to *break you!*"

She pulled back her sword and swung it high, but before she could land the blow—

CRACK!

The sound was so loud that the living rock under our feet trembled as though in fear, and my attackers went falling back all at once. I was white-hot, blinded and deafened, and lightning began to surge in my veins.

Hold fast, little bird, came his voice in my head, and *no, no, please no, not again* answered him, but I don't think he heard me, because I knew at once that he was inside of me again. I could feel him under my skin, cold and clear and brutal. *No, no, no, no,* I begged him, not sure if he could hear.

He lifted my eyes to look at them as they struggled to pick themselves up off the ground. *Not again, Umbrion, please don't hurt them, not again.*

"*So,*" he said with my voice, "*the little mongrels are rising up against me?*"

They were scrambling up to their knees. He lifted my hand and pressed it to the shallow wound on my neck. When he drew back my fingers and saw the blood, I felt his rage boil. The cut sealed itself up with a hiss of Craft, and he rounded on my attackers.

"T-traitor," Orina snarled, and with one dismissive gesture of my hand, all three of them went flying back with a force that was so sudden and so tremendous that when they crashed into the wall of the inn, the entire building thundered with the sound of it.

"*You speak of loss?*" he said, and he moved my feet so that I walked toward them. Ripples of shadow Craft followed my footsteps, swirling and hissing at my heels the same as it held them against the wall. "*You speak of vengeance? What know you of loss when nothing you have was earned? What know you of vengeance when you have never felt real pain?*"

He was choking them. *No, no, no, stop it*, I begged him, but he didn't hear me. Umbrion lifted my hand and channeled his Craft through me. My attacker began sliding up the wall, choking and spitting and kicking.

"*How dare you such presumptuousness? Everything I am is so utterly beyond your comprehension, and still you dare to pass judgment?*"

"Silas!" It was Soya, several yards away.

If Umbrion heard her, he paid her no acknowledgment. He pulled my attacker higher and higher, lifting her off the wall until she was dangling in midair, thrashing and trying to scream through the tendrils of Craft around her throat.

"*You know nothing,*" he said, and the woman started to scream. Blood peppered my chest and face. He was *ripping her open*, slowly, *excruciatingly*, and I could see individual bones snap, see strings of sinew tear as she was torn apart, piece by bloody piece. "*You are nothing.*"

"Sol's Light!" one of her cohorts screamed. The gash of gore grew higher and higher up her body until it reached her ribs, until her screaming turned to hideous gurgling, to sputtering, and then to silence. Ribbons of viscera scattered, splattering in the dust.

"*I fear your vengeance like the night-cat fears the field mouse.*"

He lifted my eyes to the other two. One was trembling, paralyzed by fear. The other had his eyes shut tight, muttering prayers.

He tugged the corner of my mouth into a smirk at the sight of it.

"*My mother cannot save you,*" he told them.

"Silas!" It was Perenor, closer. Footsteps were echoing as they came running toward the mouth of the alley.

"*Nothing can save you,*" he continued.

With the other two, at least, he was fast – so fast that I couldn't quite see what was happening despite the fact that my eyes were transfixed on them. In one instant, they were whole; in the next, with a terrible, visceral sound, they were piles of bone and meat, and I was coated head-to-toe in blood.

A hand on my shoulder. I was wrenched around, and just as abruptly as he appeared, he was gone, leaving me alone in my skin and staring at Perenor.

"Silas, what—"

His mouth was open. His gaze moved from me, to the piles of viscera in the dirt.

In my head it was a constant stream of *no, no, no, no, no, no.*

I felt fragile and nauseous and small and there were no words in me. People up and down the street were poking their heads out windows and doors. The sky was clearing, and the rumble of thunder was replaced by an eerie stillness, punctuated by muttered words and soft gasps.

"Is he still here?" Perenor managed at last.

I shook my head. There was no point trying to speak.

"I - I—" Soya, behind him, looked nauseous. "The bath house—"

"We can't take him to a public bath house, look at him!"

"Where then?" Soya demanded. "Sol's Light—" She turned from the bodies and covered her mouth with her hand.

"I saw signs of a spring—" Perenor moved to the far end of the alley and peered out between the buildings, over the thornbushes and bramble. "To the north."

"Fine," Soya said. Her voice was wan, shaking. She was pale as beach sand and her shoulders were starting to tremble. "Fine. Let's go."

"Silas, come. Hurry. Can you walk?"

I stared down at my legs. I wasn't sure. The scent of blood was choking, oppressive - I felt bile rising in my throat and it took everything in me to keep it down.

"Hurry," he said when I didn't answer, moving forward and grabbing me by one blood-slicked arm. He pulled me forward and I nearly lost my foot, but his grip held me study. "Come on. Don't look at the blood. Let's go now; we can't stay."

I found myself leaning on him heavily as I stumbled my way out of the ally, relying on his guidance, as I was all but blind from the blood and tears on my face.

BLOOD, AS IT TURNS OUT, is not an easy thing to work out of clothes or hair.

"We'll have to burn these," Perenor told me.

I didn't answer. The springs were near blistering, but somehow they were not nearly hot enough. The blood of four strangers was caked underneath my fingernails, matted in my hair, burrowed in all the little crevices of my body. I would not feel clean until I scrubbed it all off. I might not feel clean even when I had, or ever again.

"We have a few changes of clothes," he said, "but we'll probably have to buy a new cloak before we head out next."

Cleaning myself was made all the more difficult by the fact that my hands, despite the steaming heat of the spring, were trembling violently. I felt frayed, untethered – directionless and frenzied like an animal in a trap.

And I couldn't get the *fucking blood* out of my hair.

"Silas?"

No matter how hard I scrubbed, there was a tangle of blood and some vile strip of flesh that was caught in my hair, and it wouldn't come out.

"Silas – Silas, I know you're still scared—"

It's hard for me to explain it effectively – after what had happened, I felt a deep, compulsive need to be clean. I *had* to be clean. If I could get the blood and organs off of me, I could relax – or maybe that's just what I told myself, I don't know. The only thing I could focus on was the frantic desire to just get it off, get it off, why wouldn't it *come off?*

"You have to calm down enough to tell me what happened – Silas—"

Off, off, off, off, I chanted to myself. I didn't want this, I didn't want it. It was all over me and under my skin. I couldn't get it out. It wouldn't come out no matter how hard I scrubbed—

"Silas, stop."

I felt hands grab my wrists. Shoulder-deep in water, I had to lift my chin far to stare up at Perenor, who was crouched by the side of the spring.

"Stop," he said again, eyes sad and anxious.

"W-w-w-w-w-want it off," I choked. My throat was constricted.

"I know," he said. "I know, Silas. Let it soak."

Despite the heat of the water, I shuddered, and my chin fell to my chest. Perenor hesitated, then scooped up a handful of water to drizzle over the stubborn mat of blood. In another situation, I would have been surprised by such a tender gesture, but frayed and frantic as I was, all I did was let my eyes fall shut and try to get my breathing under control.

"You're safe now," he said. "You're all right."

But I didn't feel safe. In my mind, I was replaying every visceral detail of their deaths, and it was not the sort of thing that would calm me down. I began to wheeze, and I gripped the hard, rocky edge of the spring to keep myself from falling apart.

"Ssh. Silas, do you remember when we were children? When we still shared a bedroom?"

The question was strange enough to, if not soothe me, then at least distract me for a moment. I did remember, of course. Siblings always shared a room in the formative years of childhood; theirs was allegedly a sacred bond, one that was to be reinforced whenever possible. It had never really worked with Perenor and me.

"Do you remember the song?"

It took me a moment, but I did. It came back to me as incomplete melodies and disjointed lyrics.

"I remember when we came up with it," Perenor continued as he rubbed at the mat of blood in my hair with his fingers. "Grandmother was hosting a party downstairs, and you couldn't sleep because of how frightened you were by all the people, even though they couldn't see us."

The memory became clearer. I was amazed that Perenor remembered it at all. We couldn't have been more than thirty seasons old.

"I didn't want you to feel scared, so I just made up a song, and it worked. Do you remember?"

Under the milky surface of the water, I rubbed my hands into my knees. "*I'll go with you, over the ocean*," I sang, though that may not have been how it started. Out of the corner of my vision, Perenor grinned.

"*I'll take you with me, into the sky.*"

"Th-then it w-w-w-was something about a b-b-boat."

"A flying boat," Perenor corrected. "As I recall, it took you away from all the scary things in the world."

Despite myself, I smiled. I didn't have that many good memories from my childhood, but that was one of them. "W-w-w-we were s-s-so close b-back then," I said, before I could stop myself.

Perenor, by his expression, was thinking the same thing. "Yeah," he answered, massaging the mat of hair between his palms. "You used to sing that song whenever you got scared. Until one day you just stopped."

Despite my best efforts, I couldn't remember why I'd stopped. It hadn't been long before Perenor and I grew apart, but it happened so early that I couldn't remember what had done it.

"You s-s-stopped singing it to m-m-me, t-too," I said.

"Yeah," Perenor answered slowly. "I did."

He worked the bloody tangle from my hair and smoothed it out. Then he withdrew his hands from the water and leaned back on his palms.

"Better?"

I released a long breath. There was still a tight knot of dread in me, but it was no longer turning me into a shaking mess. I nodded weakly.

"Did he possess you again?" Perenor asked, gently. "Like at the confirmation?"

Carefully, haltingly, I explained. I told him about the ambush, the woman's threats, their words, the Night Father's possession of me. I stopped short before I got to the part where they were ripped into ribbons. I trusted Perenor could glean enough from context.

"Silas," he said when I trailed off. "I... shit. He just swooped in and killed them? Just like that? I suppose you are his Godspeaker, so he has a duty to protect you, but..."

I fought away the images of as best I could. "P-P-P-Perenor," I said, "I th-think you n-n-need to t-teach me d-d-defensive Craft."

I'd startled him, clearly. "What? Craft?"

"It's either C-C-Craft or physical c-c-combat," I said, "and m-most days, a s-s-stiff wind could overpower me."

I lifted my arms out of the water demonstrably. Unlike Perenor's well-constructed musculature, I was assembled almost entirely from paper-thin skin and birdlike bones.

"Silas, *I'll* protect you," he said.

"And as w-w-we've d-discovered," I answered, "there w-w-will be circum-m-mstances in wh-which you won't b-b-be there to d-do so."

I dropped my hands back into the water. Perenor frowned down at me.

"It's not..." He sighed, pushed a hand through his hair. "It's not as simple as that. You can't just *learn* combat Craft."

"I'm a q-q-quick study," I said.

"Silas, people spend *years*—"

"Then j-j-just teach m-me the b-basics!" I said, grabbing the edge of the spring with both hands. "T-t-teach me enough to incapacitate so I c-c-can run."

"That's..."

He sighed a second time.

"We've g-g-got th-thirty more days on the L-L-Long Road," I said. "T-teach me at the end of each d-d-day."

Perenor's mouth twisted. Just as I thought he was about to cave—

"He's calm now?"

We both turned. Soya had arrived from the nearby copse of trees. She had a freshly-killed rabbit over her shoulder.

"Yeah," Perenor said. "Well, I mean, he's traumatized, but he's stopped shaking."

She nodded, opened the pack to find a sheet of waxed leather to wrap the rabbit in. "So it was Umbrion?"

"Yeah," Perenor said.

"You're sure?"

"Who else would it be?"

Soya eyed me a moment as she packed the rabbit in the waxed leather, face traced with the ghost of suspicion. She looked like she had a question hanging off the edge of her tongue, held in place by the same tension that holds dew to grass. I frowned when she didn't answer Perenor's question. Did she think it was me?

"So we're dealing with a god who has a vengeful streak," she said. "Is that his goal? To just kill everyone?"

"He seems pretty good at it so far," Perenor answered.

"It seems too straightforward," Soya said. "The gods are unknowable. Why would his only goal to kill us? There's something more to the story that we don't know."

"Well, I'm sure if Silas just asks him, he'll make everything perfectly clear," Perenor said sarcastically.

Soya stilled. "Will he do that?" she asked.

"I wasn't being serious," Perenor said.

"I know you weren't, I wasn't asking you. Silas, if you ask him – pray to him – will he answer your question?"

I stared at her in silence. I had no idea. "M-m-maybe?" I answered "I m-mean, theoretically."

She finished wrapping the rabbit and stood over me, limbs akimbo. "Well, he clearly won't hurt you, so maybe try it."

"That's a stupid and terrible plan," Perenor said at once.

"Why?" Soya challenged.

"Because it could implicate Silas and anyone around him," Perenor answered. "Like you said, he's a vengeful god – what if he got word that Silas got information out of him only to betray him with it?"

"If we're not willing to talk to Umbrion, then what exactly is the point of having him?" Soya shouted.

Perenor stood up. "I'm not in love with your tone, Rhodan."

"Well, I'm not in love with the three piles of blood and viscera they're scraping off the dirt right now in Annolum!" Soya answered in kind. "I'm not in love with the city that broke in half and fell into the hot springs, nor all the people that followed it!"

"That wasn't my brother's fault, Rhodan, you said so yourself!"

"*I know!*" she bellowed, a bit too loud. I drew back away from her; a split second later, she seemed to check herself. "I know. I know, I'm just – I'm sorry, Silas."

I swallowed a knot of anxiety in my throat. "It's f-f-fine."

"I just don't want to arrive in Avenos without some kind of intel," she said.

"Well," Perenor said slowly, "if it's intel you want, then apparently there's someone after Silas. She sent those three after him, to kidnap him. Who'd be dumb enough to do that?"

"Plenty of people," she answered, setting a change of clothes for me at the side of the hot spring. I slowly climbed out and took a drying cloth. "Anyone who survived the breaking of Ellorian, and some besides."

"They'll certainly try again," Perenor said.

"I should think so."

Perenor sighed. I dried my hair first, then my limbs and torso, then set to dressing. "This is still the best course for now," he said. "He's still safest in Avenos. We'll reach out to this group that wants him from its safety, see what they have to say. After all, wanting to kidnap Silas is not necessarily a sign of bad intention. They must be against Umbrion in some capacity."

I supposed that was true, although I was hardly eager to meet them.

"Maybe they can help us," Perenor said. "Maybe they have a plan."

"Yeah," Soya answered. "I mean, hopefully."

"We should avoid staying at the inn," Perenor said. "Once they find those bodies..."

Soya nodded reluctantly. It hardly mattered to me. On a feather bed or rocky ground, I knew I wouldn't sleep tonight.

NOT ONLY DID I NOT SLEEP THAT NIGHT, I seemed to stop sleeping entirely.

I suppose it was bound to happen eventually. Apparently the number of people I could watch be ripped to shreds before I started losing sleep was somewhere between two and four.

Everything we didn't say about what happened could have filled up the palace library a thousand times over. I could see the conflict on their faces. Soya wanted to interrogate me, Perenor wanted to leave it alone.

"I thought of something," he said one morning, as we were setting up camp after a long day's trek. The dryness of the ground was slowly turning to forest-dappled plains by then, and Soya's trips to find firewood were getting longer, dryer brush getting harder to find.

I looked sideways at him. I was exhausted, and felt like I could barely see him.

"You said you wanted me to teach you defensive Craft," Perenor said. "Assuming you're as quick a study as you say you are, I think I might be able to."

He sat down next to me and started to rummage through his pack.

"Normally, using Craft is borderline impossible without a channeler," he said, "but then I remembered that I—"

"W-w-wait, stop." Craft parlance was always lost on me. "Channeler?"

"Like my staff," Perenor said. "Something, usually a weapon, carved with runes so Craft can be channeled through it more easily."

"Oh." I supposed there was quite a lot of theory that I was missing.

Perenor kept rummaging through his pack. "Anyway, a real runed weapon would take months to make and would cost more gold to buy than we have on hand at present. And besides, if I gave you a real runed weapon, you'd probably blow yourself up."

"Thanks," I said flatly.

"But then I remembered that – ah!"

He found what he was looking for at the very bottom of his bag. When he pulled it out, I didn't know what it was at first – some sort of piece of leather. When he stretched it out, I recognized it as—

"A g-g-glove?"

"A runed glove," he corrected. "It's my old training glove. Much safer than a weapon, still lets you channel Craft."

He offered it to me. It was long and thick black leather, meant to reach the elbow. Runes were stitched into the underside with silver thread, along where the palm and wrist were and extending down the arm.

"Wh-wh-what makes this s-s-safer?"

"Well, for one, it's not a weapon," he answered. I experimentally tugged the glove on. The fingers were a bit short, and the fit a bit loose, but the leather was well worn and comfortable and it flexed easily. "And the runes are fewer, meaning that the scope and power of the Craft it can channel is reduced."

"S-s-so you can t-train me with this," I said, looking up at him.

"Well, not properly," Perenor answered. "Not comprehensively. But I think I might be able to teach you the absolute basics."

"I sh-sh-shouldn't think I'd n-n-need to b-be a scholar in it," I said. I extended my newly gloved hand out toward the half-assembled fire. "H-how does it—?"

I felt a sudden recoil. I wasn't entirely sure what happened, apart from the fact that I abruptly went tumbling backwards to the sound of a loud *crack.*

"Okay, glove comes off for now," Perenor said, tugging it off my hand as I scrambled back upright. The fire was now burning enthusiastically with what little kindling was available to it.

"H-h-h-how—?"

"A complicated combination of intention and energy," Perenor answered. "Look, we'll start actual practice tomorrow. There's a whole thing with safety you should know before you put the glove on again."

"You two all right?"

It was Soya, coming back with an armful of kindling.

"Who started the fire?" she asked when she saw it.

"Silas did," Perenor said. "Quite without meaning to."

Soya eyed me. "Huh." She added some kindling to the fire; it slowly began to burn up with more strength.

"Don't worry, I took the glove away."

"For the best, probably," Soya answered. "Did you check the trap? I think I heard it go off."

"I'll go look," Perenor said. He gave me a pointed look. "No more glove."

I held up both hands in surrender and he headed off into the small forest at the edge of which we had set up camp. I rubbed the palm of my hand. I was usually competent enough at things when I set my mind to them. Hopefully I'd progress quickly out of the *accidentally setting things on fire* stage of understanding Craft.

"Burn yourself?" Soya asked.

"N-n-no." I was as surprised as she was. Soya added a few more sticks to the fire.

"I think the whole process is a little redundant," Soya said. "I mean, what's the point of self-defense when you have a god in your corner?"

The corner of my mouth twitched downward. "If I h-h-have a s-say in it," I answered, slowly, trying my best not to take offense, "I'd r-r-rather have th-those who'd d-d-do me harm unc-c-conscious, and n-not ripped apart."

Soya hesitated, then slowed to a stop shoveling in kindling. "Right," she said, belatedly. "You had no control."

It was almost a question, and I hated that she wasn't sure. I reached into the pack near my hip and produced a bag of dates. Soya sat down beside me, and the silence was tense but blessedly short.

"Didn't you say to me – after you talked to the Vizier, didn't you tell me about how you tapped into Umbrion's power yourself?"

I frowned at her. "That w-w-w-wasn't in my c-control, either," I said. "And I'd r-r-rather not have it b-be my only r-recourse."

"Right," she said again.

More silence. I plucked a dried date from the bag; Soya watched the fire crackle.

"I guess your stomach is too weak to kill anyone anyway," she continued. "Remember that time you cut your finger while cooking and passed out?"

I almost wanted to go back to the suspicion.

"You were barely even bleeding," she said, grinning, "but you just went out like a candle. Smacked your head on the counter on the way down."

"C-c-can we p-please talk about s-something else?"

"Oh! Or the time we went to the butcher's—"

"S-S-Soya."

"—and you threw up because she had blood on her hands?"

"It was g-g-gross!"

"Animals bleed, Silas," Soya laughed. "Did you expect them not to?"

"Are we making fun of Silas's weak stomach?" It's Perenor, coming back out of the woods with a rabbit over his shoulder. "I want to join in. Did I ever tell you about the time he cried at dinner because he could still see the pig's face?"

"I w-w-was forty s-seasons old!"

"That's *hilarious*," Soya said.

"Wh-why are we m-making fun of m-m-me? P-Perenor's s-stupid, l-let's laugh at him f-for that."

"I'm not stupid," Perenor snipped.

"You're kind of stupid," Soya answered, laughing.

It felt nice to laugh, even if it was only at ourselves, and even if it was only for a little while. Mostly, it felt good to think about something else – anything at all.

And though the seeds of doubt had been planted in Soya – or perhaps the seed had always been there and my attempted assassination had merely let it germinate – this was good. I could see the ghost of suspicion in everything Soya did, but this was good.

Besides, between my newly re-shredded nerves and the images of ripping flesh and snapping bone that resurfaced in my mind when things were too quiet, I found that I couldn't be too upset by her mistrust. Situations reversed, I'd be filled with doubt, too.

THE NEXT BIG LANDMARK on our way was not for two more weeks, which meant that for two weeks, until we reached Iriallum, we had nothing but the road.

Dry, rolling plains slowly turned into soggy marshland. Where once we fell asleep to wind through tallgrass and thrumming bush crickets we now slept to cooing owls and the rustle of foxes. I'd never seen a forest, only jungle, but I'd read about them. Scholars often enthused about their biodiversity, but most of the animals seemed to be smart enough to stay away from us.

Aside from the walking, all we really had was hunting and, with Perenor and I, the training.

I wasn't what you'd call a natural with Craft, not like Perenor was. It likely didn't help that we were forced to skip much of the usual curriculum that dealt with theory. Still, Perenor proved a surprisingly competent teacher.

"Craft is very physical," he explained to me one evening like most of the others. "It will feel natural to gesture when you use it, and it is encouraged. In the end, it usually comes down to energy transfer – learning to expend energy you already have by transforming it in ways not limited by your physical body."

And that made sense in theory, but in practice, it was trickier. I had spent the last few days trying to lift a stone off of a larger stone. So far I'd only made it wiggle once, although that might have been the wind.

"It w-w-was so easy wh-when it was accid-d-d-dental," I muttered. The glove was back on, my hand extended, but the rock stayed perfectly still.

"Channelers tend to react unpredictably to a mind not organized for their use," Perenor explained. "Focus. You can still feel the heat of the runes through the glove?"

I nodded. They were glowing faintly along my palm and the

underside of my arm, although it didn't seem to make a difference to the rock.

"Intention and energy," he continued. "You know how you would expend the energy to physically pick up the stone; make that your intention and expend that energy."

The rock wriggled, maybe. It was hard to tell. I dropped my hand to my side and my head fell back. I was panting, which was strange, because I'd only been standing.

"This is im-m-mpossible," I muttered.

"Don't feel too bad," Perenor said. "Remember, you're skipping a lot of required reading here."

"If C-C-Craft is j-just transfer of en-n-nergy," I said, wiping my brow with my ungloved hand, "then how w-w-were you able t-to save the ar-r-rena? I d-doubt you could have s-s-stopped that f-fireball w-with your b-bare hands."

Perenor hesitated, like he wasn't quite sure how to explain.

"There's more energy in a body than can just be expelled physically," he explained. "The same energy that lets you walk and talk and think also binds your spirit together and to your physical presence. In a pinch, a sorcerer can tap into that and expel far more energy than they would normally be able to physically."

I never paid attention during sermons, but still, "Th-th-that sounds dangerous."

"It is," Perenor said. "It's not what you'd call recommended practice. But it is good for emergencies."

"Th-th-that s-sounds like it c-could hurt y-y-you." Then it occurred to me— "Is th-th-that wh-why you w-were l-laid up for f-f-five days? D-d-did you d-damage your s-soul?"

"That's not how it works," Perenor said. "I didn't damage it, I just sort of... exhausted it. Temporarily."

"M-m-maybe y-you shouldn't d-do that again," I said.

"This isn't about me," Perenor deflected. "Focus on the rock."

I sighed and turned forward. The rock remained precisely where it had been, very much not moved.

"Frame it in your mind in the same way you'd frame physically picking it up," Perenor said. "Let yourself believe that's what you're actually doing. Once you draw that first link, the rest of it becomes pretty straightforward."

I lifted my hand again; the runes on the underside of my arm and along my palm start to glow heat onto my skin again.

"How m-m-much f-further to Iriallum?"

"Soya said another week, I think."

"And th-th-that's the h-halfway point?" The mere idea felt exhausting. We'd already walked so far.

"That is the name of Iriallum, isn't it? The Halfway City? Try to focus."

I sighed. The longer I held my hand out at a rock that wasn't doing anything, the more I felt utterly incompetent. Maybe I just wasn't meant to be a sorcerer.

"It's not w-w-working," I said through my teeth.

"Just try to concentrate."

"I *am* concentrating. It just w-w-won't *move*."

Until it did, suddenly, right as I said the word. Not only did it lift up off the rock, it went hurtling into the air several yards.

It took me by such surprise that I stumbled several steps back, and it went falling back down, cracking loudly against the larger rock and splitting into uneven halves.

"Well, then," Perenor said.

"H-h-how..."

"I guess your cues aren't physical; they're verbal, or mental," Perenor said.

"Wh-wh-what?"

"I'm a very physical sorcerer, but I'm also a very active person," he continued. "I suppose it makes sense that someone more intellectual would be more effective with words and thoughts rather than movements."

I stared at him uncomprehendingly. Perenor rephrased.

"Do the same thing I said before – frame it in your mind like you were physically moving it. But instead of holding out your hand, just say it instead."

I looked back at the rock, now lying in pieces on the ground. I dropped my hand to my side. I could still feel the runes glowing against my skin.

"*Move*," I said again, feeling that simple, one-word commands would be best – and indeed, the two halves of the rock lifted back up, arranging themselves neatly back on the large boulder. I stared in astonishment.

"Well done!" Perenor said, thumping me on the back with such force that I staggered forward. "I think that was the missing key, just adapting it to your own style."

As Perenor had said it would, the pieces were starting to fit together. I was starting to understand the delicate balance of intention and energy, how to extend it past myself. "*Spin*," I said, and the pieces of the rock began to spin on their sides, slowly at first, and then more rapidly.

"This is good," Perenor said. "*Really* good. I think we can move on to more complicated and nuanced Craft."

"I d-d-don't need m-much," I answered, looking back at him. "I sh-sh-should be f-fine with the ability to-to-to incapacit-t-tate."

"I think it's best to cover all our bases, so long as we're covering any. I can teach you how to disarm, how to knock back."

I wasn't fond of the idea of needing such abilities, but it was probably best to err on the side of caution after Annolum.

"I'll be honest, I wasn't even sure this was going to work at all," he continued, watching as the rocks continued to spin on their edges like tops. "There's a reason the Temple of Elwen is charged with the teaching of Craft – it usually requires a lot of formal education to get to this point. I didn't think it was possible to get this far without it."

"Y-y-you're a very g-good teacher," I said, and Perenor smiled at me.

I had the strange realization at that point that I was getting along with my brother. I couldn't remember the last time that had happened. I thought of our old song, though I wasn't sure why.

I WAS ABDUCTED the day we arrived in Iriallum.

Perhaps we should have seen it coming. After all, this mysterious person who had tried to kidnap me had not gone away, despite how unsuccessful her first attempt had been, and anyone who needed to go anywhere within the borders of Imlandran had to go through Iriallum.

Come to think of it, I'm not sure Iriallum will still be standing by the time this narrative of mine is read, so I'll do my best to explain the city. The two halves of Imlandran were separated by a narrow isthmus, and built right onto that isthmus, spanning coast to coast, was Iriallum.

It was a port town on two fronts – the western port, which had a straight shot to Sessyr, and the eastern port, with easy access to Myrion and Onansu. All that with the fact that it was right in the middle of the Long Road made it the ideal hub of trade and commerce and culture.

Neither Perenor nor I had ever been to Iriallum (we'd never even been out of Ellorian), and as a consequence, we were woefully underprepared when we saw it growing over the horizon.

Ellorian was big, but Iriallum was *massive*. The walls of the city alone seemed nearly as tall as the palace in the capitol, but even so we could see great stone buildings piercing the sky. Even from several leagues away, we could hear the dull thrum of the crowds, the rumble of a metropolis.

"Fuck," Perenor said, which just about summed up my reaction to the city as well.

"Welcome to Iriallum," Soya said. Having travelled several times between Ellorian and her home city of Avenos, Soya must have been used to it.

"I didn't know cities could *be* so huge," Perenor continued reverently.

"Yeah, it's pretty big," she answered offhandedly, moving up to the giant iron gates that stood open. "Just be wary of the courtesans."

The idea of being wary of courtesans was hilarious to me. Temple courtesans were famously demure and kind in their eternal effort to emulate Aemor, the god of love. I couldn't imagine why I needed to be warned about them.

"Wh-wh-what's wrong with the t-t-temple courtesans?"

"I didn't say the *temple* courtesans," Soya said, "I said the *courtesans*. Not all of them work for the gods here, and the constant competition makes them pretty pushy. But hey, it also makes them cheap, so if you're interested—"

"Pass," Perenor said at once.

"See, I was just thinking that you could do with a good romp," Soya said. "Maybe it would make you less uptight all the time."

Perenor rolled his eyes with such intensity that he likely could have seen into his own head. "Not into that, thanks."

"Not into what? Courtesans? Who's not into courtesans?"

We nodded to the guards on either side of the gates as we passed. The inside of the city was no less impressive – dense and loud and crowded and extremely, unapologetically alive.

There were vendors and bards and criers and jugglers, and everything was so interesting that I forgot entirely to be nervous about the size of the crowds milling around us.

"I'm not," Perenor said. "I'm not into anything. Never have been."

There were precious few things in all of Andelan I wanted to think about less than my brother's sex life, although a lack of interest would certainly explain why he'd never courted any of his numerous suitors.

"Well, whatever," Soya said. "If you're not keen on sex, you're going to hate this road coming up."

I was about to ask why, but when I followed her gaze, my question answered itself. It seemed to be a central hub of for-coin courtesans.

Perenor may not have thought them lovely, but I certainly did. They were clean and pretty, with tiny silver bells ringing in their hair and around their ankles. Temple courtesans may have been holier, but for-coin courtesans always seemed nicer to look at.

"Th-th-there are s-so many," I said. Ellorian had plenty, of course, but I'd never seen such a number in one place.

"Iriallum's the biggest city in the kingdom," Soya said. "More people means more courtesans. Supply and demand and all that."

"Good morning, lovely girl," said one, a pretty and willowy young man with a string of bells jingling around his neck. "Care to start your day off right?"

Soya grinned at him. "Don't tempt me, now, I have no time for pretty indulgences."

"Tempting's my job, lovely girl," he said, grinning back at her, keeping pace easily, each step ringing gently.

"Now how can you not think that's tantalizing as all fuck?" Soya asked, and even though the question must have been directed at Perenor, she wasn't looking at him – she was looking at the courtesan. Perenor, for his part, didn't bother responding; he just rolled his eyes.

I wanted to call Soya out on her lechery, but the crowd was getting pretty thick and the nervousness was finally starting to creep up alongside the fascination.

"It is tempting," Soya continued to the courtesan, "but we've been travelling all night, and like I said, I have no time for distractions, lovely and limber though they may be."

He pouted prettily, then dropped his pace until he was astride with me. I clammed up at once. "Well, what about you, then, lovely boy?"

I made a rather undignified sound en lieu of an answer, which started Soya laughing. I was never very good at talking to beautiful people.

"Or perhaps both of you at once! You're quite pretty, lovely girl, so how about two for the price of one?"

Soya laughed all the harder. "I don't think—"

"Hey!" Perenor suddenly said. "What are you—?"

He didn't sound offended, I noticed, but alarmed. I turned and saw another courtesan, yellow-haired and fair-skinned, dragging him forcefully by one arm.

Soya frowned. "Hey, easy—" she began, but suddenly there was a hand on her arm as well, and mine, and we were both of us pulled away from each other. "Hey! What are you doing?"

"Come on, lovelies," the courtesan said, and it was at that particular moment that I noticed he was armed with a small stiletto dagger tucked into the folds of his sheer linen robe.

"Let go of me!" Soya cried, struggling against the grip that kept her in place.

I was being pulled away by two people, panic rising in my throat. I had to remember my Craft - I had my glove on, if I could just—"*Perenor!*"

"Keep them separated!" barked another voice. "Take the sorcerer's staff - and get the Godspeaker!"

Shit.

I had to keep my head. If I wasn't calm, Umbrion would manifest again. I had to remember what Perenor had taught me - contextualize the energy - and—

"*Off!*" I shouted, and the two people holding me went flying back several feet. "Perenor!"

He was being dragged into an alleyway - one of his abductors was holding his staff.

Soya was being dragged in the opposite direction, though. I couldn't follow both of them. For a moment I was paralyzed, Craft burning hot on the palm of my hand—

"*Silas!*" Perenor called out as he disappeared into an alleyway.

"N-n-n-*n-n-n*—!"

I tried to run to him, but there was a sudden pain in the back of my head, and then only darkness.

MY FIRST COGNIZANT THOUGHT upon waking was wondering how many times since being chosen as Umbrion's Godspeaker I had woken up in an unfamiliar setting after losing consciousness. The tally must have been getting higher.

As my mind staggered upward through the layers of consciousness, I became aware of several things – first, that the room I was in was all but pitch black; second, that I was on a bare stone floor; third, that there was a wound on my head. I wasn't used to being wounded, though in fairness, no one really was.

I slowly took stock of my surroundings, letting my eyes adjust through the pounding on the back of my head. The room seemed like some sort of storage closet – no larger than ten feet in any direction, empty save for a bucket in one corner. There was a single door, under which a narrow ribbon of golden light was glowing faintly.

It took me a while to remember what had happened, and the moment I did it all came back at once.

Shit – Perenor – Soya – gods, where were they? Had they been hurt? Worse? All on my account?

I staggered to my feet, and then learned that head wounds make it difficult to stand. I collapsed back down onto my knees again, landing hard enough to send a lance of pain into my hip.

I had to get out of here. I didn't know where I was, but it didn't matter. I gathered up my bearings and tried once again to stand up, this time bracing myself for the wobble. Once standing, I staggered to the door and pulled hard and the handle.

Locked. Of course.

I shook it hard in its frame, pounded on the wood. "*Hey!*" I bellowed, but there came no answer. I kept shaking. The door was heavy cedar with wrought-iron reinforcement. I doubted I could kick it open.

Craft, maybe? They hadn't taken my glove, I saw when I looked down – they must not have known it was runed. I closed my eyes and pressed my hand do the door. I could see the tumblers in my head, see the prongs and the anatomy of the lock. I knew the mechanics of an unlocking door – if I could just—

The door opened. Unfortunately, with someone on the other side.

"Good, you're awake."

It was a woman standing across from me, though I could only see her by silhouette. My eyes struggled to adjust to the sudden flood of light. I took several steps backward.

"My name is Kiara," she said. "I'm a High Priestess of Aemor and second-in-command to the Godspeaker Rolen. You are in my temple. You will be staying here for quite a while."

The features of her face came into focus one by one – the clear eyes, the sharp cheekbones, the thin neck. She certainly had the look of a High Priestess, clean and commanding and patrician. It was the look in her eyes that put me on edge – dangerous, manic, possessed.

"Wh-wh-where is m-my brother?" I demanded. "Where's S-S-Soya?"

"Perhaps if you tell me everything I want to know," High Priestess Kiara said venomously, "I'll tell you everything *you* want to know."

She came striding forward, and I held my ground as best I could despite the deeply entrenched, profound fear in me.

"Where is Umbrion?" she hissed at me.

"Y-y-y-you have n-n-no idea wh-wh-what kind of d-danger—"

"*Where is Umbrion!*" she bellowed, and I flinched away from her. "Do you think I'm inclined to *show you mercy?* The only reason I haven't ripped you open like you did the Queen is because you know things I don't!"

I cowed, but only for a moment.

"Those wh-wh-who end-d-danger m-me endanger them-m-mselves," I said, flexing my hands to keep them from trembling and betraying my fear. "I am a G-G-Godspeaker. Um-m-mbrion w-will raze this t-t-temple and k-k-kill everyone in it if y-you hurt me."

"Is that a *threat,* Godspeaker?"

"*No,*" I growled, "it's a w-w-w-*warning.* Do not f-f-f-force the N-Night Father's hand! Wh-what d-do you think happened to the p-p-party you s-s-sent after m-me in Annolum?"

She narrowed her eyes at me. Her shoulders were shaking with rage, her hands clenched tightly at her sides. She looked like a cobra, wound up tight and ready to strike.

"I w-w-want n-no more b-blood spilt," I said. "B-b-but if you h-hurt me, I c-c-cannot guarantee y-y-your safety."

"If you don't want blood spilt," she said, dangerously, "then perhaps you shouldn't have killed half of Ellorian."

My throat tightened. "I d-d-d-did not b-break Ellorian."

She struck me with surprising force; a burst of pain across my cheekbone, and I tumbled onto the ground. My ears rang from the pain redoubling from the wound on the back of my head; for a moment, I could barely see.

"Do you not understand the situation you're in, traitor?" she asked me. "I am not gently asking for your cooperation. You *will* tell me what you know or I will make things very difficult for you!"

I did not immediately understand what she meant. At least, not at first.

"T-t-t-torture?" I said. How novel. Don't put my life in jeopardy, just make me wish for it to end from the pain. I wondered if torture would summon Umbrion the same as a knife to my throat, but I would have rather not found out. "How v-v-very priestly."

"How *dare* you preach to me," she hissed. "There were children in that city. Families and young lovers and infants all snuffed out in an *instant*. What sort of moral high ground is that?"

"I d-d-d-*did not break Ellorian!*"

A hand in my hair; she pulled my up with a sharp, painful tug, and new waves of pain rattled through my head in all directions. I yelped sharply and scrabbled for a hold on the wall.

"My *family* was in Ellorian," she growled at me. "My younger sister travelled all the way from here to see your confirmation. She was *eighty seasons old.*"

My throat tightened even further. I grit my teeth and shut my eyes, willing away the images of the streets buckling, of the jets of burning steam, of the city being swallowed up into the springs.

She released her grip in my hair by throwing me forward onto the floor. I landed on a hip with another jolt of pain.

"Tell me his plans," she hissed at me. "Tell me where he's striking next."

Even if I had known, I wouldn't have told her. Slowly, I pushed myself to a sit and turned around.

"D-d-does R-Rolen know about this?"

She steeled her face, but didn't answer. Her silence was more telling than anything she could have said.

"Y-y-you are a High P-Priestess, you answer only to-to-to him, b-but you w-went behind his b-back? You threaten t-t-torture w-without his knowledge?"

"Do not *preach to me, traitor!*"

"Y-you w-w-want information; I w-w-will speak only wi-with him." I turned forward, away from her, shut my eyes and willed my vision to stop swimming.

"You're not worthy to be in his presence!"

"Th-then r-r-risk the l-life of everyone in th-this b-b-building and t-torture me," I snarled. "How m-m-m-much b-blood is your v-vengeance worth?"

Silence, for a moment – then a frustrated scream. She stormed from the room and slammed the door behind her, so loudly that I jumped.

The room was dark again. My head was still screaming in pain. And now that I was alone, all the terror came creeping back in ebbs and flows like the tide.

I drew my knees up to my chest and leaned against the wall. I had to get out, but I couldn't use Craft with my hands shaking so badly. I shut my eyes and willed away the creeping darkness in my own mind.

Soya, Perenor – gods – where were they?

THE DOOR was magically sealed.

Either that or my Craft wasn't good enough to open a lock. Regardless, it had the same result: I was trapped.

I won't go into too much detail about the effects of prolonged confinement but to say that they were not pretty. I enjoyed solitude, but only by choice. Having it forced on me – for what turned out to be over a full day, in a near jet-black and dead-silent room – was more profoundly psychologically damaging than I care to admit.

I was not brought food. Occasionally, I would hear people muttering on the other side of the door, but none of them ever came in. Likely they were too scared that I would bring down the building on their heads.

I thought a lot about Soya and Perenor, wondering were they were, hoping beyond hope for their safety. In another situation, I might have prayed, but too much of my faith was gone.

I spent a full day and night cold and hungry and dirty, abjectly and utterly alone. I was reaching the point of questioning whether or not I was actually dead, and death was just a dark and empty room where you sat alone for eternity, until the door opened.

My first hope was that it was food, but the figure cut out from the bright light of the hallways was taller than any nervous, jittery servant.

"Gods, Kiara," said the figure, whose voice I recognized at once, "what have you *done* to him?"

"*Nothing.*"

His Holiness Rolen of House Chastain, Godspeaker to Aemor, strode forward, and in the darkness I could more easily make out the familiar details of his face.

"Be careful, Your Holiness!" said someone – a guard, I could only assume. "He's not safe!"

"Have you not let him out of this room, Kiara?"

"He's Godspeaker to Umbrion!" Kiara answered. "What was I meant to do, let him roam free?"

"You were meant to *not capture him!*" Rolen spun on a heel to face her. The High Priestess – I could see her now, awash in the light from the hall – buckled under his anger. "What were you *thinking?* Do you really believe this is the sort of behavior the god of love and compassion would *condone?* Do you think this is emulating Aemor?"

"Your Holiness," she protested, "he betrayed Aemor! He betrayed all the gods!"

"*Umbrion* betrayed the gods!"

"He's Umbrion's Godspeaker! He—"

"For *seven hundred seasons*, you have been my High Priestess, Kiara. In all that time, have you still not learned what a Godspeaker *is?*"

Kiara didn't seem to know what to say.

"We are *servants*," he said, "not conspirators! He has as much agency in Umbrion's actions as you have in mine!"

"He – he may know something," the High Priestess said, quietly, sounding defeated.

"And it wasn't your place to find it!" Rolen shouted back. "I know what this is, Kiara! And to your wounded heart it would sound like wisdom, but a war of gods has no place for Andel tacticians, no matter how great our stakes in the war may be!"

I realized, at that moment, that Rolen was on *my* side.

And it felt strange – almost surreal – to hear someone defending me so ardently. Perhaps the best defense would always come from a place of empathy.

And when Rolen turned again and looked down at me, I hope my face conveyed the gratitude my tongue could not express.

"Are you all right, Silas?" he asked at last.

It was a weighted question that demanded a long answer. I didn't response.

"No," Rolen sighed, "of course you aren't. Silas, I'm sorry, but I don't... I don't know what to do with you."

That didn't bother me as much as perhaps it should have. I didn't know what to do with me, either.

"I can't let you go, I can't keep you here... You should have never been brought here in the first place."

He sighed, looked briefly over his shoulder at Kiara.

"But I'm Aemor's steward, and it's my charge to show compassion, even and especially when it is difficult. Perhaps we can come up with a solution together."

He knelt down in front of me and offered both his hands.

I'd heard stories, of course, of the profound and ell-encompassing solicitude of Aemor's Godspeaker – doubtlessly the reason Aemor had chosen him at all – but it was a different thing to experience it, especially when it was so profoundly needed. I found myself blinking back tears as I put my hands into his. He helped me to my feet.

"We'll get you cleaned up," he said, gripping my wrists reassuringly. "We'll try to—"

He stilled suddenly. I wasn't sure why until I felt the air start to stir around me, a current rise around us. I remembered this feeling, and all at once I knew what was happening.

"Your Holiness?" said Kiara from behind. "Are you all right?"

Rolen and I exchanged a knowing look. My heartbeat hastened, thrumming in my ear.

"Hold fast," he told me, shortly before his eyes were filled with golden light. I wondered if my own eyes had so changed.

His expression cleared, blanked, but the grip on my wrists tightened, and I shrunk away when the golden gaze of Aemor, god of love and compassion, landed on me.

"*Brother, come out.*"

It was Rolen's voice, but the words of a god, and when I heard them, the only thing I feared more at that moment than speaking to a god was a god speaking through me.

"N-n-n-n-n-n—"

"*Brother,*" said Aemor through Rolen, "*I have your Godspeaker. You cannot hide from me now.*"

No, no, no, no, I chanted again and again, hoping that maybe this time he would hear me, *please no, please no, please no.*

"What's happening to him?" the guard asked Kiara.

"Gods above," was all the High Priestess could say.

"*You have avoided your family for long enough, brother. Answer me.*"

"*N-n-n-n—*"

But my words dried up, and I felt that white-hot pressure expanding inside of me, and before I even had the chance to sob in impotent fear, I felt Umbrion overtake me.

He swiveled my eyes first down to my wrists, then up at Rolen. He tugged my mouth downward into a dangerous scowl.

"*Get your hands,*" he snarled through my voice, "*off of my Godspeaker.*"

My hands slapped away his arms. Though the gesture was brief and short and sharp, and even though Aemor, through Rolen, barely reacted, the movement sent an audible shockwave through the room – *CRACK.*

Both guards just outside the door collapsed in a clatter of metal armor. The High Priestess was thrown back into the wall. The heavy wooden door snapped off its hinges and went crashing into the opposite wall of the hallway with a deafening sound.

Aemor lowered Rolen's hands to his sides. He did not look back as the others struggled to pick themselves up.

"*We need to talk,*" Aemor said.

"*Apparently,*" Umbrion answered. "*I can hardly do anything without hearing your nagging voice in my ear. I should kill you for what you've done to my Godspeaker.*"

Aemor narrowed his eyes, not in anger, but in confusion, as if he didn't understand the concept of killing.

"*I did nothing to your Godspeaker,*" Aemor answered. "*I merely sensed your magic on him and seized an opportunity that presented itself. If you have heard me calling for you, why have you not answered?*"

Umbrion drew the corner of my mouth into a smirk. "*That is a question wrongly asked, brother-mine,*" Umbrion said. "*It is not why I do not answer, it is why you insist on calling me.*"

"*I am owed an explanation.*"

The rage in Umbrion was sudden and brutal and all-consuming – *CRASH!*

A great sound of breaking stone and shattering wind. The front wall of my little room was blown away as though it was no more yielding than parchment, and huge chunks of rock went crashing through doorways and tumbling down the hall.

"*You are owed NOTHING!*"

Rolen took a half-step back in surprise. After a moment, the surprise shifted to anger.

"*Mother would speak to you,*" Aemor said.

"*I owe Mother even less!*" Umbrion snapped back.

"*You're being childish,*" Aemor chided.

"*And who are you to pass judgment on my actions? What do you know of everything that led me here?*"

"*You killed their queen, brother. You took away their immortality. Have you not heard their frantic prayers? You have terrified them.*"

"*Good,*" was Umbrion's only answer, dark and harsh.

"*You are bound to protect them! Mother—*"

"*I am bound to no such thing,*" Umbrion said. "*What I have always thought was my greatest weakness has become my greatest strength. I am not bound to Mother's Light like you. I never was.*"

Aemor dropped Rolen's face into a frown, as though he didn't understand - or perhaps, as though he understood, but the explanation offered no clarity.

"*I am done, Aemor,*" he hissed, and the words were venom on my lips. "*I am done sulking in the shadows and the fear and the self-loathing that you left me in.*"

"*What—?*"

"*I am done hating myself for what you let me become. I am choosing to embrace it, and I am taking you all down with me.*"

There came a sudden scream behind Aemor, but neither he nor Umbrion seemed particularly interested in it. My mind was racing, and I knew that the chances of getting out of this without someone dying were shrinking by each terrible second. In my mind, I was racing through my priorities. As soon as Umbrion left me, I need to find Soya and Perenor, get out of Iriallum as fast as possible, get to Avenos - would there be a boat I could take?

"*Umbrion,*" Aemor says, "*your foolishness is going to destroy this world!*"

Umbrion canted my head to one side.

"Silas!"

It was Soya's voice. And gods, I wanted to look at her, run to her, flee with her, but Umbrion kept my eyes focused with needle-sharp intensity on Rolen.

"And still you are surprised, brother, that I managed to come to hate you."

Pressure built within my chest, and *no, no, no, no*, I had felt this before, I knew what this was. I wanted to scream at the gathered onlookers *run, run now, he'll kill you all*, but Umbrion was still in complete control.

"Guards!" said Kiara frantically, and the guards, some of them still picking themselves up, hurried toward Perenor and Soya. I could barely see them out of the corner of my eye.

"Still you are confused as to why I rise up in anger."

But the guards, well-armored though they were, were no match for my brother and his runed staff. With a few well-timed bursts of energy, I could see him take them all out at once.

But the High Priestess had Craft of her own – a pair of sparring daggers, it looked like – and she proved more of a challenge for him. I couldn't make out the details of the battle past flashes of light. Umbrion's own Craft, in any case, was becoming deafening.

"Ten thousand ages of pain and solitude met with callous dismissiveness, and you wonder why I fight back!"

"Not that I don't love a man who can wield a staff," Kiara shouted over the roar of the energy, "but your timing is just awful!"

"We've come for my brother!" Perenor called back.

"He's a bit busy *destroying the temple!*"

Indeed, I was. The entire building was starting to quake, great rumbles from the earth interspersed with tremendous cracking and creaking in the stone and mortar from all sides.

"NO MERCY," Umbrion screamed through me, and he focused what I knew must have been a killing blow to Rolen, but Rolen vanished just before it landed, and the energy expanded outward.

"Run!" someone yelled, and the cracking turned to the sound of crumbling, collapsing. "Stop fighting, leave the intruders! Run, *run!*"

Umbrion threw forward my hand, and there was a tremendous cataclysm of light and sound expanding in all directions, and with a terrible rumble of the living rock, I could feel the temple begin to capitulate, to *break beneath my feet*, and there was screaming and screaming and screaming—

THERE WAS A DISTANT, SOOTHING SOUND of rushing water; a gentle rocking; a warmth – from nearby, someone was humming. It was a familiar melody, but somehow distant, like a hazy childhood memory or fading dream. And for a moment, it felt as though I was being soothed to sleep.

It was the memories that did more to wake me, far more than anything in my environment. When they came clawing at the edges of my mind, I felt my heart knot in my throat, and I scrambled upright—

"Easy! Silas, easy!"

It was Perenor, on the opposites side of a small, utilitarian room. My muscles were sore from disuse and my head ached from the still-healing wound. My heartbeat refused to slow. The temple – Umbrion, Aemor – what—?

"You're all right, you're safe."

I was most certainly not all right and whether or not I was ever safe was up for some spirited debate. We seemed to be alone, at least. It was the only comfort I could find – that Umbrion, if nothing else, was not actively inside me and forcing me to kill. Beyond that, I saw little that would make me feel safe.

"Wh-wh-wh-wh—"

"On a ship," he answered. "The last ship bound for Avenos before the monsoon."

That explained the rocking sensation – and likely the nausea, although that may have been from fear. I looked down at myself. I was still wearing the same clothes in which I had been taken prisoner, still dirty from several days without changing or bathing.

The echo of Umbrion in my mind was physically painful, and the pain got sharper as more and more memories came boiling up to the surface of my mind. I dug my fingers into the threadbare mattress on the bed, my shoulders shook, and *no, not again, how could he do this again?*

"How much do you remember?" Perenor asked, voice careful.

"Everything," I whispered, and every inch of it hurt.

"Are you injured?"

"H-h-how m-many are d-d-dead?"

Perenor sighed. "Silas—"

"H-h-h-how many, Perenor?"

I looked up at him. The reluctance on his face told me that the number was higher than I wanted to hear.

"A few dozen at least. The entire temple came down; we barely got out in time."

Something hard and sharp twisted in my gut.

I couldn't keep going through this. I couldn't keep having my hand forced in so much destruction. How many more people would have to die before I got to Avenos?

"They took us – Soya and I – into the barracks under the temple," Perenor said. "They tried to talk us away from you. They said that your – that you were meant to stand judgment before the gods."

At this point, perhaps I was. At what point did my own lack of complicity stop mattering? How many people would have to die before my mere existence was a threat to everyone around me?

"I didn't believe them," Perenor said. "In general, I tend not to believe anyone who says they know what the gods want if they haven't spoken to one themself. We had to fight our way past the guards to break you out, but by the time we got there..."

I drew my knees up to my chest. My memory was full of crumbling stone and screaming, of the sound flesh makes when it is ripped open slowly.

"A lot of people saw, Silas," he said after a while, voice drawn. "Aemor's temple is – was – built within the city walls. The entire building crumbled before the gods and everyone. People watched you bring it down."

I didn't want to hear more. But I could not stop myself from hearing.

"Rolen made it out, somehow," Perenor continued. "Or at least he vanished. I suppose you weren't the only one with a god on your shoulder."

Just the insinuation of Umbrion filled me with rage and heartbreak. I ended up making some pathetic sound, knotting my hands in my hair.

"I'm sorry," Perenor said at once. "I'm sorry, Silas, I didn't mean to upset you. Should – would it be better if I left?"

"N-n-n-n-n—" *No*, I wanted to say, *please don't leave, I'll fall to pieces if someone doesn't hold me together.*

"Okay," Perenor said. "Okay, I'll stay with you."

He climbed off his chair in the corner of the plain, wooden room and sat beside me. He put his hand on my back and hummed that familiar tune.

"I'll protect you," he said between notes. "I don't care if the whole world turns against you. I'll protect you. There's nothing in the world that will talk me into calling you traitor."

I hung onto his belief in my desperately, because I was rapidly running out of belief in myself.

"I'll protect you, I'll protect you."

He pulled me into his arms, and we stayed there for a while. I let my brother fight away the darkness in my mind as best he could, as best my mind could remember the light.

OUR SHIP WAS THE *SEABREAKER*, a fact I only learned because Perenor told me. I wasn't keen to do much exploring. After everything that had happened, I wasn't keen to do much of anything.

Perenor spent his days doing labor on the ship – the price of the ticket, no doubt – but in the evenings he came back to the little room and told me of his day.

The *Seabreaker* was a cargo ship, he told me, the last one to Avenos before the start of the monsoon. It would shave weeks off our journey, he told me; we would likely arrive before the storm made landfall.

In those days, Perenor proved a very assiduous big brother, which I was not used to. I would have thanked him if I'd been in any sort of shape to do so. He forced me to eat when he came back with meals, and always stayed awake until I was asleep.

I never asked why Soya did not visit me, despite being on our same boat. I think I knew the answer and was keen not to hear it out loud.

One night rather like the rest, I ventured out. Perenor was sound asleep, but I was kept awake by the ceaseless rocking, the sloshing of waves on the side of the boat. I crept from our cabin and moved slowly, quietly down the hallway, up a set of stairs, and then onto the deck.

I'd never seen this side of the ocean before. The waters were star-dappled, and the sky-river was higher than I was used to seeing. I knew enough about the night sky to know that it was a symbol of just how far I was from home.

The wind off the sea was salty and strong, and each fresh gust brought misting water over the balustrade, peppering the deck. I stood at the edge, bracing my hands on the railing.

It was at least a twenty-foot drop into the rolling, night-blackened waters. I swallowed the knot of fear in my throat.

At the time, I didn't have a word for what was going through my head, but in the weeks between that black moment and where I sit now, I have learned it: suicide. Once an obscure term, now finding its terrible niche in Andelish vernacular.

It wasn't that I wanted to die for the sake of being dead – far from it, now that I'd seen it up close – it was more the growing certainty that my death would likely mean saving many more lives. What was *my* life worth, after all, when its cost was so many other lives snuffed out? What benefit could my life bring that could possibly outweigh that terrible price?

Of course, ideation was one thing and action was quite another. The philosophy had convinced me, but what of the practicality? What happened to a thing when it died? Would it hurt? What came after?

Fear gripped me, and I gripped the railing. If I could just drop over the side – perhaps no one would even notice until morning—

"Silas?"

I shivered at her voice in time with a low howl of wind. When I turned, I saw Soya standing at the door the lead down into the underbelly of the ship. She had parchment in her hand, and she was staring at me guardedly.

"What are you doing up here?"

Without knowing the word "suicide," I had no real answer for her. Even if I had the word, I likely wouldn't have been able to say it to my best friend.

Slowly, I withdrew my hands from the side of the ship. The wind howled again, tossing my cloak and whipping my hair in front of my face.

"It's late," she said. "You should be sleeping. And you shouldn't be where other people might recognize you."

I lowered my eyes. The mistrust in her voice hurt more than I'd expected it to. I started past her, back towards the underbelly of the ship.

She caught my arm, which took me by surprise. I stopped and looked back at her. Up close, the mistrust was in clearer detail, but also tinged with now-visible traces of worry.

"Are you all right?" she asked me. "I haven't had the chance to talk to you."

"Y-y-y-you've had p-plenty," I answered. Soya flinched.

"I suppose I have," she conceded guiltily. "I'm sorry. It's just – at the temple—"

"I know."

"It was frightening, Silas. Seeing you bring down that building."

I hated this. I hated her growing mistrust of me, hated the way she hated herself for it, hated how I couldn't even be angry at her.

"I d-d-didn't bring down the b-b-building," I reminded her, doing my best to keep the heartache out of my voice.

"Right," she said. "I mean, I know. That's what I meant."

The wind on the ocean howled long and low catching Soya's long braid high in the air. She gripped the paper in her hand.

"A l-l-letter?" I asked, hoping to change the subject.

"To my father," she answered. "The ship has a rookery, so I'm sending a crow ahead to Avenos, to let him know of our imminent arrival."

I nodded. Before I could think of some further harmless comment, she said—

"Do you remember what you said to me back when you first showed me your Godspeaker's crown?"

In the time it took me to remember the conversation to which she was referring, she had continued her thought.

"Because I've been replaying it in my mind ever since..."

The conversation came back to me. I knew what she was talking about.

"You said he understood you."

He did. Or at least I thought he did. I wasn't sure anymore. My eyes trailed to the gouged, gritty surface of the deck, and my heart ached, and my mind told me to drop into the ocean and end this cloud of death that followed me.

"You said he told you that you would change the world."

I screwed shut my eyes. The only thing I wanted to think of less than my best friend's growing distrust in me was all the sweet abominations Umbrion had said. Now I had no choice but to confront both.

"What did he say to you, Silas?" she asked. "Specifically."

I knew what she wanted me to say, of course. She wanted me to reassure her that Umbrion had not told me in advance of his plans to kill Queen Nerisa and to break Ellorian, that I had not been complicit in his schemes. She wanted to know I was innocent.

"Please, Silas, I am losing sleep over this. I don't mean to pry, I just…"

But what would be the point in telling her what she wanted to hear? I could tell her every word of every conversation I'd had with Umbrion, including his gentleness, including his destiny-forging kisses, but with the seed of doubt already growing in her, how could she trust that what I said was truth? Where would her assurance be that I hadn't been in it from the start?

"I'm trying, Si," she said when I didn't answer. "I'm *really* trying."

"I b-b-believe you," I said.

"My heart knows you're not capable of such blackness but my head draws these connections anyway."

"I kn-kn-kn-know," I said.

She paused, then sighed painfully. "And my soul makes me hate myself for doubting you."

The wind howled as if in agreement. Soya gripped the letter tightly to her chest.

"I'm sorry, Silas. I shouldn't be making this any worse for you than it already is."

I doubted she could if she tried.

AND THEN, one day rather like the rest, we arrived in Avenos.

If Ellorian was a city of gold, Avenos was a city of silver. When the lookout called land and I came up to the deck to see it, the silver was the first thing I saw – gleaming silver roofs, flashing, piercing the sky.

And if there was that desperate, terrible ache still in me, it was in some way numbed by the city's exquisite beauty.

"Sol's Light," Perenor said when he came up beside me, Soya in tow.

The shining of the silver was almost painful to look at, the roar of the crowds almost deafening, even though we had not yet made it to port.

"Yeah," Soya answered, "it's pretty big." She didn't sound terribly enthusiastic.

"I never would have imagined a city could look like this," Perenor continued as though he hadn't heard her.

"Get it all out now," Soya said. "Whatever you do, don't let my father know how impressed you are, or you'll get a sixteen-part lecture on its history."

Soya's father – I'd nearly forgotten. The Lord of Avenos. Lord-Regent now, I supposed, now that the Queen was dead. It was easy to forget that Soya, rough-and-tumble, foul-mouthed, inappropriate Soya, was the firstborn and scion of a noble line. I suspect she preferred it that way, as I'd never heard her speak of her house with anything more than dry neutrality. It was one of those subjects that we never really brought up.

The anchor weighed when we pulled into port. I kept my head under my cloak until we were sufficiently masked by the thrum of the crowd.

Avenos was just as impressive from the inside as it was the outside.

Though I knew she hadn't been there in at least a dozen seasons, Soya navigated the wide stone streets with ease and familiarity, leading us on an impressively long walk right up to—

"Is *that* your palace?" Perenor asked.

"It's called Silverwatch."

Any building important enough to have a name had to be impressive, and Silverwatch did not disappoint. It was all black spires and gleaming silver roofs, shining obsidian palisades and narrow windows lit with red-orange light. The palace in Ellorian seemed a bit prosaic in comparison.

"Come to think of it," Soya said, "just don't talk to my father at all. Let me do the talking."

I wanted to ask why, but Soya was already several steps ahead, and it was a struggle enough just to keep up through the thick of the crowd.

When we made it to the front palisade, which was flanked by two guards in gleaming black armor, Soya strode right up to them with obvious intent to pass right through the open gates. The guard on the left stopped her with a pike.

"No admittance without a writ," the guard said.

Soya growled and knocked the guard's pike to the side. "It hasn't been that long," she said.

The guard paused, squinted at her. "Lady Soya?" she said.

"The very same," Soya answered.

"Shit." Both guards straightened at once. "I'm sorry, My Lady – do you need an escort?"

"It *hasn't been that long*," she repeated, more loudly. "Like I don't know the way around my own stupid palace – come on, you two."

Past the front gates was a long staircase, tapering upward toward the grand doors, black and shining, made from what I guessed was fire-glass. Soya heaved them open as though they were much lighter than they looked (but as it turned out, they were precisely as heavy as they looked, which I discovered when I tried to hold the door open for Perenor and failed spectacularly).

The inside of Silverwatch was like nothing I'd ever seen. It was all fire-glass and dark marble, beautiful but intimidating, with torches that lit the glossy surfaces in strange ways.

Soya guided us out and away of the main hallway, past the empty

Lord's seat, and into a large eastern wing. I could hear her muttering to herself about where "the bastard" would be at this time of day, but in the end, all we had to do was follow the sound of voices.

"... more refugees pouring in every day," someone said, her voice gradually growing louder as we made our way down a narrow hallway. "The inns are at capacity. There's only so much we can do further."

"What of the other Lords?" returned another voice. "Are we the only noble line in Andelan?"

"That's him," Soya sighed, turning a sharp corner and pushing through a set of ajar double doors.

The room was brightly lit with a chandelier and a large stained-glass window. Tapestries hung from the walls, and there was a large table encircled by several people in rich silks. They were all standing, save for the man at the far end of the room, who did not seem nearly so astonished as the others by Soya's sudden arrival.

"I suppose I should be more surprised."

If I had been asked to try and picture what the Lord of Avenos looked like, I would have pictured something very much like him. I could see where Soya got her dark hair and rough handsomeness, but the similarities ended there. Where Soya was firm and strongly built, her father was lanky and hawkish, with a pointed chin and sharp eyes. He was all firm lines and hard angles, severe and cross-looking.

There was some strange combination of relief and sudden anger on the hard features of his face.

"Welcome back, my only scion," he said waspishly.

"Hello, Father," Soya said. She was speaking neutrally, but I could detect measures of well-concealed resentment in her voice.

"Ellorian breaks in twain, and it is only three days ago that I hear any word," he continued, voice gradually rising in volume.

"There were extenuating circumstances."

"I sent *two crows*, Soya - two crows and a team to scout the wreckage of the city to *search for your body*."

"I made it out, Father!" she cried. "I'm fine! Please don't rush to embrace me! I sent you a crow the minute I had access to a rookery, didn't I?"

He sat back heavily in his chair, rubbing the long bridge of his nose between two fingers.

"If you are making some effort to drive me to madness, you're on the proper path, Soya."

"I'll keep that in mind." She didn't look like she was willing to budge.

"And who are these strangers?" Lord Rhodan's eyes were sharp blue, and they moved from me, to Perenor, back to Soya. "You didn't mention guests in your single, painfully brief message."

Soya hesitated, though only for a fraction of a second. "This is Perenor of House Olen, sorcerer and firstborn scion."

Perenor inclined his head.

"I have heard of you, Perenor of House Olen," Lord Rhodan said evenly. "Your pedigree precedes you. And who's this?"

"Close the door, Perenor," Soya muttered.

Perenor closed the door. I shifted in my spot and tried to look as nonthreatening as possible.

"Soya?" Lord Rhodan prompted.

"This is Perenor's brother," she continued, "Silas of House Olen, Godspeaker to Umbrion."

The silence that followed was about as tense as the reader might expect it to be. There was also a long, drawn, unnatural stillness, broken abruptly when one of the people standing at the table – a member of the Lord's council, I was willing to wager – suddenly staggered backward, knocking over a standing candelabrum with a clatter.

"Before you say anything—" Soya began, shortly before being cut off.

"You brought Umbrion's Godspeaker *here?*"

"*Before you say anything,*" Soya repeated, more loudly, "I beg you to consider the situation carefully."

"Consider the situation!" Lord Rhodan bellowed, rising from his chair. He was very, very tall, and the velvets of his station hung heavily off his shoulders. "You bring the Traitor God's hands into my palace, and you ask me to *consider the situation?*"

"It wasn't Silas who broke Ellorian!" Perenor suddenly said, stepping forward.

"I told you not to say anything!" Soya snapped at him, but Perenor wasn't listening.

"He had as much hand in it as you or I," he continued. "He needs protection, not more misdirected animosity!"

"Perenor, for Sol's sake, shut up!"

"You are trying to talk the sun into setting in the north," Lord Rhodan said, coming around the table. "I will *not—*"

"Do you know what happened to the last people who came toward my brother in anger?" Perenor said, voice dangerous.

Something cold grew in me. "P-P-P-Perenor—"

Soya grabbed him sharply by the shoulder, spun him around, and glared directly into his eyes. "This is *not helpful,*" she hissed at him, before forcefully pushing him aside. Perenor growled in the back of his throat, and Soya stepped between the space that separated me and Lord Rhodan, still advancing around the table.

For his part, Lord Rhodan seemed to hear Perenor's words with great clarity. He was no longer looking at Perenor, nor at Soya, but rather directly at me. I swallowed hard and kept my footing.

"Father," Soya said, more sedately – or at least, more sedately compared to Perenor, "I would not have brought him here without good reason. Whether you would have it or not, we are stuck in the middle of a war of gods, and Silas is the only link we have to one of its most major players. We need him."

"And what is it you think this city can *do?*" he snapped. "What could possibly be worth putting all of Avenos in such *danger?*"

"We have scholars here," Soya insisted, frustration rising again in her voice. "We have diplomats from all over the world! With Ellorian and the Queen gone, that makes our house – *you,* Father, as Lord of Avenos – the Lord-Regent of Andelan. You need him because it's your charge now to protect this world!"

Lord Rhodan's nostrils flared in anger. "You think that hasn't crossed my mind?"

"I know it has!"

"How can I be sure that bringing him into this city does more good than it would harm?" he demanded, and though he was speaking to Soya, his eyes were now on me. "How can I be sure that he is not himself *in league* with Umbrion—?"

"Watch what you say, Lord of Avenos," Perenor growled.

"These are my halls and this is my city, Scion Olen," Lord Rhodan answered, teeth bared. "My words will be as I want them to be."

"It's not only our ears that might hear you speaking," Perenor said, which brought another look of disquiet to Lord Rhodan's face.

Silence lapsed a moment. Lord Rhodan was looking at me again. I was too weary to be frightened, so I met his eyes unflinchingly.

"Can you promise me, Soya," he said, eyes swiveling to his daughter, "that you consider him no danger to this city or anyone in it?"

"Father," Soya said, "whatever danger he may pose is worth the risk. We need him. Andelan needs him. He's our only source of insight in these coming days and we cannot afford to err on the side of short-term security."

It was true in theory, but I found myself wondering what real, practical insight I could offer.

Lord Rhodan couldn't seem to decide who he wanted to more closely examine: me or his daughter. Eventually, he settled on me.

"What say you, Godspeaker?" he asked. "Do you have no words in your defense?"

"My s-s-s-stutter taught m-me long ago to n-n-never waste w-words," I answered, voice raspy from disuse.

"Words in your defense are wasted, are they?"

"They are f-f-for those whose m-m-minds are already m-made up."

"Silas," Soya muttered to me, "do you really think this is helping your cause?"

"D-d-do you think there's an-n-nything that c-can?" I returned.

Soya didn't seem to know how to respond apart from a look of frustration. I looked back at her father, breathed, and wasted some words.

"Wh-wh-what would y-you have m-me say, L-Lord Rhodan?" I asked. "That I r-r-reject the actions of my p-patron g-g-god? I reject th-them. But y-y-you would d-doubt me still, and y-you'd be r-right to do s-s-s-so. What p-proof do y-y-you have of my intentions? Wh-what proof c-c-could you ever h-have? Y-you cannot see m-my heart."

"No," he agrees, "but I can see your actions, which would tell me more of your heart than ten thousand wasted words."

"Wh-wh-what would y-y-you have m-me do?"

"Help us," the Lord answered.

"How?" I asked.

It was not a rhetorical question and never had been; I made sure the Lord of Avenos could see as much on my face. He was silent a moment, mouth half-open, as he tried to think of something.

"Tell us his plans," he said eventually.

"I d-d-d-d-do not know th-them."

"Ask him," he continued.

"I c-c-cannot s-s-summon him."

He was starting to get angry. "Pray to him!"

"And r-r-risk the l-l-lives of ever-r-ryone around m-me?"

"Then take a pilgrimage alone into the moor!" he bellowed, pointing west out the window. "Starve and chastise yourself like the priests of old until you are beset with a vision that will give us answers!"

"Father, enough!"

"But no, if we leave you alone, who knows what you'll do!" He keeps shouting, starts to pace the floor. "What, then, is the point of you, if you can do *nothing?*"

"Excell-l-l-llent question," I muttered. It must have been too low for anyone to hear, because the Lord Rhodan kept ranting.

"You've brought Umbrion's doom upon this city, Soya! The walls of the Silver City will crumble before the monsoon falls!"

"*And so will the rest of the world!*" Soya finally matched his volume. "In case it has escaped your notice, Father, this is not a battle for the fate of Avenos; all of Andelan hangs in the balance! If the Lord-Regent's city will not take the necessary risks, will not stand up and *fight,* then *who will?*"

"Take the Godspeaker to a bedroom in the east wing!" Lord Rhodan ordered the nearby guard. "Do *not* let him out. And so help me, if you hear so much as a rustle—!"

Two guards flanked me, grabbed me by the arms.

"Let him go!" Perenor cried. "Don't you dare hurt him, Lord of Avenos, or I swear by all the gods—!"

"D-d-don't worry," I said. "Th-they c-c-could not h-hurt m-m-me if they t-tried."

I could feel the guards' flinch in the tips of their fingers that gripped my arms.

"They won't mistreat him," I heard Soya say as I am marched out of the room and down the hall. "I won't let them, I swear it."

And despite the fact that I was now a prisoner in nature if not in name, despite the fact that I had a Lord and an entire palace of people who feared and distrusted me in equal measure, despite the creeping numbness ever seeping out from my core, at least, I thought, *at least* I could bathe and sleep and stay away from those who would fall into my cloud of death.

THE CLOUDS OF THE COMING MONSOON came rolling onto the horizon that afternoon, blanketing the sky in undulating waves of gray. I watched them through the window of the bedroom to which I was quarantined. My window had a sprawling view of the city and the ocean that stretched out past it. Ships came to harbor, channels of smoke rose into the sky, and I could see workers clear out the gutters and drains in preparation for the coming stormfall.

For nearly a full day, no one came to my room. The bedroom to which I had been sequestered was small but well furnished, with a desk, a chair, a hearth, and a connected bath. I mostly slept; when I could not force myself into those lapses of death any longer, I bathed and worked the knots of travel from my hair. I read from the small selection of books on the shelf by the desk. I watched the window and the muted rumble of the city. I fled from my thoughts as a shadow flees sunlight.

The next day, there came a knock on the door. I turned in time to see it opened by two well-armored, nervous guards.

"Godspeaker," said the one in front, and I rose to my feet. "The Lord-Regent and his council have summoned you to the council chambers."

I nodded slowly and rose from the bed to pull on a nondescript outer robe.

"The Lord-Regent has requested privacy," continued the guard haltingly, "from any – ah – from any gods that might have interest in the conversation."

I laughed once, humorlessly.

"Th-th-th-that is out of m-m-my control."

"Oh," said the guard, trying her best not to look nervous, to middling success. "This way."

They did not grab me by the arms this time, which was a refreshing change of pace. Instead they kept a wide berth as they escorted me down the hall, hands on their weapons, as though that might protect them.

I'd expected to be taken back to the room that Soya had first taken me to upon our arrival the day before, but we went to a different room in a different wing. This room - the council chambers, I could only assume - were much larger, with a large ring of tables and chairs on an elevated platform. The faces of some fifty people peered down at me, all of them varying degrees of wary.

There was no chair for me, but one of the guards gestured for me to stand in the center of the semicircle, so I did. I stood silent for several moments, waiting for something to happen.

In the middle of the semicircle, just in front of me, was seated Lord Rhodan, straight-backed and uncomfortable in his seat. Soya was just to his left, loose but apprehensive. Perenor was just behind them both, and he was the only one with something resembling a smile. Inexplicably, the sight of him made me feel better.

"My scion has been gracious enough to get me up to speed on recent events," Lord Rhodan - or Lord-Regent Rhodan now, I supposed - said without preamble. He was turning a crow's quill over in his hands as he spoke, and his eyes didn't move from mine. "It's quite a story."

He stopped as though he was waiting for a response, but I didn't know what it was he meant for me to say, so I stayed quiet.

"She claims that you had no agency in the Breaking of Ellorian," he continued eventually. "Is that true?"

"Y-y-yes." I looked sideways at Soya. I wondered how deeply she really believed that and found no clue on her face.

"And your brother insists that this cloud of death that follows you - the ambush, the temple in Iriallum - has less to do with you and more to do with the Traitor God's protective instincts over his Godspeaker. Would you say that's accurate?"

Protective was an interesting word for it. "Y-y-y-yes."

There was a trace of something in his eyes; I imagined it to be pity, but it was gone before I could say for sure.

"We have sent out crows to the other Godspeakers, and I have spoken with the diplomats from all the major cities. We plan to convene a moot."

"A m-m-m-moot?"

"It's usually a legislative practice," the Lord-Regent continued, "for the voting and vetoing of national laws, but we are somewhat repurposing it. If we are going to act at all, then it must be done together. And if we are going to come up with any *plan* at all, it will only be planned together."

It was not, to my fragile heart's surprise, a bad plan. In fact, with the insight of the other four Godspeakers, perhaps it may even prove useful. If there was anyone in Andelan who could do something, it was they.

"Although we are officially awaiting the responses, they will presumably be amenable to meet and come up with a plan of action, given the direness of the circumstances," he continued. "I trust that we can count on your loyalty in this?"

"It is n-n-n-not m-my loyalty y-y-you n-need c-concern yourself w-w-with."

"One can only hope," the Lord-Regent answered, voice thin. "We have also decided that extracting information must be made a priority. After all, what plan could possibly thwart a god without substantial intelligence to back it up?"

I did not understand where he was going with this, which turned out not to be a problem, because he continued:

"We will arrange to have you escorted to Umbrion's temple," he said. "We will empty it out for you, and you will pray to him to learn his plans."

I knew at once that, "There are a m-m-m-million w-ways that c-c-could b-backfire."

"There are a million ways that your mere presence in this city could backfire," the Lord-Regent answered. "You represent a walking, talking risk to the security of Avenos. We may as well get something out of it, if we can."

"But th-this could s-s-s-summon him," I said. "I am his G-G-Godspeaker; there's a ch-ch-chance he c-could manifest."

"Umbrion's temple is several leagues outside the city," the Lord-Regent said. "Any damage would be... contained."

He meant the damage would be contained to me, of course. He

didn't have to say it.

"We'll arrange it for tomorrow sometime," he continued. "Meanwhile, you're not to leave your room without an escort, nor the palace under any circumstance."

"I'll go with him wherever he needs to go," Perenor volunteered at once.

"And he *won't* be mistreated," Soya interjected suddenly. "Will he, Father?"

The Lord-Regent's mouth twisted. "No," he answered, sounding almost reluctant. "Your needs will not be neglected."

"You're not a prisoner here," Soya told me. "Your confinement is for your own safety as much as anyone else's."

"R-r-r-right," I muttered.

"For now, you'll be kept to your room," the Lord-Regent said. "We will count on your cooperation in the coming days. Guards?"

I turned around, grateful, if for nothing else, to be out of that cursed room.

"You look hungry," I heard from behind when the door shut. I looked around; Perenor was approaching from behind. "I suppose they haven't fed you yet. It's been hectic since we arrived. How are you?"

"I'm f-f-f-fine."

"You don't look fine."

"I kn-kn-know. I was l-l-l-lying."

"Oh. Right." Perenor kept stride with me. It aggravated me, though I wasn't sure why. "How are you doing, then, if not fine?"

I didn't answer, hoping I could get away with not talking long enough to get back to my room.

"Are you going to ignore me?"

"Th-th-th-that w-would be impossible, c-c-clearly."

"Is our relationship so far gone that you can't even tell your brother how you are?" he asked me. "With all those lessons in Craft, I thought..."

I stopped, and Perenor and the guards all stopped with me. The hallway between the council chambers and my room was empty.

"I want to help you, if I can," he said.

"You c-c-can't."

"I can try," he pressed. "You haven't eaten – I'll have something brought up. Would it help to continue lessons in Craft? We were getting into some pretty advanced areas, but we could keep going – you've got a talent, you know, if we just—"

"D-d-d-do you r-really th-th-think any of th-th-that will h-help me?"

Perenor's words fell off.

"D-d-d-d-do you really th-think food, d-d-distractions are wh-what I n-n-need m-most?"

"Silas," he said, though he didn't continue, so I went on talking.

"C-c-c-can't y-y-y-you s-s-see that I'm b-b-b-barely holding it t-t-t-together?" I stammered at him, and Perenor was worrying his lower lip with his teeth, flexing his hands at his sides. "F-f-f-f-ood w-won't even m-m-make a dent—"

"But it's a place to start," he said, and I swallowed thickly. I wanted to be angry with him, but I didn't have the energy. "Come on, brother-mine. What good will you be to anyone if you starve to death?"

He put a hand on my shoulder and ushered me further down the hallway. I followed along, trying to fight the welling emotion.

"We'll go walking through the gardens tomorrow, all right?" he said. "Silverwatch has a beautiful garden, you know. It's got four levels. We need to get you out of your own head, even if it's only for an afternoon."

THE MONSOON came the next day, and the heavy gray overcast split open at its seams. It was, I supposed, bound to arrive earlier this far north. It came lightly at first, a soft pitter-patter on the thin glass of the window, but within an hour it had become a familiar, pounding torrent.

Though Avenos was by all rights a similar city, geographically, to Ellorian, both being coastal cities otherwise in the middle of nothing, the monsoon here felt like an altogether different experience. The ocean was darker, cooler than the familiar topaz waters of the southern coast, and it felt somehow more sedate and more heavy; the raindrops fatter, the air more stagnant.

Perenor arrived in the morning with breakfast for two on a tray.

"They say we'll go to Umbrion's temple after breakfast," he said by way of greeting.

My stomach sank.

"They've arranged for a carriage to pick us up and take us there once we're finished eating."

I worried my lower lip. I suddenly could not find my appetite, and ended up pushing around the neatly sliced ham steak on my plate.

"You're nervous," Perenor said. It was not quite a question, nor really a statement.

"I f-f-fear wh-what he might d-d-do if I p-pray to him," I said.

"Have you prayed to him before?"

I shook my head.

"But he has manifested to you. You said so."

"In d-d-dreams, mostly," I said. "But this... I d-d-don't know wh-what will happen."

"The Lord-Regent seems to think it's for the best."

"The L-L-L-Lord-Regent is n-not a G-Godspeaker."

Perenor sighed. He poured two cups of tea from a small pot they'd provided him. "Well, he won't hurt *you*, right? I mean, you're his Godspeaker. He likes you."

"He m-m-may not l-like me quite s-s-so much if he s-s-s-senses my intentions."

Perenor lowered his head. "Do you think you can outsmart him?"

I didn't know. But I supposed it didn't matter so much when my hand was being forced like it was.

We ate the rest of our breakfast in tense silence, and when we were done, we put on our waxed cloaks and were escorted out of the palace and up to a waiting carriage, black and nondescript. What I noticed first—

"Wh-what are th-th-those?"

They were huge and hairy, pawing at the stone with their massive claws. Their fur was black and they had long snouts and rounded ears.

"They're bears," Perenor answered. "No camels in this climate."

"They're t-t-t-terrifying," I said, though they seemed domestic enough. The guards held open the carriage door and Perenor went in first.

"They're stronger than camels," he said, and I climbed in behind him, though not after giving one last look to the beasts. "Hardier, too. But you can't take them through the Wastes, so we never see them."

The guard slammed shut the door and thumped the side. The carriage took off with a rattle and groan of aging wood and metal.

It was small and cramped and dark inside, and it may have been my imagination but the bears made for a rougher ride than the camels I was used to. It wasn't a comfortable journey.

For the most part, we rode in silence. I looked out the window for a while, watching the cramped streets of Avenos until we came to the gates, and all at once the grit and the dirt and the stone was replaced with sprawling moorland. A mist had settled into the lower places, and as we rumbled away from the dull roar of the city, the sound of mayflies and cold wind and, of course, the thundering of rain on the roof of the carriage.

Eventually, I licked my lips and looked over at Perenor.

"If this g-g-g-goes p-poorly," I said, "Perenor, y-y-you must p-promise me you w-w-won't interfere."

He turned away from the window. "Won't interfere? You expect me to sit idly by while gods know what happens to you?"

"Y-yes," I answered unflinchingly, "th-that is p-p-precisely what you'll do."

"Absolutely not."

"P-P-P-Perenor—"

"You're my brother!" he interjected. "Maybe I haven't always showed it, but you are. You're my brother and I love you and I won't just abandon you."

"There are m-m-more imp-portant things than m-me," I said. "Wh-what is my l-l-life against all the l-lives in Andelan?"

"And what are all the lives in Andelan against the only family I may have left?" Perenor countered.

"Those w-w-words may s-seem like t-truth to y-y-your injured heart, b-brother, but wh-wh-when Umbrion p-p-p-possesses me to b-break the w-w-world instead of the c-c-city, you have to-to-to choose a s-s-side, and it c-can't be mine."

"Do you think that likely to happen?" Perenor asked, suddenly alarmed. "Do you think he'll possess you to break the world?"

"I d-d-don't know," I answered honestly, "b-but it w-would be irresponsible to d-d-disregard the p-possibility b-b-because it makes you unc-c-comfortable."

Perenor looked away. He didn't answer, so I knew I must have been getting to him.

"I n-n-need to know y-you will do this," I said to him. "Perenor..."

Still, he stayed quiet. But I could see the conflict in his face, even when he turned it away from me. My words had struck something n him, though I couldn't quite tell what.

"What's that sound?"

I refocused my attention. I hadn't noticed it while we were talking, but now that I was listening for it, I could hear the sound of a crowd – a mix of angry shouting, crackling fire, screaming—

"Hold!" Perenor said, and the carriage rolled to a stop. He climbed out, and I could hear the guards flanking our carriage drawing their swords. Alarmed and concerned, I poked my head out of the door.

Umbrion's temple was standing on a rock on a hill in a dryer part of the moor, small and humble, surrounded by a mob of shouting people. Its doors were standing open, and to its left was a large, burning pyre into which they'd thrown Umbrion's now flame-blackened sigil.

"Sol's Light," Perenor said.

I could only pick out bits and pieces of their angry shouting, but it was more than enough to know the context. Words like *traitor, monster, queenslayer* – I knew what they were doing, all at once. They were trying to raze his temple.

"We should leave," Perenor said to the man driving the carriage. "We should leave now, before they see us."

I stared, transfixed – my mind somehow refused to keep up with itself as it tried to process the scene. They were so angry.

"It's off!" Perenor barked to our guards. "The whole thing is off! We can't send Silas into that, and unless the two of you think you can clear out that crowd on your own—"

Someone screamed – not in anger, but in sudden, dreadful fear.

I could see a group of them dragging her out of the temple. Black-robed, long-haired – *shit*. She was one of Umbrion's priestesses. And suddenly I knew what else that burning pyre was meant for.

"Gods above," I heard Perenor say. "Silas, get back in the carriage—"

But I was not listening. The only thing in my head – *no, no, no, no—*

"*No!*"

I ran past Perenor, knocking him off-balance, sprinting those last twenty yards.

"Silas!"

"*No, stop it! Stop it! STOP!*"

But the crowd wouldn't let me through – they were all shoulder-to-shoulder, screaming death, and the priestess – gods, they had bound her hands and feet with rope, they were dragging her toward the pyre—

"*NO!*" I cried, but no one heard me.

Her screaming started a moment later. There are no words to describe the sound an Andel makes when they are burned alive. I shoved and I shoved and my heart pounded and I screamed and the crowd, *curse* this crowd, they were *cheering*, and I couldn't get through—

The glove, my mind suddenly supplied – Perenor's glove, I had it in my pocket – I fumbled for it, shoved it on.

"Silas!"

The moment it came down over my fingers, I gave one last great shove forward— "*Move!*"

There was a blinding flash of light and a force that radiated out from me in all directions. Several went flying, others fell hard into the mud, but all of them were suddenly quiet.

I ran for the pyre and realized, in the new and dreadful silence, that the priestess had stopped screaming.

I could see her body through the flames, blackened face contorted into a now-silent scream. Fire was eating away at her robes, and her flesh—

I screwed my eyes shut. I was nauseous. I gripped my stomach, fell against the wall of the temple. Behind me, the muttering started.

"*By order of the Lord-Regent, you're commanded to vacate!*" one of the guards cried from somewhere. "*This is a felonious destruction of city property!*"

Even though it had stopped, the echo of her screaming was still rattling in my head. Even though my eyes were closed, I could still see her twisted, blackened face. *No, no, no, no.*

"Th-th-this is n-n-not j-justice," I said. The muttering got louder.

"*Vacate at once!*" the guard bellowed. "*This is obstruction of the Lord-Regent's justice!*"

I lifted my face toward the crowd. I hated them at that moment, and I hated myself. Even when my will was my own, even when there were no gods to force my hand, everyone around me was *dying.*

"Th-th-this is n-n-n-*not justice!*" I cried at them vision blurring with angry, impotent tears. "Sh-sh-she w-w-was n-not Umbrion!"

The crowd was beginning to back away from me, as if all at once, they were deducing who I was.

"Silas—!"

It was Perenor, scrambling up to his feet – I must have knocked him down with the others while pushing through the crowd. He came running through the gap in the crowd.

"Th-th-this is n-n-n-not j-j-justice," I said my voice weakening as my stutter intensified. "Th-th-this is n-n-n-n-n—"

I fell forward. In all the fear and alarm and adrenaline, there was anger, boiling up to the top. My shoulders shook, my heart burned.

"*Vacate!*" the guards kept bellowing.

"Silas..."

Did you let this happen?

In retrospect – because it was always so easy to have perfect vision in hindsight – it probably was not the smartest idea for me to try and speak to him. And it was foolish of me to grow even angrier when he didn't answer.

This is your temple. Your priestess. She is dead. And you just sat by and let her?

Perenor was saying something, but I couldn't hear him. The Lord-Regent wanted me to pray, so I prayed – more fiercely and more pointedly than I had ever prayed about anything.

Your temple is desecrated, defaced, and broken by those who once worshipped you. Do you care? Do you even notice?

That horrible combination of anger and pain and fear was growing in me, strangling me. Why was he refusing to answer?

Does our prayer and devastation mean so little to you that you would allow this to happen? Has it ever meant anything to you at all?

At some point I had started to tremble. Every moment he was not answering was frozen torture on my aching heart. Why was he ignoring me, now of all times? Could he even hear me? Did he even care to listen? I felt as though I might be physically ripped apart with the mounting anger and heartache and screaming frustration in me.

Why are you doing this? Have you not noticed that I am an Andel like them, that their pain is mine? If you're going to kill them, you should give me the dignity of the same fate!

The silence that answered was deafening. Why was he not answering? I had to do *something*, I had to do *anything* – this crushing powerlessness was *eating me alive.*

I spun on my heel and turned to the temple.

"*Answer me!*" I screamed into the broken temple, and behind me, Perenor made a sound of surprise. I could hear the crowd scramble away. "Answer me! I kn-kn-know you can hear m-me!"

"Silas," Perenor hissed, "what in Sol's name are you *doing?*"

"Answer me!" I bellowed, at the temple, at the sky, loud enough, I hoped, for all the gods to hear me and tremble at my words. "I am y-y-your Godspeaker! Answer me!"

But he did not answer. And like a tide that rises in a storm and breaks over a city wall, I was left abandoned in my anger. He was *not answering*, and I was screaming at broken stones and shattered glass. And I *hated* him, and I hated myself, and I hated these monsters that would burn alive an innocent priestess, and there was *nothing* for me here. I screamed and I pushed over a piece of rubble that once was a pew and I fell to my knees and I wanted it to *stop*, I wanted people to stop *dying* because of me, was there *nothing* I could do?

Hands on my shoulders. My brother's voice, distant and indistinct. I was weak and hollowed out from emotion, and when I felt Perenor pull me into his arms, I fell against him. All I could do was sob, angry, heartbroken, lost, powerless, a wave broken over a wall and far from the ocean.

"Silas, Silas, hush, you must calm down, we cannot stay here..."

I didn't know what he meant and I didn't have the presence of mind to put it together. He pulled me tighter and I held onto him as though my life depended on it, because perhaps it did.

"Silas, please," he whispered, voice wavering from emotion as I sobbed and shook, "we can't – ssh, *I'll go with you, over the ocean. I'll take you with me, into the sky.*"

And wasn't it silly, and wasn't it childish for him to sing to me like we were both still children, and wasn't it ridiculous that it worked just like it did all those seasons ago?

"*My ship will sail far, far from here,*" he sang softly into my ear, "*away from the fear and the terrible things.* Silas, hush, you're safe, I'll protect you."

And that same foolish part of me that soothed at his words believed him when said it. I shut my eyes tightly and pressed myself into his chest. And it hurt, and I hated it, but somehow, somehow...

"*Come with me now, there's no need for tears. Brothers we are and ever will be.* You see? I remember the words."

His voice was drawn with emotion, and I still felt tattered and frayed, but I laughed, or did something like laughing. "You r-r-r-remember."

"I always remembered," he said. "Some part of me always remembered."

And I wasn't all right, and I wasn't safe, but this was good. This moment with my brother, this moment was good. I held onto it with everything left in me.

"We cannot stay here. They're watching."

I didn't know at first what he meant. I lifted my head and blinked my tear-blurred eyes.

I could see them now that I was looking. The guards were still fighting them away, shouting at them to vacate, to leave at once or be tried for obstruction, staring, muttering, hugging their waxed cloaks around themselves.

"It may not be the best idea for Umbrion's Godspeaker to be seen weeping over his broken temple," Perenor muttered to me.

"I'm n-n-n-not..."

"I know," Perenor said, "but they don't. Come on, brother-mine. We have to go."

He slid an arm around my chest and pulled me to my feet. I felt wobbly and weak with exhaustion.

"The p-p-p-priestess—" I said.

"Not now," he said. "We can't, not now, not while they're looking."

"N-n-n-no," I insisted, "n-n-no, we c-c-c-can't I-leave her—"

"We'll send for her body, I swear to you I'll see it done, but we *have to go*, Silas, we have to go *now*."

He steered me back toward the carriage, and right up until he shut the door behind me, I was staring at the pyre.

I DIDN'T LEAVE the palace again.

I slept, mostly. When I did not sleep, I walked. I paced the rain-drenched gardens, traced patterns in the hallway, wandered the library. I admired, I watched, but I never engaged. I only ever spoke with Perenor, and that was getting rarer – much of his time was being monopolized by the Lord-Regent, though I never asked why.

Every day I would find some new route through the palace, and I would walk until my legs were too sore to keep moving. Then I would go to bed and sleep until my body refused another moment of it. Then I would go back to walking.

These were some of the blackest days of my life. So many people had already died around me, but that priestess haunted my dreams. There were moments when I shut my eyes and all I could see was her charred, screaming face.

"Her name was Nara," Soya said one rainy morning.

I looked back at the door. I hadn't heard her enter.

"Her body was recovered and returned to her family," she continued. "We weren't sure what else to do with it. We've never..."

I drew my knees up to my chest. From my perch on the bed, I could see out the window, out the back of the castle, where I could see the ocean stretch into dreary gray nothingness.

"They're starting to riot," Soya said eventually. "Word has spread about what happened at Umbrion's temple. They don't want you in the city."

I could see her reflected in the glass of the window. She seemed to have aged fifty seasons in the few days we hadn't spoken. She'd foregone her usual practical leathers in favor of patterned velvets more suited to her station. She looked handsome – so handsome that I almost didn't notice the way she was staring at me, with worry, uncertainty, and fear.

"There's a rumor going around that you were seen weeping over the rubble at Umbrion's temple," she said.

I wetted my lips. "It's n-n-n-not wh-what it sounds," I said.

The answer didn't mollify her.

"I notice that you have not denied it," she returned, with a very delicate neutrality.

"It's n-n-n-n-not what it s-s-sounds," I repeated, and if my voice was edged in desperation, I did not think it unwarranted. If my dearest friend could not abate her own suspicion of me, how could I reasonably expect it from anyone else?

"Father never should have sent you to his temple," she said. "We should have known something like this would happen. All over Andelan, Umbrion's temples are being razed. We should have..."

She sighed. It wasn't that she was wrong, it was just that she knew, as well as I knew, that resentment of the past was a useless endeavor.

"Is y-y-your f-father going to-to-to oblige them?"

I looked back at her in time to see her frown. "What?"

"The r-r-r-rioters."

"He's..." she begins, but falters. "Silas, I won't lie to you. He's furious. When he heard the guard's report, he nearly had you thrown into the prison under Silverwatch. Is it true that you *screamed* for Umbrion to manifest after you saw them burn the priestess?"

I gritted my teeth. "It's n-n-n-n-n—"

"It's not what it sounds," Soya finished. "Right. Of course it isn't. I'm sure there's a reasonable explanation. There's always a reasonable explanation."

I turned fully to face her, hands knotting in the bedspread. "If y-your f-f-father's s-so angry, then wh-wh-what has s-s-stopped him from ob-b-bliging the r-rioters?" I demanded.

"*I* did, Silas, for Sol's sake!" she said, clenched hand *thump*ing loudly against the desk. "I nearly shouted myself hoarse talking him away from that edge, because I want more than anything in the world to find your innocence in the mounting evidence against you!"

I hoped the sudden surge of pain was not evident on my face.

"I saw you kill the Queen, I blamed Umbrion. I saw you kill your attackers, I blamed Umbrion. I saw you *bring down a temple*, I blamed

Umbrion. And it's so *reasonable* every time, and there's always an explanation, but somehow it gets harder every time, because I *know* you can tap into his Craft, you *said* you could, and you said he knew you, and I keep replaying those conversations in my head, and now you're at his temple, demanding for the manifest of the Traitor God, and I just—"

And it hurt, yes, more than anything, but I couldn't look away from it. My best friend was slipping away piece by piece and I was transfixed by it.

"I'm sorry," Soya said as she rubbed her eyes, and I hated myself for how much she hated herself. "I'm sorry, Silas, it's—"

"D-d-d-don't ap-pologize."

"Just – just please, Silas, promise me that if you know something – I love you so much, and I don't want to be your enemy in this. You'd tell me if you knew something, wouldn't you?"

And I believed her, I really did. That is to say, I believed that she did not want to be my enemy, and I believed that she loved me. What I found harder to believe was that she was not already halfway gone, drifting out to sea while I could only watch as the inevitable tides separated us.

And if only for that moment, I wished she could have certainty, even if that certainty was against me. At least then there would not be this agonizing tearing, this ripping of our friendship at the seams. At least then it would be easier for her.

"I kn-kn-know nothing," I said to her.

Soya flinched. "Of course," she said, and her skepticism drove the pain deeper.

For a while, we were silent. Then she sighed and pushed both her hands through her hair.

"We received some crows in response from those who will be attending the moot," she said. "Two Godspeakers have already agreed to attend, along with two other Lords and a handful of thanes. We'll be meeting on a small coastal city a day's travel from here. We'll have all the leaders and scholars and priests in one place, and – and—"

She faltered, averted her eyes.

"And then, I don't know," she finished anticlimactically. "Then we'll see if we can think up a way to survive a war of gods. Who knows? With all five Godspeakers in the same room, maybe we'll come up with something."

"It's p-p-possible," I said. Granted, it was also possible that all the stars in the sky would rearrange; that didn't make it likely.

THERE IS A VERY UNIQUE TYPE OF SADNESS, I learned in those long weeks of in-between.

"The Lord-Regent has his servants preparing for the moot," Perenor said one day as we walked together through the tiered gardens.

In my life, I had known anxiety and fear with great acuity, but this was a different beast entirely. There was no nervousness in me – not from the usual culprits of strangers and social interaction, nor even from the grander, existential threat of Umbrion's terrible vengeance on Andelan. There was no nervousness in me because there was nothing in me. No fear, no curiosity, no drive, just a sucking abyss of self-hatred and hopelessness.

"I'm not sure what level of pomp and politesse would be necessary for a meeting in these dark times, but people around Silverwatch seem to be treating it like a standard political summit, which apparently demands quite a bit of fanfare," he continued.

The rest of the world was dull, in muted colors and shades of gray. Even the resplendent four-tiered Silverwatch gardens, with their sprawling rows of blue-silver bellflowers and lush, red roses, climbing over each other in strange and wild ways, all seemed distant and foggy, holding no interest to my mind, swallowed as it was by this all-enshrouding darkness.

"Silas?"

The fog in my mind was thick, and it took me a moment to pull myself out of it at my brother's words. At some point, we had come to a stop at the top of a long set of stairs leading to the lower tier of the garden.

"You look half-dead," he said.

"P-p-p-perhaps I am."

Perenor frowned. "Don't say that."

So I decided not to say anything at all. I kept walking, moving down the steps into the lower gardens.

As we came out of the shadow of the tier above us, the rain began its relentless drumbeat on our waxed cloaks. We moved down the curving steps to the lowest tier, whose large silver gates on the far side opened into the city.

"Silas—" he began.

"Wh-wh-what p-preparations are th-there?" I asked, not because I was particularly curious, but because there was nothing I wanted to talk about less than myself.

Perenor sighed, but let it drop. "Lots of food, apparently, and a whole caravan of bears," he said. "And guards. I'm worried about the guards."

"Wh-wh-why?"

"Because they're not ready for what's coming," Perenor said. "I mean, no one is, of course, but theirs is a disrepair we can't afford. They're used to bar fights and petty thievery; they're not used to whatever foul Craft Umbrion has in store. And they're the first line of defense."

"T-t-t-teach them C-Craft, then," I said.

"What?"

"You m-m-managed it w-with me," I said. "They d-d-don't need to b-be seasoned s-s-sorcerers, do they? J-j-just teach them flame-b-b-based Craft."

Perenor frowned thoughtfully. "That would theoretically be strong against Umbrion's magic," he said.

"Shadow f-f-flees from l-light," I said, as the old proverb went.

"Maybe," Perenor said as we passed under a large olive tree. "That might not be a bad idea at all, actually. I always forget how smart you are."

I would have smiled in another situation; as it stood, I didn't have the energy.

"Silas," Perenor said when I stayed quiet, "can we please talk about the fact that you look like you're falling apart?"

"I'm f-f-fine."

"You're clearly not fine, Silas. This whole situation is clearly starting to get to you."

Our attention was drawn suddenly by the sound of a great clatter of metal. When we turned toward it, we became aware of angry shouting, growing louder as we came around the bend in the garden path.

"Stay back!" came a stranger's gruff voice, followed immediately by the sound of shattering glass. "You're standing on the Lord-Regent's palace grounds; stand back!"

There came a sudden shot of adrenaline that pierced my haze. The indistinct sounds of a crowd became more precise: shouting, chanting, jeering.

"This can't be good," Perenor said, and he hurried ahead of me. I stuffed my hand into my pocket and withdrew the glove, pulling it onto my hand before I hurried to catch up with him.

On the far side of the garden, just outside the great, vine-wreathed gate leading into the city, was a mob. The sound of it grew louder and louder as we approached.

"You are standing on the Lord-Regent's palace grounds!" repeated the voice, and I could now see that it was a guard. "Stand back! Stop this at once!"

She was holding shut the gates with all her strength, but they buckled with an answering volley of shouts as the mob pressed into them. I could pick out words like "defile" and "evil" – and, eventually, "traitor god."

At once I knew what it was. What else?

Perenor kept moving forward, apparently not having heard what I did. "What is this?" he asked the guard, though he had to shout to be heard over the riot.

The gates rattled treacherously. The guard shook her head.

"Ths gate usually stands open for the public to enjoy the garden," she said. "I noticed them coming and tried to shut it, but there's no lock—"

The gates groaned suddenly as several people rammed their shoulders into it. The guard let out a startled shout, stumbled, then pushed back against it. Perenor swung his staff off its holster over his shoulder and cracked it loudly into the ground. Blue-white threads of energy snaked around the metal bars, locking it in place.

"What do they want?" Perenor asked her, holding one hand out against the gate to reinforce his Craft.

"I'm not—" she began, before—

"*Look!*"

I could see him, standing toward the front of the crowd – some de facto ringleader, soaked through with rain, wild-eyed, frenetic. Our eyes met, and I knew at once that he recognized me.

"*Down with the traitor!*" shouted someone at the back.

"Down with the traitor!" the others chimed in. "Down with the traitor!" It became a chant. My heartbeat thundered on the side of my neck, fingers flexing in my glove.

"Shit," Perenor said, then *CRACK*. They slammed at the gates again, and the threads of Perenor's Craft shivered and quaked. "Silas, get out of here!"

"I—"

"*Go!*" he said. "Warn the palace; get the guards!"

"They're coming over the wall!" the guard cried.

Sure enough, one of the rioters came vaulting over the garden wall, wearing fitted leathers with a runed whip hanging from her hip. She was no ordinary villager – I knew a sorcerer when I saw one – and on top of it all, she was lean and deadly-looking, and I was the first thing she looked at.

"Silas!" Perenor tried to vault off the gate, but without his hand pressed into it, the Craft on the gates began to crumble treacherously. "Stay away from him!"

"You're coming with me, traitor," the sorcerer said to me.

Heart pounding, I widened my stance. "Y-y-y-you d-don't want to do this," I said to her.

"Quite the contrary," she answered, "I've been waiting to do this for *weeks.*"

Almost faster than I could perceive, her whip was off her hip and flying toward me faster than its sound could keep up with it. On instinct, I raised both hands in front of my face, and the brightly glowing runes on my forearm flashed suddenly; the whip changed its course and wrapped harmlessly around my wrist.

"Foul magic," she snarled.

"Get away from him!" Perenor screamed. "Silas, I can't—!"

"P-p-please, you m-must stop," I said. "Um-m-m-mbrion kills those wh-wh-who threaten me."

"My faith lies with the true gods," she snarled, pulling hard on the handle of her whip. My heels dug into the earth, but the Craft held me steady.

"F-f-f-faith will n-not save you!" I insisted, but she tugged again, and I tumbled forward; the snarl of lash freed my wrist, but I went rolling hard onto my side. When I heard a roar of magic, I jerked to keep rolling, out of the way of what turned out to be a powerful bolt of magic. "S-s-stop!"

"I—" Perenor said behind me, voice strained, "I can't—"

The gates rattled loudly, a sign of Perenor's waning strength. Another burst of lightning came down at me; I held up my gloved hand and met it with an arc of shielding light; the crash that resulted was blindingly bright, the recoil intense enough to press me into the ground and send my assailant flying back.

I scrambled to my feet; my attacker was picking herself up off her knees, a line of blood running down along the crux of her jaw, murder burning in her eyes.

"S-s-stop!" I begged her, holding out my hands "Please, s-stop! He w-w-will manifest in order to-to-to p-protect me!"

"*Your false god has no power over me!*" she roared, and she held her whip high—

"*No!*"

It was Perenor this time, and what happened next is almost beyond explanation.

I stood waiting for her blow to fell, arms over my head, and realized after several seconds that it had not come. Then, when I refocused enough to hear beyond the blood rushing in my ears, I noticed that my surroundings were suddenly silent.

I lowered my arms. My attacker was standing over me, whip poised to strike but hovering still in mid-air, face mid-scream, stance mid-attack. She wasn't moving - it was as though she had been suddenly preserved in ice right before my eyes.

"Wh-wh-wh-wh—"

I looked to Perenor. To my astonishment, everyone else in the garden was just as icy-still as my attacker. The gates were half-open, but the rioters on the other side were poised motionless, as if they had just started to run through them.

It was as if time, I slowly realized through the fog of adrenaline, had suddenly *stopped*.

Except for Perenor. Perenor stood precisely where he had been, the runes on his staff shining so brightly that they were hard to look at, his brow streaked in sweat.

"P-P-P-P-P-P—"

"Run," he said through his teeth, eyes screwed shut in concentration.

"Wh-wh-what d-d-d-d—"

"Silas, *run*," he snapped, "run *now*, I can't hold this forever!"

I couldn't imagine that he could hold this at all. The amount of energy it would take to *stop time* – how on earth could he possibly—?

"I th-th-th-think y-you should s-s-s-stop..." I panted. "P-P-Perenor, th-this..."

"You have to *go*," he said. The stress in his voice was starting to show; his shoulders were starting to shake. There was no way this wasn't eating him up from the inside. "Tell the castle, get more guards..."

I stumbled back on one foot, then the other. Then I turned and ran, darting for the nearest door leading into the castle. As I left, I heard the clash and clatter of the riot resume as though it had never stopped, and it made me run all the faster.

PERENOR DIDN'T REGAIN CONSCIOUSNESS for almost two days. No one knew what had happened, but it must have been something tremendous.

And though I was beside myself with fear during that dreadful in-between, there was a not insignificant part of me that was astonished that he had done something so incredible at all. Perhaps it was no less impressive than creating a shield large enough to stop a falling rock the size of a coliseum, but now that I had a proper perspective of the scope of the Craft involved, I was starting to realize something I'd never really let myself acknowledge before:

My brother might have been the most powerful sorcerer in Andelan. I wondered if it was odd to be upset by the fact that no one had warned me.

I refused to leave his side, so my brace of guards eventually gave up trying to convince me and instead took post outside Perenor's bedroom instead of mine. I sat curled up in a chair by his bed, missing the swallowing darkness and despair because it was less painful than living on the edge of my brother's death.

"It seems that no matter where you are, Godspeaker, you are a danger to those around you."

I looked up from my knees. The Lord-Regent and Soya, flanked by a set of guards separate from my own, were standing in the doorway. The Lord-Regent's hands were clasped behind his back, and Soya's eyes were underlined with dark circles. He came slowly around the far side of the bed, keeping his distance as he observed Perenor; Soya stayed in the door, looking tired and guarded.

"Your brother's skill may have prevented a very violent coup," he said, "and for that I commend him. Of course, he wouldn't have had to but for your poisonous presence in my city."

"Father," Soya hissed.

"Y-y-y-you b-blame me," I said. It wasn't really a question.

"That mob didn't swarm this castle for *my* head, Godspeaker."

"Have you c-c-come here to s-s-s-scold me?" I asked. I wished I could have put more venom into my voice, but I had never been very good at spite. "D-d-do you think th-that will h-help?"

"Stop being combative," Soya said. "Both of you."

"I am not being combative," her father answered tersely. "But I think it is becoming obvious that we must demonstrate to Avenos that their Lord-Regent is not on the side of the Traitor God; that we are not coddling his Godspeaker like a cherished guest. Why do you think they're angry? Because I am keeping *you* in this palace, while you try to summon Umbrion outside this city, and give me *no information—*"

"So l-l-lock me up," I said. "I'm s-s-sure that w-w-will make everyone f-f-feel better, and wh-what c-could possibly b-b-be more important?"

"They think me at best a fool and at worst a conspirator in your god's plot!" the Lord-Regent bellowed at me. "And meanwhile, you refuse to cooperate, giving me *no* insight into Umbrion's plans – why *shouldn't* I lock you up?"

"*No one* is getting locked up," Soya interjected. "Silas has committed no crime of gods or Andels."

"At least none that we can prove," the Lord-Regent added coldly.

"What are you trying to accomplish, Father?" Soya snapped at him. "Your quarrel is with Umbrion, not with Silas. This war has not yet even begun and already there's divisiveness among us?"

The answering silence was telling, though I wasn't sure of what. The Lord-Regent's nostrils flared, and he turned away to face the window.

"Umbrion is as much a threat to Silas he is to you and I," Soya continued, "and we have to work together or we'll die together."

More silence. The Lord-Regent looked out my brother's bedroom window, down at the streets of Avenos, busy and thrumming in the rush of midday.

"There are ten thousand people in this city," he said after a lapse of silence. "Tell me, Godspeaker, does your presence here make them safer?"

I didn't answer. I had a feeling that the question was not meant to be answered, anyway.

"Your brother insists that only those who would do you harm are in danger. But how many people is that, do you imagine? In this palace? This city? How many of them am I meant to control?"

"Wh-wh-wh-what do you w-w-want from me? If y-y-you're going to-to l-l-lock me in a c-c-cell—"

"What do I *want* from you?" He spins on a heel. "I want from you what I have *always* wanted. I want *answers*. Answers that you *conveniently* never seem to have! I want my people to know that I am not coddling Umbrion's Godspeaker while their kin die by his hand in Ellorian!"

My hands formed fists on my knees. The swallowing despair was slowly roiling up in my chest again, devouring me from the inside.

"Father," Soya said miserably, "stop. This is not productive."

"You have until your brother awakens," the Lord-Regent said in a tone that left no room for argument. "If you don't have something by then, you'll be going into the jail underneath Silverwatch, and I don't care what your brother says."

The Lord-Regent left with a spin and the fanning of his silk robes. As his footsteps echoed into silence down the hallway, Soya and I were left, staring at each other in silence.

If there was something she wanted to say to me, it was caught in her throat. Several times, she started to say something, then seemed to think better of it and shut her mouth again.

Eventually, she sighed, made a brief prayer gesture over Perenor's bed, and swept from the room.

THE NEXT FEW DAYS may not have been the blackest of my life, but they certainly were the loneliest.

I was not allowed out of Perenor's room. Food was brought to me, but I did not eat it. I sat near motionless for over a full day, staring at my brother, wishing he would wake up, dying every moment he did not.

I was starting to realize that there was no way out for me. The Lord-Regent demanded answers I did not have for a freedom he did not think I deserved. Everything around me turned to death and chaos. And despite how desperately I wanted to, I could do nothing to fix it.

On one cold and lonely night, when the air was too close and the room too dark, I stepped out onto the balcony, facing west out of the room. I was met with howling wind and hissing rain; within moments, I was drenched with cold water.

I came to the edge, planting my palms on the wide, rain-slicked fireglass balustrade, and looked down. It was a sheer, six-story drop onto one of the lower tiers of the garden.

Rain had soaked my hair, saturated my robes. My vision blurred and my heart pounded.

It would hurt. Of course it would. But not for long, surely. It wasn't the fall that killed you, it was the sudden stop.

Slowly, slowly, I lifted myself onto the railing. In the howling wind and sheeting rain, it took some time for me to find my balance, but I was able to eventually rise to my feet. My robe whipped around my ankles, my rain-soaked hair blowing in front of my face.

If I was lucky, perhaps death – whatever it might bring – would be easier than what my life had become.

"One," I whispered. The wind answered with a howl that sent my legs wobbling.

"Two," I continued, and my hands started to shake.

"Three." And I dropped.

And then, quite to my surprise, I was caught by my shoulders. My eyes flew open—

My little bird...

Shaking, I was lowered back down onto the railing, down onto my knees, and when I looked up through my rain-slicked hair—

My little bird, my little bird, what has this world done to you?

He hovered in the air like ink in water, formless, nebulous, ever changing. My throat constricted. I could have never predicted my own heart at that moment when I stared up at the Night Father's face. I had expected the fear, but not the surge of affection when he gently leaned his forehead against mine.

Have they turned all things against you? he asked me. *Have they even made you a danger to yourself?*

And I knew this was bad, of course; I knew this was dangerous. But *gods*, when his hands lifted to my neck, his current softened all my edges as the ocean softens jagged glass.

"Um-m-m-m—"

I know this blackness you're in, he told me. *For all the ages of your world, I have lived in it. And I am telling you that despite the treachery of your own mind, you are strong enough to live through it, and you will come back from it all the stronger.*

I hated that my eyes were burning with tears. I hated that after everything Umbrion had done, he could still cup me in his hands and make me feel precious and safe and wanted and loved.

Your story doesn't end here, my dear little bird, he said to me. *Soon, you will be leading my armies. Soon, you will be king of all Andels, and you will never taste this darkness again.*

My breath stuttered. "Arm-m-m-mies."

It won't be long now, he told me. *The fruits of my labors will come soon, like shadows in the dark, and all those who caused you this pain will eat their cruelties.*

Fear was bubbling up through my treacherous affection. "Sh-sh-shadows in the d-d-d-dark."

Warn them if you will, he said. *The wise will follow you. You're the only one who can protect them.*

I swallowed a growing knot of fear. "I am?"

Little bird, he said, *surely by now you've learned that I will never hurt you, and neither will anything under my command.*

Even through everything, I knew that what was said in these next few seconds was absolutely critical. With my heart thundering in the side of my neck, I asked, "Wh-wh-when?"

First light, he said, and dread swallowed me. *At first light, all your pain will be ended. At first light, you'll know what it means to rise from the ashes of your own despair.*

I opened my mouth, but the question I nearly asked him was swallowed by a kiss. My mind blanked. The wind howled, the rain poured, but Umbrion's kiss still dissolved me into stardust.

"Silas! No! *Silas!*"

His voice was indistinct at first, as though he was shouting from the other end of a very long tunnel. But as I kissed Umbrion and his hands threaded through my hair and his starlight thrummed under my skin, his words became clearer.

"No! *No!*"

Hands around my waist. I was suddenly pulled back with tremendous force, off my perch on the wide railing, tumbling backward and landing hard on my hip.

"Silas!" It was Perenor, gasping, teary-eyed. "Silas, gods, why would you – how could you ever—!"

My head was still spinning – I looked up toward where Umbrion had been hovering only moments before, but he was gone. There was a void in the air where he had been, as empty as though he'd never been there at all.

"Silas, brother-mine, gods," Perenor sobbed, holding me tightly, burying his face in my chest. "Silas, I'm so sorry – please, gods, please promise me, promise me you won't ever—"

There were a lot of questions going through my mind at that moment. Somehow, the first one to occur to me was, "Y-y-you're aw-w-wake—"

He was pale and worse for wear, but he was awake, holding me tightly by the midsection and shaking.

"Please," he said, "please, Silas, I would never forgive myself if I ever lost you—"

I swallowed hard. Was *that* why he'd come rushing out? "D-d-d-did you n-n-not s-see him?"

"Please, please, Silas, come inside, come inside..."

He hadn't seen Umbrion. Perhaps he could not. Perhaps only Godspeakers could see them.

"P-P-P-Perenor—"

"You must promise me," he said, staring at me tearfully, "*promise* me you'll never do this again. I could never—"

"P-P-*Perenor*," I said urgently, "I am v-v-visited b-by Umbrion!"

Confusion tempered his sudden grief. "What—?"

"He's g-g-g-going to-to-to attack at dawn!"

"HOW DO WE KNOW this information is accurate?" the Lord-Regent demanded. Perenor had woken him up only moments ago, and his foul temperament matched. He stood in the darkened hallway, dressing gown clutched tightly around his chest.

"Why would he lie?" Perenor snapped.

"Get my daughter," he barked to a nearby guard. "*Now.*" The guard nodded and sprinted off, armor clattering.

"This is what you wanted from him, isn't it?" Perenor said. "You demanded information, and now that he gives it to you—"

"This could be a trap of the deadliest kind," the Lord-Regent said. "Who knows what foul machinations the Traitor God has laid out?"

"We *do not have time for your skepticism*, Lord-Regent!" Perenor bellowed. The mere act of shouting seemed to knock the wind from him, and he doubled over against the wall. Alarmed, I stepped to his side.

"Y-y-you sh-should not be up," I said.

"I'm fine," he answered through his teeth. He wasn't fine, of course, he was just proud. "Lord-Regent, you have word of the Night Father's attack, straight from the mouth of his Godspeaker. What further proof do you need?"

"I cannot simply put the entire city on alert because this *traitor*—"

"*How much is your cursed prejudice worth?*" Perenor thundered. "Is it worth the lives of everyone in your city? Yours? Your daughter's?"

"What's going on?" came Soya's voice, as if summoned by her mention. She was hurrying down the hallway in her night-clothes, long hair braided down her back.

"Umbrion is going to attack Avenos at daybreak," Perenor said.

"*What?*"

"So says his traitorous Godspeaker," the Lord-Regent snarled.

"It's past midnight already!" Perenor said. "If we don't move quickly to fortify the city, Avenos will share Ellorian's fate!"

"I will not be held responsible for the fruit of a tree of lies—!"

"*Guards!*" Soya called. "Fortify Avenos! Wake up the Guard Captain!"

The Lord-Regent spun. "Soya, you do *not* have authority—!"

"*Then I will take it if you do not!*" she roared at him. "I will not let your petty distrust take down the Silver City, not while your scion draws breath!"

Two of the guards hurried off in the opposite direction to follow Soya's orders.

"Soya," Perenor said, "wake up all the members of your guard. I can teach them how to summon magical fire."

"Magical fire—?"

"It's strong against Umbrion's magic," he said. "Shadow flees from light."

"You can do that in – what – six hours?"

"The basics, yes. Just enough to hopefully give us an edge. I trust you have a supply of runed weapons?"

"This is preposterous—!" the Lord-Regent began, but Soya talked over him:

"Yes, in storage. There should be enough for most of the guard."

"We may have to deputize citizens who can fight. Silas, do you know how many are coming?"

"N-n-n-n—"

Bu then I realized I did. At some point, Umbrion had laid out his entire plan in my head, and the numbers were staggering.

"A l-l-l-lot," I said, nervousness rising in my throat. "They're going to c-c-c-come from the ocean."

"Shut down the ports," Soya said to another guard. "No one goes in or out. Start building barricades at all the gates, strongest nearer the coast. Wake up everyone."

"Yes, ma'am," the guard said before hurrying away.

"Get the families with young children under the castle!" Soya bellowed to whoever was in earshot; already, people were starting to wake up, poking heads out of doors and coming around the hallways. "Wake up the Lord-Regent's council and get them to the chambers! We are a city under siege!"

"Soya—" the Lord-Regent began.

"Either cooperate or stay out of my way, Father," she snapped at him, striding off.

IT TOOK ME no more than ten minutes to stammer my way through everything I knew about the attack. Every time I managed a sentence, one of the councilors or the Guard Captain would shout something out the door of the council chamber that would cause more people in the hallway to start running.

I had nearly finished my explanation when Soya came barging in.

"The families are starting to arrive," she said to her father.

"What are you *wearing*," the Lord-Regent answered, and though it was phrased like a question, it sounded much more like an accusation.

"Armor," she returned flatly. I had to admit that she looked absolutely ferocious. She was wearing a set of gleaming black armor, outfitted with a long cloak in her house colors of violet and silver. She had a broadsword on her back and an expression on defiance on her face.

"No," the Lord-Regent said. "I forbid you to fight."

"Oh," Soya returned glibly, "finally taking the threat seriously now?"

"You are my only scion; I will not allow you to put yourself at risk!"

"Then you'll have to tie me up, Father, because this city is under siege and I will not sit idly by and let it fall without falling myself."

"Is P-P-P-Perenor with the g-g-guard?

Soya looked back to me. "Yes," she said. "Quite a teacher, your brother."

"He m-m-managed it with me," I answered, holding up my gloved hand.

"But even with Craft, we'll be stretched thin. I've deputized the sorcerers from the monastery, and those willing and able to swing a sword, but even then..."

"The walls of Avenos have survived harsher storms," said someone on the council.

"I'd not make the mistake of underestimating a god," Soya said. "Can we send out crows to neighboring thanes, Father? Do we have time?"

The Lord-Regent's nostrils flared. "Maybe," he said. "It won't amount to much, but I suppose we're not in a position to refuse anything."

"Thank you for finally getting on board," Soya returned venomously. "I need to borrow Silas."

"What for?" the Lord-Regent asked at once.

"A guard thinks he's found one of Umbrion's scouts."

I looked back at the council. No one had explicitly given me permission to leave, but with the rules about where I was allowed to go suspended in a time of crisis, I decided to listen to Soya, who was proving to be more of a leader than her Lord Father. I followed her out.

"We're repurposing some of the dynamite used in the mines to the north," she said as she walked, "and the blacksmiths have agreed to use their kilns to heat oil for traps."

"H-h-heated oil?" I asked.

"Fire is fire, even in liquid form," she answered. "We can mount cauldrons of the stuff over the walls."

It was a good idea. Grisly, but good. I'd forgotten how clever Soya was. I was an academic, but Soya always had the ability to think laterally.

We were going down, I noticed, into a corner of Silverwatch I had never been, one of little ornamentation and utilitarian furnishings. Guards were milling every which way, pulling on armor, gathering weapons, barking out and listening for orders. We turned into a small room and saw—

"Wh-wh-wh-what the f-f-f-*fuck*—"

"We have no idea," Soya answered at once.

I looked at it, and I kept looking at it, and for some time my mind couldn't quite make sense of what I was seeing, despite how closely I was studying it. I had never seen anything quite like it in my life.

It was black-skinned, hulking, about the size of a large goat, though the similarities ended abruptly. It walked on two short black legs with, so far as I could see, cloven hooves, and it had two large, sinewy arms and fingers tipped with massive claws. Its face was flat, its eyes were black and glassy, and it was snarling and thrashing in its bonds – iron chains that the guards, I could only imagine, had freshly fastened on it.

"Are these the foot soldiers you told us about, Silas?" Soya asked me. "Is this the Night Father's vanguard?"

I had no idea. The information he had planted in my head had told me how many and when, but had not included what. My expression must have shown my answer.

"Well, whatever it may be, it seems to speak, although not in any language we can recognize."

"*Filthy warmbloods! Filthy, filthy!*"

I took a half step back in surprise. Its voice was high and throaty, its long black tongue clumsy between syllables.

"W-w-warmblood?"

Soya glanced at me. "What?"

"*Filthy warmbloods! Rip and tear and rip and tear!*" It started shrieking, bouncing as high as it could in its heavy iron chains, flailing its claws manically.

"It..." I began haltingly, "it's s-s-saying..."

"*Rip the flesh and break the bone, send them into Shadow!*" It would have sounded almost singsong but for the frantic warble in its voice. It was shaking violently, like a mad dog, gnashing its teeth between each word. "*Kill the warmbloods! Kill!*"

"You can understand it?" Soya asked me.

I looked back at her. "Y-y-y-you can't?"

"It's not speaking Andelish, Silas," she said guardedly.

"Y-y-yes it is," I replied. "It's s-s-s-saying... c-can't you hear it?"

"*Kill, kill, rip, kill, tear, kill, rip!*" It was getting less coherent by the moment, in any case, devolving from sentences to strings of words, and then into grunting and shrieking. It was a vile little thing, hateful and viscerally repulsive for reasons I couldn't quite articulate.

"Can it understand *you?*" Soya asked. Her voice had never sounded so suspicious.

"I..."

She was staring at me expectantly, if reservedly. I swallowed, wetted my lips, and took a few steps forward, crouching down in front of it.

It was still thrashing and screaming violent nonsense when I interjected, "C-c-c-can you und-d-derstand m-me?"

The shouting stopped abruptly. It turned its large, oblong head toward me, and stared at me with its fireglass eyes.

"*Speaker*," it said.

I recoiled.

It didn't take me long to put it together, of course: it recognized me. Surely it had been created with that in mind.

"*Speaker!*" it said a second time, louder, suddenly throwing itself toward me. I staggered away from it at once, and the beast reached out toward me. "*Speaker is king of the krashth-gar! Speaker, Speaker!*"

"What is it saying?" Soya asked, still sounded guarded.

I looked back at her, swallowed. I could only imagine what the answer would do to her already suffering opinion of me, but it would have been dangerously dishonest to keep it from her.

"I..."

Feeling suddenly cold, I pulled my robes more tightly around my midsection.

"It c-c-c-calls itself k-k-krashth-gar, whatever that m-m-m-means," I said. "And it c-c-calls me k-king."

"King," Soya echoed, voice flat.

I averted my eyes. Of course I was its king. Umbrion had promised me a kingship, hadn't he? I was the voice of its maker.

The room, I noticed somewhat belatedly, had gone very quiet. The guards around us seemed to finally recognize what they were seeing.

"S-S-Soya," I said. "I'm n-n-not..."

I couldn't find the words. It didn't seem to matter, because Soya didn't seem to want to respond. She stared at me with such intensity that I felt as if she was trying to see through my soul.

Several further moments of silence passed, and then she turned on one plated boot and addressed the other soldiers, now staring in uniform silence.

"Did you hear that, guards?" Soya asked. "It calls itself krashth-gar."

Not having expected to be addressed, the guards exchanged looks among themselves in unsteady silence.

"Do you want to know what I call it?"

She reached over her shoulder, and before my mind was able to perceive the movement, she had unsheathed her broadsword, swung it high, and cut the thing in two before it had a chance to react. Slimy black viscera spilled onto the floor. I covered my mouth with my hand and looked away while Soya turned to face the guards.

"I call it *fucking dead.*"

There were a few hesitant chuckles, though only a few.

"I call it unholy. I call it Shadowspawn. I call it demon. But mostly I call it dead."

She pointed her sword toward its bisected corpse, still twitching gruesomely.

"It has no Light to protect it," she said, "and that means we can kill it. That means we can win. That means that the night does not yet fall on the Silver City, not while your Lord-Regent draws breath, not while your swords are sharp and your Craft is hot."

By some combination of the direness of the situation, her startling display, and her own charisma, she had them spellbound, and as she walked toward the nearby table full of weapons and armor and related miscellany, they watched in reverent silence. She snatched a rag and used it to clean her broadsword of the black blood.

"You're scared," she said. "That's fine. I'm scared, you're scared, everyone in fucking Andelan is scared. So quickly after we lose the Worldmother's Light, we're forced to confront a real possibility of death. That's fucking scary.

"But it's also good. Fear keeps you sharp. And it's liberating, too. These ugly bastards are coming for all of us – every last one. There's no hiding, no clemency. So why not go down swinging and screaming Skyfire?

"Umbrion may have taken the Worldmother's Light, but her fire still burns in all of us. Has not Perenor been showing you that, bringing it out in you? It can still burn through any shadow!"

The corpse began to glow white-hot. One of the guards, runed sword shining, was bringing it to a burn with rudimentary, but effective, Craft. Bells of white-hot flame began to consume the body. The other guards noticed and watched in kind.

"I'll not ease your minds with pretty, false promises," Soya continued, "and I won't say that we *will* win, only that we *can*, that we *must*. Ours is the greatest city in Andelan, and if we are to die, then we will be the last ones to go, Craft blazing, swords shining! We will defy the darkness till our last breaths!"

One guard called for a cheer – then another, and another. Soya continued, shouting over the growing sound:

"So fight like our world depends on it, my friends, because I assure you that it does!" she cried. "Fight and scrape and claw and bite, because we must believe that the Light will always be stronger than the Shadow, and because we will *not* be collateral damage in a war of gods without going down *fighting!* We are *worth the fight!*"

Soon, the room was pulsing with their cheers, and with the words of House Rhodan (*"Glory in Light!"*), and Soya stood at the center of the room, sword in hand, eyes burning.

She was ferocious and brave and handsome at that moment. It's how I'll always remember her, I think, for the rest of whatever days I have left.

"Not a bad leader, that friend of yours," said a voice from behind.

I spun – Perenor was standing behind me, looking exhausted, but smiling. Behind us, the crowd still chanted – *"Glory in Light! Glory in Light!"*

I smiled weakly at him. "Almost l-l-l-like she was b-born for it."

"I need to talk to you, Silas."

I nodded, looking back to the chanting crowd only for a moment before I followed him out into the hallway. There was little else but a small, dirty window looking out onto the city. The gray overcast was dark – far darker than it should have been so close to daybreak – as though in warning of tidings to come.

"H-h-how g-goes the crash c-c-course in Craft?"

"I think I've done all I can for them," Perenor said. "They have no finesse or control, but they can summon fire well enough, and I suppose that's all they need." He rubbed his eyes with the heel of his palms.

"G-g-good," I said. "Y-y-you should r-rest."

"Would that I had time," he answered. "There's yet more work to be done."

"P-P-Perenor, you're in n-no sort of sh-shape for that."

"I don't imagine anyone ever could be, but that won't stop me from fighting."

I started. Perenor leveled me with an even stare.

"F-f-fight?" I repeated. "Perenor, y-y-you can't f-fight."

"I can," he answered. "I'm a sorcerer, and this city needs defense. It would be irresponsible to sit out because I'm tired."

"Y-y-you're m-more than tired, P-P-Perenor, you're stretching y-y-yourself past your l-limits—!"

"But I *can* fight," he interjected, "and in the current circumstances, that means I must."

"Being th-theoretically c-c-c-capable of combat d-d-doesn't m-make you real-l-listically ready for a b-battle!" I said. "Y-you woke up only hours ago f-f-from two d-days of unconsciousness! W-w-would you ask m-m-me to fight, s-s-since I'm n-now a s-sorcerer by some r-r-rudimentary definition?"

"Of course not. You're not fully trained in Craft and you're not trained at all in combat."

"Th-then I'd ask the s-s-same of a m-m-man who can b-barely stand up!"

"Silas, I *want to fight.*"

"Wh-wh-*why?*"

"Because it's worth fighting for!"

"Y-you could *die!*"

"*It's also worth dying for!*"

I reeled back. Perhaps I shouldn't have been shocked, but I was. My brother was willing to die? What would I ever do without him?

"Don't you remember what you said to me?" he continued, dropping his voice. "Back before the riot at Umbrion's temple, you said that there were things more important than you. And at the time I didn't want to believe it, but now that this battle is so near, I think I understand."

I stared at him in furious silence. Why did he have to have this clarity *now?* Why couldn't he be selfish for a while longer?

"There *are* things more important," he said. "More important than you, than me, than any one Andel. All of this shared progress of our people, our society – we can't allow it to just be wiped off the map by some doom-driven god. The sum of all Andel achievement, all our history and culture – isn't that worth fighting for? Isn't that worth dying for?"

My eyes burned with tears as I realized that I couldn't talk him out of this. Perenor was going to fight, and maybe die, and the worst part is he was right to do so.

"I d-d-d-don't w-w-want you to d-die," I whispered, with the infinite naïveté of a boy.

"I don't want to die, either, but I will if I have to," he answered with the patient wisdom of a man. "If it means defending this city, this world. I will, Silas."

"I'm guessing you don't want heavy armor," Soya said behind him, softly.

I lowered my head to hide the tears now falling down my face. Perenor looked back. Behind where Soya was standing in the doorway, the guards were still chanting and cheering.

"Yes," he answered after a lapse. "Light. Leathers, if you have them. They're better for combat Craft. That was a nice speech you gave in there, Rhodan."

"We can rustle something up for you," Soya answered, foregoing the compliment. I wiped the tears now rounding my jaw. "Silas, you should stay here."

"I-I-I—"

"Yes," Perenor said, as though driving home his point, "he should."

"We need your connection to Umbrion," Soya told me. "We can't risk you."

I couldn't risk either of them, but they were going off anyway. It seemed so tremendously unfair somehow, for them to go and put themselves at risk while forcing me to stay behind.

"I-I-I-I—"

"Perenor, let's get you suited up. Then we should get you out to the southern docks; that's where the vanguard will come, according to Silas, and where we'll need the most help."

Were they really going now? What if they died? What if this would be the last time I ever saw them? I stared uselessly at them as they walked away and I didn't know at that moment what I wanted, but I knew it wasn't this.

"Er, Your Holiness?"

The voice was coming from behind. I looked back, but only briefly. It was one of my usual guards.

"Lady Soya asked me to take you down to the underbelly of the castle, where the families are."

I looked back. Perenor and Soya were exiting through a large iron door. I watched them leave, wondering if I could ever really stay here while they were out there, weighing questions of love and death and fate that I was not equipped to answer.

In the end, though, I found that there was only one question that mattered – would I ever forgive myself if anything happened to either of them and I was not there?

THERE IS A SAYING – and I know not whether it will survive in common parlance after all that's happened – that says the gods do not deal in chance. It's often used as a comforting platitude, a reassurance that all pain is part of some grander design. The implication, however veiled, is that our lives are fundamentally out of our hands; that we are pawns in a greater game of destiny.

I don't know that I ever really believed that, but after all I've seen, I know for certain that I do not now.

There is no tide without ripples, and similarly, there is no destiny without the million-million insignificant choices in every person's life. It is the insignificancies that drive the tides of history, not vise-versa. One foolish boy goes running headlong into battle and dooms a kingdom; one brave sorcerer does the same and saves it. Both acting and reacting, both forging fate with each breath and each step with everyone else.

I wonder, then, what that implies about my choice to shake my guards, to leave the castle and go out into the fray.

Because of course I did, because *obviously* I did, because my brother and best friend were out there, and I could not let them risk their lives without at the very least standing by their side. The moment I was shepherded into the jail beneath Silverwatch, repurposed as a makeshift shelter for the families and their young children, I knew I could not stay. Already I could hear the clash and clamor of battle far above my head. It was dawn; the fight had started.

I ignored the guard's shouting and I left with an armful of stolen armor off a nearby rack. I ran, not thinking of fate, but forging it anyway, unwilling to leave those I loved behind.

And in that ever-advancing tide of destiny, I made a choice, and here at the end of all things, I am forced to wonder whether it was the right one.

IT SHOULD COME TO THE READER as no surprise that despite all these pretty ideas about love and death and destiny, I remained entirely unsuitable for actual battle.

When I pushed through the front doors of Silverwatch, down the steps, and into the city, the first thing that hit me was the sound of it.

The demons that Umbrion had made had already broken through the barricades. All around me, the black-skinned monstrosities were loping, slouching, snaking through the streets, hissing and snarling. But the sound of it, gods, the sound – I could hear people screaming, the sound of ripping flesh and snapping bone and clattering metal.

I'd swiped a set of ring mail on leather, the smallest size I could find, but it still ill fit me. Fat raindrops drummed my hooded cloak, and my runed short sword felt entirely useless and clumsy in my hand. I was not and never would be any kind of fighter; the sword did little else but remind me.

Every sensible part of me was screaming to go back, to get out, to flee while I could. Every other part of me was desperate to find Perenor and Soya.

So I hefted my useless sword and pulled forward my hood and pushed into the bedlam.

Those demons, those monstrosities, they came in every shape and size, small and impish to massive and hulking. The only common features they shared were their black, scaly skin and their taste for flesh.

I ducked and weaved through the madness, shouting my brother's name through the cacophony of wind and rain and screaming. All around me, people were dying, throats and hearts and viscera ripped out before falling into an eerie silence as their demon assailants set to eating them as a night-cat would eat its prey.

I had nearly given up all hope until I saw a familiar flash of blue-white light further into the city, near a large square built around a fountain.

"Perenor!"

There he was, Craft and teeth flashing, his runed staff in one hand and a sword in the other. He was cutting demons down with terrifying efficiency, with ferocious bursts of Craft and precise swings of his swords.

And by the gods, some quiet part of me supplied, was he ever impressive. Among mere mortals, he wielded Craft like a lesser god, all righteous vengeance and deliberate fury. For a moment I could only watch, awestruck, spellbound, as he took on some half-dozen of the black-skinned abominations at once, burning through them with searing blue-white light.

My attention was drawn by a looming shadow, growing even in the darkness.

It was small at first, but rapidly grew in size. By the time it came over the hill coming up to the square, it was the size of a building. Its features came into definition – a massive, sinewy arm gripping a chimney, its legs spread wide. It was as tall as a house, and soldiers and guards went fleeing before it, scrambling away.

"Perenor! Behind you!"

He did not hear me. He was so focused on the creatures in front of him that he did not notice the massive demon thundering towards him until—

"No!"

The demon dipped its hand down and swatted him as one might swat away a gnat, and Perenor went flying, soaring through the air and crashing into the fountain with a dreadful, ominous *CRACK*.

I ran forward, my sword clattering to the ground.

Perenor collapsed in the basin of the fountain, and as I grew closer, I could see blood snarling through the water. I did not have time to think; I ran in front of him and stretched my arms out as the demon came lumbering forward to deliver a killing blow—

"Stop!"

The demon stopped.

It stared down at me, its massive hand still raised and primed to strike. Rain sluiced down its black scales, and its massive eyes were fixed on me.

All the other demons in the square had also stopped.

"D-d-d-don't hurt him!" I said, arms still outstretched. "Don't hurt him!"

Slowly, slowly, the demon lowered its arms. My head spun. To what degree would it follow my commands? Would they do whatever I said?

"D-d-don't hurt an-nyone," I continued, hoping they could understand me. "J-j-just leave! G-go back to the sh-shadow!"

A tense lapse of silence. Then, from the side—

"*Speaker orders us to stop?*" It was one of the smaller demons, currently half-finished devouring the corpse of a guard; I was nauseous just looking. The demon appeared to be addressing me.

"Yes!" I sobbed. "P-p-please, just g-g-go back to the ocean, d-d-don't hurt an-nyone!"

"*Speaker orders us to stop!*" another demon said, sounding surprised. "*Maker says one, Speaker says another! Who follow?*"

What ensued was what I can only describe as several moments of bickering. The demons – and there were quite a few listening, by this point – were all squabbling amongst each other, saying things like *Maker says kill* and *Speaker says stop*.

At a wider radius, the guards who had stopped fighting due to the sudden discussion were watching. It was doubtlessly not a good picture, seeing a huddle of demons around me that were not ripping me apart.

"I am y-y-y-your Speaker!" I said, drawing myself up as much as possible, projecting all the authority I could manage. "I order y-y-you to s-s-stop!"

This seemed to ignite even more discussion, as though it was the most profound philosophical question yet posed to them. Perhaps it was.

But it was not until one great, booming voice superseded the rest that everything came to a sudden stop:

"*I answer only to Maker,*" the massive demon above me boomed, its voice as loud as thunder. And with one hand, it punched a hole in the roof of a nearby building.

People started screaming again. The fighting resumed. I staggered back.

"N-n-no!" I cried. "I'm y-y-your m-maker, you m-m-must answer to me!"

"Silas—"

I spun. Rain blurred my vision, but I could see Perenor lying in the shallow pool of water, now stained read with blood. Everything else in the world suddenly stopped mattering. I fell to his side.

"Perenor," I said, grabbing him by the shoulders. He howled in pain and I withdrew my hands. "G-g-g-gods, you're hurt—"

His pain seemed to subside a moment later. "You saved me," he said. There was blood in his mouth, and he was delirious.

"*Help!*" I shouted into the battle, but no one could hear me over the clamor. "Help, s-s-s-someone help!"

"I remember why we stopped singing," he said to me.

"Sh-sh-shut up, Perenor, for f-f-fuck's sake, you're w-wounded—"

"They told me," he kept talking, like he hadn't heard me, "they told me that you would never be the sort of scion House Olen needed. They told me not to bother trying to help you, that you would never change."

I simultaneously wanted to hug him and knock him unconscious, if only to keep him from wasting breath. "Sh-sh-shut up, Perenor!" I wasn't sure I could take much more of this. "*Someone help!*"

"I believed them," he told me, and he was choking on the blood filling his mouth. "I believed them. I'm so sorry, I didn't want to disappoint them—"

"I f-f-f-forgive you, you b-bastard, n-n-now *please* stop t-t-talking—"

"I stopped singing and I lost a brother—"

"You d-d-didn't lose m-me, I'm r-right here!"

There came a look of vague, delirious joy on his face then, after a moment's pause. I could see blood welling behind his lips, and no, no, no, *please no, please no, not now, not after everything.*

"You are," he said. "You are, you're here. I'm glad, before the end—"

"It's n-n-not the end!" I was past the point of trying to pretend that tears weren't pouring down my face. I held him tightly by the shoulders. "It's n-n-n-n-n-not the end—!"

"I'm glad I could be a brother again," he said, "I'm glad I could sing to you—"

"*Stop,*" I begged him, "d-d-don't, don't d-d-do this—"

"Brother, I have to," he said. "I told you, I told you. There are things worth dying for."

Talking, seeing, thinking – it was all so far beyond me. This was dying, he was dying in my arms, and despite everything, I couldn't stop it. My hands fisted in his leathers and I fell forward into ugly, broken sobbing.

"I give everything I have to protect you, to protect this city, this world," he said, and his voice was getting fainter, and to the left of me I could see a growing source of white light. "I give it gladly, I give it all gladly. I love you, brother-mine."

"I l-l-l-l-l-love y-y-you—"

"I'm glad I remembered..."

The light was building brighter. My vision was foggy with tears, but I could see the runes burning brighter than the sun on his runed staff, blazing, trembling with mounting energy, the sum total of everything Perenor was building into one point of light and heat and Craft, growing and growing until—

—there came a great cataclysm of light and sound, blinding, deafening, ever-expanding around me. I was reminded of that day, half a season and ten lifetimes away, where Perenor's Craft domed over the Queen's Ring and saved Ellorian from the falling star, but this was so much brighter, and so much stronger, and I was breathless, falling back.

I could hear the demons all around us, shrieking and sizzling and turning to dust, and the dome of light grew ever wider, screaming out in an impenetrable wall of light that eclipsed the mighty Silver City. And I knew, without looking, without thinking, in a deep and visceral way, that he was dead, my brother was dead, having sacrificed everything for this victory.

I lay still and silent, and the sounds of battle faded, though whether it was to the sudden triumph or to my own fading consciousness, I cannot say. I lay staring at the sky, rain falling on my face, and I dropped away.

PERENOR. Ay, gods, the wound still cuts.

If I had time, brother-mine, I would write your eulogy. I would sing your praises in a thousand pages. If I had time, I would tell stories of our youth, of the sunlight and the sand, when we two were so young and inseparable, and close as two brothers were ever meant to be.

And in this eulogy, I would not shy away from how we had drifted. I would tell every gruesome detail of your cruelties, of my withdrawal, and when I came to the end it would make our rekindling, those final weeks together, seem all the sweeter.

And it was, brother-mine, in its own way, despite the circumstances. I would not have traded those last few weeks for any treasure. I had not realized how terribly and all-encompassingly I had missed my brother until, for those brief moments, I had him again.

I know that time will write your eulogy for me, Perenor. You are now, always were, and ever shall remain a hero of Andelan. They will write songs about you, whisper legends of you, you who saved Avenos in its darkest hour.

You fell into some great perhaps, a long and cold sleep, and since I cannot wake you, I can only bid you sleep well, sleep well, brother. You have earned your respite.

I don't think I'll be long to join you.

BY THAT POINT, I had seen death. I'd tasted it, choked on it. But this was the first time I had felt it.

It was a bitter draught to swallow, but edifying. There is no better way to truly understand the nuances of death than to outlive someone you love.

I spent the next few days sequestered in my room as the city struggled to put itself back together. From my window I watched the scene below – the bodies of the fallen picked up and carried away in carts, roofs patched, walls rebuilt.

Every now and then I would look toward the door and think, *I should talk to Perenor.* Then, *oh.*

And then I would go back to looking out the window.

No one bothered me. Every day, a servant would come by with a meager meal, which more often than not went back uneaten. I had lost my brother, and along with him, my appetite, my desire to sleep, my drive, and much of the goodness left in my life.

And then, on one day rather like the rest, Soya appeared in my room without knocking.

She was silent for a while; I didn't even notice her until I shifted and caught her reflection in the window.

We stared at one another for some time. She hesitated there in the doorway before she finally spoke:

"They're rioting," she said.

I knew, of course. I'd seen them out the window, heard their screaming. They were pooled by the front palisade circling Silverwatch, growing every day in number, screaming obscenities about me.

Perhaps I should have felt something, but I did not. There was an ocean of grief inside me that felt no noticeable change at the rains of fear.

"They saw you," she said.

I didn't know what she meant, and my grief prevented me from caring.

"*I* saw you, Silas," she continued, voice rising. When I didn't look back at her, she said, "*Silas.*"

I reluctantly turned my head away from the window. She was standing just inside the door, looking frayed and weak and heartsick, face full of betrayal.

"I *saw* you, do you hear me?" she said. "*Everyone saw you.* They saw you commiserate with the demons, they saw you hold him down. They saw you *try to kill your own brother.*"

My mind was still heavy with anguish and slow to pick up on her meanings. Was that what they'd seen? But then, in the eyes of those who already had reason to hate me, I could see how such a conclusion would be the most obvious. They'd been too far to hear me speak, to see what I was doing when I was bent over my brother before he died.

If it were me, I'd likely have been convinced, too.

"And *every bone in my body* denies that you would ever do something so *black*, Silas, but I watched you do it! I saw you over him before that burst of Craft knocked you back and saved the city. Tell me I'm wrong, Silas!"

I stared at her in silence.

"*Answer me!*" she bellowed.

There may have been some part of me that wanted to reply, but there was no voice left to say it.

And Soya, poor Soya, was staring at me with furious tears in her eyes.

"No words?" she asked, voice thin.

I slowly shook my head.

"No words," she said. "How convenient."

The words stung like needles, but what was a needle when my chest was ripped open?

"I don't know what to think," she said. "You give us warning for an imminent attack, and then you stain your hands with the blood of your own brother. I can't fathom what twisted game this is, Silas, but I can no longer be part of it."

I could only answer with more silence. It seemed to infuriate her.

"The Court Sorcerer is coming up with something to... bind you," she said. "I do not know what it is, but she assures us that it will contain whatever foul magic you have in you."

I dropped my head against the window, feeling nothing.

"It will have to be ready for the moot," she continued, "because we cannot let you leave this room again without some measure of protection from the evil that follows you."

Further silence. I had nothing to say, so I stayed quiet and stared out the window, where the city struggled to rebuild itself, where the rioters were still gathered, and I listened to the pulses of their chanting.

"We've have word from your mother."

I'd though that perhaps there was nothing left in me to feel anything at all, but that managed it. I looked back at her again.

"They're going to be at the moot," Soya continued, voice flat. "Your mother and grandmother are two of six surviving members of the Queenscourt. They sent you a letter."

She threw a letter down onto my bed. For a while I could only stare at it, searching for some way to feel about it. How did they survive? Were they safe? How much did they know about what had happened to me since the breaking of Ellorian?

"If you want to respond," Soya said, "give it to the guards."

She turned and swept from the room. When the door closed behind her with a resounding sound, I went back to staring at the letter. It took more courage than I thought it might to pick it up and slowly unfold it.

Silas, are you hurt?

We hope that you will respond by crow if you can, but regardless, we will see you at the moot, my dear. After everything, all we want is to see you again, you and your brother both. There is nothing we want more.

I covered my mouth with one hand. I didn't even realize there were still tears in me left to fall, but as I finished the note, I doubled over myself and fell to pieces, sobbing and screaming until emotion hollowed me again and exhaustion took me.

GRIEF DRAGGED ON, ceaseless, limitless, a great and swallowing dark. I remained sequestered in my gilded prison cell. At night, I could hear only rain, and during the day, only the chanting of the rioters calling for my death.

I slept little, but when I did, I dreamt of Perenor, smiling and laughing as though nothing had happened, strong and brave and singing our song. And it was wonderful until that inevitable end when the truth came back like a blow to the stomach. Still, I didn't begrudge myself my dreams. They were one of the few things left that brought me any comfort.

I knew that there must have been preparations for the moot underway, but only because I could hear – and, to some degree, see, through my rain-streaked window – people moving equipment and supplies into large carts lined up along the inner side of the palisades surrounding Silverwatch. I suppose that I should have been eager for the moot to come, as the only hope left in the world would be waiting there, but that creeping numbness swallowed whatever hope there was in me.

One day rather like all the others – I couldn't say when, as I'd long ago stopped trying to remember – the door to my room opened again. This time, it was one of the guards posted outside my door.

"Your presence is requested," he said to me, and I stared blearily at him. "You're being summoned to the council chambers."

I'd barely moved in days, certainly no further than the length of my bedroom, and I was sure that I was by no means presentable to the Council of the Lord-Regent, though I couldn't find the will in me to care.

So I pulled myself to my feet, ignored my own swaying, and followed the guards out of the room. They kept their eyes forward and their hands on their swords as they escorted me down into the castle.

When I arrived in the council chambers, it was to a markedly smaller number of councilors than there had been before. I wondered if it was because they were frightened of me or if it was because they were dead.

There were at least two familiar faces: the Lord-Regent and Soya, both regarding me with various intensities of distrust.

"Godspeaker," the Lord-Regent said, the first to address me after several lingering moments of silence, "It seems that your god's attempts to snuff us out have not worked, at least not entirely."

If he expected me to feel some sort of shame, he underestimated how numb I had become to everything around me. He sat waiting for an answer for a while, but when none came, he slowly continued:

"In six days' time, we will all of us be leaving for the moot. Every politician and diplomat and statesman and priest of station will be meeting us in Andwelum, a little fishing village about two days from here. You can imagine our apprehension at bringing you with us, after everything that's happened."

I kept my silence. It seemed to anger him somehow.

"Still, we acknowledge that your presence is... necessary. Despite the *marked* delay in your warning, it proved that you do have some use. So our Court Sorcerer has developed a device that she says will bind you and whatever Craft you would wield or would be wielded through you. Miara?"

A woman off to the side rose. She had a small metal contraption in both hands, and she came toward me slowly, unsteadily, like a frightened animal.

"Your hands," she said as she came closer, and after a moment, I lifted them toward her, palms up.

She fastened two large, brass manacles around each wrist, joined by a short chain in the middle. They were heavy and snug, with runes carved into the metal. The moment they snapped shut, there was a short hiss of Craft that sealed them into unbroken bands. I stared down at them for a moment, not sure what to think.

"Sorcerers call them nullifiers," she explained. "Often, nullifiers are used in construction, to make certain rooms Craft-proof. I took that concept and made this."

I tugged weakly at them. They held firm. My hands could not move more than six inches apart. The chain between them, at least, rotated freely on both ends, allowing me some small amount of mobility. When I tried, mostly out of curiosity, to conjure a simple flame, nothing happened.

"Any sort of Craft that is channeled through you will cancel itself out," she elaborated, stepping away from me. "This combined with total sequestration will, with any luck, keep you... contained."

It might work on me, but I doubted very much they would hold back the full wroth of a god if he chose to possess me.

Still, I suspected this demonstration had less to do with me and more to do with them. I looked back up at the councilors and saw the fear in them, some well hidden and others obvious. They were terrified of me, and I could not blame them for it.

The sorcerer Miara returned to her seat, leaving another lapse of silence to stifle the room.

"You should know," Soya said, after a lengthy pause, "that we burned your brother's body yesterday."

Something small and broken twisted in the back of my throat, but I said nothing.

"At first we weren't sure what to do with the dead," the Lord-Regent said, somewhat brusquely. "We'd never had to deal with them before, let alone in such numbers."

I wondered how many had died, then wished I hadn't wondered.

"Committing their remains to the Worldmother's Flame seemed like a—" (the Lord-Regent stumbled here, though only for a moment) "—respectable choice."

My hands twisted in the manacles.

"Despite everything that's happened," Soya said, "you ought to know that your brother was and forever will be honored. His tutelage of the guards, showing them how to channel Craft, saved many lives. His final sacrifice saved even more. He'll be remembered as a hero."

That small and broken something twisted in my throat all the tighter.

"Take him back to his room," Soya said to one of the guards unhappily.

I was turned and marched back to where I came, shackled, hating myself for the tears now pouring down my face.

AFTER A WHILE, the body rejects overwhelming heartbreak and despair as a method of self-preservation and falls into a sort of emotional numbness. Where once I had been mourning my brother, hating myself, being swallowed by the void in my own heart, I now felt nothing. And while logically I recognized that this was likely the farthest thing from progress, emotionally I was grateful for the reprieve. Numbness was better than the alternative.

The monsoon raged, the riots grew ever louder, and the days ticked on. I dreamt of Perenor every night.

Four weeks into the season, the entire castle had packed itself up. The Lord-Regent, his council, Soya, every guard in Avenos, a fleet of functionaries, and a handful of servants all gathered a few weeks' worth of provisions and assembled the caravan that would take us south along the coast, to the nondescript little port down of Andwelum. I had never even heard of it before, though I was willing to wager neither had most of the others on their way to it.

We set out on a dark, cold morning. The monsoon was in full force, drowning the city and surrounding moors with sheets and sheets of water.

Mine was a carriage in a line of dozens. I was covered by a nondescript black cloak. My head was down. I was unornamented – save for my new manacles, of course – and virtually indistinguishable from any of the others as we made our slow, plodding way out of Avenos.

The citizens, lined up along the street as we passed, must have recognized me through the windows of my carriage anyway, because as soon as the crowds were thick enough, I could hear them start to shout.

They screamed out things like "death to the traitor god" and "kill the treacherous Godspeaker." They shrieked obscenities and threats, and despite what I knew to be my better judgment, I watched their faces as we passed.

I marveled at the absolute, all-encompassing hatred. They knew nothing about me past my station, but already they loathed me with such force that they wanted to kill me. And despite everything, I couldn't blame them. I wondered how many of them had lost a spouse or a child or a parent in the attack. I'm sure I would have felt better if I'd been able to blame someone in Perenor's death.

"*You bring ruin to our city!*" screamed one, a blacksmith by the look of her.

"Kill the Godspeaker!" shouted another. "Let him taste the ruin he brought on us! Kill the Godspeaker!"

"Kill the Godspeaker!" they began to chant. "Kill the Godspeaker! Kill the Godspeaker!"

There was a tingling in my fingertips, a feeling that I could not immediately identify. After a while, I realized it was anxiety. After everything, I thought myself numbed to my fears of other people - or at the very least, more occupied with a far grander terror - but there it was, raising pinpricks along my flesh. It was almost comforting to feel it again.

At that moment, there was a tremendous sound, and my entire carriage rocked to one side. I screamed once, hoarsely, and nearly fell over.

"Stay back!" one nearby guard shouted - or tried to shout - over the mob. "Do not approach the Godspeaker!"

There was another shove, not as strong as the first. Outside my carriage, two of the guards were physically holding back the mob, bloodthirsty and shouting.

The old anxieties were thrumming now, in the deepest part of me, but I found it frighteningly easy to ignore. I gripped my knees and stared forward, sinking back into the numbness.

"Kill the Godspeaker!" they chanted. "Kill the Godspeaker! Kill the Godspeaker!"

Numbness was not good, but it felt safe. The crowds roiled and hated and chanted, and the caravan marched on, the caravan marched on.

WE MADE CAMP only once. I was not let out of my carriage. I curled up on the wooden floor and didn't sleep.

Andwelum, as it turned out, was a dingy little coastal town, nondescript, made up mostly of squat buildings with weathered tin roofs. It had neither the splendor of Ellorian nor the mightiness of Avenos. It didn't even have a wall; the city just sort of happened at one unremarkable spot where the moor met the coast.

And yet when we arrived, it was overrun. There were people everywhere, although none of them seemed to like it much. When the head of our caravan came into the city, someone shouted, "*Make way for the Lord-Regent!*" There was an echoing answer of, "*Make way, make way!*"

Andwelum remained unimpressive the closer we got. Its buildings were weatherbeaten, its streets muddy, and I could detect the stink of blood lingering beneath the wood smoke and dirt. Though I tried not to imagine to what had happened to such a poorly-defended coastal town this close to Avenos, images appeared in my mind anyway, unbidden.

The other members of the caravan were dismounting their camels, climbing out of their carriages, beginning the process of unpacking and settling. As I was wondering whether or not I would be let out of my carriage this time, I heard voices from outside.

"... large building on the north side of the city," said a familiar voice. "So far as we can tell, it once served as a town hall of sorts. It should be sufficient.

"Good," said another voice that I knew to be the Lord-Regent's.

"Ours was the first caravan to arrive," said the other voice. I recognized it, too, though I couldn't immediately tell from where. I moved closer to the door of my carriage. "The city was abandoned."

"Not abandoned, I don't think," said a third voice, Soya's.

"No," agreed the Lord-Regent grimly, "not abandoned."

"Is this him?"

They had stopped outside my carriage.

"Yes. Please, Your Holiness, for your own safety, stand back."

I sat up a little straighter. Could it possibly be—?

"I have no fear for my safety, Lord-Regent."

The carriage door was pulled open, and I squinted against the sudden light. In long waxed cloaks streaked with rain stood Soya, her father the Lord-Regent, and—

—and, gods, it was Rolen, Godspeaker to Aemor. It felt as though an age had passed since I last saw him. He was worse for wear, though no worse than me, I was sure.

Incredibly, there was not a trace of suspicion on his face. I was so unaccustomed to seeing an expression of trust that it took me a moment to identify the emotion that was on his face. I eventually recognized it as eclipsing sadness.

"Silas," he said. "It's so good to see you."

He reached out both hands into the carriage toward me. The gesture seemed to not only surprise but offend the Lord-Regent, the guards outside my carriage, and many of the onlookers standing in the mud outside. At once I could hear frantic whispering.

I hesitated a moment, swallowed the knot in my throat, and took his outstretched hands.

"Please, fetch him a waxed cloak," Rolen said to a nearby functionary.

"Your Holiness—!" the Lord-Regent began.

"*Now*, please," he interjected, firmly but not unkindly, with the exact inflection needed to silence dissent. The Lord-Regent growled in the back of his throat, but the functionary was already scurrying off to fetch one from a trunk secured to the back of my carriage.

Rolen helped me gently from my carriage. Rain began drumming at once on my hair and face, but it was worth it to breathe fresh air. I looked slowly at my surroundings. Soya was frowning; the Lord-Regent looked about ready to scream, and all the servants and guards were staring at me with outright distrust. It was only Rolen who was putting one arm around my shoulders, and I tried not to be stunned by the gesture.

The functionary soon came back with a waxed cloak. Rolen swept it over my shoulders for me. I shivered, though whether from the cold or the staring onlookers, I couldn't say.

Rolen once again put his arm around my shoulders and started to move toward a large building that looks like an inn. The crowd parted in the middle, creating a long but narrow path up toward its front door.

"I can't help but notice those manacles you wear, Silas," he said to me softly as we walked, and I kept my eyes down. "Did the Lord-Regent force this indignity on you?"

I deeply and thoroughly owed him an answer, but it had been over a week since I'd used my voice, and all that came out at first was a dreadful croaking sound. I tried again.

"It's – it's f-f-f-fine."

"It is most certainly not fine," Rolen said, "but you are lovely to bear these cruelties with such grace. These people stare at you as if you're some monster in need of caging."

"P-p-perhaps I am," I said.

"Silas, if there is no respite for a man of your supreme patience and graciousness, then there is no respite for anyone."

I didn't quite know what to say, so I stayed quiet. Compliments of any sort were entirely alien to me, especially lately.

"Your mother is waiting for you, Silas."

I took in a sharp breath. I looked up at him just as we made it to the lobby of the inn and he shrugged of his cloak. I had a lot of tangled, painful emotions tied up in her, but one rose far above the rest: I wanted to see her. "Wh-wh-wh-wh—?"

"Upstairs," he said. "You can go now, if you like."

"We can't allow him to just *go* anywhere, Holiness," the Lord-Regent interjected, having followed us inside. His cloak was removed by a servant.

"Then we shall have to pull rank on you, won't we?"

The voice had come from the side. I turned to see Greatmother Amira, dark hair rain-streaked, boots up on a table by the fireplace. She looked tired, and somehow more dangerous than usual.

"Holiness," the Lord-Regent said, quickly adjusting to the sight of Sol's Godspeaker in his presence, "I'm afraid I'm going to have to insist. The boy has proven—"

"He is not a boy, Lord-Regent," Greatmother Amira interjected harshly. "He is a Godspeaker. And he is *not* your prisoner."

"He has proven time and time again that he is a threat to everyone around him!" the Lord-Regent said.

"Don't mistake your perceptions for proof, Lord-Regent," Rolen returned without missing a beat. "You are absolutely incapable of knowing his experience."

"He is a threat that must be controlled," the Lord-Regent said.

Clang. It was the sound of Greatmother Amira's mug of something – ale, perhaps – hitting the table. It was loud enough to silence everyone all at once.

I watched as she rose to her feet, as she crossed the weathered, aging wood floor toward me. She hooked a finger under the chain linking my manacles and lifted them up to inspect them.

"Show me a man who thinks he can control a god," Greatmother Amira said pointedly, "and I'll show you a fool."

"I'd be careful about preaching wisdom, Holiness," the Lord-Regent said, slowly. "Wisdom is lovely in theory, but in practice, I have an entire kingdom now under my protection."

"Gods help them all, then, because they don't seem to be helping you," Greatmother Amira said.

I stood for a while in stupefied silence. Although it made perfect sense for them to empathize, I still found it mystifying. I'd prepared myself to live the rest of my life at the mercy of no one. I swallowed the knot of welling emotion in my throat.

"P-p-please," I said. "My m-m-mother—"

"She's upstairs," Rolen said, smiling warmly. "And rest assured, you may count on privacy. We still outrank the Lord-Regent."

I stared up at him gratefully, hoping my expression could convey everything my stubborn tongue could not. I hurried past him, up the creaking stairs, and into a narrow hallway, where standing at the far end—

"Silas!"

She was haggard, sleep-deprived. Her eyes reminded me of Perenor's.

At once, tears went streaming down my face.

"M-M-M-M—!"

I ran for her, and she crashed into me, holding me so tightly that all those years of mistreatment felt like some evil, distant dream. I was awash in that uniquely childlike security - what son is ever afraid of anything while in his mother's arms, after all?

"Silas," she sobbed into my hair. "Gods, you're alive - I'd feared—"

She didn't have the words for it - so few of us did, despite how many had already died - but I knew well enough what she meant. She held me all the tighter in her arms, and with my own hands bound, I could only bury my face in her shoulder and press into her as tightly as I could.

"You've lost weight," she told me, voice thick, and it took everything in me not to sob. "Don't they feed you in Avenos? And you're in chains! Gods, what happened? We've had no word!"

But for my stutter, I would have been espousing how deeply and profoundly wonderful it was to see her, how much I had missed her, despite the fact that I'd never had the time to notice.

"Come inside - they have a room for you—"

She ushered me inside the door outside of which she'd been standing. It was a plain, dirty, nondescript little room, but I don't think anything could have made me notice. Together we sat down on the edge of the bed, and she carded her fingers through my hair like when I was still a little boy.

"I never thought I'd see you again," she said as she kissed my temple. "Thank the gods, thank the gods. When we heard word that Umbrion's Godspeaker was in Avenos, we could hardly believe it. What happened? Where's Perenor?"

The wounds were still fresh, of course, and her question pulled them open again. Gods, how could I answer her when grief had all but stolen my voice for weeks? How could I tell her what she needed to know when I was a useless, stuttering mess?

"Silas?" she asked when I didn't answer. "Where's your brother?"

She withdrew and looked down at me. Some shadow of an answer must have been visible on my face, because all the blood drained from hers.

"Silas?" she said again, more urgently.

I swallowed a hard knot in my throat.

"He f-f-f-f-f-f-fell," I stammered. "In b-b-b-battle, he f-f-f-f-fell..."

She clapped a hand over her mouth.

"A g-g-g-great d-d-demon," I choked, fighting back as best I could the ever-encroaching tears. "He w-w-w-was th-thrown..."

"No," she said, and my tears came anyway.

"He d-d-d-died to s-s-s-save the c-c-city," I told her, though my throat was growing ever tighter. "He g-g-g-gave up his l-l-l-life, everything in he c-c-c-could g-give..."

"No," she said again. "No, gods, please no—"

"I'm s-s-s-s-s-sorry," I stammered at her. "I'm s-s-so s-s-sorry, it's m-m-my fault—"

"Silas—"

"I sh-sh-shouldn't have l-l-let him g-g-g-go," I said, face not wet with tears, shoulders shaking, hands wringing in my manacles. "He w-w-w-was in n-n-no c-condition to f-f-fight, I sh-shouldn't h-h-h-have—"

"Don't you dare," she said, pulling me into her arms again. "Don't you dare, Silas. I'm not going to lose another son. Not to war, and not to his own grief. Do you understand me?"

I understood her; whether or not I could believe her was another matter entirely. We sat together a while, her hand in my hair, as I curled up against her and tried to hide from my grief for no other reason than I was not sure how much more I could live through.

"I will not lose you," she whispered to me, over and over. I was not sure if it was meant to reassure me or herself. "I will not lose you."

MOTHER AND I had dinner that night in that room at the end of the hall, with two guards posted outside my door. The food was sub-par and all my old wounds were aching, but for the first time the ache felt more like healing and less like dying. A pain shared, it seemed, truly was a pain halved.

We didn't talk much. Every time one of us tried, the subject inevitably turned dark, and my mother would grip my wrist and say, "There's no point in discussing it here, like this." And she was right, of course - what point was there in trying to make sense of tragedy when the tragedy had not yet ended? - and we would drop the subject and fall into silence.

And it wasn't ideal, but it was good. Good to be with her, good to share the burden of our losses.

"Wh-wh-where's G-Grandmother?" I asked eventually, half-wondering if I really wanted to know.

"With the Lady Queen, I'd imagine," Mother answered, picking at her breast of roast duck. I sat up straighter in the flimsy wooden chair.

"The L-L-L-L-Lady Queen yet l-lives?"

"'Survives' may be the better term," she replied grimly. "The loss of her wife nearly broke her. But yes, she lives."

I took a sip of the weak, cooling tea. Part of me wanted to seek her out and offer condolences, but the rest of me knew better. Even if I would be let out of my room - which seemed unlikely - I doubted she would want to see the face of the man who reached out his hand and ripped her wife apart.

"Your grandmother does want to see you," she said, and I looked up at her. "She's just busy. She's one of the most senior on the Queenscourt, and she's been trying to make sense of this new political chaos."

"Th-th-th-that is the d-d-duty of House Olen," I sighed.

"Silas," Mother said gently, "don't be too hard on her. She was as wounded as any of us by the Breaking. Her sense of duty is strong. You can't fault her that."

I felt as though I could, but for Mother's sake, I wouldn't. I took another sip of tea.

There came a few muffled voices through the doorway. I couldn't make out the words at first, but as they came closer, they got clearer:

"The Godspeaker is not allowed unscheduled visitors." It was one of the guards. "Lord-Regent's orders."

"I could give a fuck about the Lord-Regent and his orders," came the answer, and I knew at once who it was. "He's not *my* Lord-Regent and he never has been. Are you going to move aside or aren't you?"

"It's G-G-G-Greatmother Amira," I said to Mother, who straightened in her chair.

"Should we – do we stand? What's the form of address—?"

"It d-d-doesn't matter," I assured her.

The door opened a moment later.

"Silas," Greatmother Amira said, striding into the room. She was still in her fitted leathers and knee-high boots. "I apologize for interrupting, but—"

"No, no, no," my mother said, rising respectfully from the table. "Please, I'm sure you have much to talk about."

"I won't be long," Greatmother Amira said.

"Of course," Mother obliged. "Silas, I'll come find you after dinner. I'll try to find your grandmother."

I smiled as best I could, though I fear it came out more like a grimace, as I wasn't sure I wanted to see her at all. I watched as Mother left, then looked back at Greatmother Amira.

"You've had no further contact with...?"

It took me a moment, but only a moment. I shook my head.

"Good," she said. "That's good. On the grand scale of things, at least. The moot begins officially tomorrow, and though there have been no formal discussions, most of the Godspeakers are already in agreement on the plan of action."

I stared up at her in confusion.

"It's something that hasn't been attempted in an age," she said. "Not since my people were stranded on Onansu."

For a few moments I couldn't glean the meaning of her words, until I could. It was something I'd only ever heard of through history books, and I realized, somewhat belatedly, that Greatmother Amira was the living embodiment of that history.

"Y-y-y-y-you're talking about—"

"When the gods came down in what your kingdom calls the Manifest, we – the Ansu – were too far to hear them, too far to know," she said, sitting down across from me. "But we saw the Worldmother's Light on the horizon and we yearned for it. Back then, Onansu was an unforgiving place, rocky and unyielding.

"For weeks, we prayed to that far-off light for some respite, for some aid and understanding. And eventually, it worked. The Worldmother came down from the sky, burning white, and she grew the jungles up around us."

"She m-m-m-made you her Godspeaker," I said. "The f-f-first."

"Yes," Greatmother Amira said, "with a kiss. She blessed me and all of my people with great knowledge and strength. It led us across the waters, to your fledgling kingdom of Imlandran. It led us to develop horticulture, husbandry, mathematics, philosophy."

"And w-w-w-we're g-going to r-r-repeat that p-process?"

"If it worked with a few hundred people praying and fasting for a few weeks, imagine what all five Godspeakers could do in just a few hours."

Something cold twisted inside of me. "Y-y-y-you m-m-mean to summon the gods? Can s-s-such a thing b-b-b-be done?"

"It happened once," she said. "Perhaps it can be done again."

It seemed wholly and absurdly dangerous. Summon the Night Father? Here? Had she not seen all the destruction he'd wrought?

But then again, it would not be him alone that would be summoned. All his siblings and his mother would also be there. Would they be able to keep him under something resembling control? More to the point, was it worth risking everything on the assumption that they could?

"It's v-very r-r-risky," I said.

"Yes, it is," she answered. "Extremely. But these are desperate times and they call for desperate measures."

"I d-d-don't think it's a g-good idea."

"Have you got a better one?" she countered, raising both eyebrows.

"N-not this," I said. "Umbrion only b-b-b-brings d-destruction in his w-wake. It w-w-would be a f-fool's errand to try and s-s-summon him."

"It would be a far greater error to do nothing," she said.

"F-f-forgive me, G-Greatmother, b-b-but any t-time I've d-d-done anything, it has only r-r-resulted in d-d-death."

I regretted speaking at once. The words came from a place too close to my heart, were too revealing. Greatmother Amira gave me a long, measuring look, and I averted my eyes. There followed a very, very long pause.

"I heard about what happened to your brother."

I wet my lips. Of course she'd heard.

"I'm so sorry, Silas."

I appreciated her words of comfort for what they were, but drawing any real comfort from them was impossible. I stood up and walked to the window, rubbing at the manacles around my wrists.

"I can't help but wonder if that's the seed of your defeatism," she said. "I certainly wouldn't blame you if it was. I heard your friend's story – Soya. She told me everything that's happened. Everything around you breaks. People die, temples topple, and then you lose your brother."

"G-G-G-Greatmother—"

"There's a word in the Ansu tongue that doesn't have a direct translation in Andelish," she told me. "It expresses a loss so profound, a heartbreak so complete, that you start to forget what it meant to be whole. *Inwari.*

"But there's a famous idiom about *inwari*," she continued. "*Mori ite anda inwari do.* It means that *inwari* follows only where there was truest love."

I felt her hand on my shoulder. My throat constricted, but I wouldn't let myself cry. I'd done too much of it already.

"It hurts because it meant something," she told me. "It hurts because he was your brother. So don't begrudge yourself your own *inwari*. Let it hurt. And for your own sake, don't let it make you forget what it is to be whole."

I nodded, though I scarcely knew why. To end the conversation, likely.

"I'll see you tomorrow at the moot," she said. "Until then, find what peace you can. It's in short supply these days."

Her hand fell from my shoulder. I heard her leave out the door and down the hallway, knowing that if I had ever been whole, I was sure I never would be again.

"—DO NOT THINK it *wise—*"

"He has lost a brother."

"His is not the only loss in Andelan!"

I wondered if they knew how thin these walls were.

"He needs us right now, Mother. Who else would be there for him?"

"We do not yet know his loyalties."

"*Mother!*"

I leaned my head against the wall. I was sitting cross-legged on the bed, wondering if I was meant to feel offended by the fact that my own grandmother thought me a traitor to the gods. On top of everything else, I found it difficult to feel anything at all. I twisted my wrists in my shackles and wrung the brass chain.

"You know as well as I do that Silas had no hand in the Breaking. There isn't a conspiratorial bone in his body! You're only resisting because—"

"Because it *hurts?*" my grandmother said, voice harsh. "Because seeing him will always remind me of his brother, who's dead and burnt? Because Perenor is dead and that *kills me?*"

"It kills him, too!"

"I c-c-can hear you," I said, loud enough to be heard through the flimsy wooden door. If I had to listen to them argue a moment longer, I was going to lose my mind.

Their words, at least, abruptly stopped.

It took them a while, but eventually the door opened. Mother came first, uneasy but apologetic.

"The walls are thin," she said.

Grandmother entered. She looked so much older, somehow, and

she stared at me with what I'm sure she hoped to look like suspicion, but I could see right through her. The flimsy veneer of mistrust was hiding nothing but heartache and exhaustion.

"S-s-s-so are we," I answered.

"Always so clever," Grandmother snapped.

"So d-d-does it k-kill you to-to-to l-look at m-me?" I asked.

Her response wasn't immediate. I watched all the subtle lines of her face shift one by one. Traces of doubt, of remorse, of anger, all of it masked almost perfectly. Almost.

"Yes," she answered after the lapse of silence. "Your mother tells me he died in battle."

I nodded slowly.

Grandmother swore under her breath. "Foolish boy," she said. "As soon as I felt the city breaking, I knew, I *knew*..."

"We shouldn't talk about this," Mother said softly.

"I-I-I-I had h-half expected y-y-you to-to b-b-blame me f-f-for his d-death," I said.

"There's much I blame you for," she said, "but not for this. "There's a reason Perenor was so skilled in Craft. More than anyone, he was unafraid of sacrifice. He was always so ready to put others before himself, to—"

"Please," Mother said, voice drawn, "please, let's not speak on this."

"Mother..."

I moved toward the edge of the bed and took her hands in mine. She offered me a valiant smile and sat down beside me.

Grandmother watched us, face studiously blank.

"You've been in Avenos," she said after a moment.

I nodded again.

"How find you the new Lord-Regent?" she asked. "Is he a reasonable man?"

I wasn't sure where this was going, but I had my suspicions. "Qu-qu-quick to anger, p-p-perhaps," I answered, "and one who d-d-does n-not operate t-t-terribly well under p-p-pressure, but n-not unr-r-reasonable."

"Good," she said. "Good. Then perhaps all hope is not yet lost for a stable Andelan."

I frowned.

"Y-y-y-you think of p-p-politics," I said.

"Someone must."

"Now?" I asked, feeling anger rise in me. "Wh-wh-when there are g-g-g-gods who would s-seek to destroy y-you?"

"What good does fear do?" she snapped at me, like she had been waiting all evening for an excuse. "Nothing! Especially in times like these, Andelan cries out for leadership, for order in the chaos!"

"Y-y-your grandson is n-n-not five w-weeks dead!"

"And would you have him *die in vain?* He gave up his *life* for this world—!"

"Stop it!" Mother said suddenly, shrilly. "Stop it, both of you! For so long, you've been at odds with one another! Can you not find common ground in these most desperate times?

We both fell silent for a while. Grandmother looked out the window; I stared down at the floor.

"This is a family that is so much smaller than it used to be," Mother said. "Our husbands, our son. Surely here at the end of all things, we can overcome our differences?"

When I reluctantly lifted my eyes back to Grandmother's, I found her looking back at me, still angry, still suspicious, but now with traces of something like guilt.

"I don't know," she said. "How deep do they run?"

She seemed as though she wanted a real answer, so I considered the question a moment. Outside, rain pattered on the glass.

"Quite d-d-deep," I said at last. "M-m-my chief c-complaint has ever b-b-been that m-matters of the state have alw-w-ways taken p-p-precedence."

She stayed quiet, her eyes running me through.

"I have d-distant m-m-memories of y-your affection, b-b-but they w-w-were so l-long ago. I s-s-spent the bulk of m-my childhood b-b-being trained to f-f-feel inadequate," I continued. "I s-s-struggle to recall the l-l-last time I f-felt wanted."

Perhaps I'd said too much. I wrung my hands in my lap.

There was a lapse of silence. I'd never felt so vulnerable. Despite our long and tangled history, never once had we let these things out in the open - and now there they were, all my scars, fresh and bloody as they day they were carved, open and awaiting judgment.

But none came, because before too long, there was a knock at the door.

Beside me, Mother straightened. "Yes?"

The door opened. It was a young woman, a servant at Silverwatch, one who'd come with the caravan. "His Holiness's - er, your dinner's been prepared, sir."

I nodded my thanks. The functionary ducked back out at the words before the door opened wider so she could carry in a large tray.

"Let's eat," Mother said, voice wan.

I nodded again. All that was said and unsaid were still hanging in the air like a choking fog, and as the servant went to set the small, rickety table, we languished in the unsteady silence.

"IT'S FAR TOO DANGEROUS!" bellowed Lady Aevor from the side of the table.

"There's no other option!" shouted Greatmother Amira back at her.

(The reader must forgive me for not including the whole text of the moot. Though I'm aware it would have some historical significance, there was very little said that didn't boil down to the above two points. I'm rather pressed for time, so some truncation is necessary.)

"You would put all of Imlandran in peril – all of Andelan!"

"We need answers," Rolen said, sounding nearly as angry as he did exhausted. "And more to the point, the gods need answers. All the Godspeakers have prayed for guidance, and we have all been met with the same answer – that Umbrion will not speak to them, that they cannot find him."

"If there is any hope in stymieing this, it lies in the other gods," Fiyera continued, and I was amazed by her patience – this must have been the twentieth time she'd reiterated that very point. "We have his Godspeaker, which means we have leverage. We can force Umbrion into the open, force him to confront his family."

"There are ten thousand ways that could backfire," the Lord-Regent said, voice clipped. "There are ten thousand ways it could make everything worse!"

"Do you really think there's any fate worse than what he doubtlessly already has in store?" Soya demanded. She was sitting at her father's right hand, literally as much as symbolically. "You heard Silas before those demons came crawling out of the water – he called them the vanguard! I would rather hazard this than whatever else the Traitor God has planned."

"Umbrion answers to Silas alone," Greatmother Amira said, and I felt fifty pairs of nervous eyes move to me, and then quickly away.

It must have taken more effort to ignore me than to look at me, because I was chained to a chair in the center of the room, manacles on and shackled to the floor by both ankles. Undignified, perhaps, but I didn't have much dignity left to preserve anyway.

"Umbrion manifests for Silas alone. This is the only way to ensure that the other gods can't get to him."

"This is foolish," Lady Aevor growled, sitting back in her seat.

"This is the only way," Fiyera said.

Everyone collectively seemed to realize that this was the fiftieth time they'd been round this point. Many sat back; others rubbed their eyes; some muttered to servants to bring them food or wine.

The large hall had felt comfortable at one point – the tables had been set up in a great U-shape, the outer half-ring lined with chairs to seat the most important people in Andelan – the Lord-Regent, all four other Lords and Ladies, the Godspeakers, the surviving Queenscourt, the councilors, the diplomats, a smattering of thanes from larger cities.

But after five long hours, it had stopped feeling comfortable. My legs ached from disuse. My head pounded from all the shouting. My wrists and ankles chafed from their bindings. None of the functionaries had dared come close enough to serve me any food, though without a table, I wouldn't have been able to eat it anyway.

I wondered on more than one occasion if there was any point in my being here. No one had asked me anything – they were all too nervous to even look at me longer than a few seconds at a time. My function in this discussion appeared to be a prop.

"And what if this is all a trap?" Lady Aevor asked, following a lengthy pause.

"Careful," Greatmother Amira said lowly.

"You're all thinking it," Lady Aevor growled. "Don't try to lie and say you aren't. What if this is precisely what the Traitor God wants? He would have plenty of reason to get the other gods in the same place at the same time. How can we even be sure of where the boy's loyalties lie?"

"This is not a *boy*, Lady of Aevorlum," Greatmother Amira said. "This is a Godspeaker – a Godspeaker who has as much skin in this conflict as any of you. I'd suggest that you keep your tongue behind your teeth on subjects with which you are woefully unfamiliar."

Not that it wasn't nice to have someone come to my defense, but it was rather aggravating being spoken about as though I wasn't there.

Still, I've always been one to pick my battles.

"The kingdom have always valued your counsel, Your Holiness," the Lord-Regent said, "but surely you must realize why we're so hesitant to trust him in any capacity."

"I realize it fine," she answered. "I am merely pointing out that you're wrong to do so."

In a room full of powerful people unaccustomed to being so spoken to, it was an interesting – and, I admit, rather amusing – study in their facial expressions. They were by turns horrified, indignant, aghast, embarrassed, and none of them were willing to talk back to Sol's Godspeaker.

"What does the Worldmother think of him?" the Lord-Regent asked suddenly.

It was a good question, and the room reacted accordingly. Every head swiveled in the Greatmother's direction.

"She has said nothing about him one way or the other," she admitted.

"Troubling," muttered a woman on the Lord-Regent's council.

"What of your seers?" the Lord-Regent asked. "Onansu has an entire council of seers. Have they no prophecies on him? On anything?"

"Your question misunderstands the theory of prophecy," she answered. "And time as a concept." Her patience was starting to wear thin, clearly.

"Fine. Then what of the other Godspeakers?"

I turned my head to the left. They were all lined up at the table across the way.

Fiyera sighed. "We are Godspeakers, same as him. We don't need to know his mind to know his innocence. Even if he conspired as you all seem to believe he has, we know that he would not have had a choice in that conspiracy."

"You'd be so apologetic to him?" said one of the thanes, sounding off-put. "Even if he was willing?"

"There can be no willingness where there is no choice," Fiyera said. "We are *servants* to the gods. We have *always* been—"

"Don't bother," Greatmother Amira said. "They will not and cannot understand."

I stared at them, heart aching. Empathy - it wasn't something I'd ever anticipated feeling again. Emotion knotted in my throat and I looked down at my knees.

There came another lapse of silence. Every pair of eyes turned to the Lord-Regent. In the absence of the Queen, he was the ultimate authority, and it would be his decision on what course of action to take.

And after a long pause, the Lord-Regent sighed. "Be it at your peril, then, Godspeakers," he said.

"My Lord—!" began one councilor, aghast.

"You cannot seriously—" began another.

The Lord-Regent held up one hand to silence the detractors. "We'll empty this city of all those not necessary to assist the Godspeakers in their work," he said. "I am sure they'd be willing to give us a day's start to flee the area."

Greatmother Amira hesitated a moment, then nodded. "A day."

"Therefore whatever happens," the Lord-Regent continued, "we'll have a day's ride on it."

The shouting started up again, this time with more volume. Words like "absurd" and "madness" were thrown around quite a lot. Several people stood. I heard some accusing the Lord-Regent of abusing his new power, and others start shouting about what Queen Nerisa would do in this situation.

It carried on for quite some time, a jumbled cacophony of hurling insults and outrage, before it was all silenced by a sudden, loud, thunderous *crack* of metal on wood.

Soya, now standing, had neatly impaled the crest of her hand-axe into the table in front of her. She was seething with rage.

"*What, then?*" she bellowed. "If not this, then *what?* What would the detractors have us *do?*"

No one answered, or at least not for quite some time.

"The gods—" began Lady Aevor, but Soya shouted her back down:

"*The gods can't find him!*" she thundered. "Or were you not paying attention? Would you wait for them? Would you have us hide from it all, barricade ourselves in our homes and cower like children, hoping that the Night Father fails, *somehow?* Or would you stand and *do something?*"

Soya stood waiting for a response, challenging them all with smoldering brown eyes. No answer came.

"If I am to die, I would die like Perenor!" she said, and his name lanced straight through me. "I would die standing in defiance of destiny! I would go down *fighting!* The Night Father took our immortality. Let's show him that it has not broken us!"

Greatmother Amira leaned over to Fiyera and muttered, "The girl is more a leader than her Lord Father."

Fiyera smirked, and I could not say a word to the contrary even if I cared to.

"From where I'm standing," Soya said, voice finally starting to settle, though her conviction had not wavered, "we have two paths before us. One is the path of action – and yes, it could bring us ruin. But the path of inaction erases all doubt of it!"

Tense silence choked the room like smoke. After a moment, the Lord-Regent rose and placed a hand on his daughter's back.

"My scion speaks with wisdom beyond her years," he said, "and courage beyond all expectation. Are there any who would find fault in her words?"

No one spoke. How tremendous Soya was at that moment. Had it only been a season ago when we were getting drunk together and stargazing? When had she grown from my rough-and-tumble friend to a Lady-Regent of Andelan?

"Then it is so decided," her father said. "In the absence of the Queen, I decree it in her stead: the Godspeakers will set their plan in motion. The rest of us leave at first light."

IN THEORY, the mass exodus from Andwelum wasn't to start until the next morning, but by the time I was escorted back to my main room in the inn not an hour after the end of the moot, I could already see several caravans lining up in preparation for departure. I could only imagine that for many it felt less like leaving and more like fleeing, and I found myself incapable of resentment. If it were me, I'd be fleeing, too.

I sat by my window for a time, wringing my aching wrists in their manacles, watching the bustle, wondering if I could sleep if I tried, wondering what tomorrow might bring, lost in the numbness of it all until there came a knock at the door.

I looked up, and before I could even gather the wherewithal to speak, it opened. A familiar head of long, red hair poked through.

"Sorry," said Arana, Godspeaker to Lilline, smiling, but looking deeply tired, "is this a bad time?"

I didn't answer, which turned out to not be a problem, because someone behind her did it for me:

"He's effectively being held prisoner, Arana." I recognized the voice as Fiyera's. "I can't imagine there would ever be a *good* time."

The door opened wider. All four other Godspeakers came inside, one by one. I looked on in a clouded combination of confusion and fatigue – Arana, Fiyera, Rolen, and finally Greatmother Amira.

"Everyone's leaving already," Arana said, sitting down on the bed beside me. Rolen sat at the table, Fiyera stood by the window, and Greatmother Amira leaned against the wall nearest the door after it closed behind her. "They must be eager."

"I suppose I can't blame them," said Fiyera as she peered out the window, "though it does make me wonder if they truly understand the scope of this. They flee Silas as though he's the enemy, or as though any amount of distance from him could shield them from the Night Father's wrath."

"Please, Fiyera," Greatmother Amira said coolly, "your optimism is embarrassing."

Fiyera turned around. "Don't expect me to apologize for the truth, Greatmother."

"Let's not think unkindly of them," Rolen said. "They're just scared. We're all scared."

"Which is why we need to talk about tomorrow," the Greatmother returned. "So far as I'm aware, I'm the only person in this room who's ever made any concerted effort to summon a god."

"That was a rather unique circumstance, wasn't it?" Arana asked.

Greatmother Amira shrugged. "This isn't?"

That was a fair point, the room seemed to collectively decide.

"It's not a Godspeaker's natural purview to directly ask the gods to do anything, so I can't imagine it ever would be anything but a unique circumstance."

I looked between them. For a time, none of them said anything.

"So what will we be doing?" Fiyera asked. "Specifically. What did you do all those seasons ago?"

Greatmother Amira shifted her weight from foot to foot. Remembering seemed to make her uncomfortable.

"It was myself and several of my closest friends," she said. "It was during the monsoon. We spent months praying to the distant light on the horizon for some respite."

"So you just—" Arana paused, hunting for the word. "You just willed her to you through prayer?"

"It was closer to meditation," the Greatmother admitted. "A circle of us, sitting on a rocky outcropping, heads bowed in concentration. We had spent so long on the inhospitable rock that was Onansu and morale was low. There were some who wanted to give up on the light on the horizon, but I urged them onward anyway, because there was nothing left but the hope of something better.

"And when she finally came..."

It wasn't relevant, strictly speaking, but we all hung on her every word anyway. The parallel wasn't lost on us.

"A great slice opened up in the clouds, and the sun came through," she said slowly. "She was brightly burning, skin like dark copper, hair flowing like smoke in wind – the most ecstatically beautiful creature I had ever laid eyes on. And when she landed on the rock, lush grass and meadow flowers rolled outward from her feet like ripples in water, spreading so quickly that the great rainforests were growing around us, towering trees and distant birdsong.

"And she came toward me, and the first thing she did was apologize."

"Apologize?" Arana repeated, startled.

"There was a great deal more she said besides, but yes. She told us she hadn't realized how careless she had been, spreading out all her children so far, even in places where there was no other life. That's why she gave us the rainforests, why she bent down to give me the Benediction, a kiss that gave the Ansu the greatest gift she could give – courage, even in the face of terrible darkness."

"The Worldmother's Flame," Rolen said, and Greatmother Amira nodded.

I swallowed thickly. Little pinpricks of emotion were seeping into me. That was what Perenor had been bringing out in the Avenos guard, and even in himself in his last moments alive. The Worldmother's Flame, as strong as everything in him, that saved the city.

"Umbrion took her Light from us," Fiyera said slowly. "Do you think he could take her Flame as well?"

The Greatmother hesitated. "I don't know," she admitted.

"I know that Aemor would never allow it," Rolen said at once. "He was wrought from that Flame, and he loves it dearly."

"How does the god of love spring from the flame of courage?" Arana asked, mostly to herself by the tone.

"There's no greater act of courage than to love," Rolen answered, smiling smally, "completely and selflessly."

I thought of Perenor again, Perenor and his sacrifice, and for a moment I even thought of Umbrion. He had never known the Worldmother's Flame. He was wrought of the shadow it cast. I wondered if it had made him lonely, if anyone had loved him. I wondered if I had. I think there's still some part of me wondering that.

This silence was longer than the first, all of us falling into our thoughts until Arana spoke, voice small:

"Will this work?" she asked.

It was the question on all our minds, perhaps. No one said anything for a time.

"I don't know," Greatmother Amira answered after a moment. "But I don't think the knowing is what's important. What's important is the trying."

"And if it b-b-b-backfires?" I said. I was looking away, but I could feel their eyes on me. "W-w-will it have b been worth it to t-t-t-try then?"

"Yes, Silas," Greatmother Amira said. I'd expected her to sound cross, but she only sounded sad.

"This is f-f-f-folly," I said. "If th-th-this curse has t-t-taught me anything, it's th-th-that there is n-n-no reward for effort wh-wh-when you align y-y-yourself against the g-g-gods. This c-c-can do n-nothing but h-hasten the end."

"Good," said Greatmother Amira.

It hadn't been the response I was expecting. I looked back at her. "Wh-wh-wh-wh—?"

"I said good," she repeated. "I would rather that be the alternative outcome. Either end this apocalypse now or hasten it. What would you rather see, Silas? A long, protracted, bloody, and inevitably pointless war? It's like your friend said – inaction may save us now, but not forever."

I opened my mouth as if I wanted to speak, but no words came. I shut my mouth again a moment later.

"Greatmother, be kind," Rolen said. "He's been through much."

"I know he has," Greatmother Amira answered. "And that's why I harbor no anger for him. Silas, if I'd been through what you've been through, I would spurn the mere idea of action, as well. But inaction isn't a rejection of any outcome, it's a submission to all of them."

I tried – so, so hard, I tried – to make myself hear and believe the wisdom in her words, but after having everything around me crumble and break, it was the hardest thing in the world.

The floorboards creaked in front of me. I looked up from my lap and saw Greatmother Amira crouched in front of me.

"Do this knowing it could backfire. Do this knowing all the world could end because of it. Do this because despite what this world has done to you, you know it's still worth saving. Do this because no one else can and because there's no other way."

Perhaps there was no wisdom in her words. Perhaps there didn't need to be. Perhaps my injured, mourning heart had mistaken necessity for philosophy. I swallowed hard and nodded, resigning myself again to what felt like an inevitable chasm of doubt.

Greatmother Amira bent forward and kissed my forehead. I squinted back the threat of tears.

"We'll leave the day after tomorrow," she said, rising to her feet. "We'll go to the temple outside Andwelum to avoid collateral damage, if it can be avoided."

I could not imagine it would be. By the way the silence lingered, neither did anyone else.

CARAVAN BY CARAVAN, starting at the earliest hours of pre-dawn, the sleepy-little coastal down emptied. The caravan bound north for Stormhold left first, followed by the caravan bound south across the water, to Whiterock. The crowds thinned and the hum of people gave way to the hiss of rain.

"Your Grandmother went back with the Lord-Regent to Avenos," Mother told me as we stood by the window and watched the last caravan leave, bound for Onanwa. It was likely the caravan Greatmother Amira would be going with, if she could go at all.

"Ever the p-p-p-p-politician," I said under my breath.

"Don't be unkind, Silas."

I wanted to ask her why not, ask her why Grandmother deserved my kindness after everything, but I was too tired, too nervous. In less than a day, I and the other Godspeakers would be attempting a thing against all odds, and despite the likely doom it would bring down on us all. Being angry with my grandmother was not high on my list of priorities.

"But I'm staying," Mother said after a moment, and I felt her hand on my back.

I looked over at her, startled. I thought she would just spend the last night before leaving in the morning. Despite my better judgment, I asked, "Wh-wh-wh-why?"

"Because I spent nine long, painful hours birthing you," she answered. "Because I don't think I ever dedicated enough time to being your mother. Because I love you."

The words felt strange and foreign to me. I couldn't remember a time when I'd ever heard them uttered to me with such sincerity and warmth. It set my heart to beating faster against my ribs, made y eyes burn.

"You sh-sh-sh-shouldn't," I said. "It's n-n-not s-safe."

"There's nothing safe left," she answered. She was trying to sound lighthearted, and it would have been funny, except that it was desperately grim.

"M-Mother—"

"You're my boy," she interjected, firmly by gently, "the only one I have left. I'm not leaving you, Silas. Especially not now."

Even if I knew the words that would talk her out of it, I doubted my own ability to stammer through them without breaking down into tears.

"Besides, if any god is going to lay a hand on you," she continued, smiling through suddenly mist eyes and stroking my hair, "they'll have to go through me first."

"D-d-d-don't s-say that," I muttered. "He w-would."

She smiled weakly and sidestepped the comment.

"And your friend is staying, too," she said. "Soya."

That was far more surprising than hearing Mother was staying behind. I hadn't spoken to her once since Perenor died "Sh-sh-sh-she is?"

"She must be," Mother said. "I saw her watch as her father left on his own caravan. I'm sure she just wants to assure your safety."

I didn't have the heart to tell her all that had changed between us, so I remained silent. Mother watched me, frowning, eyes sad.

Eventually, she sighed and kissed my temple. "I wish we had the time to get to know each other again," she said, and I found myself settling against her shoulder. "Perhaps we can, after this is all over."

"P-p-p-perhaps," I lied, knowing that however this ended, my life would not be a part of it. I think she knew it, too, deep down.

So we watched the last caravan leave, watched the rain beat against the glass and tried, desperately and unsuccessfully, to think of other things.

I DIDN'T SLEEP that night. I felt as though I might never sleep again.

My mind was white-hot with questions without answers. Would this work? Would it make any difference either way? Did Umbrion already know?

Speculating, of course, achieved nothing, but I did it relentlessly anyway, until dawn came fighting its way through the clouds and one of the few functionaries who'd stayed behind with the Godspeakers came knocking on my door to wake me up.

I washed my face and was escorted down into the main room of the tavern. Apparently there was no longer any call to keep me sequestered to my room – after all, the city was all but empty. Rolen, Fiyera, Arana, and Greatmother Amira were all pulling on boots and gloves and waxed cloaks.

"Good morning, Silas," Rolen said. "Did you sleep well?"

"No," I answered, seeing little point in lying.

"Neither did I," he returned with as much humor as he could manage.

"I suppose we're skipping breakfast," Arana said. She was braiding her long, red hair and knotting it into an elaborate bun at the back of her head.

"Why?" Fiyera asked. I could tell she was trying for glibness, but mostly she just sounded tired. "Hungry?"

"Not at all," Arana answered with a sigh.

The conversation quickly dried up. I threw on a cloak – a much easier task since Greatmother Amira had managed to magic them off my wrists – and together we departed from the inn, a small team of nervous, jumpy functionaries keeping a wide distance behind us.

"Wh-wh-wh-where's this t-t-temple?" I asked no one in particular.

"Further away, toward the coast," Greatmother Amira answered. "Just an hour's ride, I'm told."

There were five bears waiting for under the hutch extending out from the tavern, freshly groomed, saddles polished. And maybe it was stupid, but somehow the prospect of riding one of those monstrous beasts was more immediately terrifying than the inevitable apocalypse.

"We must do what we can to ensure that Umbrion is the last to be summoned," Fiyera said as she swung onto her camel. "At least that way, the balance of power will be favorable. More favorable."

"But whatever you do," Greatmother Amira said, and though she was speaking as though she was addressing everyone, she was looking right at me, "do not engage them. Once they're summoned, if they're summoned, let them to each other."

I couldn't imagine what it is they would say to each other, but I supposed I'd find out, one way or another.

The bulk of the ride east toward the coast was in silence. The monsoon was heavy and unforgiving, and the bear made for a strange and wobbly ride, and my waxed cloak felt like it was made of sheer linen for how dry it kept me. I did my best to fight away thoughts that I'd die looking like a drowned rat.

We rode for nearly two hours before I saw, poking up over the horizon, a small, nondescript, humble little temple. It was neither grand nor dedicated to any particular god – it was the temple of a small city like Andwelum, who did not have the resources to dedicate a temple to each god, but did the best they could with what they had. It was hewn of gray stone, with plain glass windows streaked with dirt and rain, standing on the edge of a cliff that overlooked the choppy, gray water.

"Leave the bears here," said Fiyera, shouting over the ever-rising roar of the ocean. "We want them far enough away from any danger. We may need them for a quick escape."

I'm sure most of us were thinking of what unlikely danger bears could save us from, but no one said anything.

The temple, for its part, was all but intact. Dusty and cold from disuse, but serviceable. As the rest of us shed our waxed cloaks and hung them on the hooks by the wooden door, Fiyera used an impressive, controlled burst of Craft to move all the rows of pews to the sides of the main chamber.

"Your friend Soya has followed us," Rolen whispered to me as I pulled off my cloak.

I looked at him, then back through the window at which he was standing. I didn't see anything at first, until I noticed several shadows standing a half-league away.

"The eye and ears of the Lord-Regent, no doubt," Rolen said.

I stared through the window at the shifting smudges on the rainy backdrop. For one absurd moment, I wanted to go to her, to try and make up with her in whatever time I had left.

"And I think your mother might be with her, too," he continued.

I certainly wouldn't have put it past her.

"We must remember that the gods do not understand time the way we do," Greatmother Amira said, moving toward the center of the emptied area. "We must be patient, willing to wait for them."

"Patience," Rolen said thoughtfully, "at the end of all things."

"Especially at the end," Arana said. "Where's your wife?"

"Back in Sariah, or on her way," he answered. "She wanted to stay. I shouted myself hoarse talking her out of it.

I stared down at my feet, wishing Mother had done the same.

"Where's yours?" Rolen asked her.

"Dead," she answered softly.

"I didn't know," Rolen said.

"Neither did I, until I went back to Whiterock."

"Form a circle," Greatmother Amira said gently.

We formed a circle.

Greatmother Amira took my hand in one of hers, and Rolen's in the other.

"Joining hands should help to amplify our natural Craft," Fiyera explained at Arana's look of confusion. "It should help us to be heard more clearly."

"I've never prayed for something so direct of Aemor before," Rolen said, taking Fiyera's outstretched hand. "How long do you think it will—?"

I had just taken Arana's hand when his sudden silence came. His eyes were open, but he was still, save for the steady rise and fall of his chest.

"Rolen?" Arana asked, slipping her hand from mine to move toward him. "Rolen, what's wrong?"

He didn't answer. He looked almost as though he was falling asleep for the glazed expression on his face.

"Arana," Greatmother Amira said, "you may want to step back."

"Why?" Arana asked, concern growing in her voice. "What's wrong with Rolen?"

"*Rolen isn't here right now.*"

We all took several steps back. None of us had ever really seen it from the outside, but we knew it by sound. His eyes were glowing golden and the tenor of his voice had changed. He was an avatar.

"Aemor," Arana whispered, and after a few seconds of floundering, she bowed deeply.

Aemor, through Rolen, didn't seem to notice. "*Mother?*" he said with Rolen's voice, and though his expression was searching, he remained completely stationary. "*They've called us together, Mother, and not a moment too soon.*"

We all looked at Greatmother Amira, but we could tell that the Worldmother had not manifested in her.

"*So desperate are they that they call us here,*" said Fiyera, beside me, and I jumped. Her eyes were a luminescent deep blue. "*Our brother's actions must have taken quite a toll.*"

"*I saw it firsthand,*" Aemor answered, not missing a beat. "*I watched those vile creatures he made come shambling up out of the waters. They're an abomination.*"

"*I'm more concerned that he took our mother's Light from them,*" said Arana, and I stumbled back a few steps. "*When did he gain such power?*"

"*There's much our brother would hide from us,*" Aemor answered, voice low.

I looked at Greatmother Amira, and she looked back at me, but neither of us had been possessed. I opened my mouth to ask if there was something I should do, though I doubted my own courage to speak in the presence of not one but *three* gods, when all of a sudden—

"*Jealous, brother?*"

The voice came out of me, but not from me, and at once I was overtaken. The incredible pressure of the Night Father's presence expanded in me, in all directions at once. My body loosened, my breathing steadied. But in the back of my head, panic screamed.

All eyes in the room turned to me at once. I felt the Night Father pull the corner of my mouth into a smirk.

"*You need not get so testy,*" Umbrion said through me, and he set my feet to walking toward Rolen. "*After all, I always was the one with ambition.*"

"*Ambition?*" Aemor answered, anger rising in his voice. "*You call this senseless slaughter ambition? This is not ambition, this is murder!*"

"*I call it coming to my full potential,*" Umbrion said. He kept advancing toward Rolen. "*I call it finding strength and purpose when I was provided with neither.*"

"*Does it make you feel strong?*" Elwen asked through Fiyera, and Umbrion stopped, swiveling my head around to look at her. "*Unmaking everything on this world, spitting on all Mother has given you?*"

"*What has Mother given me?*" he asked, spinning me on my heel to address all three of them at once. They looked on in silence. "*Well? Feel free to answer, siblings-mine. What has Mother given me?*"

"*Life,*" said Lilline through Arana.

He spun me around again. Arana's eyes were shining deep violet, and mine – black, I could only imagine – bored into them.

"*What is life worth when you're alone?*" he snarled at her.

"*You are not alone,*" she answered.

"*I have always been alone!*" he bellowed back at her, but she did not flinch. "*From the day of my making, I was alone! She wrought me from the shadow her Light cast! Do you not understand? I did not know her Light; I could not know her Light! I exist in diametric opposition to her Light!*

"*And then you came – all of you – burning and bathing in it, one with it – a part of something I could never understand, never have! Where were you when I was choking? When I was lost in the darkness that she forced me into?*"

Their expressions had changed, Rolen's most of all.

"*Where were you?*" he asked again, more desperately, as though he genuinely wanted their answer. "*You knew, you saw, you were there! Where were you?*"

And with a cold and terrible realization, I suddenly understood. I knew why Umbrion chose me as his Godspeaker. I knew why he called us alike. And my soul *ached* for him, and I felt the threat of tears burn in my eyes – mine or his, I didn't know.

There came no answer to his question. I could feel my shoulders trembling, my heart hammering in the side of my neck.

"*Fine,*" he said, straightening. "*I suppose I should not have expected an answer.*"

There followed in me a great sensation of tearing, starting at my navel and ending in my skull. Unlike last time, when his presence had simply vanished, I could feel him screaming his way out of me. The pain was intense, but mercifully brief, and I collapsed onto the floor.

There! I am manifest!

My vision clouded. My mind screamed.

Our Godspeakers would force our hand, Mother, he continued, no longer with the aid of my voice. My vision was still swimming, pain pounding between my temples. *Let us oblige them. Come out!*

I lifted my head with a great concentration of will. The Night Father had manifested, caped in swirling twilight, arms open in defiance. He was advancing on Greatmother Amira, whose shoulders were set, and who had, I could tell, still not been possessed by the Worldmother.

Come out, Mother! he called. *I know you're watching! I can feel the venom of your gaze on me even now!*

I wanted to shout something at him – anything – no, don't, wait – but I still felt dizzy from the fading waves of pain. I struggled to pull myself to my feet.

Before he reached Greatmother Amira—

"*Umbrion.*"

I had never seen anything quite like what I saw when I looked back at Greatmother Amira. When Sol possessed her, not only did her eyes glow silver-white, but the whole of her body seemed illuminated. Threads of silver light circled her wrists and climbed up her arms like unearthly tattoos, and the very air around her vibrated, as though warped by heat.

"*Why are you doing this?*"

Umbrion stopped halfway between me and Greatmother Amira.

The rags of twilight pooled at his feet and began to tint with red.

You know why I am doing this, he said. *You have ALWAYS KNOWN!*

The rigid lines of Greatmother Amira's face softened; the silver of her eyes dimmed. For a moment, she was the most tragic creature in all of Andelan.

"*I know,*" she answered.

It was not the right response. Umbrion's fury boiled over, and he screamed in rage and pain, and the living rock rumbled beneath his feet, and the wind of the monsoon howled to deafening volume—

—and in that great cataclysm of sound, the rock and mortar of the temple began to crack, to crumble. Great slabs of stone were carried away as though they were no more substantial than paper, and the monsoon became more of a typhoon, screaming wind and rain and great flashes of lightning.

YOU KNEW! he roared at her as the temple came down around us. *YOU ALWAYS KNEW! YOU KNEW AND YOU DID NOTHING! YOU HAD THE POWER TO CHANGE ME AND YOU LEFT ME TO THE ANGER AND THE PAIN AND THE LONELINESS!*

Arana and Fiyera and Rolen were looking around at the unfolding cataclysm, but Greatmother Amira's burning silver eyes were fixed on Umbrion.

"*Because I loved you as you were,*" she answered. "*What right does a mother have to change her child?*"

Still not the right answer, apparently. He screamed again. Four great bolts of lightning struck the ground behind me; the force of it rattled my bones and sent my ears ringing. I wrenched around—

"*What are those?*" demanded Aemor through Rolen.

Four figures, dark and terrible, standing toward the far end of what used to be the temple – all that remained was the stone foundation at this point – and robed in black. Gods, I could tell, but gods of what? Who were they? Where had they come from?

These are my children, Umbrion bellowed, and something cold grew in me. *Children of hatred and war and madness and deceit. They will undo this world and everything on it!*

A man with skin as white as bone; a woman with hair as dark as ink; a man with a smile that made my mind snarl in protest; a woman in heavy armor with a bloodied axe - these were his gods? This had been his plan from the start?

"*Abomination*," said Elwen through Fiyera. "*Abomination!*"

"*Umbrion*," said Sol through Greatmother Amira, heartbreak in every line of her face, "*what have you done?*"

I have done what you made inevitable!

"*Umbrion*," said Lilline through Arana, "*we will have to stop you.*"

I do not fear you! he cried. *A thousand ages of pain and darkness has made me stronger than you can possibly imagine!*

I could see their hands as they began to glow with Craft. They advanced on Umbrion, and as I was just behind him, I scrambled away - I did not want to be near any great battle of the gods - but before I could even gather my bearings enough to stand—

"No!"

And all of a sudden, Mother was there in front of me, standing with her arms outstretched. She was staring at the other Godspeakers, but directly through Umbrion - and I suddenly remembered that, like Perenor, she couldn't see him. She could only see the other Godspeakers.

"Don't hurt him!" she begged the Godspeakers, but it was Umbrion whose attention she had truly ensnared. He circled her like carrion as she spoke, looking her up and down. "Please, don't hurt him! He's only a boy!"

Well, well, well, Umbrion said. *The greatest playwrights in the land could not have planned it better. Yet another example of a mother who claims to love but only hurts!*

No, no, no - was he - he wouldn't—?

"Please don't hurt him," Mother said, blind to Umbrion's presence and deaf to his words. She was speaking to the Godspeakers, assuming they were advancing on me. "Please, please!"

Isn't her remorse pretty, Worldmother? Umbrion asked, looking back at Greatmother Amira. *Isn't it so easy after the fact? A lifetime of abuse and neglect, and now look how she weeps! Where were her tears when she left her son alone in his misery? Where were her pleas for his safety when he drowned in his own torment, when this world chained and imprisoned him like an animal?*

"M-M-M-M-M-M-M—!" Curse my stutter! I couldn't even tell her to leave, to run, to get away for her own safety! "*M-M-M-M-M-M—!*"

But her love comes too little, Umbrion said, raising one hand toward her, *her concern too late!*

Before I knew what I was doing, I scrambled to my feet and grabbed Umbrion by the forearm with both hands.

It may have been the most foolish thing I'd ever done, but it was a gesture that stopped him dead in his tracks. His too-dark eyes focused on me with needle-sharp intensity.

"Don't," I choked at him. "P-p-please."

There was confusion on his face – hurt as well.

This woman sat by while you suffered, he said. *Your whole life, she left you in your misery! And you would spare her?*

"Yes," I sobbed, tears pouring down my face. "Sh-sh-she's f-f-f-family."

"Silas," Mother said behind me, unsure. Of course, she could only hear half the conversation.

He wrenched his arm out of my grip. The confusion hadn't faded from his face; if anything, it had only intensified.

"D-d-d-do you n-not understand?" I stammered at him as the wind howled and the rain beat down. "W-w-w-will you n-n-not even t-t-try?"

My breath left me. For a few moments of deafening silence, he looked from me, to Aemor in Rolen, to Sol in Greatmother Amira.

And for an instant, one brief ephemera, the ghost of something like remorse whispered at the edges of his face.

"*Brother,*" said Aemor through Rolen—

—and like that, the moment shattered like so much glass.

I am betrayed by my own Godspeaker!

Fear rose in my chest. "N-n-n-n-n—"

I chose you because I thought you knew my pain!

I wanted to scream, *I do, I do know your pain,* but my voice was gone. It had been a small miracle that I'd spoken at all. I stood swaying in front of him, made heavy with rainwater, and my skin crawled under the mounting certainty and the end of all things.

And now you would choose your tormentor over me! he said, and though he was angry, I would have had to have been deaf not to hear the underpinnings of intense pain and betrayal. *I who loved you when no one else did!*

No mercy! he screamed, and CRACK—

I spun in time to see my mother's body hit the floor - *no, no, no—*

No forgiveness! he roared, and *BOOM—*

"*Mother!*" screamed Aemor through Rolen.

I fell to my mother's side, my head a screaming tangle of conflicting thoughts, and she wasn't breathing, gods, Mother wasn't breathing, her eyes were empty like Perenor's—

Only vengeance!

I lifted my eyes, and through the blur of tears, I could see her—

Greatmother Amira, held by the neck in Umbrion's hand, and the silver of her eyes was draining, and the very earth trembled, and in the sky, the clouds churned and boiled and split open, and I could see—

Through the wounds in the overcast, slashes of sunlight, white sunlight, but there was something moving in front of it, a great black shadow that swallowed the sun—

And the silver of Greatmother Amira's eyes faded, and there was a tremendous and familiar sound of ripping flesh—

"*No!*"

"*Mother!*"

But she was in pieces on the floor, chunks of viscera and bone and blood, and Umbrion glowed white-hot with the strength of the devoured Worldmother, electric, pulsing with primal energy.

VENGEANCE.

Arana and Lilline vanished in a hiss of violet light. Fiyera and Elwen followed. Umbrion, the Night Father, the Sun Eater, turned to Aemor, still in Rolen, still standing, face full of horror.

Umbrion lifted his hand, but Rolen and Aemor were vanished before he could fell the blow.

Where they went, I didn't know - I still don't know - but it didn't seem to matter to Umbrion. He turned forward and looked down at me, kneeling over my mother's lifeless body, soaked with rain, shaking, utterly broken. He stared at me and I stared back at him.

I sat and I waited for that final blow. In that moment, death was a certainty. He would not spare me. I did not want him to. What was there left for me to live for?

But he hesitated when he saw me, and though his hand was still outstretched, there came no killing blow.

Perhaps he did love me, after all. I could see something very much like love in the shifting starlight of his eyes. And I think some part of me loved him. I think that part of me still does, despite everything.

He clenched his hand and vanished.

And still I sat, drenched in rainwater, surrounded by corpses, in a surreal twilight of a swallowed sun. The sun, the sun, where had the sun gone? It was nothing but a ring of white light around a great, black shadow. What had Umbrion done to the sun?

Far beyond the edge of the temple, the ocean began to boil. Great shapes undulated, shifted in the twilight-blackened waters.

"Silas! Silas!"

The shapes emerged from the surface of the water. Heads, I could see, and horns as well, black scales and burning eyes. They came out of the deep, taller than the tallest buildings, shaking the earth as they moved. This was no vanguard – this, *this* was Umbrion's true army, great leviathans.

"*Silas!*"

I was grabbed by the shoulder and wrenched around.

It was Soya, aghast, thunderstruck. I did not need to ask to know that she had seen everything – everything except that which might have exonerated me.

"What have you done?" she asked.

I stared at her. There would be no answer. My words were gone.

"How could you—" she began, but faltered. "Why did you—?"

And what could I say to her? She'd been outside the temple, no doubt, just like my mother. She'd seen it. She'd seen me break open the temple, summon down a typhoon, rip open Greatmother Amira. She had seen everything except Umbrion.

If it were me, I'd be thunderstruck, too.

A great pain in the back of my head – the heel of her sword, no doubt – and I collapsed atop my mother's corpse.

COULD THIS have been avoided?

The question eats at me as rot eats through flesh. I find myself looking over all these pages in piles around the room, going over these fateful events with great obsession, and wondering if there was anything I could have done, anything at all, that could have mitigated all this death and darkness.

The answer, despite how much I should wish to deny it, is yes. Yes, they could have been avoided.

Everything around me broke catastrophically, as though destiny was soldiering on without me, but that wasn't true. I had one thing that offered me power, and I should have made use of it: I had understanding, and I had love.

Though he denied it in the end, I knew Umbrion's pain - better, perhaps, than any thinking creature in Andelan. I knew the shame and the fear and the unworthiness that ate away at him. And if I had been born a shade darker, a touch stronger, perhaps my hands would have been just as bloody as now are his.

I'm not trying to excuse what he did. There is no excuse. I'm just saying that I am aware - painfully, acutely aware - that things could have been different. I could have just talked to him. I *should* have talked to him. I should have been the love he needed. I nearly was.

I have prayed to him. During these last few days, I have written until my hand refused to move or my heart refused to remember, and I have laid down in my cot and prayed to him. I have told him that I understand, begged him to come speak to me, offered every sweet word of love and comfort I could think of.

If he has heard me, he has not deigned to respond. And regretting, perhaps, is pointless - but what else is left to do?

FIVE DAYS AGO, I awoke in this prison cell.

Even through the thick walls and the living rock beyond them, I could hear the clash and clamor of battle.

I knew where I was. I had been here once before. The jail far beneath Silverwatch.

There was only me this time, in a cell with thick bars at the far end of the row. I was alone, and far on the other end of the long hallway I could see one of two guards hurry up the steps leading into the castle.

My head was pounding in pain, and it took me a while to climb back up out of the fog of my memory, to remember what happened.

Over the course of several minutes, memories came back to me one by one, each more venomous than the one before. The moot, the summoning, the gods, the sun. How many had we lost? What had happened?

"When does it stop?"

I looked up. Soya was standing on the other side of the barred door, looking down on me with a set expression. She was in her battle armor, a helmet under her arm, a sword in her hand painted black with blood. She looked like she was out of breath.

"Tell me," she said, voice hard. "Tell me when the assault stops."

I did not know what assault she meant, but I could guess. I saw the great leviathans lurching out of the deep, tall as mountains. I wondered how many he had made.

"*Tell me!*" she cried suddenly, rushing at the bars. They clattered against her plate armor and I sprang backward in the cot on which I was sitting. "Our line cannot hold forever! Tell me how many there are! Are we fighting for nothing? Should we flee and hide or stand and defend what we have? What path will save the most lives? Tell me!"

I swallowed hard. Even if I'd had my voice - which I decidedly did not – I had no answer for her. I knew nothing.

She threw her helmet to the floor in rage; it hit the stone with a mighty, reverberating *clang*. She turned back to me, eyes afire with fury.

"Everyone is dying, Silas!" she screamed at me. "The combined armies of Avenos, Stormhold, Whiterock, Sariah, Onanwa – they are not enough! Their numbers are too many and our supplies are too low! Have you lost all loyalty to your own people?"

All that answered her was the echo of her own voice. She bared her teeth at me.

"Don't look at me like that!" she snapped. "How do you have the nerve to feign such innocence? I *saw you!* I was there, Silas! I watched you, I saw what you did – to Greatmother Amira, to your own mother! I watched you break open the clouds and *black out the sun!*"

And how could I have ever hoped to argue with such conviction? With a voice or without, there was nothing to be said to such anger.

"And still you would try to convince me of your innocence? That you knew nothing, did nothing?"

There were angry tears rimming her eyes. I wanted to comfort her, but I dared not move.

"My father is dead thanks to you," she whispered. I swallowed the heart that had lodged itself in my throat. "He died defending this city from the scourge of your master. And now I am left to lead a falling city in a losing battle and you will not help? Why will you *not help?*"

I wondered for a while if I deserved this viciousness, but quickly decided that such things were not productive to think about.

When Soya's breath evened, she said, "They call for your death."

I looked back up at her.

"Those that are left to call for it, at least," she continued. "They no longer seem to care for whatever vengeance the Night Father may have in store. They would see your head separated from your shoulders."

At this point, I was all but deadened to any outside stimulus. The immediate and present threat that my best friend would see me executed hit me like raindrops hit glass. I was no longer sure what my life was worth, in any case. What did it matter?

"I do not yet know if I will oblige them," she said. "But the longer you refuse to help the more tempting it feels."

She turned on her plate heel and stormed back down the long, long hallway leading out of the jail. I watched her until she vanished, listened until her the sound faded from earshot.

I sat down against the bars. My cell was spartan. A cot, a bucket, a blanket, a pile of dirty parchments and charcoal.

I stared at the parchments for some time. One way or another, I knew I would be dead soon. Perhaps I should make the most of the time I had left.

I picked up the parchments and I set to writing.

THREE DAYS AGO, I received a second visitor.

I lifted my head from writing - my pile of written papers was nearly knee-high by that point - when I heard the footsteps. They were not as heavy as Soya's, nor with the same purpose, and when I lifted my eyes, it took my heavy, addled mind a moment to recognize her.

"They say they will execute you in two days."

She was familiar, of course, but somehow completely different. It had been less than a season since I'd last seen her, but there was a weariness in her eyes and a sadness in the lines and furrows of her face that made Lady Queen Roslin seem like a different person entirely.

I wondered if bowing would be inappropriate. In any case, I was too hungry and fatigued to try standing. I had already arrived at the conclusion that I would not speak again for so long as I drew breath - which, apparently, wouldn't be much longer - so still I said nothing.

"They advised me not to go down here," she told me. Her voice was strangely neutral, almost detached, like she was narrating someone else's life. "They said it was too dangerous, that you are a demon in Andel form."

The Lady Queen looked back toward the two guards at the very far end of the hallway.

"They're afraid to approach you," she said. "They say you are a lesser god, like Umbrion - that all who come too close to you find death."

Erroneous conclusions, but sound deduction. I looked down the hallway at the guards. Over the last few days I'd noticed that they would occasionally look back at me, as though expecting me to lash out at any moment. I was mostly surprised they had any guards at all to spare. The sounds of battle above my head had not abated. I could only imagine how desperate things were in the world above my prison.

When I looked back I saw her eyes burn with tears. Her fists clenched at her sides. Her shoulders set.

"They said I should not approach you, but I had to. I wanted to look into the eyes of the man who killed my wife."

The words should have stung more, but I was swallowed almost entirely by a dreadful, gnawing numbness. There was nothing in me left to hurt.

So I looked up at her, and she looked into my eyes, and I hoped that she found whatever answers she was looking for.

"It's strange," she said, voice drawn taut, "you don't look like a killer."

I wondered what it was I did look like. Nothing good, assuredly. I hadn't eaten in over two days - food was reserved for refugees and families, not for me - nor bathed, nor really slept.

"She liked you," the Lady Queen continued. "She found you charming, intelligent. She looked forward to having you on her Council."

In my mind's eye, I could see her, Queen Nerisa, dark-haired and bright-eyed, strong and beautiful and confident. I am sure that was what the Lady Queen wanted - she wanted me to remember her with perfect clarity, wanted me to hurt from the guilt.

She could not have known that I was already dead from it.

"And now she's dead," the Lady Queen said. "And the kingdom she spent her entire life building from nothing is crumbling to dust.

"The sun is swallowed in the sky, great black leviathans come up from the oceans in endless numbers, and everyone is dying, dying without the Worldmother's Light. My wife is dead, and dead in vain. And you *killed her.*"

She was silent a moment. I could detect a subtle, pervasive trembling in her. She gripped the bars of my cell tightly with both hands.

"And I want to *hate you for it,* but I *can't.*"

My hands wrung around the nub of charcoal.

"I want to hate you for killing her, hate you for undoing everything she ever worked for, hate you for dooming your own people and I *can't,* I can't *do* it, because I hear her voice in my head telling me - she always told me, *my love, there is never a point to hatred.* But what else is left but the hatred? Hatred, and the memory of the woman I loved - she is dead now, *dead,* and I can't even manage to hate you for killing her—!"

She turned away, covering her face with both hands. I wanted to offer her words of comfort, but there were no words left in me. I lowered my eyes to the floor of my cell, respectfully averting my gaze while she collected herself.

"Two days, they say," she said, voice shaking. "Two days – such as they are in this evil, unending twilight. Two days and you'll be dead. And it won't make anything better. Even justice offers no comfort.

"If it was our spirits your master was trying to break," she said, "he has accomplished his goal."

She departed from whence she came, leaving me alone with my papers and my thoughts and my solitude.

And there was nothing else for me to do, so I kept writing.

YESTERDAY, I had one last visitor - one I did not expect. All the ages of this world could have passed and I never would have expected to see her.

"Silas?"

By then I was over halfway finished with this little narrative. I was lost in my thoughts and my papers, and when I looked up, I thought perhaps that I'd slid into a dream.

But there she was - my grandmother, tall and graceful as ever, worse for wear but still standing, eyes underlined with dark smudges that betrayed her careful poise.

I stared at her in astonishment but didn't answer.

"I'd ask how they're treating you, but the question seems redundant." She looked briefly around my cell. "What are you writing?"

I didn't answer, of course. I still couldn't, and likely never again would, speak.

"Not speaking?" she asked. Surprisingly, I found no judgment in her voice. "Can't say I blame you."

She came toward my cell door and sat down on the floor so that she was just on the other side. The cell was small enough that I likely could have reached out and touched her if I so wanted - but circumstances as they were, I didn't feel any particular inclination.

"I heard that your mother is dead," she said, voice neutral.

She paused as though waiting for a response, then seemed to think better of it and carried on.

"I heard that you killed her."

When I still did not answer, she sighed.

"I'll be honest, Silas," Grandmother continued, "I don't know what or who to believe. Soya calls you traitor and can barely speak of you without sobbing. But I am told Perenor believed in you to the last. Accounts of your loyalties are numerous and varied – and they are all pointless."

I looked to her. She looked back at me. I saw my own exhaustion in her eyes, my own despair and brokenness and lack.

"What does your motivation matter now? What does anything matter now? What is done is done. I would not spend my last moments trying to make sense of this tragedy. I would rather do what I can to stopper your suffering."

I'll admit, it wasn't what I was expecting her to say. There must have been some surprise on my face, because she smiled sadly at me and leaned her forehead against the bar of my cell.

"Don't look so surprised," she said. "I know it may be hard for you to believe, Silas, but I have never wanted you to suffer."

That was indeed hard for me to believe.

"Looking back..."

She drifted off a moment. Some great and soft tragedy settled into the lines of her face.

"I remember when you were little," she said. "You couldn't have been more than 50 seasons old. You had built your first spyglass. You brought it to your mother and I, and you were so excited. You went on and on about how you had used glass and refraction to make distant objects larger, and I remembered thinking to myself, *Gods, my grandson is a genius! What a boon he'll be to House Olen!*"

She laughed, and I nearly laughed with her.

"I had Perenor, who was strong and fierce and loyal, and I had you, who was quick and sharp and careful, and I thought between the two of you, House Olen will change Andelan for the better.

"But things didn't turn out that way, did they, Silas?"

No, indeed. I fussed with my piece of charcoal and watched her in silence.

"You withdrew," she said. "I thought it was just a phase for a time. I thought you'd grow out of your shyness. But seasons came and went and you never did. If anything, your fears intensified. And I came to realize that you never would be what I wanted you to be. You could not. What is a politician who can't speak in public? What is a diplomat who can't be in a crowded room?

"And somewhere along the line, I started to resent you."

That I was willing to believe. I rubbed my thumb along the tip of my piece of charcoal and stared into my lap.

"And I was cruel to you," she went on. "And I treated you unfairly. Not because of anything you'd done, but because of how upset I was at the situation. I had so many high hopes for you and I had to watch them crash and burn. I'm not trying to excuse it, Silas, just explain it.

"But you must understand," she said, "you *must* understand, Silas, that I never wanted you to *change*. I didn't want you to be anything other than what you were. I *loved* you, Silas, and I still love you, for exactly what you are. I just – at some point, I..."

And even though it would have been nice to hear this 100 seasons ago, even though it felt like too little and too late, it was nice. In a cold, sweet, aching way, it was nice.

"And that's why I'm going to stand for your crimes," she said, and at once I sat up straight. "I am still the matriarch of your house, and I can still declare myself responsible for your actions under Imlandranian law. If they want to execute someone, they can execute me."

I sat forward, moving to scoot across the papers toward her, but she held out a hand.

"No, Silas, don't," she said. "It's all right. What does it matter now? What does any of it matter? House Olen is forfeit. Our sun is swallowed, our world plunged into an endless twilight. What does my life matter now?

"If you would doom this world, then you would only bring it quicker. But if there is any hope left at all, it is in you.

"Besides..."

She reached through the bars and put her hand on my hair, and she smiled at me, and it was nothing but pain.

"If I have a choice in it, I would die like Perenor," she said. "Like your mother. Defending something I love. That is the strongest Craft there is."

And tears blurred my vision, though I thought I'd long run out of them. And I curled up against my grandmother's chest, though the bars tried to keep us apart.

And in the back of my head, I knew what I had to do.

TODAY, I will die.

In less than an hour, the guards will come and reluctantly release me, my crimes paid for on the head of my grandmother. They will be too scared to approach me too closely. They will hope that I go up into the city and try to leave. They will hope that I will die in the fray.

But I will not die in the fray. I will walk through the battle and his demons will not harm me; they will never harm me.

I will know where he is. I will sense him, feel him, as I always feel him. I will walk until I find him, even if it is halfway across Andelan.

I will find him, and I will pay the same price paid by my brother, my mother, my grandmother. I cannot kill him - nothing can kill him - but I can give everything in me to bind him. The binding Craft will be little more than threads to him, but I know it will hold him, stop him, end this terrible assault. I know the demons will stop their attack.

This sundering will end when I bind him for the same reason Umbrion did not kill me back in Andwelum. It will end for the same reason Perenor saved Avenos. It will end for the same reason my grandmother saved me. There is power in love, and power in sacrifice.

Soya, I've left these pages for you. If you made it this far, I can only hope that they gave you what you wanted, whether it was answers or closure or justification for your feelings. I hope you rule your father's city with the strength and grace of which I know you are capable. I hope this darkness has not broken Andelan. I hope you can rebuild.

Hold out the night, Soya. The siege will break tomorrow.

I hear the guards coming now; I have to go.

Goodbye.

I could feel you draw nearer. I could have stopped you, of course, but I let you come.

When you appeared, it was to the sound of crunching gravel under your feet. And little bird, how you ached. Not just in body from all the miles you walked to meet me, but in spirit. You were in so much pain.

And in our little alcove by the water, we stood staring at one another. And I told you to leave, and I warned you of my wrath, and you should have run, but you stayed. You stumbled toward me and you kissed me.

And what power you have, little bird, what tremendous power.

I could feel it ensnare me before I knew what it was. Little threads of bluish light, fragile enough for me to snap with a movement, but strong enough to hold for all time. How could I ever break them? Those threads are the only thing left of you.

The sum total of your magic – everything you were, all the energy that bound you together – is in those threads. You died to bind me, little bird, and even though I could break them in an instant, I know, as you knew, that I never will, I never will.